Woods & Waters Wild

COLLECTED EARLY STORIES
VOLUME 3:
HIGH FANTASY STORIES

Charles de Lint

SUBTERRANEAN PRESS 2008

First Edition

ISBN
978-1-59606-229-0

Subterranean Press
PO Box 190106
Burton, MI 48519

www.subterraneanpress.com

Copyright Notices:

Contents:

for Leslie Howle

I should have known you way back when,
but at least we're pals now

Introduction:

HERE WE ARE IN the final stretch: the third and last collection of these early stories of mine (fourth if you count *What the Mouse Found*, though in some ways, it's more like a sidebar). As with the previous volume, I'm going to assume that if you've bought this book, then you probably have the others, so I don't need to repeat the apologia from the introduction in volume one. But I will note that this one has some of my earliest work in it (the stories collected under "Pastiches," which were a little painful for me to reread) but also some of my favourites (such as "The Graceless Child").

Most of them fall somewhere in between.

YOU'LL NOTICE that many of these stories initially appeared in small press magazines. I loved the 'zines. Their boom time was pre-Internet, so this collective of like-minded individuals publishing and reading each other's 'zines was the only way to connect with other people who loved this kind of storytelling—especially for someone living in the boonies like Ottawa.

At that time Canada was still a decade or so away from having a single publisher with a dedicated f/sf line.

I'd heard of conventions, of course, but they usually had the words "science fiction" in their name and that didn't really interest me. I read some sf, but my heart lay in fantasy. I liked the pulps, but I loved the sort of fantasy exemplified by Lin Carter's classic Sign of the Unicorn series from Ballantine. I can't recall how often they published a new title (probably once a month), but I can certainly remember scouring the shelves of the local book stores for a new one every time I went in.

This was where I was introduced to the work of William Morris, Lord Dunsany, E.R. Eddison, James Branch Cabell and so many other classic practitioners of the field. Every book was different from the others, but they all had one thing in common: a sense of wonder.

And they were good.

They also inspired me to try my own hand at writing prose (as opposed to the verse and songs I'd been writing for years).

Pastiches

UNFORTUNATELY, MY early writing, like that of many authors, was so inspired by other writers that my first efforts might as well be considered pastiches, rather than homages. Of course, I *thought* I was writing something fresh and new at the time. But this is how we learn—apprenticing ourselves to the masters to learn the craft and eventually develop our own voices and follow our own Muse.

These stories owe their debt to Lord Dunsany and William Morris, though they don't come remotely close to what those writers were able to do. They're also the reason I started seriously considering a career as a writer, since three of them sold to the first place I sent them for the remarkable (to me at the time) sum of ten dollars each.

Thanks to Charles Saunders for recommending the magazine to me, and to Loay Hall for buying them.

Angharad

THESE STORIES were rewritten and put together to form the first part of **Into the Green**, published by Tor in 1993.

But before that novel was even a gleam in the eye of Terri Windling who suggested I do it, before I'd even had the good fortune to meet her and eventually get to work with her, the late Marion Zimmer Bradley was having a huge impact on the fantasy field. There were her

Darkover books, of course, which, like a great deal of Andre Norton's work, was as much fantasy as sf. But there was also her anthology series, *Sword and Sorceress*.

I knew from people who'd worked with her that she was a tough taskmaster. She didn't abide second-rate anything in the stories she accepted for this series. But she was also willing to work with authors to help them get their stories in shape. That's pretty much a fairy tale now, when editors are overworked and don't have that kind of time, but it was already becoming rare in the eighties.

Anyway, the point is, I wanted to get into those anthologies, and after some back-and-forthing with Marion on one of my stories (during which I learned a lot) I finally got in with "Cold Blows the Wind." I had to work just as hard with the next couple of stories I placed with the series, but at least I finally thought I was getting somewhere with my short fiction.

Dennet & Willie

I CAN'T remember much about the writing of these two stories, though I do know I wrote them a long time before I finally placed them in *Night Voyages*.

Thomas the Rhymer

THE IDEA here was to retell traditional ballads as fantasy stories. I wrote three of them; two were published, and again, as with the Dennet & Willie stories, they were all written long before two of them finally appeared in *Mythic Circle*.

It seemed like a good idea at the time—and still is, as shown by, say, Ellen Kushner or Diana Wynne Jones—but as I was writing them I became more interested in writing stories set in a contemporary setting, so I abandoned the series. That previously unpublished third story, "The Cruel Sister," has been sitting as a first draft in my files for years.

The Fane of the Grey Rose

"THE FANE of the Grey Rose" wasn't the first story I wrote, nor even the first I had published. But it was the first longer piece I managed to finish, and it was my first professional sale.

Like many new writers, I would begin longer projects, but then abandon them as soon as a more intriguing idea came along. Nothing wrong with that, if one is simply writing for a hobby, but if you want to be published and reach a wider audience, the first rule is to actually finish the story.

"The Fane of the Grey Rose" I managed to finish.

I sent it to Andrew J. Offutt, a writer with whom I'd been having a correspondence in the late seventies, sending it for the same reason that so many unpublished writers pass their stories around: you want to be read. Imagine my surprise when, some time later, Andy wrote back to tell me he'd like to use it in an anthology series he was editing for Zebra Books called *Swords Against Darkness*. The only catch was, it had to be a lot shorter to get into the book.

So "The Fane of the Grey Rose" also gave me my second rule on the road to becoming a professional writer: listen to the editor.

By that I don't mean slavishly do whatever he or she might suggest simply to make the almighty sale. But it is important to consider their input. After all, a good editor is only interested in making the story you've written the best it can be. Good editors don't ask for arbitrary changes. There are always viable reasons behind their requests. Some might be artistic, some commercial (as the case was here—my story was simply too long for the collection as it stood). It's the writer's job to consider the requested changes and decide whether or not they'll improve the story. Or at least whether you can live with them. I could, and Andy's editorial suggestions did improve the story.

So in 1978 I made my first professional sale and a year later "The Fane of the Grey Rose" appeared in *Swords Against Darkness VI*. Let me tell you, it was a serious thrill to be in the same anthology as authors I'd long admired such as Manly Wade Wellman, Ardath Mayhar, Poul Anderson, Tanith Lee, and Orson Scott Card, as well as some of my talented peers: Charles R. Saunders, Gordon Linzner, Diana L. Paxson, and others.

By the time the book came out it would still be another four years before I finally sold a novel, but this was the sale that made it all seem viable to the young hopeful writer I was at the time. And while I've thanked him before, I can never thank Andy enough for all his support and interest in my writing at that early point in my career, when it seemed I was only writing for the four walls of my study.

A Kingly Thing

BACK IN the seventies, when I was only getting published in the small press (and even that was spotty), my friend Charles Saunders and I started up our own small press magazine called *Dragonbane*, which was focused mostly on heroic fantasy. Charles edited the magazine and I published it under my Triskell Press imprint. I enjoyed being on the other side of publishing so much that I decided to publish and edit a companion magazine, *Beyond the Fields We Know*, which was more fantasy oriented, and named after a phrase used by Lord Dunsany.

Now, in those days, many of the 'zines only paid their contributors in copies, but Charles and I were determined to actually pay for the material we used. Though I can't remember how much we paid, it was probably in the neighbourhood of a half cent a word. But even at that piddling rate, when you added in payments to artists and printing costs, we had to find a way to cut expenses. So Charles and I each put stories in our magazines, because we didn't have to pay for those.

"A Kingly Thing" was published in *Beyond the Fields We Know*.

I don't remember actually writing it, but rereading it I can see that, like my unpublished novel *Eyes Like Leaves* and many other stories I wrote around that time, it owes much of its inspiration to the music of Robin Williamson and Marc Bolan. I just wish I could have done more justice to that inspiration.

Woods and Waters Wild

THIS STORY grew out of reading fairy tales and Irish poetry, playing Celtic music, and listening to Seamus Ennis telling stories about the origin of fiddle and pipe tune titles. It ended up in a convention program book many years after I wrote it.

The White Road

THERE WAS a time when I wouldn't read science fiction, mostly because I thought I wouldn't like it, but the truth is I hadn't really tried much, and what I had tried were lesser books. I preferred fantasy, and in the seventies that didn't mean books where a motley group of adventurers went off on a quest, or set off to gather an army to fight in some huge war between Good and Evil. The legacy of Tolkien's trilogy came later.

This was a time when fantasy books were all different from one another. I read them for the sense of wonder they instilled in me, not because I liked a certain kind of plot.

But you had to work a little to find these books.

I can remember one day how I was jonesing for a new title, but I already had, or had read, everything on the store's bookshelves (this was actually possible back then, since there were less than a dozen or so titles published a month, period). So I went further afield and found myself in a department store where I came across a book called *Huon of the Horn* by Andre Norton. I loved it, and was delighted to go back to the book store and find that there were so many other books available by this author. The only problem was, they were all science fiction.

But I'd really liked *Huon of the Horn*, and I had nothing else new to read, so I tried one of the Witchworld books, and between the two, I've been hooked on Norton's work ever since.

Now you could quibble and say that her books are more science fantasy than science fiction, but there were spaceships and aliens and other planets, and you know what? From there I went on to read

Clifford D. Simak, Roger Zelazny, Jack Williamson, and any number of other sf authors, and my reading life has been the better for it.

All of which is to say, when I was asked to write a story for *Tales of the Witch World*, I jumped at the chance.

The Graceless Child

WHENEVER I have an agent (as I do now with the wonderful Russ Galen), I usually handle the short story sales myself. But back when I was one of Richard Curtis's clients, he was asked if I'd like to contribute a story to an upcoming Warner anthology.

I hadn't done a lot of high fantasy for some time by this point (early nineties) and the idea appealed to me. I'm glad it did, because this is one of my favourites of my own stories. So thanks to Richard and the anthology editors Baird Searles and Brian Thomsen for thinking of me.

— ❦ —

THE ONE story missing from here that I really wanted to include is a collaboration I did on a high fantasy novelet with a fellow named James E. Coplin who used to write under the name "J.E. Coplin." If you've been reading the introductions to these early story collections, you know I lost touch with him years ago.

Since the first volume came out I've done everything short of hiring a private detective to try to track him down, but without any luck, so that story has to stay in my file drawer, more's the pity.

— ❦ —

IF ANY of you are on the Internet, come visit my home page at www.charlesdelint.com or on MySpace.

—Charles de Lint
Ottawa, Summer 2008

Pastiches

A Tale of Tangle
Who Has Many Names

i.

O TANGLE NAY-SAID THE love of Weste the Song-smith, with his moon-light eyes and tiny binding lays, and would not bide in the lands she knew. Nay, needs must she journey, 'pon windy feet and laughing with the sun, to Lands of Far Away where she might be one with herself and ken her own inner peace.

So she sat with him then upon that last day with a smile as sweet as the dawn and the sun spilling magic upon her freckled back. With meadow eyes, she spoke more than words to him, though she left him in the dayspring of their love.

She would return and sing once more with him, she said, but first must she dance the aelfin woods with her feet bare and a green kirtle wrapped loosely about her fair slim body. In moonlit wolds and 'pon starry hilltops she would learn to pipe windy reels 'pon a silver flute that she had acquired when once she danced for men in their cities and had drawn fancys for their eyes with her aelfin form.

And he said: "Forget me not."

She would return and hold his aching body, she said, and ease his heart once again; and she said: "Farewell for awhile."

And he said: "Farewell."

So, with a toss of her head that set her golden-brown curls a-tumbling, she left him and went upon her way…

ii.

TANGLE AWOKE from a bed of moss to meet the dawn with laughter and skirling tunes and dancing in meadows. She bathed in forest streams and broke her fast with the gifts of the wood: nut, fruit, root and berry. And what were days for her passed as years in the lands she once knew.

O copse and lea, shore and sea, she knew through her wanderings, for restless as a gypsy wind was she. Still, oft she would bide in some chosen place where Peace lay pleasing upon the air and there she would pipe a few tunes and rest as Time passed her by.

Where she bided the flowers grew more fair, the air more sweet, and all the Woodland Folk rejoiced though often they knew not the cause of their joy.

iii.

THEN ONE day, as she lingered in a quiet glade learning the ways of her fingers and flute, there came to her Avenal, Mother of the World, and she told Tangle a tale of long ago:

"O once of a time, when the Gods were younger and the land wore Elder names, there dwelt in the court of one King Wellstarre a young maid whose name was Fancy…and a fair maid was she. Now, she was loved by a shepherd's son hight Waine, but she disdained his love for she would be away to other lands in search of the fabled Key of Happiness which, she deemed, lay not in his arms, nor in the hills and fields she knew.

"So of a day, she took herself from Estelleaad and the court of King Wellstarre and wended a-west—for to the west lay Wellande, the Home of the Gods. There, her heart bid her, was the Key of Happiness to be found.

"O long she journeyed over the lands of Eldwolde and many a beauty and marvel she knew, and many an adventure came her way, until at last she sailed upon the waters of the Westron Sea and came at length to the Home of the Gods. By now she was aged, indeed an old woman, but still she sought an audience with Them, for the Key was like a molten image that burned in her mind driving her onward as it had done for lo! so many years...

"She landed her small craft on Wellande's golden shores and stepped from it eagerly, though her frame was feeble and not so swift to obey even the simplest of her commands. From its wooden bow, she hobbled along that aelfin strand until she met with Jarl, Lord of the Seas, where He sat mending His nets of the ages. She asked of Him the secret of the Key of Happiness and He said to her:

"'Ah! maid, I have watched you pass over Eldwolde from Wellstarre's court, lo! these many years, and much sorrow do I wear for you. For, Fancy, you left the Key in Wellstarre's court and in the hollows of the Hills of Bre, where Waine tends his sheep; in your father's heart as he grieves your hasty leave-taking and in each step you have taken in your journey over the lands of Eldwolde. Let it be known that Happiness dwells where you would find it and needs not lie ever over the next hill or across the great wide sea.

"'Yea, each land bears its own Happiness for its children and more besides, and the Key to it lies within you and about you wheresoever you are if you would but see it and then use it to open your own inner doors wherein lie Peace and sweet Joy.' And with the sorrow of the seas in His deep eyes, Jarl returned her to Estelleaad and the court of King Wellstarre upon the wings of the Weste Wind.

"There she was a young maid once again and but a few years had passed since she had been away. Within her heart she found her Key and with it she opened many doors with her love for those she knew. But Waine she found not, for the aelfin folk had stolen him away to the Lands of the Undying to ease his sorrow and loss. So now, though she had, indeed, found the Key, she had lost the one door which she fain would have opened."

iv.

THEN TANGLE saw that she sat by a bed of rustling Forget-me-nots and upon her finger, the golden ring that was the love of Weste glinted and sparkled in the bright sun.

Holding her flute close to her breast, she asked of Avenal, "And did she ever find him?"

And Avenal answered her saying: "Aye, so the tale is told…but in other lives and other times."

Drawing a deep breath, Tangle said quietly: "I will return to him, but yet must I bide here for a spell and do what I must do. For I have in my heart a weird and, for my own peace of mind, I must follow it."

Avenal rose wearily then and stood, gazing thoughtfully upon her. Though but a short space of time seemed to pass, the afternoon sun was nigh unto its setting when at last She spoke and said:

"Twas a tale and no more that I told and holds only what any tale may. Let it not trouble you with unbidden thoughts. Mayhap, he will await your return with a light and trusting heart, as the seasons slip into years and the years fade beyond counting. Still, I think not…lo!" She paused as the sweet peal of horns rang through the wood and searched for their source; but Tangle heard them not. Through the glimmering twilight She saw the aelfin host come riding and in their midst, She caught the downcast features of Weste the Song-smith; but Tangle saw it not.

Then She said: "The night draws near and I must away. Peace be with you, Tangle, and may you find your Key without o'er-much sorrow…"

And even as She spoke, the night was full-come and She was gone, leaving Tangle alone with naught but her thoughts, a heavy heart and her weird—and they must see her through to the end of days

Of the Temple In the City of the Burning Spires

LADEN AND BEJEWELED WITH eyes of bright lights, the golden-tressed Mistress of the Morning 'rose from her bower in the dark wood and sent its shadows whirling and spinning into rainbows. O that wood, where the boughs hung heavy with the memories of night and naught stirred but a dream-restless faun and the fair winged song-smiths with their endless beaming songs. Aye, that wood where the mushrooms grew in secret all night long 'neath the pale gaze of the moon; where the stars sent their hearts to dream as they lay bespeckling the midnight skies.

After a long feline stretch, She gently trod the mossy forest floor and then, thrice, sent Her blessèd form a-spiraling into the blossoming air. Upon the third time, the sky quivered and the sun 'rose full and golden and bore Her light into the day.

"Whither now?" She asked the wood in a soft voice and a Wind 'rose and carried Her with a sweet swirl and rustle of leaves, to Jalanell the City of the Burning Spires. There She stood in no man's sight and watched the priests in their temple hallowing the dawn—intense thin men, too preoccupied with their rituals to appreciate the reality of their devotion. Morgane—for so was She named in the lands of men—frowned. Her gaze sped from the splendor of the temple, the ornate furnishings, the jeweled robes of the priests and the glory therein, to the squalor in the streets outside, and a great sadness fell upon Her.

Awhile She stood and pondered 'till a small glad thought stole into Her heart. With a tiny spell, She breathed new life into the still form of a sleeping slave and clapped Her hands with glee as he 'rose wingèd into the air. He cast a shimmering golden light upon the temple floor ere he passed through its walls and danced laughingly upon the Wind. Far away over the hills and into the Lands of Dream he was drawn to where the aelf-folk welcomed him with joy and twined his heart with peace and contentment as they bade him: "Ever stay…"

While lo! In the temple the priests gaped and their consternation was written upon their unbelieving brows with deep wrinkled lines. Then a sudden understanding came to the high priest and he threw his jeweled garments upon the temple's marble floor and strode through its portals into the clean light of the sun and smiled. And Morgane was well-pleased.

But his brethren stood yet in the taper-lit temple—breathing the incense-laden air—and their bewilderment was a deep troubling in their hearts. Long after Morgane had passed on into the lengthening of the day did they abide within that gloomy fane until, at last, a candle flickered and went out. Then they filed from the temple to find the high priest where he basked in the light of both his new-found knowledge and the bright gleaming sun high overhead. Seeing him, their confusion and anger found a focus.

The first rock struck him above his eye and a thin trickle of blood mingled with the shock etched in his anguished face…

WHEN MORGANE passed by Jalanell on the wings of the following day, She found the broken body of the high priest upon the temple steps. Her merry features clouded over with a terrible wrath as She held his limp form in Her trembling arms.

And when She was gone, that temple in the City of the Burning Spires was no more…

Nareth the Questioner

IN TARANANN, BY THE shores of the Lake of the Seven Sorrows, Nareth the Questioner came walking. There was none could say how far or how long he had wandered save that he was known in all lands, on all worlds. His weird had led him from fabled Marad, whose shining towers stood moon-high and sullen, through Eldwolde's golden woods, and as far as the doomed reaches and wastes of the Greylands. And for what? What but the insatiable quest for knowledge.

Nareth sighed and sat down upon a well-worn rock near the water's edge and, adjusting his cloak comfortably about him, he brooded. Time passed unnoticed as he relived the weary years of his journeyings, a lifetime spent unravelling the Great Mystery to which there is no answer save the quest itself. And yet…dimmed, but never forgotten…there was the memory of an almost-heard name…the name of a Hidden One who held the answer…

So he sat until, after what might have been days, might have been years, he felt a presence behind him. Half-rising, he turned with sword drawn only to see the bent figure of an old man leaning on a staff, staring at him through hooded eyes; a half-smile playing about his lips. Sheathing his blade, Nareth sat down again and let out a heavy sigh.

The old man shuffled feebly to the edge of the lake and laid aside his staff. He bent down and, cupping his hands, drank deeply of its waters. Then, rising slowly, he turned to face Nareth. Leaning on his staff, he murmured:

"What Nareth? No questions today?"

Nareth looked up with a start at the old man's use of his name and said: "Who are you? How have you come to know my name? Are you here to mock me, as all the others do? To fill my mind with yet more lies so that I must search out Truth all the more desperately?"

The old man straightened suddenly. With a fluid movement, he tossed aside his staff and stepped closer to Nareth. There was a gracefulness in his step that belied his seeming senility of a few moments past.

In a purring voice—strangely rasping and unlike the speech-patterns of man—he said: "I am Jaalmar."

Nareth's eyes widened. That name...it was He! Nareth knew all the old tales...the legends of Jaalmar...the Lord of Secrets and Quiet Walking. He had been worshipped by the elder races in First Land for—more cat than man—He was of the Old Gods. It was said that His knowledge was deeper than the reaches beyond the stars; He whose voice was the Murmur of Peace and the Howl of War, from whose loins the cat-folk had sprung; He whose days have never begun and will have no end. Jaalmar! Here was the Hidden One who knew the answers to all questions. But how to pry that knowledge from Him?

Nareth looked out upon the waters of the Lake of the Seven Sorrows and tossed a pebble into its still waters. As the ripples spread out from where the pebble had dropped, he turned to Jaalmar and said slyly: "Tell me of its sorrows."

Jaalmar smiled and answered in a hypnotic murmur that spun and chanted words like the moon rising on Beltane Eve, like waves roving in the depths of the sea:

"They are...That Which Was and That Which Might Have Been... That Which Is and That Which Is Not...That Which Will Be and That Which Might Be...and That We Are Not...for we dwell but in a glamour and dream dreams therein and yet...All That Is, Is Not...

"You speak in riddles," said Nareth, "and yet, if all this is but a glamour—or a dream within a dream—tell me this then: who is it that dreams?"

Again the Master of Secrets smiled and with eyes of which the cat-folk's be but reflections, watched the winds of Taranann journey over His words; saw All That Is and Is Not; and then said quietly:

"To your own peril I will tell you the Secret, my curious friend: there is no dreamer and you have never been!" And Nareth knew the words as Truth and was no more...

— 🔥 —

IN TARANANN, by the shores of the Lake of the Seven Sorrows, Jaalmar, the Lord of Secrets and Quiet Walking, stood alone.

Looking across the lake's shining waters, He spoke without speaking and said:

"There is a different Truth for each and every being and woe be to he who would know them all. Poor Nareth the Questioner. A lifetime spent seeking what can never be known. A lifetime unlived. Poor Nareth the Questioner. Poor Nareth the Fool!"

And then He laughed and walked from Taranann into other tales, tales of which only He knows the telling…

Llew the Homeless

HARK NOW! FOR THIS is a tale the Wessener tell, and heed its telling, for 'tis a tale true-told. A tale of Mid-wold, when that world was yet young and there was war and trouble between the folk of Lyonesse, the south sea-bound land, and Kernow, to the north, a land of moors and stone hills.

And who knows now how that strife began? Indeed, the years of its waging seemed endless until, of a day, Drustans, the High Lord of Lyonesse, called unto him his Chief Bard, Llew, and to him said:

"Ah! Llew, I weary of this war! The land, itself, withers and spoils and there is no joy left among my people. I yearn for peace. So now, this task I set upon you: go you to Carth Caer and ask of King Marke a meeting between we twain. Say unto him that I will meet with him on the borders of our land and there, where the standing stones alone may bear witness, shall we take rede for the coming days and speak of peace. Be swift, my friend, and let naught detain you on your way, save the need for rest and let that be only when the need is great. Go now."

"As you wish, m'Lord," said Llew when Drustans was done with his speech and he bowed low to his liege. He slung his small harp over his shoulder and took his staff in hand. Then he withdrew from the High Lord's hall and was upon his way.

NOW THE tale tells that Llew was faithful to his lord and strode for a day and a night without pause for food or drink or rest. When fell the second night of his journey, he was well within the borders of Kernow and there was a weariness upon him. Before him was a dark wood of elder and oak and a path that led therein—a small crooked way that seemed but little trod—and this he followed as the night thickened upon his shoulders.

Then there was a light before him and, when he came anigh, he saw that it spilled from the window of a rudely-built cottage. With his staff, he rapped lightly upon its door and a voice bade him enter. Within, there was an old carline sitting by the fire, spinning. She glanced up from her work and brushed a thin strand of grey hair from her wrinkled brow.

"Play me a tune, Harper," she said.

But he said: "No, good dame, for I am hungry and have traveled o'er far without breaking my fast."

The carline rose from her work and brought to him meat and cheese and sweet fresh-baked bread and let him eat.

"Play me a tune, Harper," she said when he was done.

He shook his head and said: "No, good dame, for there is a great thirst upon me. Not a drop of wine or water has passed my lips for two days and a nights"

Then the old woman brought to him a flagon of mulled metheglyn and let him drink.

"Play me a tune now, Harper," she said.

But the warm honey-brew made his eyelids heavy and brought his fatigue full upon him.

"No, good dame," he said, "for I weary from my long journey and fain would I take my rest."

Then the carline led him to a shut-bed, the bedding of which was feather-filled and sweet-smelling, and let him sleep. When the sun woke the day with a fresh morning, Llew arose and made ready to take his leave. The old woman stopped him at the door.

"I have guested you well," she said, " with meat and wine and rest. Come now, Harper, play me my tune."

But he looked at her and said: "No, good dame, for I must be away upon my journey. I have a task of great import to fulfill for my liege and naught may detain me from it."

Then was the old carline wroth and she cursed him, saying:

"So be it, Harper. Sorrow you may have known, aye, and mayhap despair as well, yet now I lay this doom upon you: may you never again know the comfort of hearth and hall but walk ever the wild woods and wastes of the world!"

As she spoke, her words fell upon Llew's ears with a dismal certainty that turned his heart to ash. He opened his mouth and was about to speak, to somehow explain to her his seeming thanklessness, but then he saw the darkness in her eyes—and was there not a hint of satisfaction in her malice? Without a word, he turned from her and continued upon his way.

Now let it be said that it was no small asking that this carline had demanded of him, for in those days, when a bard sang, that song might take a day, and yet a day again, in its singing. The Bards of Lyonesse sang no common tales, but held in their lays all the sacred histories of their land. Tales of the ancient heroes and the Old Gods spilled from their hearts and were heard only at the sacred meets and motes, when all the folk might gather to listen and so be uplifted. Aye, there were they heard and in the halls of the High Lord.

And let it be remembered that his Lord, Drustans, had laid a task upon him that must be fulfilled with all speed and so his time was not his. Yet still, it was a deed ill-done and there was a dooming to be paid for it that far surpassed any reckoning that Llew might have deemed fair.

NOW THE tale tells that Llew came to the court of King Marke at Carth Caer, where it lay high in the moored hills of Kernow, and having fulfilled his task, made a speedy return to the hall of his Lord in Lyonesse. And the tale tells further that Drustans and Llew left that hall and fared one even toward the border of Kernow and came, in time, to the place of the standing stones, yet it tells no further.

But it is known that upon a newly-wrought cliff, where once the moors of Kernow met those of Lyonesse, two travelers came upon the grief-wracked broken form of Llew, once Chief Bard to the High Lord Drustans of Lyonesse, and from him they heard a bitter lament. It was a long ballad, sung in the ancient language of the Bards, yet through his skill of song-weaving they had no difficulty in understanding that secret tongue. In the common speech, it tells this tale...

O dig a grave and dig it deep-o
line it with ferns and flowers fair
and lay me down there within-o
that death may ease my dark despair...

there lay a land hight Lyonesse
Drustans the Blessed was her Lord
her golden shores held back the sea
her cliffs were high, her caernar low

one eve my Lord and I did stride
did stride the moor-wens, soft and slow
we strode to meet King Marke of Kernow
in his fey wolds of hill and stone

along the way I plucked my harp
her murmur made the night less grim
yet still a brooding weighed the air
as though the Dakath rode the wind

the moors grew dark, the stars were dimmed
no man we met upon that road
'till we did fare the hills of Kernow
'till 'mongst grey dolmen, hushed we rode

then rose three shade-shapes from the gorse
intent they were us to detain
and we did 'bide what might befall
that they might speak or else give way

the first it spoke and said: "Drustans
when you seek joy, I give you pain

that you will nevermore ken peace
your own deceit shall be your bane!"

the second spoke and to me said:
"Harper, I take from you your hearth
through ages you will ever fare
seeking what ne'er more may be yours!"

the third he spoke and cracked the sky
his voice was like the booming waves
that beat like thunder 'gainst sea cliffs:
"Lyonesse lies in her grave!"

a roar of doom rose from the south
and pierced our hearts with nameless dread
the anguished cry of hill and wood
—we knew, in truth, our land was dead

then wroth was Drustans, gentle Lord
then mad was Drustans, ever sane
and he did show to them his rage
—for with one blow, the three were slain

lo! then we strode our homeward way
onto this cliff, but newly-wrought
and we did gaze into the sea
that fell and dusky 'neath us tossed...

And here, or so the travelers have told it, Llew's voice broke and his grief overwhelmed him so that he could sing no further.

For a long while, naught was heard save the piteous sobbing of the broken Bard, but then he stood straighter and, leaning upon his staff, he sang...

a darkness swept across my mind
I can recall but one last sound:

departing footsteps 'pon the rocks
as I lay swooning on the ground

Drustans is gone, I know not where
as you have found me, I have lain
now take my harp and cast it far
into those dark and troubled waves

and dig a grave and dig it deep-o
line it with ferns and flowers fair
and lay me down there within-o
that death may ease my dark despair...

And when his refrain faded, Llew's staff fell from his grip and he lay upon the cold stone and wept.

The travelers were much-moved by his sorrowful tale and did for him as he had bade them. His harp they cast into the tumultuous sea, but the raging dark waters would not take it and flung it back to them. They dug a grave for him. For two days they laboured in the rocky ground and then gathered ferns and flowers, heather and bracken. Tenderly, they laid him therein, but the earth would not accept his body and heaved it from her bosom.

Hollow-eyed and spirit-broken, he left them then, with his harp slung over his shoulder, staff in hand, and his doom a cursed weight that he must bear unto the very end of days. Through the wilds and the wastes he fares and there is no rest for him, he who is hight Llew the Homeless, forsaken by all.

NOW IT is told that Drustans made his way to Carth Caer and took service with King Marke and served so well that he became Marke's most trusted knight. And the tale tells also that Drustans stole from King Marke his promised bride—Isolde, the blessèd maid of the Westron Isle—making her his own speech-friend, and so fulfilled the prophecy of his own treachery. But that is another tale.

There are some who say that he was be-spelled and that this treason was not his doing, but those same folk know not the true tale. They know not how Llew was set a task by his liege and how, in its undertaking, he brought doom to Lyonesse. They know not how the Bard was forsaken by Drustans when he lay broken and grieved in that place now named Land's End, where the cliffs of Kernow meet the tides of the raging sea.

Aye, they know not the true tale of the sinking of Lyonesse, those that even recall its name, and how its rending was wrought by one who loved that land dearly, to wit, Llew, now named the Homeless. He is gone now from this tale and from the eyes and knowledge of men, yet still he walks the world and is cursed therein, forever and for always.

And ere the full-telling of this tale be done, it must be said that the old carline in the wood of elder and oak was none other than Myken, the Mistress of Torment and Spite, and she is of the Dakath, the Dark Gods, who have no love for anything that is noble and true.

And here is the tale ended.

Angharad

Cold Blows the Wind

My lips they are as cold as clay,
my breath smells earthy strong,
and if you kiss my cold clay lips,
your days they won't be long...

—from "The Unquiet Grave";
traditional ballad (Child 78).

DON'T GO BY NIGHT, they said. But she did. Don't stray from the road, they said. But she did. Don't follow the fire; don't listen to its music. But she did. They meant well, she knew, but they didn't understand. She sought the blue-gold fire and the fey music of Jacky Lantern's elusive kin. It was all she had left.

IT WAS the night they camped by Tiercaern, where the heather-backed Carawyn Hills flow down to the sea, that Angharad's people met the witches. There were two of them—an old winter of a man, with salt-white hair and skin as brown and wrinkled as a tinker's hands, and a boy Angharad's age, fifteen summers if he was a day, lean and whip-thin with hair as black as a sloe. They both had the flicker of blue-gold in the depths of their eyes—eyes that were old and young in the both of them, of all ages and of none. The tinkers had brought their canvas-topped wagons around in a circle and were preparing their supper when the pair approached the edge of camp. They hailed the tinkers through a sudden chorus of camp dogs and

Angharad's father Herend'n went out to meet them, for he was the leader of the company.

"Is there iron on you?" Herend'n called, by which he meant, were they carrying weapons. The old man shook his head and lifted his staff. It was a white wood, that staff, cut from a rowan. Witches' wood.

"Not unless you count this," he said. "My name is Woodfrost and this is Garrow, my grandson. We are travelers—like yourselves."

Angharad, peering at the strangers from behind her father's back, saw the blue-gold light in their eyes and shook her head. They weren't like her people. They weren't like any tinkers *she* knew. Her father regarded the strangers steadily for a long heartbeat, then stepped aside and ushered them into the wagon circle.

"Be welcome," he said.

When they were by his fire, he offered them the guest-cup with his own hands. Woodfrost took the tea and sipped. Seeing them up close, Angharad wondered why the housey-folk feared witches so. This pair was as bedraggled as a couple of cats caught out in a storm and, for all their witch-eyes, seemed no more frightening to her than might beggars in a market town square. They were skinny and poor, with ragged travel-stained cloaks and unkempt hair. But then the old man's gaze touched hers and suddenly Angharad *was* afraid.

There was a distance in those witch-eyes like a night sky, rich with stars, or like a hawk floating high on the wind, watching, waiting to drop on its prey. They read something in her, pierced the scurry of her thoughts and the motley mix of what she was to find something lacking. She couldn't look away, was trapped like a riddle on a raven's tongue, until he finally dropped his gaze. Shivering, Angharad moved closer to her father.

"I thank you for your kindness," Woodfrost said as he handed the guest-cup back to Herend'n. "The road can be hard for folk such as we—especially when there is no home waiting for us at road's end." Again his gaze touched Angharad. "Is this your daughter?" he added.

Herend'n nodded proudly and gave the old man her name. He was a widower and with the death of Angharad's mother many years ago much of his joy in life had died with her. But he still had Angharad and if he loved anything in this world, it was his colt-thin daughter with her brown eyes that were so big and the bird's nest tangle of her red hair.

"She has the *sight*," Woodfrost said.

"I know," Herend'n replied. "Her mother had it too—Ballan rest her soul."

Bewildered, Angharad looked from her father to the stranger. This was the first *she'd* heard of it.

"But, da'," she said, pulling at his sleeve.

He turned at the tug to look at her. Something passed across his features the way the grass in a field trembles like a wave when the wind touches it. It was there one moment, gone the next. A sadness. A touch of pride. A momentary fear.

"But, da' ," she repeated.

"Don't be afraid," he said. "It's but a gift—like Kinny's skill with a fiddle, or the way Sheera can set a snare and talk to her ferrets."

"I'm not a witch!"

"It isn't such a terrible thing," Woodfrost said gently.

Angharad refused to meet his gaze. Instead, she looked at the boy. He smiled back shyly. Quickly Angharad looked away.

"I'm not," she said again.

But now she wasn't so sure. She wasn't exactly sure what the *sight* was, but she could remember a time when she'd *seen* more in the world than those around her. But she'd been so young then and it all went away when she grew up. Or she had made it go away…

ANGHARAD SMILED as she left the road, remembering. The forest closed in around her, dark and rich with scent and sound. The wind spoke in the uppermost branches with a murmur that almost, but not quite, buried the vague sound of a fey and distant harping that came to her from deeper in the wood. Her witch-sight pierced the gloom, searching for the first trace of a will-o'-the-wisp's lantern, bobbing in amongst the trees.

— ❦ —

AS THOUGH the coming of the witches was a catalyst, Angharad found that she *could* see what was hidden from others. There was movement and sound abroad in the world that went unseen and unheard by both tinkers and the housey-folk who lived in the towns or worked the farms, and to *see* it, to *hear* it, was not such a terrible thing.

Woodfrost and Garrow traveled with the company that whole summer long and will she, nill she, Angharad learned to use her gift. She retained her fear of Woodfrost—because there was always that shadow, that darkness, that secrecy in his eyes—but she made friends with Garrow. He was still shy with the other tinkers, but he opened up to her. His secrets, when they unfolded, were of a far and distant sort from what she supposed his grandsire's to be. Garrow taught her the language of the trees and the beasts, from the murmur of a drowsy old oak to the quick chatter of squirrel and finch and the sly tongue of the fox. Magpies became her confidants, and badgers, and the wind. But at the same time she found herself becoming tongue-tied around Garrow and, if he paid particular attention to her, or caught one of her long dreamy glances, a flush would rise from the nape of her neck and her heart begin to beat quick and fast like a captured wren's.

THE SMILE grew bittersweet as Angharad moved deeper into the forest. It was on a night like this, between the last days of Hafarl, the Summerlord's rule and the first cold days of autumn, on a night when the housey-folk left their farms and towns to build great bonfires on the hilltops and would sing and dance to music that made the priests of the One God Dath frown, that she and Garrow made a mystery of their own. They made love as gently fierce as the stag and moon in the spring and, afterwards, lay dreamy and content in each other's arms while the stars completed their nightly wheel and spin above them.

The tears that touched Angharad's cheeks as she continued through the trees, remembering, were not the same as those that night. *That* night she'd been so full of emotion and magic that there was no other release for what she felt swelling inside her. Now she was only... remembering...

— 🍃 —

THE TINKER company wintered in Mullyn that year, on a farm that belonged to Green George Snell who once traveled the roads with Angharad's people. There they prepared for the next year's traveling. Wagons were repaired, as were harnesses and riggings. Goods were made to be sold at the market towns and the horses were readied for the fairs. When the first breath of spring was in the air, the company took to the road once more. Angharad and Garrow still rode in Herend'n's wagon, though they had jumped the broom at midwinter. Newly married, they were still too poor to afford their own wagon.

The road took them up into Umbria and Kellmidden that summer where the company looked to meet with the caravans of other travelers and to grow rich—or at least as rich as any tinker could get, which was not a great deal by the standards of the housey-folk. They looked forward to a summer of traveling and the road, of gossiping, trading and renewing old acquaintances. Instead, they found the plague waiting for them.

— 🍃 —

THE MEMORY of that first devastated town was still too fresh in Angharad's mind. It cut like a sharp sliver of mandrake root thrust deep into her heart. She stumbled in the forest, foot caught in a root, and leaned against the fat bole of a tree. The bark was rough against her skin and snagged at her hair as she moved her head slowly away from it. As though echoing her pain, the fey and distant harping faltered and grew still. She lifted her head, afraid of the sudden silence. Then faint, faint, the music started up once more and she went on, trying to keep the memories buried, but they rose, constant as air bubbles in a sulphur spring, the pain spreading through as pervasively as those noxious fumes.

— 🍃 —

THE CORPSE had lain in the town square, black and swollen. Surprised, the tinkers' shocked gazes found more—in alleyways, in doorways—sprawled bodies, black from the plague. Too late, Herend'n realized their plight. The town had been silent, empty, but there had been no hint, no rumour of this. Too late, he turned the wagons. Too late.

Two nights later the first of the company took sick. In retrospect, Herend'n realized that one of the dogs must have spread the sickness. Angharad and the witches *saw* the plague spreading under the skin of Marenda's son Fearnol and Herend'n turned the wagons into their circle and they set up camp. Too late. By nightfall, half the company was stricken. In two weeks' time, for all the medicines that Angharad and the witches and the rootwives of the tinkers gathered and prepared and fed to the sick, the greater part of the company was dead. Nine wagons were in that circle and sixty-two tinkers had traveled in them. On the morning that the last of the dead were buried, only one wagon left the camp and only three of the company rode in it. They were thin and gaunt as half-starved ravens. Jend'n the Tall. Sheera's daughter, Benraida. And Crowen the Kettle-maker. There was a fourth survivor—Angharad. But she remained behind with her dead. Her father. Her husband. Her kin. Her friends.

She lived in her father's wagon and tended their graves the whole summer long. She cursed the *sight* that had made her *see* the black sickness speed and swell inside the bodies of the stricken, killing them cell by cell while she stood helplessly by. Garrow…her father…She cursed what gods she knew of, from Ballan the Lord of Broom and Heather to Dath, the cold One God and Hafarl's daughter who had always seemed the most real to her. Gentle Tarasen, who kept safe the beasts of the wood and the birds of the air. Even she had failed Angharad in her time of need.

She stayed there until the summer drew to an end and then she remembered a tale once heard around the fires of a tinker camp, of marshes and Jacky Lantern's kin and how the dead could be called back in such a place if one's need were great enough, if one had the gift…She took to the road the next morning with a small pack of provisions slung over one shoulder and Woodfrost's white staff in her hand. She went through a land empty and deserted, through villages and towns where the dead lay unburied, past farms that were silent and as forsaken as broken dreams. She traveled through the wild north highlands of Umbria and when she crossed Kellmidden's borders it was to come to a land that the plague had never grasped in its diseased claws, and she still did not understand why she had been spared when so many had died.

Hafarl's grip was loosing on the land as the autumn grew crisp across the dales and hills of Kellmidden's lowlands and the constellations that wheeled above her by night were those of Lithun, the Winter Lord. She stopped to sup in a last inn, ignoring the warnings of the well-meaning housey-folk that stayed warm by the fire when she went out into the night once more. She went empty-handed now, her provision bag depleted and the rowan staff no longer needed for she knew she was approaching the end of her journey. As she had eaten her supper in the inn, she'd *heard* the sweet fey music…calling to her, whispering, drawing her on, unattainable as fool's fire, but calling to her all the same. When she left the road and entered the dark forests, Garrow's features swam in her mind's eye, a familiar smile playing on his lips, keyed to the fey unearthly music that came to her from the depths of the forest, and she knew her journey was done.

NOW THE land sloped steadily downward in the direction she was traveling. The forest of pine, birch and fir gave way to gnarly cedar and stands of willow. Underfoot, the ground softened and her passage was marked by the soft sucking noise of her feet lifting from the marshy footing. A sliver of a horned moon was lowering in the west. Last quarter. A moon of omens. The muck rose to her ankles and the long days of her journeying and sorrow finally took their toll. Weary beyond belief, she collapsed on a small hillock that rose out of the marsh. The fey harping was no louder than it had ever been, but somehow it seemed closer now.

On arms trembling from fatigue, she lifted her upper body from the ground and rolled over to see the makers of that music all around. They were tall ghostly beings, thin as reeds and glowing with their own pale inner light. Their hair hung thin and feather soft about their long and narrow faces. The men carried lanterns filled with flickering light; the women played harps that were as slender as willow boughs with strings like spun moonlight. Their eyes gleamed blue-gold in the darkness.

"Strayed," the harping sang to her, a ghostly refrain. "Too far…too far…"

She looked amongst their ranks for another slender form—a familiar form, with black hair and no harping skill—but saw only the ghostly harpers and lantern-bearers.

"Garrow?" she called, searching their faces.

The harping fluttered like a chorus of bird calls, grew still. Angharad's heartbeat stilled with it. She held her breath as one of the pale glowing shapes moved forward.

"You!" she hissed, her breath coming out in a sharp stream as she recognized the man's features. Her pulse drummed suddenly, loud in her ears, driven by a mingling of fear and anger.

Woodfrost nodded wearily. "You are still so stubborn," he said.

She glared at him. "What have you done with Garrow?" she demanded. "I didn't come for you, old man."

"As a child you could *see*," Woodfrost said as though he hadn't heard her, "but you saw soon enough that others couldn't and, rather than be different, you ignored the gift until you became as blind as they were. Ignored it so that, in time, all memory of it was gone."

"It was a curse, not a gift. How can you call it a gift when it allows you to *see* those you love die while you must stand helplessly by?"

"So many years you wasted," Woodfrost continued, still ignoring her. "So stubborn. And then we came to your camp, my grandson and I. Still you protested, until Garrow drew the veil from your eyes and taught you your gift once more—taught you what you had once known, but chose to forget. Was your gift so evil, then?"

Angharad wanted to stand but her body was too tired to obey her. She managed to sit up and hug her knees. "Garrow was alive then," she said.

Woodfrost nodded. "So he was. And then he died. Death is a tragedy—no mistake of that, Angharad—but only for the living. We who have died go on to…other things; as the living must go on with the responsibility of being alive. But not you. Oh, no. You are too stubborn for that. If those you love are dead, then you will go about as one dead yourself. It is a fair thing to revere those who have passed on—but only within reason, Angharad. Graves may be tended and memories called up, but the business of living must go on."

"I could call him back…in this place, I could call him back," Angharad said in a small voice.

"Only if I let you."

Anger flickered in Angharad's witchy eyes. "You have no right to come between us."

"Angharad," Woodfrost said softly. "Do you truly believe that I would stand between you and my grandson if he was alive? When you joined your futures together, there was none happier than I. But we no longer speak of you and Garrow; we speak now of the living and the dead, and yes, I will come between you then."

"Why is it so evil? We *loved* each other."

"It is not so much evil…Let us leave the talk of evil and sins to the priests of Dath. Say rather that it is wrong, Angharad. You have a duty and responsibility while you live that does not include calling forth the shades of the dead. Death will come for you soon enough, for even the lives of witches are not so long as men would believe, and then you will be with Garrow in the land of shadows. Will you make a land of shadows in the world of the living?"

"Without him there is nothing."

"There is everything still."

"If you weren't already dead," Angharad said dully, "I would kill you."

"Why? Because I speak the truth? You are a woman of the traveling people—not some village-bound housey-folk who looks to her husband for every approval."

"It's not that. It's…"

Her voice trailed off. She stared past him to where the will-o'-the-wisps stood pale and tall, silent harps held in glowing hands, witchy lanterns gleaming eerily.

"I could live ten years without him," she said softly, her gaze returning to the old man's. "I could live forever without him, so long as I knew that he was still in the world. That all he was was not gone from it. That somewhere his voice was still heard, his face seen, his kindness known. Not dead. Not lying in a grave with the cold earth on him and the worms feeding on his body. If I could know that he was still...happy."

"Angharad, he can be content—which is as close as the dead can come to what the living call 'happiness.' When he knows that you will go on with your life, that you will take up the reins of your witch's duties once more—then he will be at peace."

"Oh, gods!" Angharad cried. "What duty? I have no duty, only loss."

Woodfrost stepped towards her and lifted her to her feet. His touch was cold and eerie on her skin and she shrank back from him, but he did not let her go.

"While you live," he said, "you have a duty to life. And Hafarl's gift—the gift of the Summerblood that gives you your *sight*—you have a duty to it as well. The fey wonders of the world only exist while there are those with the *sight* to *see* them, Angharad, otherwise they fade away."

"I see only a world made grey with grief."

"I have known grief as well," Woodfrost said. "I lost my wife. My daughter. Her husband. I, too, have lost loved ones, but that did not keep me from my duties to life and the gift. I traveled the roads and sought blind folk such as you were and did my best to make them *see* once more. Not for myself. But that the world might not lose its wonder. Its magic."

"But..."

The old man stepped back from her. In his gaze she saw once more that weighing look that had come into his eyes on that first night she'd met him.

"If not for yourself," he said, "then do it for the others who are still blind to their gift. Is your grief so great that they must suffer for it as well?"

Angharad shrank back, more frightened by quiet sympathy in his eyes than if he'd been angry with her. "I...I'm just one person..."

"So are all who live..., and so are all who have the gift. The music of the Middle Kingdom is only a whisper now, Angharad. When it is forgotten, not even an echo of that music will remain. If you would leave such a world for those who are yet to be born, then call your husband back from the land of shadows and live together in some half-life—neither living nor dead, the both of you.

"The choice is yours, Angharad."

She bowed her head, tears spilling down her cheeks. I'm not as strong as you, she wanted to tell him, but when she lifted her anguished gaze he was no longer there. She saw only the wraith-shapes of Jacky Lantern's kin, watching her. In their faces there were no answers, no judgments. Their blue-gold eyes returned her gaze without reply.

"Garrow," she said softly, all her love caught up in that one word, that one name. There was a motion in the air where Woodfrost had stood, a sense of some gate opening between this world and the next. Through her teary gaze she saw a familiar face taking shape, the hazy outline of a body underneath it. "Garrow," she said again, and the image grew firmer, more real. For a long strained moment she watched him forming there, drawing substance from the marsh, breaching the gulf between the land of shadows and the hillock where she stood, then she bowed her head once more.

"Goodbye," she said.

The grief swelled anew in her. He was lost now, lost forever, while she must go on. She could feel his presence vanish without the need to watch. Her throat was thick with emotion, her eyes blinded by tears. Then there was a touch on her cheek, like lips of wind brushing against the skin, here one moment like a feather, then gone. In the midst of her grief a strange warmth arose in her and she thought she heard a voice, distant, distant, whisper briefly, *I will wait for you, my love,* and then she was alone in the marsh with only the ghostly will-o'-the-wisps for company.

Through a sheen of tears, she watched one of the harpers approach her, the woman's pale shape more gossamer than ever. She laid her harp on Angharad's knee. Like Woodfrost's hands, it had substance and weight, surprising her. It was a small plain instrument—more like a child's harp than like those that the itinerant barden carried and played. She touched the smooth wood of its curving neck.

"I...I'm a witch," she said in a low soft voice, the bitterness in it directed only at herself. "I can't make music—I never could."

But her fingers were drawn to the strings and she found they knew a melody, if she did not. It was a slow sad air that drew the sorrow from her and made of it a haunting music that eased the pain inside her. A faery gift, she thought. Was it supposed to make her grief more bearable?

"It must have a name," the wraith said, her voice eerie and echoing like the breath of a wind on a far hill.

A name? Angharad thought. She watched her fingers draw the music from the instrument's strings and wondered that wood and metal could make such a sound. A name? Her sadness was in the harp's music, loosened from the tight knots inside her and set free on the air.

"I will call it Garrow," she said, looking up.

The ghostly company was gone, but she no longer felt alone.

THE TINKER company was camped by a stream with good pasture nearby when the young red-haired woman with her old eyes came to their wagons, a small harp slung from her shoulder. She called out to the tinkers in their own secret tongue and they welcomed her readily with a guest cup and a place by the fire. Sitting in the flickering firelight, she looked from face to face and smiled as her gaze rested on a lanky girl named Zia who was thirteen summers if she was a day.

Zia blushed and looked away, but inside her she felt something stir that had been buried a year ago when she learned the ways of a woman and set aside her favorite doll with its cloth face and broom and heather body.

The red-haired woman smiled again and began to play her harp.

The Weeping Oak

SHE FOUND HIM IN Avalarn, one of Cermyn's old forests, the one said to have been a haunt of the wizard Puretongue though that was long ago. He lay in a nest of leaves, sheltered in a cleft of rocks. Above them, old oaks clawed skyward with greedy boughs, reaching for the clouds.

"I know you," he said, dark eyes opening suddenly to look into her face. They glittered like a crow's.

"Do you now?" she said mildly.

He was a reed-thin feral child and she felt an immediate kinship with him. He had her red hair, and the same look of age in his eyes that she had in hers. He could have been her brother. But she had never seen him before.

"You lived in an oak," he said.

Angharad was a tinker with the blood of the Summerlord running through her veins, which was just another way of saying that she had a witch's *sight*. She rocked back on her heels as the boy sat up. A small harp was slung from her shoulder. Her red hair was drawn back in two long braids. She wore a tinker's plaited skirt and white blouse, but a huntsman's leather jerkin overtop. A small journeypack lay by her left knee where she'd set it down. By her right, was a staff of white rowan wood. Witches' wood.

"Are you hungry?" she asked.

When he nodded, she drew bread and cheese from her pack and watched him devour it like a cat. He took quick bites, his gaze never leaving her face.

"I lived up in the branches of your tree once," he said, wiping crumbs from his mouth with the back of his hand. "I'd hear you playing that harp, when the moon was right."

Angharad smiled. "You heard the wind fingering an oak tree's branches—nothing else."

The boy smiled back. "So you *were* there, or how would you know? Besides, how else would a treewife play the harp of her boughs?"

His voice was soft, with a slight rasp. There was a flicker in his eyes like fool's fire.

"What's your name, boy?" she asked. "What are you doing here? Are you lost?"

"My name's Fenn and I've been waiting for you. All my life, I've been waiting for you."

Angharad couldn't help smiling again. "And such a long life you've had so far."

The boy's eyes hooded. A fox watched her from under his bushy eyebrows.

"Why have you been waiting for me?" she asked finally.

Fenn pointed to her harp. "I want you to sing the song that will set me free."

— 🕯 —

ANGHARAD CRAWLED through the weeds with the boy, keeping low, though out of whose sight, Fenn wouldn't say. The foothills of the West Meon Mountains ran off to the west, a sea of bell heather and gorse, dotted with islands of stone outcrops where ferrets prowled at night. But it wasn't the moorland that he'd brought her to see.

"That's where he lived," Fenn said, pointing to the giant oak that stood alone and towering in the halfland between the forest and the sea of moor.

"The wizard?"

Fenn nodded. "He's bound there yet—bound to his tree. Just like you were, treewife."

"My name is Angharad," she said, not for the first time. "And I was never bound to a tree."

Fenn merely shrugged. Angharad caught his gaze and held it until he looked away, a quick sidling movement. She turned her attention back to the tree. Faintly, amongst its branches, she could make out a structure.

"That was Puretongue's tree?" she asked.

Fenn grinned, all the humour riding in his eyes. "But he's been dead a hundred years or better, of course. It's the other wizard that's bound in there now. The one that came after Puretongue."

"And what was his name?"

"That's part of the riddle and why you're needed. Learn his name and you have him."

"I don't want him."

"But if you free him, then he'll finally let me go."

Somehow, Angharad doubted that it would be so simple. She didn't trust her companion. He might appear to be the brother she'd never had—red hair, witcheyes and all—but there was something feral about him that made her wary. The oak tree caught her gaze again, drawing it in like a snared bird. Still there was something about that tree, about that house up in its branches. Silence hung about it, thick as cobwebs in a disused tower.

"I'll have to think about this," she said.

Without waiting for Fenn, she crept back through the weeds, keeping low until the first outriding trees of Avalarn Forest shielded her from possible view.

— ❧ —

"WHY SHOULD I believe you?" Angharad asked.

They had returned to where she'd first found him and sat perched on stones like a pair of magpies, facing each other, watching the glitter in each other's eyes and looking for the spark that told of a lie.

"How could I tell you anything but the truth?" Fenn replied. "I'm your friend."

"And if you told me that the world was round—would I be expected to believe that too?"

Fenn laughed. "But it is round, and hangs like an apple in the sky."

"I know," Angharad said, "though there are those that don't." She studied him for another long moment. "So tell me again, what is it you need to be freed from?"

"The wizard."

"I don't see any chains on you."

Fenn tapped his chest. "The bindings are inside—on my heart. That's why I need your song."

"Which can't be sung until the wizard is loosed."

Fenn nodded.

"Tell me this," Angharad said. "If the wizard is set free, what's to stop him from binding me?"

"Gratitude," Fenn replied. "He's been bound a hundred years, treewife. He'll grant any wish to the one who frees him."

Angharad closed her eyes, picturing the tree, its fat bole, the lofty height to its first boughs.

"*You* can't climb it?" she asked.

"It's not a matter of what I'm capable of," Fenn replied. "It's a matter of the geas that was laid on me and the wizard. I can't stray, but I can't enter the house in its branches. And the wizard can't free me until he himself is free. Won't you help us?"

Angharad opened her eyes to find him smiling at her.

"I'll go up the tree," she said, "but I'll make no promises."

"The key to free him—"

"Is in a small wicker basket—the size of a woodsman's fist. I know. You've already told me more than once."

"Oh, treewife, you—"

"I'm *not* a treewife," Angharad said.

She jumped down from her perch on the stones and started for the tree. Fenn hesitated for a long heartbeat, then scrambled down as well to hurry after her.

"HOW WILL you get up?" Fenn whispered when they stood directly under the tree.

Though the bark was rough, Angharad didn't trust it to make for safe handholds on a climb up. The bole was too fat for her to shimmy up. She took a coil of rope from her pack and tied a stone to one end.

"Not by witchy means," she said.

The boy stood back as she began to whirl the stone in an ever-widening circle above her head. She hummed to herself, eyes narrowed as she peered up, hand waiting for just the right moment to cast the stone. Then suddenly it was aloft, flying high, the rope trailing behind it like a long bedraggled tail. Fenn clapped his hands as the stone soared over the lowest branch, then came down the opposite side. Angharad untied the rock. Passing one end of the rope through a slipknot, she pulled it through until the knot was at the branch.

Journeypack and staff stayed by the foot of the tree. With only her small harp on her shoulder, she used the rope to climb up, grunting at the effort it took. Her arms and shoulders were aching long before she reached that first welcome branch, but reach it she did. She sprawled on it and looked down. She saw her belongings, but Fenn was gone. Frowning, she looked up and blinked in amazement. Seen from here, the wizard's refuge was *exactly* like a small house, only set in the branches of a tree instead of on the ground.

Well, I've come this far, Angharad thought. There was no point in going back down until she'd at least had a look. Besides, her own curiosity was tugging at her now.

She drew up the rope and coiled it carefully around her waist. Without it, she could easily be trapped in this tree. Her witcheries let her talk to the birds and the beasts and to listen to their gossips, but they weren't enough to let her fly off like an eagle or crawl down the treetrunk like a squirrel.

She made her way up, one branch, then another, moving carefully until she finally clambered up the last to stand on the small porch in front of the door. She laid a hand on the wooden door. The wood was smooth to her touch, the whorls of the grain more intricate than any human artwork could ever be. She turned and looked away.

She could see the breadth of the forest from her vantage point, could watch it sweep into the distance, another sea, green and flowing, to twin the darker waves of gorse and heather that marched westward. Slowly she sank down onto her haunches.

She remembered the foxfire flicker in Fenn's eyes and thought of the lights of Jacky Lantern's marshkin who loved to lead travelers astray. Some never came back. She remembered tinker wagons rolling by ruined keeps and how she and the other children would dare each other to go exploring within. Crowen's little brother Broon fell down a shaft in one place and broke his neck. She remembered tales of haunted places where if one spent the night, they were found the next morning either dead, mad, or a poet. This tree had the air of such a place.

She sighed. One hand lifted to the harp at her shoulder. She fingered the smooth length of its small forepillar.

The harp was a gift from Jacky Lantern's kin, as was the music she pulled from its strings. She used it in her journeys through the Kingdoms of the Green Isles, to wake the Summerblood where it lay sleeping in folk who never knew they were witches. That was the way the Middle Kingdom survived—by being remembered, by its small magics being served, by the interchange of wisdom and gossip between man and those he shared the world with—the birds, the beasts, the hills, the trees…

Poetry was the other third of a bard's spells, she thought. Poetry and harping and the road that led into the green. She had the harp and knew the road. Standing then to face the door, she thought, perhaps I'll find the poetry in here.

She tried the wooden latch and it moved easily under her hand. The door swung open with a push, and then she stepped through.

The light was cool and green inside. She stood in the middle of a large room. There were bookshelves with leather-bound volumes on one wall, a worktable on another with bunches of dried herbs hanging above it. A stone hearth stood against another and she wondered what wood even a wizard would dare burn, living here in a tree.

The door closed softly behind her. She turned quickly, half-expecting to see someone there, but she was alone in the room. She walked over to the worktable and ran her hand lightly along its length. There was no dust. And the room itself—it was so big. Bigger than she would have supposed it to be when she was outside.

There was another door by the bookshelves. Curious, she crossed the room and tried its handle. It opened easily as well, leading into another room.

Angharad paused there, a witchy tickle starting up her spine. This was impossible. The house was far too small to have so much space inside. She remembered then the one thing she'd forgotten to ask Fenn. If the wizard had caught him, who had caught the wizard and laid the geas on them both?

She wished now that she had brought her staff with her. The white rowan wood could call up a witchfire. In a place such as this that had once belonged to a treewizard, fire seemed a good weapon to be carrying. Returning to the work bench, she looked through the herbs and clay jars and bundles of twigs until she found what she was looking for. A rowan sprig. Not much, perhaps, but a fire needed only one spark to start its flames.

Twig in hand, she entered the next room. It was much the same as the first, only more cluttered. Another door led off from it. She went through that door to find yet one more room. This was smaller, a bedchamber with a curtained window and a small table and chair under it. On the table was a small wicker basket.

About the size of a man's fist…

She stepped over to the table and picked up the basket. The lid came off easily. Inside was a small bone. A fingerbone, she realized. She closed the basket quickly and looked around. Her witcheries told her that she was no longer alone.

Who are you? a voice breathed in her mind. It seemed to swim out of the walls, a rumbling bass sound, but soft as the last echo of a harp's low strings.

"Who are *you?*" she answered back. No fool she. Names were power.

She felt what could only be a smile form in her mind. *I am the light on a hawk's wings, the whisper of a tree's boughs, the smell of bell heather, the texture of loam. I dream like a fox, run like a longstone, dance like the wind.*

"You're the wizard, then," Angharad said. Only wizards used a hundred words where one would do. Except for their spells. Then all they needed was the one name.

Why are you here?

"To free you."

Again that smile took shape in her mind. *And who told you that I needed to be freed?*

"The boy in the forest—the one you've bound. Fenn."

The boy is a liar.

Angharad sighed. She'd thought as much, really. So why *was* she here? To spend the night and see if she'd wake mad or a poet, or not wake at all? But when she spoke, all she said was, "And perhaps you are the liar."

The presence in her mind laughed. *Perhaps I am,* it said. *Lie down on the bed, dear guest. I want to show you something.*

"I can see well enough standing up, thank you all the same."

And if you fall down and crack your head when the vision comes—who will you blame?

Angharad made a slow circuit around the room, stopping when she came to the bed. She touched its coverlet, poked at the mattress. Sighing, she kept a firm hold of the basket in one hand, the rowan twig in the other, and lay down. No sooner did her head touch the pillow, than the coverlet rose up in a twist and bound her limbs, holding her fast.

"You *are* a liar," she said, trying to keep the edge of panic out of her voice.

Or you are a fool, her captor replied.

"At least let me see you."

I have something different in mind, dear guest. Something else to show you.

Before Angharad could protest, before she could light the rowan twig with her witcheries, the presence in her mind wrapped her in its power and took her away.

THE PERSPECTIVE she had was that of a bird. She was high in the oak that held the treewizard's house, higher than a man or woman could climb, higher than a child, amongst branches so slender they would scarcely take the weight of a squirrel. The view that vantage point gave her was breathtaking—the endless sweep of forest and moor, striding off in opposite directions. The sky, huge above her, close enough to touch. The ground so far below it was another world.

She had no body. She was merely a presence, like the presence inside the treewizard's house, hovering in the air. A disembodied ghost.

Watch, a now-familiar voice said.

Give me back my body, she told it.

First you must watch.

Her perspective changed, bringing her closer to the ground, and she saw a young man who looked vaguely familiar approaching the tree. He looked like a tinker, red-haired, bright clothes and all, but she could tell by the bundle of books that joined the journeypack on his back that he was a scholar.

He came to learn, her captor told her.

Nothing wrong with that, she replied. *Knowledge is a good thing to own. It allows you to understand the world around you better and no one can take it away from you.*

A good thing, perhaps, her captor agreed, *depending on what one plans to do with it.*

The young man was cutting footholds into the tree with a small axe. Angharad could feel the tree shiver with each blow.

Doesn't he understand what he's doing to the tree? she asked.

All he understands is his quest for knowledge. He plans to become the most powerful wizard of all.

But why?

A good question. I don't doubt he wishes now that he'd thought it all through more clearly before he came.

Angharad wanted to pursue that further, but by now the young man had reached the porch. He had a triumphant look on his face as he stood before the door. Grinning, he shoved open the door and strode inside. The presence in Angharad's mind tried to draw her in after him, but she was too busy watching the footholds that the young man had cut into the tree grow back, one by one, until there was no sign that they'd ever been there. Then she drifted inside.

Look at him, her captor said.

She did. He'd thrown his packs down by the floor and was pulling out the books in the treewizard's library, tossing each volume on the floor after only the most cursory glances.

"I've done it," he was muttering. "Sweet Dath, I've found a treasure trove."

He tossed the book he was holding down, then got up to investigate the next room. After he'd gone, the books on the floor rose one by one and returned to their places. Angharad hurried in after the young man to find him already in the third room, dancing an awkward jig, his boots clattering on the floorboards.

"I'll show them all!" he sang. "I'll have such power that they'll all bow down to me. They'll come to me with their troubles and, if they're rich enough, if they catch me in an amiable mood, I might even help them." He rubbed his hands together. "Won't I be fine, won't I just."

He was not well-looked upon, her captor explained. *He wanted so much and had so little, and wasn't willing to work for what he did want. He needed it all at once.*

I understand now, Angharad said. *He's—*

Watch.

Days passed in a flicker, showing the young man growing increasingly impatient with the slow speed at which he gained his knowledge.

It was still work after all, Angharad's captor said.

"Damn this place!" the young man roared one morning. He flung the book he was studying across the room. "Where is the magic? Where is the power?" He strode back and forth, running a hand through the tangled knots of his hair.

Can't he feel it? Angharad asked. *It's in every book, every nook and cranny of this place. The whole tree positively reeks of it.*

She felt her captor smile inside her mind, a weary smile.

He has yet to understand the difference between what is taken and what is given, he explained.

Angharad thought of ghostly harpers in a marsh, Jacky Lantern's kin, pressing a harp into her hands. Not until she'd been ready to give up what she wanted most—as misguided a seeking after power as this young man's was—had she received a wisdom she hadn't even been aware she was looking for.

She watched in horror now as the young man began to pile the books in a heap in the center of the room. He took flint and steel from his pocket and bent over them.

No! Angharad cried, forgetting that this was the past she was being shown. *We can't let him!*

Too late, her captor said. *The deed's long past and done. But watch. The final act has yet to play.*

As the young man bent over the books, the room about him came alive. Chairs flowed into snake-like shapes and caught him by the ankles, pulling him down to the floor. A worktable spilled clay jars and herb bundles about the room as it lunged towards him, folding over his body, suddenly as pliable as a blanket.

Flint fell with a clatter in one direction, steel in another. The young man screamed. The room exploded into a whirlwind of furniture and books and debris, spinning faster and faster, until Angharad grew ill looking at it. Then, just as suddenly as it had come up, the wind died down. The room blurred, mists swelled within its confines, grew tattered, dissolved. When it was gone, the room looked no different than it had when Angharad had first entered it herself. The young man was gone.

Where...? she began.

Inside the tree, her captor told her. *Trapped forever and a day, or until a mage or a witch should come to answer the riddle.*

Before Angharad could ask, the presence in her mind whisked her away and the next thing she knew she was lying in the bed once more, the coverlet lying slack and unmoving. She sat up slowly, clutching basket and rowan twig in her hands.

"What is the riddle?" she asked the empty room.

Who is wiser, the presence in her mind asked. *The man who knows everything, or the man who knows nothing?*

"Neither," Angharad replied correctly. "Is that it? Is that all?"

Oh, no, the presence told her. *You must tell me my name.*

Angharad opened the wicker basket and looked down at the tiny fingerbone. "The wizard in the tree—his name is Fenn. The boy I met is what he could be, should he live again. But you—you live in the tree and if you have need of a name, it would be Druswid." It was a word in the old tongue that meant the knowledge of the oak. "Puretongue was your student," she added, "wasn't he?"

A long time ago, the presence in her mind told her. *But we learned from each other. You did well, dear guest. Sleep now.*

Angharad tried to shake off the drowsiness that came over her, but to no avail. It crept through her body in a wearying wave. She fell back onto the bed, fell into a dreamless sleep.

— 🌿 —

WHEN ANGHARAD woke, it was dawn and she was lying at the foot of the giant oak tree. She sat up, surprisingly not at all stiff from her night on the ground, and turned to find Fenn sitting crosslegged beside her pack and staff, watching her. Angharad looked up at the house, high in the tree.

"How did I get down?" she asked.

Fenn shrugged. He played with a small bone that hung around his neck by a thin leather strong. Angharad looked down at her hands to find she was holding the rowan twig in the one, and the basket in the other. She opened the basket, but the fingerbone was gone.

"A second chance," she said to Fenn. "Is that what you've been given?"

He nodded. "A second chance."

"What will you do with it?"

He grinned. "Go back up that tree and learn, but for all the right reasons this time."

"And what would they be?"

"Don't you know, treewife?"

"I'm *not* a treewife."

"Oh, no? Then how did you guess Druswid's name?"

"I didn't guess. I'm a witch, Fenn—that gives me a certain *sight*."

Fenn's eyes widened slightly with a touch of awe. "You actually saw Druswid?"

Angharad shook her head. "But I know a tree's voice when I hear it. And who else would be speaking to me from an oak tree? Not a wet-eared impatient boy who wanted to be a wizard for all the wrong reasons."

"You're angry because I tricked you into going up into the tree. But I didn't lie. I just didn't tell you everything."

"Why not?"

"I didn't think you'd help me."

Angharad gathered up her harp and pack and swung them onto her back. Fenn handed her her staff.

"Well?" he asked. "Would you have?"

Angharad looked up at the tree. "I'm not dead," she said, "and I don't feel mad, so perhaps I've become a poet."

"Treewi—" Fenn paused as Angharad swung her head towards him. "Angharad," he said. "Would you have helped me?"

"Probably," she said. "But not for the right reasons." She leaned over to him and gave him a kiss on the brow. "Good luck, Fenn."

"My song," he said. "You never gave me my song."

"You never needed a song."

"But I'd like one now. Please?"

So Angharad sang to him before she left, a song of the loneliness that wisdom can sometimes bring—when the student won't listen, when the form is bound to the earth by its roots and only the mind ranges free. A loneliness grown from a world where magic as a way of life lay forgotten under too many quests for power. She called it "The Weeping Oak" and she only sang it that once and never again. But there was a poetry in it that her songs had never had before.

Thereafter, as she traveled, that poetry took wing in the songs that she sung to the accompaniment of her harp. It joined the two parts of a bard that she already had, slipping into her life as neatly as an otter's path through the river's water. She continued to range far and wide, as tinkers will, but she was a red-haired witch, following a bard's road into the green, which is another way of saying she should be content with what she had.

And so she was.

Into the Green

STONE WALLS CONFINE A tinker; cold iron binds a witch; but a musician's music can never be fettered, for it lives first in her heart and mind.

THE HARP was named Garrow—born out of an old sorrow to make weary hearts glad. It was a small lap harp, easy to carry, with a resonance that let its music carry to the far ends of a crowded common room. The long fingers of the red-haired woman could pull dance tunes from its strings, lilting jigs or reels that set feet tapping until the floorboards shook and the rafters rang. But some nights the memory of old sorrows returned. Lying in wait like marsh mists, they clouded her eyes with their arrival. On those nights, the music she pulled from Garrow's metal-strung strings was more bitter than sweet, slow airs that made the heart regret and brought unbidden memories to haunt the minds of those who listened.

"Enough of that," the innkeeper said.

The tune faltered and Angharad looked up into his angry face. She lay her hands across the strings, stilling the harp's plaintive singing.

"I said you could make music," the innkeeper told her, "not drive my customers away."

It took Angharad a few moments to return from that place in her memory that the music had brought her to this inn where her body sat, drawing the music from the strings of her harp. The common room was half-empty and oddly subdued, where earlier every table had been filled and men stood shoulder-to-shoulder at the bar, joking and telling each other ever more embroidered tales. The few who spoke, did so in hushed voices; fewer still would meet her gaze.

"You'll have to go," the innkeeper said, his voice not so harsh now. She saw in his eyes that he too was remembering a forgotten sorrow.

"I..."

How to tell him that on nights such as these, the sorrow came, whether she willed it or not? That if she had her choice she would rather forget as well. But the harp was a gift from Jacky Lantern's kin, as was the music she pulled from its strings. She used it in her journeys through the Kingdoms of the Green Isles, to wake the Summerblood where it lay sleeping in folk who never knew they were witches. That was how the Middle Kingdom survived—by being remembered, by its small magics being served, by the interchange of wisdom and gossip between man and those with whom he shared the world.

But sometimes the memories the music woke were not so gay and charming. They hurt. Yet such memories served a purpose, too, as the music knew well. They helped to break the circles of history so that mistakes weren't repeated. But how was she to explain such things to this tall, grim-faced innkeeper who'd been looking only for an evening's entertainment for his customers? How to put into words what only music could tell?

"I...I'm sorry," she said.

He nodded, almost sympathetically. Then his eyes grew hard. "Just go."

She made no protest. She knew what she was—tinker, witch and harper. This far south of Kellmidden, only the latter allowed her much acceptance with those who traveled a road just to get from here to there, rather than for the sake of the traveling itself. For the sake of the road that led into the green, where poetry and harping met to sing of the Middle Kingdom.

Standing, she swung the harp up on one shoulder, a small journeypack on the other. Her red hair was drawn back in two long braids. She wore a tinker's plaited skirt and white blouse with a huntsman's leather jerkin overtop. At the door she collected her staff of white rowan wood. Witches' wood. Not until the door swung closed behind her did the usual level of conversation and laughter return to the commonroom.

But they would remember. Her. The music. There was one man who watched her from a corner, face dark with brooding. She meant to leave before they remembered other things. Before one or another wondered aloud if it was true that witch's skin burned at the touch of cold iron—as did that of the kowrie folk.

As she stepped away from the door, a huge shadowed shape arose from where it had been crouching by a window. The quick tattoo of her pulse only sharpened when she saw that it was a man——a misshapen man. His chest was massive, his arms and legs like small trees. But a hump rose from his back, and his head jutted almost from his chest at an awkward angle. His legs were bowed as though his weight was almost too much for them. He shuffled, rather than walked, as he closed the short space between them.

Light from the window spilled across his features. One eye was set higher in that broad face than the other. The nose had been broken— more than once. His hair was a knotted thicket, his beard a bird's nest of matted tangles.

Angharad began to bring her staff between them. The white rowan wood could call up a witchfire that was good for little more than calling up a flame in a damp camp fire, but it could startle. That might be enough for her to make her escape.

The monstrous man reached a hand towards her. "Puh-pretty," he said.

Before Angharad could react, there came a quick movement from around the side of the inn.

"Go on" the newcomer cried. It was the barmaid from the inn, a slender blue-eyed girl whose blonde hair hung in one thick braid across her breast. The innkeeper had called her Jessa. "Get away from her, you big oaf." She made a shooing motion with her hand.

Angharad saw something flicker briefly in the man's eyes as he turned. A moment of shining light. A flash of regret. She realized then that he'd been speaking of her music, not her. He'd been reaching to touch the harp, not her. She wanted to call him back, but the barmaid was thrusting a package wrapped in unbleached cotton at her. The man had shambled away, vanishing into the darkness in the time it took Angharad to look from the package to where he'd been standing.

"Something for the road," Jessa said. "It's not much—some cheese and bread."

"Thank you," Angharad replied. "That man…?"

"Oh, don't mind him. That's only Pog—the village half-wit. Fael lets him sleep in the barn in return for what work he can do around the inn." She smiled suddenly. "He's seen the kowrie folk, he has. To hear him tell it—and you'd need the patience of one of Dath's priests to let him get the tale out—they dance all round the Stones on a night such as this."

"What sort of a night is this?"

"Full moon."

Jessa pointed eastward. Rising above the trees there, Angharad saw the moon rising, swollen and round above the trees. She remembered a circle of old longstones that she'd passed on the road that took her to the inn. They stood far off from the road on a hill overlooking the Grey Sea, a league or so west of the village. Old stones, like silent sentinels, watching the distant waves. A place where kowries would dance, she thought, if they were so inclined.

"You should go," Jessa said.

Angharad gave her a questioning look.

The barmaid nodded towards the inn. "They're talking about witches in there, and spells laid with music. They're not bad men, but any man who drinks…"

Angharad nodded. A hard day's work, then drinking all night. To some it was enough to excuse any deed. They were honest folk, after all. Not tinkers. Not witches.

She touched Jessa's arm. "Thank you."

"We're both women," the barmaid said with a smile. "We have to stick together, now don't we?" Her features, half-hidden in the gloom, grew more serious as she added, "Stay off the road if you can. Depending on how things go…Well, there's some's as have horses."

Angharad thought of a misshapen man and a place of standing stones, of moonlight and dancing kowries.

"I will," she said.

Jessa gave her another quick smile, then slipped once more around the corner of the inn. Angharad listened to her quiet footfalls as she ran back to the kitchen. Giving the inn a considering look, she stuffed the barmaid's gift of food into her journeypack and set off down the road, staff in hand.

— ❦ —

THERE WERE many tales told of the menhir and stones circles that dotted the Kingdoms of the Green Isles. Wizardfolk named them holy places, sacred to the Summerlord; reservoirs where the old powers of the hill and moon could be gathered by the rites of dhruides and the like. The priests of Dath named them evil and warned all to shun their influence. The commonfolk were merely wary of them—viewing them as neither good nor evil, but rather places where mysteries lay too deep for ordinary folk.

And there *was* mystery in them, Angharad thought.

From where she stood, she could see their tall fingers silhouetted against the sky. Mists lay thick about their hill—drawn up from the sea that murmured a stone's throw or two beyond. The moon was higher now; the night as still as an inheld breath. Expectant. Angharad left the road to approach the stone circle where Pog claimed the kowrie danced on nights of the full moon. Nights when her harp played older musics than she knew, drawing the airs more from the wind, it seemed, than the flesh and bone that held the instrument and plucked its strings.

The gorse was damp underfoot. In no time at all, her bare legs were wet. She circled around two stone outcrops, her route eventually bringing her up the hill from the side facing the sea. The murmur of its waves was very clear now. The sharp tang of its salt was in the mist. Angharad couldn't see below her waist for that mist, but the hilltop was clear. And the Stones.

They rose high above her, four times her height, grey and weathered. Before she entered their circle, she dropped her journeypack and staff to the ground. From its sheath on the inside of her jerkin, she took out a small knife and left that as well. If this was a place to which the kowrie came, she knew they would have no welcome for one bearing cold iron. Lastly, she unbuttoned her shoes and set them beside her pack. Only then did she enter the circle, barefoot, with only her harp in hand.

She wasn't surprised to find the hunchback from the village inside the circle. He was perched on the kingstone, short legs dangling.

"Hello, Pog," she said.

She had no fear of him as she crossed the circle to where he sat. There was more kinship between them than either might claim outside this circle. Their Summerblood bound them.

"Huh-huh-huh…" Frustration tightened every line of his body as he struggled to shape the word. "Huh-low…"

Angharad stepped close and laid her hand against his cheek. She wondered, what songs were held prisoner by that stumbling tongue? For she could see a poetry in his eyes, denied its voice. A longing, given no release.

"Will you sing for me, Pog?" she asked. "Will you help me call the stones to dance?"

The eagerness in his nod almost made her weep. But it was not for pity that she was here tonight. It was to commune with a kindred spirit. He caught her hand with his and she gave it a squeeze before gently freeing her fingers. She sat at the foot of the stone and brought her harp around to her lap. Pog was awkward as he scrambled down from his perch to sit where he could watch her.

Fingers to strings. Once, softly, one after the other, to test the tuning. And then she began to play.

It was the same music that the instrument had offered at the inn, but in this place it soared so freely that there could be no true comparison. There was nothing to deaden the ringing of the strings here. No stone walls and wooden roof. No metal furnishings and trappings. No hearts that had to be tricked into listening.

The moon was directly overhead now and the music resounded between it and the sacred hill of the stone circle. It woke echoes like the skirling of pipes, like the thunder of hooves on sod. It woke lights in the old grey stones—flickering glimmers that sparked from one tall menhir to the other. It woke a song so bright in Angharad's heart that her chest hurt. It woke a dance in her companion so that he rose to his feet and shuffled between the stones.

Pog sang as he moved, a tuneless singing that made strange harmonies with Angharad's harping. Against the moonlight of her harp notes, it was the sound of earth shifting, stones grinding. When it took on the bass timbre of a stag's belling call, Angharad thought she saw antlers rising from his brow, the tines pointing skyward to the moon like the menhir. His back was straighter as he danced, the hump gone.

It's Hafarl, Angharad thought, awestruck. The Summerlord's possessed him.

Their music grew more fierce, a wild exultant sound that rang between the stones. The sparking flickers of light moved so quickly they were like streaming ribbons, bright as moonlight. The mist scurried in between the stones, swirling in its own dance, so that more often than not Angharad could only catch glimpses of the antlered dancing figure. His movements were liquid, echoing each rise and fall of the music. Angharad's heart reached out to him. He was—

Something struck her across the head. The music faltered, stumbled, then died as her harp was knocked from her grip. A hand grabbed one of her braids and hauled her to her feet.

"Do you see? Did you hear?" a harsh voice demanded.

Angharad could see them now—men from the inn. Their voices were loud in the sudden silence. Their shapes exaggerated, large and threatening in the mist.

"We see, Macal."

It was the one named Macal who had struck her. Who had watched her so intently in the commonroom of the inn. Who held her by her braid. Who hit her again. He stank of sweat and strong drink. And fear.

"Calling down a curse on us, she was," Macal cried. "And what better place than these damned Stones?"

Other men gripped her now. They shackled her wrists with cold iron and pulled her from the circle by a chain attached to those shackles. She fell to her knees and looked back. There was no sign of Pog, no sign of anything but her harp, lying on its side near the kingstone. The men dragged her to her feet.

"Leave me alo—" she began, finally finding her voice.

Macal hit her a third time. "You'll not speak again, witch. Not till the priest questions you. Understand?"

They tore cloth strips from her skirt then to gag her. They tore open her blouse and fondled and pinched her as they dragged her back to town. They threw her into the small storage room of the village's mill. Four stone walls. A door barred on the outside by a wooden beam, slotted in place. Two drunk men for guards outside, laughing and singing.

It took a long time for Angharad to lift her bruised body up from the stone floor and work free the gag. She closed her blouse somewhat by tying together the shirt tails. She hammered at the door with her shackled fists. There was no answer. Finally she sank to her knees and laid her head against the wall. She closed her eyes, trying to recapture the moment before this horror began, but all she could recall was the journey from the stone circle to this prison. The cruel men and the joy they took from her pain.

Then she thought of Pog…Had they captured him as well? When she tried to bring his features to mind, all that came was an image of a stag on a hilltop, bellowing at the moon. She could see…

THE STAG. Pog. Changed into an image of Hafarl by the music. Left as a stag in the stone circle by the intrusion of the men from the inn who'd come, cursing and drunk, to find themselves a witch. The men hadn't seen him. But as Angharad's assailants dragged her from the stone circle, grey-clad shapes stepped from the stones, where time held them bound except for nights such as this when the moon was full.

They were kowrie, thin and wiry, with narrow dark-skinned faces and feral eyes. Their dark hair was braided with shells and feathers; their jerkins, trousers, boots and cloaks were the grey of the Stones. One by one, they stepped out into the circle until there were as many of them as there were Stones. Thirteen kowrie. The stag bellowed at the moon, a trumpeting sound. The kowrie touched Angharad's harp with fingers thin as rowan twigs.

"Gone now," one said, her voice a husky whisper.

Another drew a plaintive note from Angharad's harp. "Music stolen, moonlight spoiled," he said.

A third laid her narrow hands on the stag's trembling flanks. "Lead us to her, Summerborn," she said.

Other kowrie approached the beast.

"The cold iron bars us from their dwellings," one said. Another nodded. "But not you."

"Lead us to her."

"Open their dwellings to us."

"We were but waking."

"We missed our dance."

"A hundred moons without music."

"We would hear her harp."

"We would follow our kin."

"Into the green."

The green, where poetry and harping met and opened a door to the Middle Kingdom. The stag pawed at the ground, hearing the need in their voices. It lifted its antlered head, snorting at the sky. The men. Where had they taken her? The stag remembered a place where men dwelt in houses set close to each other. There was pain in that place…

— ❦ —

ANGHARAD OPENED her eyes. What had she seen? A dream? Pog, with that poetry in his eyes, become a stag, surrounded by feral-eyed kowrie…She pushed herself away from the wall and sat on her haunches, shackled wrists held on her lap before her. The stone walls of her prison bound her. The cold chains weighed her down. Still, her heart beat, her thoughts were her own. Her voice had not been taken from her.

She began to sing.

It was the music of hill and moon, a calling-down music, keening and wild. There was a stag's lowing in it, the murmur of sea against shore. There was moonlight in it and the slow grind of earth against stone. There was harping in it, and the sound of the wind as it sped across the gorse-backed hills.

On a night such as this, she thought, there was no stilling such music. It was not bound by walls or shackles. It ran free, out from her prison, out of the village; into the night, into the hills. It was heard there, by kowrie and stag. It was heard closer as well.

From the far away place that the music took her, Angharad heard the alarm raised outside her prison. The wooden beam scraping as it was drawn from the door. The door was pushed open and the small chamber where her body sat singing grew bright from the glare of torches. But she was hardly even there anymore. She was out on the hills, running with the stag and the kowrie, leading them to her with her song, one more ghostly shape in the mist that was rolling down into the village.

"St-stop that, you," one of the guards said.

His unease was plain in voice and stance. Like his companion, he was suddenly sober.

Angharad heard him, but only from a great distance. Her music never faltered.

The two guards kept to the doorway, staring at her, unsure of what to do. Then Macal was there, with his hatred of witches, and they followed his lead. He struck her until she fell silent, but the music carried on, from her heart into the night, inaudible to these men, but growing louder when they dragged her out. The earth underfoot resounded like a drumskin with her silent song. The moonlit sky above trembled.

"Bring wood," Macal called as he pulled her along the ground by her chains. "We'll burn her now."

"But the priest..." one of the men protested.

Macal glared at the man. "If we wait for him, she'll have us all enspelled. We'll do it now."

No one moved. Other villagers were waking now—Fael the innkeeper and the barmaid Jessa; the miller, roused first by Angharad's singing, now coming to see to what use Macal had put his mill; fishermen, grumpy, for it was still hours before dawn when they'd rise to set their nets out past the shoals; the village goodwives. They looked at the red-haired woman, lying on the ground at Macal's feet, her hands shackled, the chains in Macal's hands. His earlier supporters backed away from him.

"Have you gone mad?" the miller demanded of him.

Macal pointed at Angharad. "Dath damn you, are you blind? She's a witch. She's casting a spell on us all. Can't you smell the stink of it in the air?"

"Let her go," the innkeeper said quietly.

Macal shook his head and drew his sword. "Fire's best—it burns the magic from them—but a sword can do the job as well."

The mist was entering the village now, roiling down the streets, filled with ghostly running shapes. Lifting her head from the ground, Angharad saw the kowrie, saw the stag. She looked at her captor and suddenly understood what drove him to his hate of witches. He had the Summerblood in his veins too.

"There…there's no need for this," she said. "We are kin…"

But Macal didn't hear her. He was staring into the mist. He saw the flickering shapes of the kowrie. And towering over them all he saw the stag, its tined antlers gleaming in the moonlight, the poetry in its eyes that burned like a fire. He dropped the chains and ran towards the beast, swinging his sword two-handedly. Villagers ran to intercept him, but they were too late. Macal's sword bit deep into the stag's throat.

The beast stumbled to its knees, spraying blood. Macal lifted his blade for a second stroke, but strong hands wrestled the sword from him. When he tried to rise, the villagers struck him with their fists.

"Murderer!" the miller cried.

"He never did you harm!"

"It was a beast!" Macal cried. "A demon beast—summoned by the witch!"

They let him rise then to see what he'd slain. Pog lay there, gasping his last breath, the poetry dying in his eyes. Only Macal and Angharad with their Summerblood had seen a stag. To the villagers, Macal had struck down their village half-wit who'd never done a hurtful thing.

"I…" Macal began taking a step forward, but the villagers pushed him away.

The mists swirled thick around him. Only he and Angharad could see the flickering grey shapes that moved in it, feral eyes gleaming, slender fingers pinching and nipping at his skin. He fled, running headlong between the houses. The mist clotted around him as he reached the outskirts of the village. A great wind rushed down from the hills. Hafarl's breath, Angharad thought, watching.

The wind tore away the mists. She saw the kowrie flee with it, thirteen slender shapes running into the hills. Where Macal had fallen, only a squat stone lay that looked for all the world like a crouching man, arms and legs drawn in close to his body. It had not been there before.

The villagers shaped the Sign of Horns to ward themselves. Angharad held out her shackled arms to the innkeeper. Silently he fetched the key from one of Macal's companions. Just as silently Angharad pointed to the men who had attacked her in the stone circle. She met their shamed gazes, one by one, then pointed to where Pog lay.

She waited while they fetched a plank and rolled Pog's body onto it. When they were ready, she led the way out of the village to the stone circle, the men following. Not until they had delivered their burden to the hilltop Stones did she speak.

"Go now."

They left at a run. Angharad stood firm until they were out of sight, then slowly she sank to her knees beside the body. Laying her head on its barreled chest, she wept.

It was the kowrie who hollowed the ground under the kingstone and laid Pog there. And it was the kowrie who pressed the small harp into Angharad's hands and bade her play. She could feel no joy in this music that her fingers pulled from the strings. The magic was gone. But she played all the same, head bent over her instrument while the kowrie moved amongst the stones in a slow dance to honour the dead.

Mists grew thick again. Then a hoofbeat brought Angharad's head up. Her music faltered. The stag stood there watching her, the poetry alive in its eyes.

"Are you truly there?" she asked the beast. "Or are you but a phantom I've called up to ease my heart?"

The stag stepped forward and pressed a wet nose against her cheek. She stroked its neck. The hairs were coarse. There was no doubt that this was flesh and muscle under her hand. When the stag stepped away, she began to play once more. The music grew of its own accord under her fingers, that wild exultant music that was bitter and sweet, all at once.

Between her music and the poetry in the stag's eyes, Angharad sensed the membrane that separated this world from the Middle Kingdoms of the kowrie growing thin. So thin. Like mist. One by one the dancing kowrie passed through, thirteen grey-cloaked figures with teeth gleaming white in their dark faces as they smiled and stepped from this world to the one beyond. Last to go was the stag; he gave her one final look, the poetry shining in his eyes, then stepped away. The music stilled in Angharad's fingers. The harp fell silent. They were gone now, Pog and his kowrie. Gone from this hill, from this world.

Stepped away.

Into the green.

Hugging her harp to her chest, Angharad waited for the rising sun to wash over the old stone circle and tried not to feel so alone.

Dennet & Willie

Dennet & the Fiddler

"...for mony's the rantin' time
ma fiddle an I hae had..."

—from "Rattlin', Roarin' Willie";
attributed to Robert Burns.

DENNET LOVED TO HEAR a fiddle played. She was a trim maid, fair of face, well-favoured of form, with hair the colour of winter hazels and wise, bright eyes that twinkled with all the sparkle of hearth cat's curiosity. Her smock was a deep rust this day, worn overtop a white, knee-length shift that seemed the whiter when contrasted against the sun-brown of her rounded limbs. Kneeling on the floor of The Otter's Holt Inn, she scrubbed its hardwood surface with the single-minded determination of one getting an unpleasant task over with as quickly as possible.

And she loved to hear a fiddle played. Whether it be the sure, swift notes of a dance tune, or the plaintive, mournful sighs of a slow air, she loved the sound that plain horsehair could coax from string and wood. No matter the season or the time of day, whether asleep, a-dream, or busy with whatever task was at hand, she would drop all at the first familiar scrape of a bow across a string.

So it was that, with her knees red from her kneeling and her hands red from the soapy water, she paused in the midst of her work to sit up. Brushing a willful strand of hair from her brow, she cocked her head to listen the better to the sound that had caught her ear. Though it was not a fiddle playing, there *was* someone lilting a fiddle tune outside—a fiddle tune that leapt and swirled, filled and rounded out with all its appropriate grace notes; a fiddle tune that she knew, and knew well, though she couldn't quite recall its name. Dropping her wash-rag, she wiped her hands dry on the front of her smock and stepped to the door to investigate its source.

There was a man drawing water at the well, his bearded chin bobbing as he mouthed his tune. Dennet leaned against the doorjamb and regarded him with interest, taking in his lean frame and the way his hair fell in tangled waves down his back—hair as brown as her own, though darker. He wore a patched coat that was mostly mottled green, tan trousers tucked into red woolen socks at the knee and a pair of dusty shoes with worn brass buckles. His shirt was the blue of a robin's egg, his cap a darker blue, and he'd a bag over his shoulder that bounced against his side as he drew the pail up from the well. He drew on the rope in a curious manner—as though he'd only strength in, or the full use of, one arm.

The tune ended as the pail topped the lip of the well. With the same curious manner as he'd drawn it up, he lifted the pail and drank deeply.

"Ho, tunesmith!" called Dennet impulsively. "We've a better brew indoors."

The newcomer looked up with water dripping from his moustache. "Aye, an' I'm sure you do. But with never a coin to my name, I could scarce afford it." He grinned, adding, "Less you'd be offering it free of charge?"

"Were it my inn..." Dennet shrugged and the stranger's grin grew broader.

"...an' if dirt were coin," he finished, "we'd all be rich. Ah, no matter. The water's free an', more an' likely, 'tis a good deal cooler than your ale besides."

Dennet smiled. "You've the truth of it there."

She crossed the courtyard to join him. Since their first exchange of words she'd felt an unfamiliar feeling steal over her, as though she and this stranger were old friends, meeting after a long absence. It was a pleasant feeling, and more, she was enjoying this unexpected excuse to set aside her chores for a few moments. When the days fared all the same, the one into the other...well, any respite, no matter how short, was a treat. She sat down on the lip of the well and kicked her heels against its stones.

"What was that tune you were just lilting?" she asked. "And where're you from? Where're you going?"

"Ah, so many questions. What's your name, lass?"

"Dennet."

"Dennet," he repeated, enjoying the sound of it. "Well, Dennet, 'tis Willie Wistel I am, from Tamawain…or at least 'twas there I was born and bred. I've been walking the roads for so long I can scarce call any place my home now. As to the tune, I picked it up from a flute player—in Fairwillow 'twas, I believe—some half-dozen years ago an' I never did learn its name. I'm bound for Estelleaad."

"The Grey City," murmured Dennet, her curiosity fully aroused now. Estelleaad had been the High Seat of King Wellstarre in the elder days, or so the legends had it. South it lay, past the Tanglewood, its spires tumbled down, its streets forsaken. Of that once-proud city all that remained now were deserted ruins. The Grey City, the folk of the Vales named it and said it was haunted. "What takes you there?"

A shadow passed over Willie's face, immediately replaced with a smile. "Twould be too long a tale for such a fine summer's nooning. Come, though. What of yourself? Do you dwell in yon inn?"

If Dennet saw the shadow, she made no mention of it. "For now," she said, answering his question. "When my own coin ran out, Jolser— he owns the inn—Jolser let me work here for bread and board and a small weekly wage. If all goes well, I'll be on my way when the Barley Moon takes to its waning, faring northward. I was born on Pridmore, in the Alban Isles, and've been road-faring since my fifteenth summer."

"On your own?" asked Willie.

"Surely. Why not?"

"But does no one trouble you, being a lass on your own an' all?"

Dennet smiled mischievously. "I run fast," she said and they both laughed.

"What's in your bag?" she asked a moment later.

The shadow returned to Willie's face. He seemed to withdraw into himself at the question, his brow growing furrowed, his eyes taking on a haunted look as though some memory—better forgotten—had come to the fore. A stiff silence fell between them and Dennet wondered how she'd upset him. For all that he was a stranger, it was not in her distress anyone. She tried to think of something she might say to make amends when Willie said softly, "Tis a fiddle."

The concern that she'd upset him slipped away at that word. She clapped her hands together and leaned towards him. "A fiddle? Would you play it for me? There's naught I love dearer."

"I..." he began, then stopped. He'd thrust his left hand into his coat pocket when she'd approached. Now, as though he were speaking some shameful secret, he drew that hand forth and held it before her. It seemed more a claw than a hand. The bones were twisted out of shape, the fingers stiff, the skin wrinkled and parchment dry. He watched her face, awaiting the usual reaction—the drawing away, the pity—only her eyes rose from the crippled hand to look guilelessly into his own.

He dropped his gaze to mutter, "Are you not going to say, 'Oh, what a shame. How terrible it must be?'"

Dennet shook her head. "No. You've heard that often enough, I'm sure. How did it happen?"

"A harvesting accident, two years past now. I've been unable to play, unable to use the damn thing since." His voice was laced with a self-pity he seemed unable, or unwilling, to hide. "I don't know why I even carry yon fiddle about," he continued. "It does nothing but 'mind me that once I *could* play it." He lifted his eyes to hers once more. "Twas my gran'dad's though, an' 'tis all I've to remember him with. Ah, an' I 'mind when I could play it. Twas as though the fiddle was enchanted betimes, as though my gran'dad was with me, was putting the tunes in my head. There were times I could play tunes I'd never heard before...tunes I'm sure he alone'd ken. He was a grand fiddler, he was, an' his fiddle... 'twas to be my luck, he said. Now...ah, now the luck seems gone."

Dennet touched his arm. "Your hand...is that why you're faring to the Grey City?" As he'd spoken, a sudden insight had gripped her...that and the memory of an old tale she'd heard. The tale had it that Cablin, the Wild Lord of the Middle Kingdom, was said to visit Estelleaad on certain nights of the full moon. The Grey Harper he was called in some tales...Grey Harper, Grey City. And was not Cablin also named the Healer?

Willie nodded. "Aye. There was a tinker from Lillowen told me of it. How'd he put it? Ah…'When the full moon rises, Twilight shrouds the grey stones of Estelleaad and the Wild Folk walk; and in the Twilight, all things are possible.' I'll not hide it from you that I see little chance of finding aid there…but what've I to lose?" He held up his hand. "Since this, I've had no joy out of life. An' I've a feeling about that place…"

Abruptly, he stood and thrust his crippled hand back into his coat pocket. "Is there a market-town that's not too far? I'd like to try an' earn a few coppers with a song or two. A meal'd do me good, an' I'll be needing journeybread for the road as well."

The Otter's Holt Inn stood at a crossing of five roads. Dennet pointed to one that ran southward. "A half league'll bring you to Dunfielding. There's always a market there. They'd…" She stopped in mid-sentence, realizing that she'd been about to say they'd love to hear his fiddle. "They'd surely listen," she finished lamely.

"Then 'tis there I'll give it a try."

He stood awkwardly before her, suddenly not wanting to go, though not understanding what drew him to her. She was fair, to be sure, but he'd met fairer maids before. No, he realized, there was something in her that seemed the perfect match for something in himself and more, he could sense that she felt much the same.

"Will you be back this way for your supper?" she asked.

"Aye," he said, glad of a reason to return. "If my luck's good." With that, he tipped his cap to her and strode away.

Dennet watched his receding back with mixed feelings, wondering if he would indeed return. With his mind off his hand he seemed to be a right merry fellow and she was attracted to him in a cheerful, tingly way. But she didn't care for the bitter edge to his spirit, the shadow that appeared to eat away at him like a canker. Still, what did she know of how he felt? She held her own hands up to her eyes and regarded them thoughtfully. How would _she_ feel?

She shook her head, confused. She did know, however, that she'd like to know him better. He drew her as surely as the moon drew the tides of her home isles. Perhaps he would return. He'd said he would if his luck was good.

"Then let his luck be good," she murmured and rose. Returning to the inn, she suddenly recalled the name of the tune he'd been lilting. It was *The Fiddler's Farewell to Sorrow.* Smiling to herself, she went back to her chores.

— 🦢 —

THE OTTER'S Holt was crowded that evening. Dennet weaved in and out amongst the tables bearing large flagons of ale, stoups of wine and trays piled high with food, taking orders and filling them, wiping the beads of perspiration from her brow. When Willie entered, their eyes met for a moment, then he seated himself in an empty chair by the hearth. He looked about himself with interest. The inn's patrons drank and ate boisterously, telling tales and outrageous jokes, slapping their knees or banging the tables for emphasis. Though there were two traders in the crowd—northerners by their looks—for the most part it was made up of locals, farmers and shepherds fresh in from the fields, their homespun shirts and trousers giving off the rich aroma of earth and manure, their hair tousled, their eyes ale-bright.

"How'd it go?"

Willie looked away from them to find Dennet standing before him. He dug into his pocket with his right hand. Grinning, he brought forth three coppers. "Well enough to pay for a meal."

"Veal stew, then? With an ale?"

As he nodded, she slipped away. It seemed scarce a moment later that she returned to his table with a flagon of ale, its foaming head dripping over the rim, and a plate of steaming stew.

"I asked Jolser if you could sing here this eve," she said, setting plate and flagon before him. "And he agreed. Will you?"

The shadow was forming in his eyes again. Dennet frowned and wagged a finger at him. "Don't be an ass, Willie Wistel. If you do well, you can make twice as much here as ever you could in the mart. It's not out of pity that I asked for you…it would never be out of pity. And list, afterwards, we can sit and talk."

With an effort, Willie raised a smile. "My…my thanks, Dennet. An' afterwards…well, I'd like that."

So Willie Wistel sang in the inn that night and, when the night ended, he was the richer by ten coppers and a piece of silver. He'd sung the songs of the lands he'd traveled through, lands where he'd once played his fiddle, exchanging tunes and songs with the local musicians. The silver piece he received from one of the traders after he'd sung a song from the man's homeland, north of the Wall of the World.

When the inn finally closed, he helped Dennet clean up as best he could. Later, with the floor swept and the chairs straightened, they sat and spoke long into the night. The hearthfire died to low coals, its pale glow lighting Dennet's face so that it shone with an unearthly beauty. Willie felt his heart skip a beat and a wondrous contentment took hold of him. Then he thought of his crippled hand, no longer in his pocket, and the simple pleasure of the evening turned sour for him. He stood, hiding the hand in his pocket once more, and retired to the bed Dennet had prepared for him in the stable. Lying in the sweet-smelling straw, he resolved to be on his way come the morning's light.

But the next morning, he awoke late and, when Dennet came to wake him with a cheery hello, his resolve fled him like dawn mist before the rising sun. That day passed with him helping her about the inn with her chores and, come the night, he sang again in the main room. He received only five coppers that eve, but it was not for coin that he stayed. It was for the quiet talk that followed the evening, when the crowd was gone and Dennet and he had the hearth to themselves.

THE DAYS wended into a week and half-way into a second. On a night when the Barley Moon was a crescent of silver light in the sky, Dennet told him that she would come to the Grey City with him and would hear no word to deny her.

"For," she said, "life is short enough as it is and with a chance to fare to such a magical place smack before me…ah, how could I not take it?"

She danced for him that eve. He lilted a wild reel 'neath beaming moon and twinkling stars and watched her dance on the green sward behind the inn—her legs flashing in the pale light, his voice strong and carrying the tune truly. Breathlessly he reached its end and, as breathlessly, she collapsed on the grass beside him. She laid her head on his knee and looked up into his face, a contented smile on her lips.

During these past days she'd discovered a well of love within her at which there was no need to draw the water, for it came bubbling up like a fountain, of its own accord, spreading throughout her, setting every nerve a-tingle. Now that love spilled over and washed through her so that she lifted her arms to draw Willie's face down to her own. Their lips met, brushing gently at first, then the tongues touched, their spirits merged.

Willie's gaze swam and he felt lightheaded. Dennet guided his right hand to her breast and he stroked her hair with the other, the crippled one. But in the midst of their joy, he saw that hand in the moonlight, the claw touching her brown-gold hair, and a look of horror twisted his face. He drew back and rose, all in one motion, staring at it with a hatred as rancid as curdled milk.

Dennet sat up, the wash of her love still pounding through her veins, befuddling her senses. "Willie...what is it...?"

"I'll not touch you with...with *this*! I'll not!" Trembling, like a man in the grip of a fever, he turned from her to stagger away.

"Willie!" she called after him, understanding dawning on her. She rose to her feet. "It doesn't matter. I love you, hand or no hand."

He stopped to look back at her. "I feel that...deep inside, I know it. An' yet, I can't but help think 'tis for pity." He shook his head. "No, I'm being unfair to you...I...I don't know what to think. Let me...ah, let me sleep on it. I'm sorry, Dennet. Truly I am."

Dennet dropped the arms that she'd held open to him and watched him walk slowly away, his head bowed. "It was never pity," she murmured, tears brimming in her eyes. "Never that."

But he was too far away to hear.

WHEN WILLIE crawled into the hay, all he could do was stare at the wooden crossbeams above his head, scarce visible in the poor light.

He clutched at his head, his emotions running rampant through him so that he hardly knew who he was. When at last some semblance of sanity returned to him, he cursed himself as the prize fool of all time. What mattered the hand, when compared to Dennet? She paid less attention to it than he did. Was she not worth a hundred times a hundred hands? What mattered it that he could no longer play the fiddle? Had he missed it at all in the past week? His heart was caught sure and fast, there was no denying it.

He felt that he should run to the inn that very moment to tell her, but knew that Jolser would have his hide for it. Thinking of Jolser, he realized that the innkeeper—aye, and the inn's patrons too—had given scarce a second glance to his hand. It was *he* that built up the horror of it, *he* that read the pity, the drawing away that wasn't even there. And if there was a drawing away, it was more from his own bitterness than from any physical aspect of his hand.

With it clear in his own mind, he prayed that Dennet would forgive him, that she would understand. In the morning—first thing in the morning—he would talk with her.

His heart felt lighter then. He knew that he'd not change overnight, that he'd have to fight at times to keep the mood from him, but at this moment he felt assured that he could. And there was still Estelleaad. Together, if Dennet was still willing, they could seek out this Cablin of which she'd spoken. The Healer she called him. Ah, and if there was nothing, if there was no one there, he promised himself that then and there he'd put an end to all further yearnings.

With half-formed resolutions drifting through his mind, sleep came to him, and with sleep, came a dream. Dennet's face appeared therein, flushed with joy, her eyes alive and bright, her lips half-parted in a merry grin. Then he saw the whole of her and she was dancing, dancing on a tabletop in the inn, encircled by the men of the countryside who were clapping in time to a wild tune, shouting encouragement. But her eyes, her eyes were only for the fiddler, and the fiddler was he.

He looked at her down the length of his fingerboard, saw his crippled hand whole again, the fingers leaping to the swirl of the tune, fingering the strings with a lighter touch than he'd ever imagined was possible. The bow was a blur to his sight, his fingers growing more so. But clear and crystalline in his eyes was Dennet, Dennet dancing, dancing for him.

On he played, the tune growing, swelling until it was the only sound to fill the whole of the world—that, and the sound of Dennet's feet slapping the tabletop. The clapping and shouting of the men faded, until they were the only two that remained; the only two in all of the world. On he played, the tune becoming a wild, living thing. On she danced, her dance becoming life itself.

Then, to his terror, his fingers began to change on the strings, to draw in on themselves, to twist and deform until they were only parodies of themselves. The tune faltered as his fingers stiffened into the too well-known claw and the fiddle fell from his hand to splinter on the floor. Aghast, he stared at the wreckage, unable to comprehend what had happened.

"Don't stop!" he heard Dennet cry. "Play on! Play on!"

He looked up to meet her eyes. Their brightness turned from joy into coals of anger.

"I...I can't," he said, holding up his hand.

All around the inn, the men stood and stared at him. Laughter erupted, seemingly from hundreds of throats, and they pointed at his hand.

"Play on!" cried Dennet. "Play on, or lose my love, cripple!"

He put his hands over his ears and shook his head, moaning to himself. He felt himself swaying, the floor bucking beneath his feet.

"Play on! Play on! Play on!"

"I can't!" he screamed and woke from the dream bathed in a cold sweat, trembling from head to foot, his cry still echoing in his ears.

Willie felt the taste of bile rise up in his throat. Clutching his head, he wept. Dennet was not like that. He felt as though he'd soiled her with his dream. But he remembered something she'd said, when first they'd met. *A fiddle? There's naught I love dearer.* Naught she loved dearer. What use would a crippled fiddler be to her?

With a leaden heart, he reached for his fiddle sack to draw out pen, ink and parchment. Mixing the ink, he dipped the quill into it and began to write.

— 🖋 —

COME THE morning, the sun arose over The Otter's Holt to find Dennet crossing the courtyard. A foreboding grew in her heart as she put her hand on the doorlatch of the stable. All her fears became realized when she saw the small piece of parchment lying on the straw, lying where Willie's head should have lain. Trembling, she picked it up and as she read, the tears streamed down her cheeks.

Ah, Dennet…

Deep within your hallowed soul
enchantment lies like burnished gold;
nor, never does its shining fade
in 'midst of all that might it shade.
Sweet lady, be a gentle friend,
ever, always, without end.

I fare but a short ways, an' if you'll
wait, be sure I'll return for you…

Willie Wistel

"The fool," she managed through her tears. "The thrice-damned ass." She knelt in the straw, the parchment folded and clutched in her hand. Not until the full force of her sorrow was spent did she rise, red-eyed, to return to the inn.

Once in her chamber, she doffed smock and shift, exchanging them for trousers, a woolen sweater and walking boots. With her journeysack over one shoulder and a long green mantle over the other, she made her way to the kitchen to take her leave of Jolser and gather what foodstuffs she would need for her journey. Jolser was displeased to see her go—both for his liking of her and the short notice—but he gave her journeybread, nuts and dried fruit, and paid her her wages with an understanding nod.

Standing outside the inn, Dennet looked away to the south, along the road Willie must have taken. There was only one place he would have gone and that was Estelleaad, the Grey City. She took out the parchment to look at it once more, then thrust it back into a pocket. With a sigh, she set out.

— 🌿 —

WILLIE'S ROAD led him over hill and heath, through long sweeps of trackless gorse, into the Tanglewood and beyond. Above, night by night, the Barley Moon waxed to its fullness. Below, he stumbled and dragged his feet over the unfamiliar terrain, his heart wavering between the fulfilling of his quest and returning to Dennet.

The bread and cheese he'd bought in Dunfielding tasted stale to his palate, though it was still fresh. His sleep was troubled with dreams, ill-omened terrors that left him weak upon awakening. Betimes he would grope for Dennet, weeping that she was so far from him, that he had forsaken her. Other times he awoke moaning from his dreams with her voice still ringing in his ears—*Play on! Play on!* But ever he fared southward.

He remembered a time—before the scythe had ruined his hand— when his fingers could move as freely as anyone's, aye, and twice better on a fiddle. He remembered a time when confusion was alien to him, when he'd been content with his lot, happy enough and accepting his limitations without frustration. But that was before the accident, before his spirit had soured within him. Now he begrudged everything he couldn't do, begrudged any who could do what he himself could not. And his one hope—that somehow his hand might be healed— he realized that, couched as this desire was in magic, there was little chance of his ever being whole again.

Magic. For all the ballads he'd sung of it, the old tales he'd heard, he was still unsure as to its reality. He'd seen small magics in marketplaces: a dowser once in Marad, conjurers and palm-readers, an old woman who could cure warts. But to heal a hand in which the nerves and muscles were long dead?

On the sixth night since his leaving the inn, he knew within himself that his goal lay but another day's march ahead. Squatting on a low outcrop, he peered southward into the growing dusk, bemusedly eating the last of his journeybread. The same instinct that told him he was so near his goal, awoke a growing elation that pervaded his being.

Ah, soon, he thought. Soon we'll see.

Swallowing his last bite, he lay down amidst the gorse and fell into a—for once—dreamless sleep.

DENNET WAS road-wise, experienced at fending for herself in the wilds, and had been since she first left her home isle of Pridmore. How else to survive for five years on her own? But two months at the inn had taken away a little of her stamina. The life had been easy there, easier than road-faring in any case. At the end of her first day her legs ached with weariness and she realized that she might not catch up with Willie before he reached the Grey City. She could not match his pace-eating stride, for one thing.

Stopping to eat, a curious mixture of sadness and confusion washed over her. She was sad for she wouldn't be with him to share either his triumph or his failure, confused that she was even following him in the first place. She touched the parchment in her pocket then and the confusion, at least, fled. She knew why.

He'd not forsaken her. No, he'd gone so that he could come back to offer her a whole man, never understanding that she was well-content with the man he already was. Her years of traveling the roads had given her a certain callousness towards the advances of men, to their promises. With Willie it was different. It was—she searched for the word—it was right. They were like two parts coming together to make a perfect whole wherein neither would be overshadowed by the other.

That was it. Where other men had sought to bring her in under their own shadow, Willie—for all the bitterness that gnawed at his spirit—had offered her an equal sharing. It had been there from the first night. All that kept them apart was his own misguided notion that he was unfit for her.

Should his seeking meet with success she knew all would be well. But what if he failed? The more she thought of it, he was doomed to fail. For all the tales told of magical healings, she'd never met the one to whom it'd actually happened. And what of this Grey Harper that the Valers said dwelt in Estelleaad...this Healer? He was of the Wild Folk, the willful ones that were neither good nor bad, but rather a bewildering mixture of the two. Saying he was there, how could he be trusted to help? Had Willie thought of that? Oh, what if he failed? Could he overcome his bitterness for her sake?

In the days that followed Dennet was filled with these questions, worrying over them, turning them round and round in her mind. By the third day all her road-strengths had returned and she began to make good time. Yet the road she took was not the most conducive for swift traveling. It was not even a road. She merely fared southward, across the downs and low hills and through the Tanglewood.

On her sixth day she topped a hill, clambering over granite and loose shale until she reached its crest. She paused for a moment to catch her breath then made for the opposite slope. The loose stones slipped beneath her feet and suddenly she was tumbling down the hill—a hill that was much steeper than she'd supposed from its top. She scrabbled about herself, trying to break her fall, but only succeeded in starting a small avalanche to follow her. Stones bruised her face where they landed and a small boulder bounced by, narrowly missing her.

There was a drop at the bottom of the hill. She went over it to land with jarring force on the stones below, the bones of her left leg snapping beneath her body's weight. A flood of pebbles showered over her. Twisting aside, she could not dodge the boulder that smashed into that same leg, crushing the already broken bones. Pain roared up from her leg, lancing through her body, tearing a scream from her throat.

Shock froze her. She sat still, biting her lip, her mind numb. Beneath the shock, she realized the full weight of the calamity that had befallen her. Here, so far in the hills, there was no one to turn to for help, no one that would be passing by, save by chance. Perhaps Willie would return this way, but come aid or not, she would never walk again.

Glancing at her leg brought a sour taste to her mouth. Her trousers were stained a deep crimson and twisted into an awkward angle. She tried to move it, but the motion brought such a wave of agony that her mind escaped into a wash of darkness…away from the horror of what had befallen her, away from the mind-numbing pain.

— 🖋 —

WILLIE CAME to Estelleaad just before the nightfall of his journey's seventh day. He wended the deserted, overgrown streets for over an hour, staring wide-eyed at the immense empty buildings, the crumbled spires and arches. As shadows lengthened with the deepening dusk he found a garden filled with stone statues. He rested there, sitting in the tall grass, and looked about himself, his heart filled with a growing awe.

Along one wall hawthorns and brambles vied for space with apple trees, the boughs of which were laden with green fruit, already turning rosy. Amidst the grass and clover that carpeted the garden, blue harebells, white campions and yellow coniguefoils merged into one colour with the encroaching twilight. The opposite wall was hung with ivy, bordered by woad and fennel, while the foremost wall was hidden by a rough thicket of hazels and rowan.

There was a fountain in the centre and all about it, the statues: grinning fauns and slender wood nymphs, wild beasts and birds poised for flight. Centermost of all was a cloaked figure, tall and foreboding, with one hand raised in a salute, the other resting on a stone harp, so intricately carved that each of its strings was depicted, separate and distinct. There was a hare crouched at its feet.

Cablin, thought Willie, looking at the centre figure. This must be he…the Grey Harper. Was this the place then? Would he come here, where his statue stood?

Willie held his breath. The whole of the garden gave off an air of expectancy that froze his limbs. Then the moon rose above the ruined buildings—the Barley Moon, full and swollen. The first ray of light that touched the garden bathed the face of the stone harper, throwing its features into bold relief. For a moment Willie thought it lived. Caught up in anticipation as he was he might imagine anything, he realized. He grinned foolishly and shook the thought from him.

But the grin fled his lips, for the statue did live and was stepping from its pedestal.

Willie fell back from it. He'd expected magic—sought it at least—but now that he was confronted with its reality, his very soul seemed to shiver and withdraw within itself. The stone folds of the statue's cloak billowed impossibly in the wind, the stone eyes shone golden in the moonlight. The flesh, though it took on a living hue, retained a tinge of greyness, of stone. The figure dropped the hand that was held up in a salute and smiled.

At that smile, the fear that had blossomed in Willie's heart seemed to expand until it encompassed and permeated his entire being. At that smile, the dark night took to itself the moon's light and twilight filled the garden—an unearthly shimmering half-light that placed the garden in a world beyond time.

The statue looked curiously at the trembling man before it. "What have we here?" it asked. "Not in three times three score mortal years has there been one to greet me in this place. Man…how are ye named? What would ye of me?"

Now was the time, thought Willie amidst his fear. His throat felt constricted, dry, and he swallowed with difficulty. He opened his mouth to speak, but couldn't find his voice. Then a vision flashed in his mind, of Dennet as she'd been that last night, her head upon his knee, drawing his face to hers. With the vision came courage and the resolve to see the thing through, not just for himself, but for both their sakes.

"Wistel," he said at last, cursing the quaver in his voice. "I am named Willie Wistel, O Twilight Lord. I…I give you greeting…"

"And I, Cablin, give ye greeting, Willie Wistel. Step forward, man, and tell me what ye would have of me. This night is sacred to my folk, to my kin. Ye are within the circle—" and indeed the statues had come to life, encircling them "—and the full moon is high. Ask what ye will and, mayhap, it will be granted."

Willie took a cautious step forward. Again his voice forsook him. Mutely, he held his crippled hand up to Cablin's golden eyes, thinking with all his heart on what he wished. Cablin shook his head sorrowfully.

"So much bitterness I see in thee, Willie Wistel, so much self-pity. Yet I can grant ye thy wish. What do ye offer in return? What payment have ye brought?"

Willie shrank in upon himself. He remembered the old tales and realized that he'd forgotten the price of magic, he'd never thought of payment. Desperately, he cast about for what he might offer. There were the coins he'd earned…

"I have no need for such trifles," said Cablin, reading his thoughts.

"But…but I have naught else…" mumbled Willie. Naught save his fiddle.

Cablin smiled. "Yon instrument will do."

Willie took his fiddle from its sack and held it before him, regarding it as though for the first time. His fiddle? To have the use of his hand again, he must give up the fiddle? Another'd be easy enough to find, but another'd not be this one. He stared at it, his eyes unfocused, the spirit of his grandfather rising up to overshadow all. Never sell the fiddle, he'd told him. It'll be your luck.

Willie rubbed his temples, trying to clear his thoughts. What luck had the fiddle brought? He looked to Cablin, searched the calm face with its haunting gold eyes, but could find no answer there. His gaze turned to the fountain. Reflected in the strangely still waters of its pool was his grandfather's face.

The years since his death slipped away and once more Willie felt himself standing by the bier—a gangly youth holding a fiddle in his hand, looking down at the old man's corpse lying thin and forsaken of life on a woolen blanket. The lines of the aged face swam in his sight. Now he was looking down on the hills he'd traversed so recently. He was looking down from a great height, as though he were a hawk or an eagle, as though he rode in the moon. The vision narrowed to draw closer to the earth.

Suddenly before his eyes, the pool reflected a face he knew all too well, a face that had been clear in his mind the whole of his journey south. Yet where he remembered it gay, it was twisted with pain now. He saw the terrible ruin of her leg and felt his heart die within him.

"Dennet!" he cried, reaching for her. As his hands touched the water, the image disappeared. "Dennet!" He looked up to Cablin, despair plain in his eyes. "Was that a true far-seeing? Was it? Where is she?" His voice rose shrill, edged with panic.

The Grey Harper nodded solemnly. "Aye, 'tis a true far-seeing. She lies in the hills, a good day's walk from here."

"I must go to her. I must help her. Her leg…"

"Though ye run as swift as the wind, there is still nothing ye might do for her, save offer her comfort. She has lain there for two nights and a day, Willie Wistel. Her spirit is fast slipping from her body and, should she live, she will never walk again." Cablin shrugged his shoulders. "So is the way of things."

Dennet's pain was burnt into Willie's mind. She'd been following him, he realized. Not content to wait, she'd followed and now she would die. With scarce another thought, he thrust his fiddle into the Grey Harper's hands. "Then save her. This is the boon I ask of you, nothing more. Only save her."

"What of that?" Cablin motioned to the crippled hand.

"Damn the hand! Is she not worth a hundred such?"

"To thee perhaps," murmured the Grey Harper. A strange look passed fleetingly over his face, then he lifted his arms, saying, "So be it!"

The words echoed and rebounded in the walled garden. Cablin touched the strings of his stone harp and the notes that rang forth swelled to join the reverberating words. Willie covered his ears, but the sound grew louder, in his mind as surely as outside of it. Before him, the rim of the pool glowed, flaring into a blinding brilliance, then Dennet lay there amidst a fading shimmer. He reached for her.

"Touch her not," he heard Cablin say and found he could not move.

The Grey Harper gestured and the cloth of Dennet's trousers fell from her leg, revealing the terrible reality of its ruin. Willie tried to look away, only his gaze was locked onto the sight whether he would see it or not. Cablin ran his hand along the swollen flesh and the leg began to heal. The bones reformed from their shards, twisted to regain their former shape. The cuts sealed, the flesh became smooth once more.

Standing back from her, Cablin looked to Willie. "So. It is done. She will live and walk and be as whole as ever she was. As for thee, ye had the one chance to heal thy hand…now it is gone for all time." He gazed curiously on Willie, reading the whole of his past two years, the longings and yearnings, the bitterness and self-pity. "Ah, Willie Wistel, do ye regret it?"

Willie met his gaze without flinching. "No. How could I? Dennet… she is all that matters. The hand I can live without…she I could not. I can see that now."

Cablin smiled. "That was well-spoken, Willie Wistel." He took up the fiddle and handed it back to Willie who took it without looking at it. "Ye thought for another, Willie Wistel. I offer ye thy instrument back. Play me a tune and that will be payment enough."

Utter silence fell. Willie dropped his gaze from the Grey Harper's.

"Why do you mock me?" he asked in a low voice.

"Mock thee?" The words blasted into Willie's mind, sending him reeling backwards. "Do ye think me so craven? Can ye not hold the bow in yon crippled paw? Pity ye may receive from others, man, but none from me. If ye lack the courage to play me a tune, then return to me thy fiddle and begone from my sight!"

To hold the bow in his crippled hand? Aye, and finger with his right? Willie looked at the fiddle and saw that it had become a mirror image of itself. Where the bridge had sloped to the right, it now sloped left. Where the bass string had lain, now the fine high string was wound. Where the chin rest had fitted his left chin, it now fitted under his right. He flexed the fingers of his right hand. Perhaps it could be done.

Unsurely, he fitted the bow into the stiff fingers of his left hand. For all that the hand was useless, the wrist was still supple. There was where the secret of bowing lay, after all: in the wrist. With growing confidence, he put the fiddle to his chin and drew the bow along a string. Moments later—with the fiddle tuned—he began to play a tune, the one he'd lilted when first he'd come to The Otter's Holt Inn.

The sound that came forth was more like a pig's squealing than music, but he didn't stop. He'd never played so poorly before, at least not since he'd first begun to play. He knew all the notes, the finger positions, to be sure, but he had to reverse them all in his mind. The smoothness was lacking, the tone that took years to perfect was missing. Yet for all that he played the tune through, both parts repeated, and then the whole of it again.

When he was done, he turned to the Grey Harper with a huge grin on his face. Rather than being embarrassed at the poorness of his playing, he was elated that he had even done as well as he had. All that time...he'd never thought of such a thing.

Cablin's smile joined his. "I have heard better music howled by cats, Willie Wistel, yet I will consider the payment fulfilled." He beckoned to the statues that encircled them. "But my companions...they would dance. For this one eve I will grant ye thy skill of old. Though it be gone with the morning's light and the true re-learning then begins... for tonight, join with me and we will play that tune once again."

Willie put bow to strings and began the tune once more. This time the notes flowed from his instrument like molten silver, like the wild rushing of a moorland stream, like the fey wonder of a mountain wind. The Grey Harper touched the strings of his harp in accompaniment and the statues began to dance, capering around and around in a wild fling.

From memories of deep pain, Dennet awoke to see it all. She felt her leg, marveling that it was whole.

How...? she thought.

Then the music took hold of her and she could think no more. Standing, she removed her boots and the tatters of her trousers. She kicked her heels and leapt into the dance, swirling about with the living statues, her eyes on the fiddler, and the fiddler only. Willie met her gaze and, if the tune had seemed alive before, now it truly took on life.

They saw only each other. Between their eyes, a new world formed, a world that held a promise that they would never sunder again, that no matter what their trials, they would be together, for ever and for always. And when the dance finished at last, when the Barley Moon dropped behind the ruined buildings of Estelleaad, they collapsed on the grass before the fountain. All around them were statues on their pedestals, unmoving stone once more, and naught remained of the tune but a fading echo.

They could not stop smiling, Dennet and Willie. Their lips met, their hair mingled and they lay together, clasped in each other's arms. Dennet sat up in the midst of their love-making to ask, "What...what of your hand?" She touched it and knew in that moment what had befallen, what Willie had given up for her sake.

Willie cupped her chin with it and kissed her soundly. "What of it?"

He ran the hand down the length of her leg. Dennet sighed and clasped him the tighter.

"Aye," she murmured. "What of it?"

Above them, the statue of the Grey Harper smiled.

THEY AWOKE in the morning, entwined in each other's arms. Dennet sat up and stretched, content with the world. She touched Willie's cheek with her lips and stood.

"The world is wide," she said. "Where will we fare?"

Willie shrugged. "Everywhere." He took up his fiddle and bow, adding, "An' how do *you* care for the sound of a cat's howling?"

Dennet raised her eyebrows quizzically. Instead of replying, he played a half-dozen dissonant notes. She laughed.

"Oh, I like it well enough."

Dragonwood

THEY'D FARED WELL THAT night, the wise-eyed maid who'd danced barefooted on the tabletop, her green shift hiked to her knees, and the crippled fiddler—the long bow held in his maimed left hand as he fingered the fiddle's strings with his right. The ale had flowed while the rafters rang with the fiddler's wild tunes, the shouts of encouragement from the onlookers, the infectious clapping of callused hands. And though the uproar of the inn's patrons drowned the sound of the maid's feet slapping the wooden tabletop, never once was the tune lost.

There was a feyness in the fiddler's playing so that each note, graces and all, could be heard through the din. The tune carried itself to every corner of the room, out the open shutters and wide-propped door, to skirl across the courtyard, lost at last where the inn's lane met the road and the hawthorn hedges grew.

Alone, they sat by the hearth now, dancer and fiddler, smiling with a cheerful weariness—the inn empty, the hour late. They counted their earnings and the coals in the hearth awoke twinkles in the handful of copper coins and one silver piece. Mugs of hot honeyed-milk steamed on the table before them, still too hot to drink.

"Ah, Dennet," said the fiddler, whose name was Willie Wistel. "You danced so well I near lost the tune a time or two for watching you too close'."

Dennet stretched lazily and brushed a lock of nut-brown hair from her eyes. "And there was a time or two," she said with a teasing grin, "when you played the tunes so fast I could scarce keep up. More 'n' likely you were just waiting for my feet to tangle."

"I?" asked Willie innocently.

"You!" She gave his beard a sharp tug and jumped to her feet, out of his reach. "Come," she added, keeping the table between them. "Let's to bed. The road's waiting us tomorrow, bright and early. There'll be no time for sluggards then."

She was off and up the stairs to their room before ever Willie could frame a reply. Chuckling, he loosened his bow, placing it in a bag to join the fiddle. With the bag over his shoulder, he took up the two mugs in his right hand—thankful for their large handles—and followed her.

"The road," he repeated to himself as he mounted the stair. "Aye... the road to Dragonwood..."

— 🔥 —

THEY SOUGHT a way into the Middle Kingdom, these two, that fey realm where Cablin, the Grey Harper, held sway. One night—long past now and lost in a handful of years—they had met with him, shared the sweet wildness of his touch, savoured the timeless wonder of his presence. It had been in Estelleaad, the ruined city where once King Wellstarre held his court in days long past. Now only ghosts flitted over the cracked cobblestones of its avenues, wandered amidst its tumbled towers.

They'd tasted magic that night. Subtly, it settled in their hearts, nestled deep and hidden, awaking a vague discontent that neither could quite find words to adequately express. A year passed, and another. Rather than fading, the discontent grew, blossoming until finally they understood what it was they sought...magic. Yet how to find it?

Oh, sometimes when feet and fiddle caught a tune with a certain edge, they transcended the mundane to know its peripheral essence— wildness, wonder, moon and mist. But when the tune ended, when feet and fingers were still, it would slip away from them, swift and sudden, leaving only a yearning in their hearts and the vague sense of something like a will o' the wisp flitting near—very near—though ever just out of reach. So they sought, their feet wandering many roads on a quest with no clear direction, until that first mention of the Dragonwood.

They heard of it in Colswain, while sharing a roadside dinner with a tinker whose name they never learned. Over roasted hedgehogs and rosehip tea, the talk turned to things not quite of this world and the tinker'd spoken then of the wood.

"Far in the south it lies," he'd said, "a dark wood of stunted trees an' twisted thickets in the midst of a wasteland of barren hills. Tis said that the wood holds a wisdom…a key…perhaps a gate to the realms of the weren, the Wild Ones of the Middle Kingdom." He'd shrugged, adding, "A perilous place, to my mind, an' from what I've heard, not fit for honest folk."

"An its naming?" asked Willie. "Is there a dragon there in truth?"

The tinker smiled, teeth white against his dark skin. "Who can say? A tinker hears a thousand tales. Can even the half of them be true?"

But the name awoke something in Dennet and for her it rang true.

"Dragonwood," she'd murmur, nestled in Willie's arms, in an inn somewhere, or along a roadside neath a sheltering tree, and a faraway look would come into her eyes. "Dragonwood," she'd say in a low voice and a tiny chill would run up her spine.

Dennet was one to have her way, once her mind was set upon a thing, and Willie felt the same stirrings, though in him they were not so strong. So at length they did fare southward, asking after the wood at inn and cot, manor and thorp, whatever came their way.

They heard a hint here, an assurance there. They paid their way with songs and tales of their travels, with the fiddle tunes that Willie could play all the night without tiring and the sweet dances that the trim maid Dennet could step to those same tunes.

"Dragonwood?" repeated an innkeeper once, his thoughtful frown disappearing as a copper found its way into his hand. "There's a wood named so beyond Yeynd's borders, east of the mountains."

But there was no Dragonwood there. No forest at all, in fact, only rolling heaths and granite outcrops that poked through the browning furze and gorse. They cursed the innkeeper soundly for a day or two, but continued southward all the while.

They crossed those heaths on Yeynd's borders, coming to a wide river that proved shallow enough to wade across. Once through the sucking mud and thickets of shoulder-high reeds on its southern bank, they walked the wooded hills of Doon to the grasslands of Kilbey. More downs and hills, another river, and they came to a fair land of wide pastures and grainfields, bordered with neat hedges and walls of fieldstone.

"How is this land named?" asked Dennet of the first soul they met.

He was a burly farmlad, his brow and shoulders wet with perspiration. Leaning on his hoe, he took a break from his labour to look over the travel-worn pair.

"The Borderlands," he said at length, with a slow drawl.

"Why is it named so?"

"Why?" He gave them an only-a-fool-would-ask look. "Because it borders the waste, is why."

"And is there a wood in its midst?"

Now his eyes grew guarded. "Now how would I know?" he replied and returned to his hoeing.

Dennet and Willie exchanged glances, but said nothing. They left him to his work and fared on, walking the long day until they came to a small village. From the brow of the hill whereon they stood, they could see an inn along the one main thoroughfare of the burg, built of good sturdy timber and fieldstone. And beyond…beyond spread the waste, grey and misty with the day's end pale upon it.

Willie touched his pack. "Our food's low. What say we play for provisions in the inn—the landlord willing—an' fare the waste in the morn?"

Dennet nodded agreement, though she only half-heard him. Her attention was drawn fully to the grey hills of the waste. There was a gleam in the bright depths of her eyes, a glimmer of anticipation that she made no effort to conceal. As they neared the inn, Willie turned to her.

"No word of what we seek," he cautioned her. At the question spoken with her raised eyebrows, he added, "Remember the farmlad. He was welcome enough till we mentioned the wood. It's food we need to fare those heaths, so it's a welcome we should seek to earn that food."

"But…

"Aye. I can sense it too. It's there, or not in all the world. But remember: without provisions we'd not get far an' I'll not turn thief this late in my life."

Dennet smiled. "Oh, aye. And you're so old…all of twenty-nine. What of me then? I'm but the two years younger. Am I nigh a hag as well?"

Willie took in her dusty hair and the road-grime that clung to her clothes. "No. More an unkempt ragamuffin," he said and dodged the mock blow she aimed at his chin.

By then they were come to the inn.

— ❦ —

THE NEXT morning found them in the market buying smoked meats and journeybread, dried fruit and a half-dozen candied tarts for Willie, who had a sweet tooth. With their packs loaded and a pair of waterskins filled and hanging from their shoulders, they left the village, heading southward, into the waste.

That first day brought them into lands where there was as much bare stone and raw earth—sun-dried and poor footing in the rises and hollows—as there was vegetation. There were thorn trees along ridges, spindly rowans and the naked stems of bog violets and bell heather, their blooms long withered and fallen. And ever the brown-grey gorse. Nightfall heralded the rising of a horned quarter moon. The minute high-pitched squeaks of bats cut across the silence of the heaths, sending shivers along their spines. They huddled together seeking comfort in each other's arms. A wind arose as the night grew chiller, playing mournfully across the hills. When they finally slept, it was not deeply.

Two more days brought them within sight of what must be their goal, for surely that wood spread out below them was the wood they sought. A shadow hung over it that was deeper than the sun's setting might bring. The twisted trees lifted their boughs upward in strange patterns, like the thin arms of haggard beggars demanding coins from the sky. Looking upon the wood awoke unpleasant feelings in the pits of their stomachs, so they turned away, meaning to brave it on the morrow, in dawn's light.

There was a menhir on the hill where they stood, old and grey, but somehow reassuring. They put their backs to it, away from the view of the wood, and ate, attempting jokes to still their untimely fears—jokes that rang hollowly, without raising a smile. At length they fell silent and let that silence wrap about them, to fall like an invisible wall between them that grew the firmer, the longer they kept to their own thoughts. Perhaps this wood was their goal; perhaps not. So close to it they felt a foreboding steal over them and wondered at the wisdom of seeking the Grey Harper, the Wild Lord, of asking admittance to his realm.

Dennet especially considered the wisdom of this quest of theirs, now that a possible ending had come to it. Below the wood lay. Not a clean wood of healthy growth and seasonal beauties, but a shadowed place filled with some unknown—perhaps perilous—thing that seemed the worse for being unknown. The need that had driven her this far flooded away as she thought of the wood. It left behind a coldness that chilled her very marrow, an acidic taste that was sour in her throat. Ah, but Willie…she'd egged him on, wheedled to have them come this far…

Willie thought of Cablin, remembering him clearly as he'd been in the moon-garden of Estelleaad—all grey, truly a Grey Harper, a statue filled with godhood come to life, unconcerned with mortal, mundane things, otherworldly, unpredictable…wild. He feared what might await them in that wood just over the crest of the hill. Not for himself did he fear, but for Dennet who was life and breath to him. He bore no weapon should danger arise. He walked peaceful ways, shunning the warrior's sword, the sharp edge of violence that changed something in one's soul. What if danger *should* arise? What would he do?

When worry plagued Willie, there was but one thing that might drive it away. Sitting up from the rough stone at his back, he drew his fiddle-bag to him, pulling out instrument and bow. Tightening the bow, he rosined it fiercely before he tuned the fiddle. Dennet stirred, startled at his first abrupt movement, then smiled, albeit thinly. Yet when the first measure of the tune awoke from the strings, she felt her heart lighten, the smile blossomed, and she tapped her foot on the ground, humming an accompaniment.

It was an old tune that he played. She knew it well and relaxed within the set boundaries of its familiarity. Then something crept into it, an impossible sweetness, the feyness that sometimes came from deep within Willie—as it lies in all musicians that love their craft, putting heart and soul into the measures they caught with fragile reed or string, in the lipping of a flute, the tapping of a tipple against a goatskin drum.

It was an impossible tune that was for them and them alone. It rebuilt their confidence, reaffirmed the love that had somehow grown less strong as one road became another and another...ever the endless searching. The love that had blazed star-bright when first they'd become one arose again in Dennet, thrilling her spirit, sending the blood pounding through her veins. She saw Willie's face flushed with emotion as their eyes met in the wan light of stars and horned moon. Like the first dance of bodies becoming one, they felt the rush grow between them, swelling...but then they were no longer alone.

The tune faltered and they turned as one to see what their love, what the sweet music had drawn to them. Friend or foe, he stood a half-dozen paces away, swaying still though the tune no longer played. He'd a small torso for his height, with long spindly legs and arms, a heart-shaped face, owl-like eyes and a wide mouth. Straggly hair hung down past neck and shoulder to fall over the ragged cloak that fell to his knees in long tatters. His tunic and leggings were in little better repair, but he was no tinker come upon hard times, no beggar far from a city's streets. Two small horns sprouted from his brow and the tips of his ears ended in tiny points.

"You fare for the wood." His voice was like a wind through reeds, husky, breathy. The words spoke a fact, asking no question.

They nodded, Dennet and Willie, words forsaking them in the afterush of their moment of wild emotion. But it was plain in their eyes that a myriad riddles had awoken, begging for answers.

The strange being inclined his head to them. "Ennis was I named, when first I awoke to find the world about me. A hobogle I am." His body continued to sway as though he still heard Willie's air. "That tune... it slipped through stone and earth to draw me here. Fair playing...fey playing...like a pale shadow of the Wild Lord's music and so, for a mortal, playing beyond compare. Why do you fare for the wood?"

Dennet found her voice first. "We...we seek the realm of...the Middle Kingdom..."

The hobogle nodded. "Aye, there is indeed a gate there, from Mid-wold to Cablin's realm. But not for naught is yon forest named the Dragonwood. Draigdd is the creature's name, he who guards the way, who holds all the wisdoms of Mid-wold betwixt his claws. Perilous would it be to awaken him. How can you dare?"

Again the two were silent. The hobogle's owl-eyes bored into them, reading there what was perhaps hidden even to them.

"So it goes," he said at last, softly, almost sadly. "List."

He lilted a tune that was like moonlight in a deep glen, like the quietest time of the night, when naught stirs, the one moment when even badger, owl and polecat pause, ere they shake themselves and continue their hunt.

"Play it," he demanded of Willie.

Willie pursed his lips and shaped a *why?* But there was an insistence in the hobogle's eyes that could not be denied. Putting bow to fiddle then, Willie played.

He had a way with tunes that made others green with envy—once heard, never forgotten. Again the air hung about them, stronger on the fiddle's strings. A stillness fell over them, like a pause in time. A moment it lasted—perhaps an age—then he drew the bow from his instrument and time seemed to flow once more.

"Such might stay him," said the hobogle. "Played from the heart."

Another unspoken question formed on Willie's lips.

"It will be needful...should Draigdd awake. And awake he shall, if you walk his wood."

Willie's voice returned. "Why? What is the danger? *Is* there even danger?"

"There is always danger with the dragonfolk. What form it will take is another matter. Who can say how it will come?"

"Why do you tell us then? Why do you aid us?" Willie was growing more puzzled as his questions were answered, rather than less.

"Aid you?" replied the hobogle in his breathy voice. "Say rather that I would aid all the world."

"I don't understand. But...if it is better for us to leave him undisturbed...why then you, Ennis. Could you not show us the road to Cablin's realm?"

The hobogle shook his head. "I cannot. There are laws and there are laws. If you seek a way, it lies below. Return safely from the wood, from Draigdd, and perhaps…we will see what we will see. Comfort I can offer, a healing of the soul, if the need be there…"

Like waking from a dream, they blinked and he was gone. Over their limbs crept a great weariness that could not be denied. Riddles were forgotten, fiddle laid upon the gorse, bow beside it, and they slept, curled in each other's arms.

— 🌿 —

THE MORNING dawned with a golden promise so it was with lighter hearts that they essayed the slope leading down into the dark forest.

Dragonwood.

Was a dragon evil then? Willie asked himself as they passed between the first few trees. He could remember tales—knew songs himself—that told of the great battles between the heroes of old and the dragonfolk. But once or twice he'd heard as well that dragons were among the first folk. Mys-hudol. The word crept from nowhere into his mind. The talking beasts. Such were the dragonfolk, in certain tales. And the mys-hudol, they were said to be among the wisest of wise.

They fared a few more paces into the wood, its uncanny stillness and the ominous umbra between the trees banishing the lightness from their hearts as though it had never been. The trees themselves were grim parodies of oak and pine, ash and elm, twisting above and about them in shapes that seemed more like intertwined serpents than the boughs of an honest wood. There was no undergrowth, only a thick carpet of mouldering leaves and pine needles. Directly before them, scarce two score paces into the wood, was a small clearing. The grass therein was mottled and brown, rocks protruding in a haphazard scattering from one length to the other. Hand in hand they stepped closer, when the stones stirred.

From the dead grasses and leaves a grey shape arose, refuse and dirt clinging to what were not stones, but dull scales. Heavy lids opened slowly revealing eyes that seemed all dark pupil and were as large as the spread of both Willie's hands. Like misty breath on a chill morning, steam trickled from nostrils and a great mouth opened in a half-yawn, revealing row upon row of yellowed teeth. The body that stirred before them was six times the height of a tall man, as wide as the height of two more.

The head lifted. Slowly the unfocused eyes grew clear and the dragon saw them. They stood frozen in their tracks, clasping each others' hand tightly, each lending the other strength, for there was a madness in those eyes, and undying hate for all things mortal.

WHERE IS THE SWORD?

The words startled them, echoing horribly in their minds. A reptilian reek assailed them, accentuating the volume of the dragon's speech that pounded within their skulls.

OR DO YOU COME WITH A GREAT SPELL TO SLAY ME? A SLIP OF A GIRL AND A HERO WITH A CRIPPLED PAW THAT CAN BEAR NO WEAPON…HID, IS IT?

Willie feared, his legs trembled and his whole body shook, but his fear was not for him alone. It was for Dennet as well, for the harm that might come to her. That fear lent him courage to speak boldly. "No. I bear no sword, for my heart would never let me."

Laughter like thunder roared in their minds, shook their very souls.

WHAT? A COWARD COMES BEFORE ME?

"If to desire peace be cowardly…aye…"

The dragon's great muzzle swung back and forth, letting first one eye, then the other regard the pair. *YOU LIE. I SMELL IRON. WHERE IS THE SWORD?*

Willie stepped back from the glare, puzzled. He searched his mind until he remembered the small dagger stowed away in his pack. Fumbling with the pack's drawstrings, he took out the dagger and cast it far behind them, to the very edge of the first trees. "If you fear iron, see: I have cast it from me."

Now Draigg looked puzzled, if such an expression could be read aright on a face that bore no resemblance to anything human. *I DO NOT FEAR IRON. YET THEY BEAR IT…ALL THOSE HEROES THAT SEEK TO SLAY ME. AND YOU, MANLING, IF YOU DO NOT SEEK MY DEATH, WHY THEN HAVE YOU COME?*

Dennet answered, her voice low. "We seek a way into the Middle Kingdom…" She paused as anger flared in the dragon's eyes, an anger that kindled an echo within her own. She took a deep breath. "Why do you anger? We have come in peace. We ask but directions—a small thing."

SO. YOU WOULD HAVE MY WISDOM, WOULD YOU? YOU WOULD SUCK IT FROM ME LIKE THE LEECHES YOU ARE, UNTIL I LIE LIKE A HUSK, AN EASY VICTIM FOR THE HEROES THAT WILL COME THEN AND SLAY ME. SLAY ME! I WHO HAVE BIDED SO LONG, OUTLIVING ALL OF MY RACE. MY WISDOM IS THE POWER THAT WILL NEVER BE REVEALED.

"Wisdom," said Dennet, ever willful and fully angered now, no matter the behemoth's size, "is for all, so that the world may be the better for it. The world changes. How many have sought to slay you in these later years? None, I'll wager. For five hundred years or more, none have come. And none will come, save such as we, seeking directions, not death. Tell me I lie, but know that you be wrong."

Red fires burned in the dragon's eyes and a spout of steam gusted from his nostrils. *NO! WHAT YOU SAY COULD NEVER BE TRUE. THEY WILL COME, THE HEROES, THEY WILL ALWAYS COME.*

"I say the world changes, old thing that knows naught." Willie took her arm and squeezed it warningly, but Dennet shook him off. "The warriors of old are not so many. Swords are melted down into spades and hoes, folk *are* learning the wisdoms of this world, aye, and seeking the worlds beyond. And that wisdom lies not in the musty learnings that you hoard—festering and twisting within you so that it is nothing, not wisdom, not anything."

NO! WISDOM IS STRENGTH, THE MIGHT OF POWER AND STRIFE. IF WHAT YOU SAY BE TRUE, I WILL COME FORTH FROM MY WOOD AND TEACH THE WORLD MY WISDOM. WITH FLAME AND DEATH I WILL BURN IT INTO THEM!

The dragon reared upon its hind legs to tower over them. Flame burst from its wide mouth, igniting the trees above.

Mad, thought Willie, utterly mad. Once it might have been wise, but the turnings of too many years had twisted his mind, even as the wood was twisted. He could see the dragon's head bending to seek them. Desperately, he pushed Dennet aside, following in a leap that barely let him escape the second burst of flame. Lifting Dennet from her crouch, he took her arm, propelling her deeper into the wood, where the trunks of the trees grew too close together for the dragon to follow.

More flames erupted and those trees were a sudden inferno.

I WILL REND YOU! The words burned in their minds as fiercely as any flame. *I WILL REND YOU AND ALL YOUR WORLD!*

They ran. Branches with fetid moss clinging to them slapped their faces, roots tripped them. But they gained distance, for they were swift-footed with fear, while the dragon must burn his way to them.

He would rend the world, thought Willie as he ran and his heart stopped cold. Even could they escape the dragon's wrath, they had loosed his horror upon the world, a world that had no defense against it. What Dennet had spoken was true. Men had laid their weapons aside. They tilled the earth, harvesting corn, barley and other grains, rather than reaping harvests of men's souls upon their bloodied blades of war. There were no more heroes in the world. There was naught to stop this thing they'd loosed…naught save…

Willie remembered then the tune the hobogle had showed him. The notes rang crystalline in his mind. If he must fight, it was music that would be his weapon. If he had magic, there was only the one spell: the one his fiddle might weave.

He stopped his headlong flight to kneel on the ground. Clumsily, he drew forth fiddle and bow. He cursed his cripple hand—for the first time in many years—for he lost precious seconds tightening the bow one-handedly, setting it to the strings, checking the tuning…and the dragon was upon him.

He laid the bow across the strings. Before the first note could sound, flame erupted over his head, a great taloned paw lashed out to strike him, sending him tumbling, fiddle still clutched in his hand. His head struck a tree and his consciousness fled him.

Dennet stared in horror. Blood washed Willie's face and brow, blood stained the pale blue of his shirt—the blood of her beloved. Her anger grew to become a living thing. Words formed in her mind to lash out at the thing that towered above them, words that grew like swords from the steel of her spirit, and as they were forged she could sense the hobogle's tune growing in her heart.

Away from her the words flew, striking into the deep mind of the dragon, that mind twisted by who knew what mad dreams the years might propagate. If there were flames about her, she felt them not. If Draigdd struck her—struck her as her Willie'd been struck—the striking had no force. Only the words were real, burning like golden flares, brighter than any dragon's flame—her words striking the maddened old one. And all the while that tune-spell of the hobogle underlaid her words, driving them into the dragon's mind with ever-increasing intensity. She'd not Willie's way with tunes, but her subconscious had heard it, remembering it well enough for it to come swelling up through her now.

The words told things for which there were no words, truths that could not be denied. They were words, yet wordless. Tongued, they might have sounded so:

There is wisdom and wisdom. There is wisdom that is hoarded like gold and jewels, deep within caves and secret places of the mind, like that written in books to be pored over by scholars who have forgotten how to live, hoarded and treasured in a miserly grip so that its use falters, its wiseness becomes lost though the ink remains darkly scratched upon the parchment, though the wisdoms be truths not even time might alter. When those truths are taken forth, twisted out of context, in the end, naught remains but chaos.

But there is wisdom that is open and free as well, like the windings of a reel, on a harp or a fiddle or a flute, in the dance of feet upon green swards. That wisdom writes itself upon glistening water, in oaks that grow tall and clean in unshadowed woodlands. A wisdom that is the sweet thrilling of moonlight upon moors, of stars speckling the sky, of the sun, that brightest of all stars. A wisdom that is of honest folk toiling the land, growing their foodstuffs and being content with what they own, not raising the war-banner, sword and shield, to take from another. Fey or worldly, that wisdom is clean and for all...

As each word raged from her, the sword-like thrusts of them became tempered with compassion, became like light birch-rods switching against the dragon's mind, became a warm kindness...for the hobogle's tune brought peace and her words were both wise and true. The red lines thinned and disappeared in the dragon's eyes, the madness faded and forgotten understanding came to him. He remembered that he who held all wisdom, might learn still; he remembered that to have wisdom, one must use it wisely.

Thousands of years of troubled sleep, of rising to slay errant knights who sought glory in his death, of slumber once more wherein their blind hatred festered in his dreams…Dennet's sheer belief in her rightness, her compassion behind that rightness, the sweet trembling of the tune-spell that promised a sleep free forever from those dreams of madness…

The dragon, Draigdd, the heart of Dragonwood, collapsed before the maid and the very ground shook with his falling. The flames that roared about them vanished as though they'd never been, but the trees were charred and smoldering still, speaking plainly that once they'd been real.

Dennet gazed about herself with the weight of the dragon's knowledge within her. Somewhere amidst it lay the road to the Middle Kingdom, but she was too filled with their alien mess to sort the one bit from the rest. She saw the sleeping dragon and knew that peace was his. She looked to the wood and knew that it would grow clean once more, its shadow lifted, though men would still shun it. She looked and knew and all wisdom was hers until she could bear it no longer.

Whirling, it spun from her, that her sanity might remain, for this was wisdom that should not be a mortal's. Whirling, it spun her so that she fell to the ground in a swoon, one outstretched hand reaching for Willie's still form.

DENNET AWOKE first, dazed, only half-comprehending what had been wrought. She saw the dragon lying like stone once more and her Willie lying like one dead. To him she ran. She washed the wound on his brow with water from the skins in their packs, marveling that he was not more sorely hurt. She held him till his eyelids fluttered and he looked up at her. His head was ringing so that he could scarce think, but he smiled.

"Ah, surely," he murmured in a voice so low that Dennet had to bend low to hear him, "ah, surely, I am beyond death an' this is the Mother of the World, sweet Anann herself, that holds me so." His eyes twinkled beneath his pain. "But see Anann. She's so dusty. More a ragamuffin with her hair all singed an' a tangle of uncombed locks…"

Dennet returned his smile, her eyes brimming with tears. "Be still," she said. "Be still and hold me. The way was within me and I have lost it. Ah, hold me…"

Willie clasped her tightly and they remained so for a long while. At length they rose, gathered their scattered belongings—Willie marveling that his fiddle was yet whole—and made to leave. One long look they gave Draigdd.

"He has peace now," said Dennet. "May it always be his. But he might have shown us the way. Where can we go now? What have we left?"

Willie put his arm around her. "We have each other. We can search the more. An' though the way be lost to us for now, let us never lose this: that we have each other."

Dennet said nothing, but pressed closer to him. Sighing, she repeated his words. "Aye, we have each other…

Wearily, they forsook the wood and made for the hobogle's hill, for the menhir that stood tall and grey upon it.

Thomas the Rhymer

Thomas the Rhymer

"Harp and carp, come along with me,
Thomas the Rhymer…"

—from "Thomas Rymer";
traditional ballad (Child 37)

WHEN THOMAS RYMER WAS seventeen, the Lowlands were still wild with
the sudden mysteries and impossible beauties of the Middle Kingdom. But the
days of the Elder Folk were numbered. Year by year, the priests of the White
Christ forged northward, bearing the cross of repentance and the sword-edged
creeds of the bitter desert with them. Love they preached, and burned the
Dhruides for following another faith. Peace they declared, and burned the
wise-wives and hill-walkers.

But when Thomas was still seventeen, the folk of the Lowlands knew of
the White Christ's priests only by hearsay, and the realm of faerie was closer.
Magic still walked the world in those days.

MIDSUMMER CLASPED the land with a lover's embrace and the twilight
was stealing over Tickhill Dale and Cragby Wood when Thomas saw
the faeries ride. Thomas had the witch-sight—as the old folk still call
it—for he was born in the twilight. So where another might have heard
the sighing of winds, seen only grass stirring in the last light of a sweet-
scented day, Thomas saw the faeries ride.

He sat under an elder tree, its bark rough through his thin woolen
shirt and the grass damp under him. Half-dreaming, he started awake

when the first jingle of bells came to his ears. He looked around, peering through the dusk, but saw nothing. He heard only the tinkling bells and a high clear laughter of voices that set his heart to trembling. Then his deepsight, his twilight gift, sharpened and he saw them.

They were neither the stately old ones of the Highlands, nor the diminutive sprites of nursery tales. Rather they were as tall as a child of thirteen, slender as saplings, graceful as wind-blown willows. They rode shaggy ponies with glittering harnesses and delicate saddles that gleamed palely in the waning light. They rode by him—scarcely a dozen yards from where he sat open-mouthed—as though they were alone in the growing night and there was no gawky youth watching their every move with greedy eyes.

Gossamer hair floated to their shoulders. Their robes sparkled and shone with a myriad jewels and fine metals woven into the cloth. And on each sleeve and harness were the lovely golden bells. Their features were pale and thin—high cheekbones, high brows—with dark eyes that held all the age their young-seeming bodies showed not.

Foremost of all was a lady mounted on a chestnut palfrey, her own shimmer of hair matching the hue of her mount's as it lost itself in its mane. Behind her came other maidens, each almost as fair, though not one outshone her. There was a harper amongst their company. He was fair-haired and wore a cloak of rougher cut than the rest, its colour pale beside the bright mantles of his companions.

The whole company numbered some three-score. There were a half-dozen in mottled jester's colours, and many of the rest—male and female—had shining armour peering from under their cloaks.

Thomas watched them pass, his heart in his mouth. He was undecided as to whether he should be afraid—for there were tales of the Elder Folk's terrible punishments meted out to prying mortals— or whether he should jump up from his hiding place to lose himself amidst their sparkling humour.

Last in line came a couple. One was a young maid—for her eyes, too, were young—the other obviously an unwelcome suitor. The maid cast her eyes about, avoiding her companion's gaze, then saw Thomas. Her pony stopped under the sudden pressure of her knees and she stared at the youth.

"He sees!" she cried.

The whole column stopped. Swords whispered out of hidden scabbards and a score of the riders surrounded the elder tree in less than a breath's passing. Thomas's own breath caught in his chest. He crouched, half-risen, to look fearfully about himself. Better he had run the moment he'd cast his eyes on these folk. Now there was no place to hide.

The riders that encircled the tree held their weapons ready, though not yet threateningly. Directly before Thomas, their circle parted and the lady who'd ridden at the head of the company stepped her palfrey into the opening. Her eyes were like the deep tarns of the Highlands and Thomas felt his senses swim as he was drawn into their depths. Then he looked at the ground and stood trembling, listening to the feathery sound of the lady's mount whisper through the grass. When the sound stopped, he looked up. The lady's expression was unreadable.

Silence held the tableau for what seemed an eternity to Thomas. Screwing up his courage, he looked at his feet once more and found words.

"I...I meant no harm," he began. "I couldn't help b-but...see..."

"Gently, lad. Do you think we mean you harm?"

The lady's voice was sweet and low and it drew Thomas's eyes upward once more. Mutely he shook his head. He wasn't really sure, to be honest, but prudence bade him make no mention of that for the nonce.

"Many leagues have we ridden," continued the lady, "through husbandman's field and cheaping burg, and never a mortal's eye did see our passing. How does it come about that *you* see us, then?"

Thomas read an implied threat in the question, for all the lady's gentle speech. Any answer he might have framed died stillborn inside him.

"Deepsight," said the harper, appearing at the lady's side. "He has the twilight-sight. Isn't it so?"

This second query directed at him, Thomas could answer with a simple nod of his head.

"What god or gods rule these dales?" the lady asked.

The question startled Thomas. Then he thought of the moon's sweet light and a new courage filled him. He stood straighter and replied boldly, and it seemed that the Goddess washed his fears from him as though they had never been.

"Anann," he said, and the name rang through the dusk. "Anann and the Horned Lord."

A sigh rippled through the company. The lady smiled and that smile dispelled any lingering fears that Thomas might have retained.

"Then these are fair dales," she said softly. "And you, lad. Long has it been since we guested a mortal. Would you join our company for awhiles? There will be music and feasting and dancing, aye...and a hallowing of our withered spirits under Anann's sweet light."

Numbly, Thomas nodded, casting caution to the winds.

THERE WAS such a dance that night, where Eldale Hill rises out of Cragby Wood, that the stars themselves, looking down from their heights, would never forget it. In and out, between a scattering of longstones, the faerie dancers wove their steps. Their movements were light and airy, like winds rustling barley fields, or a brook winding down a sharp incline.

Goatskin drums and handclaps kept the rhythm, pipes and flutes skirled overtop, while deep and throaty harp notes rang underneath. The company's harpers were two: one the lady's own brother Padwell, the other the one who had questioned Thomas. His name was Finan and he was kin to the Elder Folk of the Highlands, whereas the lady and her company were not. It was he who had led them here, promising them homes.

The lady's name was Glamorgan. As she was fairer than any other in the company, so was her dance fairer as well. She swept and swirled with such grace that the liquid movements of the others paled and seemed awkward beside hers. And when the moon rose to shine on Eldale Hill's heights, she leapt higher than any other, as though the swelling music would carry her into the night's bosom so that the Goddess and she might dance together.

Thomas stood to one side, eyes wide, his head spinning with fiery elf-brew, his blood pounding to the wild and strange music. When it rose to a final crescendo, the youth sensed a power crackle between the longstones. The company—dancers, musicians, all—froze and trembled. Thomas sensed that otherworldly power seep into his own spirit. It came like a brightness that filled his every cranny, that sent his spirit soaring, his body shivering. Then it was gone.

He stood in silence, his soul leagues away, drifting and laughing in a deep joy. When the dance began again, slow and stately now, Thomas joined the winding line, never questioning the right or wrong of what he did. Glamorgan appeared at his side to take his hand and Ninen—she who first discovered him *seeing* them—took the other. His fingers tingled where they touched faerie flesh. Thomas grinned from ear to ear, and they danced on.

In time, couples broke off from the dance to sit on the longstones or stretch out on the grass. Cups of elf-brew began their rounds again. Padwell took up his small harp and commenced a dreamy air. It whispered across the hilltop, soft and fey—more a distant murmur of far off wild places than a tune of here and now.

Thomas found himself sitting with Glamorgan and Finan on the hill's crest where it looked northward across the low wooded hills. They sat quietly, contemplating the view. When the lady broke the silence, her words seemed more a part of Padwell's harping, and almost passed unheard.

"What would you be, young Thomas? Where does your life lead you?"

Thomas sighed and remained silent, hearing her voice as though from a great distance. But when at length he realized that he was spoken to, he tried to shake his light-headedness from him and answer.

"A storyteller," he said, his eyes meeting the lady's. "Once I wanted to play an instrument, but my fingers..." He smiled self-consciously. "They were always playing the fool. My father was a tinker, see, always on the road. One day he didn't come back and there was my mother with ten of us brats to bring up. So in my fifteenth summer I took to the roads and prenticed to a harper. When I saw the uselessness of that, I decided to tell tales.

"I've worked in fields, I've fished, but always I've sought out tales. And one day I'll get my courage up and stand in some marketplace or inn and see what manner of response my telling might bring me."

Thomas smiled suddenly, throwing out his arm to encompass the hilltop.

"And here this eve," he added, "surely I've the matter for a dozen tales."

His companions returned his smile, but Thomas sensed a certain sobriety under seeming happiness.

"Tales," Glamorgan murmured. "I've a tale for you, my fledgling teller. A tale of sadness and exile." Her eyes took on a bitter and faraway look. "We lived in a fair land—we few you see gathered here. Far to the south it lay, on the shores of an inland sea. Merry and prosperous we were, keeping to our own dales, never troubling mortals—not like the mischievous wee folk that we shared those lands with.

"But the Dead God's priests came and laid their terrible doomings on all our hallowed places. Many of my people died. Only we few survived to flee.

"We have powers and magics, but they availed us not. For what can withstand the gathered might of these desert folk? Cold iron they bear and words we may not hear. And what have we? Nothing that might stay them. Not wind-speech nor wood-rune; not sea-word nor flame-spell. So north we have fled, seeking new lands…seeking peace. And this hill, the wood below, the dales and hills….ah, Finan. Whose lands are these?"

"They are Lord Huntlings," the harper began, but the lady cut him off with a quick motion of her hand.

"I care not what mortal lord plays ruler here. What of the Elder Folk, if any?"

Finan was silent a long while. At length he shook his head. "Glamorgan. Forget settling here. True, the lands I found for you are not so fair…but again, they are unclaimed. Better, ah, far better it would be to fare onwards."

"Whose?"

"Lucan's," Finan replied wearily. "An old one. An earth-mover. Your company has not the strength to best him."

"But we wish for peace—not to take these lands by war. That would make us no better than the desert priests. Surely we could share them?"

"Not with Lucan. He is bitter and spirit-withered, this stag-browed one, my lady. Once he and his folk were a mighty clan, but he waged a war with the sea-folk—Aylwin's people—over a thing so slight that neither of them remembered what they fought over almost before the first blow was struck. In the end, the sea-folk prevailed, for they stole Lucan's horn of plenty.

"He is the last of his kin now and would let none share this land with him, be they ever so peaceful and soft-spoken. Believe me. Let us fare on to the Highlands—to the hills of which I spoke. Only a few hobogles dwell in them. I have bespoken your plight to them and they are ready to welcome you."

Glamorgan looked thoughtful. "Perhaps you are right," she said. "I seek no warring—especially not with kin, be they ever so distant. And yet…this land is so deep-hearted. It calls out to me. Is there no way Lucan might be appeased?"

"Perhaps if he had his horn once more," Finan said with a shrug. "He is alone now—his kin have all gone on to the Far Shores. I think he longs to follow them, but he will never leave without his horn. And Aylwin…he will never give it up."

"Have any tried? Asked?"

"Oh, aye. At first. But Aylwin will have naught to do with his land-kin now. My own father was the last to try and such was Aylwin's wrath that my father scarce' escaped with his life. Bitter would that have been. To lose my father, aye. But worse, there would have been blood-war between our people. So none have tried since—by fair-speaking, guile or plain theft."

"What of an exchange?" Thomas asked, following their talk with keen interest.

Finan smiled. "An exchange of what? What could Aylwin need? He has the wealth of both sea and land—for the ships that fail in the waves…where else would their spoils go but into his troves?"

"Then north we will fare tomorrow even," Glamorgan said and the talk turned to other matters.

It was much later, long after moon-set when the dawn was pinking the eastern skies, that the faerie company slept. Thomas, though, remained awake, going over in his mind all that had befallen him these past few hours. Such wonders. There were tales bubbling in his mind and, such was his excitement, that he could scarcely have slept even if he'd wished to.

Yet amidst all the marvels he remembered, one stood out above all others and that was Finan's talk of this stag-lord Lucan. What a tale that would be, could one win his horn back from the sea-lord. Then Lucan would rejoin his kin and Glamorgan's people could dwell in these dales.

Thomas regarded his hosts again and now perceived the weariness in them. In repose, their smooth faces had worried lines etched in them—a pinched look that their usual glee hid well. And he thought again…the tale that would be therein…the regaining of the horn, the stag-lord's passing, the new home for these travelers from afar.…

The how of its doing was lost in Thomas's sudden excitement. Stealthily he arose and crept through the camp. By the time that dawn was full upon the land, he was a good league from Eldale Hill, faring east towards the sea.

Behind in the camp, all save Finan slept through his leaving. Feigning sleep, the harper watched Thomas go. With the insight of the Elder Folk, he'd known what passed through the youth's mind and smiled now to see him go. It was better this way. Glamorgan seemed to have taken a fancy to the lad, but their trek north was no place for a mortal. And as for him meeting the sea-lord Aylwin well, there was as much chance of that as there was of the sun rising in the west. Yet…

A strange foreboding shadowed the harper's thoughts. He shook it from him, letting his mind empty of further musing. Soon he, too, was asleep.

"I WILL not go."

"But, lady," Finan pleaded.

The twilight was upon them once more and the lady refused to go on once she understood where Thomas was gone. And in that knowing she saw too—in Finan's mind—the harper's foreseeing.

"We cannot abide here," he continued earnestly. "Lucan minds not the trooping folk faring through his land—and so we would appear having bided but the one night. But to stay longer would be to court disaster. He has power, Glamorgan. Power that even the Dead God's priests might fear."

"Then let us follow Thomas."

Finan shook his head. "All the land, from here to the sea, is Lucan's." He the uncomfortably before the fiery-eyed lady, wishing he'd never let the mortal go. "Why?" he asked. "What do you see in the manling?"

Glamorgan's eyes grew dreamy. "I see the spark of genius in him— held back only by the narrowness of his experience. I would loose that spark." She reached out to touch Finan's cheek. "Surely you are not jealous, Finan?"

The harper smiled. "Never that. What we have, you and I..." He shrugged eloquently. "But I see now what it is you've seen. There is something in the youth—no doubt of it. And a fair thing it would be to see it freed."

They stood silently then, neither willing to yield to the other, but unwilling to speak and perhaps give life to words that would later be regretted.

"I have it," Finan said. "If this pleases you, lady. Let me take you northward to where others can guide you and I will return and seek out young Thomas. And finding him, I'll bring him north to you."

Their eyes locked while Glamorgan weighed his words. Then she smiled.

"To horse!" she cried to the company. "We ride for our new land!"

The company mounted with a jingle of bells and then swift as the wind were gone from Eldale Hill, the countryside flashing beneath the hooves of their ponies.

— 🌿 —

THAT FIRST morning Thomas used the last of his meager supply of coins to buy provisions for his journey in the small town of Willenwee. The sea was not a long ways, but an ending to his quest he couldn't predict. He didn't regret his decision. He could no longer forego it. Foolish as it might well be, it lay upon him like a geas now. So, rather than working for meals along his way—as was his wont—he bought as much as his coins would buy. That gave him food for two weeks. A beginning if nothing else.

From Willenwee he fared on, heading due east. The pastures and grainfields gave way once more to woodlands until he walked the wilds where few men fare. There was a road that ran southeast, from Willenwee to the sea, but Thomas judged that the sea-lord's tower would lie more to the north—close to the wild Highlands.

He hummed as he walked, recognizing the sweet air as one that his hosts had played the eve before. He wondered if they'd think him a poor guest, taking his leave without a word of thanks as he had. But he put that thought to flight as he imagined their faces—especially Glamorgan and Finan's—when he met them again, Lucan's horn in hand. Now that would be a sight.

Deep in the wilds, Thomas widened his perceptions with his deepsight. It was a thing he seldom did, for the denizens of faerie were as changeable in their moods as a fickle breeze. Did a man pass them by, unaware of them, they simply ignored him. But did a man let on that he saw them—ah, who could know how they might react? Still, Thomas needed directions and only those of the Middle Kingdom could give them to him. Could he find himself one.

He trudged the morning steadily into afternoon. When shadows grew long he began to look for a place to sleep. He'd walked a long day with little sleep the night before. Now weariness washed over him in waves so that he could hardly keep his eyes open. He lifted his feet dully, stumbling often, and at last simply collapsed where he stood. Lying on the sweet grass of a meadow, he looked skyward to watch the twilight chase the day into night. Then he slept.

— ❦ —

IT WAS at noon on his third day after parting with the faerie company that Thomas met with his first Elder Folk. There were three of them— small, gnarled tree-men dragging a long rounded log a good four times their own weight. They cursed fluently, slipping between the common tongue that Thomas knew into their own musical language, ignoring Thomas as though he were no more than the log they struggled with.

The log—a great weight for the three—was only eight feet long, two feet around. Smiling, Thomas stepped up and put his own back into the work. The three stopped in their tracks, letting loose their grips so that Thomas was left holding the whole of the log's weight.

"Ware your feet!" he cried as the weight proved too much for him.

The three little men skipped out of the way as he dropped the log, then stood poised near him, ready to flee at the slightest hint of danger. Thomas kept a firm smile on his lips, though he was beginning to feel a little queasy inside. Though the tree-men were no taller than his knee in height, he saw now the long wicked knives at their belts. And there were three of the little men.

"If we all take a grip," Thomas said bravely, "I'm sure we could manage this thing."

One of the tree-men pulled at his beard and cocked his head.

"Now, he'll be a man," he said as if talking to himself. "That's plain enough for even a piskie to see, though 'nann knows they can scarce' see past the ends of their noses. But how is it he sees us, then?"

"Perhaps he's a goblin," offered another.

The first cuffed him. "Oh, aye. A gob' do you say? Where's *your* sense, then? No, he's a man. It's plain as porridge. Eye can see him. Nose can smell him."

"Maybe he's a…" began the third, but the first cuffed him as well before he could even finish his sentence.

"Well," Thomas said, a little taken aback with their manner that was so unlike that of the lady's company, "I'll be off…seeing how you're in little need of my aid after all."

He began to walk away.

"Now hold on!" the first cried. He was obviously their spokesman. "Not so swift, lad!"

Thomas stopped and turned to look at them, half-afraid he'd see those knives drawn after all. But the tree-men were all smiling.

"It's just that you're the first man we've met—you are a man? Aye, good. But we've never met the one could *see* us before, if you follow my meaning. And…that is…if you *would* help us, we'd surely be grateful." The little man's words quickened into a tumble as he warmed to his subject.

"See, the foresters chopped down old Cory's home, and we're trying to rescue at least a wee bit of it so's the new place will have the smell of the old, so's to speak, at least for awhile, and the load *is* heavy—a bit too heavy for us if you come right down to it…"

Thomas grinned. "Then let's be at it," he said, breaking into the babble. He took a hold of the log once more. "My name's Thomas Rymer."

"We've only one name each," said the spokesman of the little men. "I'm Haben, and these're Jold and Cory."

"Pleased," Thomas said, nodding to each in turn.

Haban smiled, while the other two looked at their feet, scuffling them in the grass.

"The log?" Thomas added.

"Oh, aye," Haban said.

With the four of them all lifting, the log was soon hoisted and they trudged off into the wood.

— 🌿 —

"IT'S BREW we want now," Haban muttered, "for it's hard work, this wood-hauling, and naught'll help us forget it save a draft or two or three of thorn-brew—freshly-brewed, mind you. None of that month-old dwarf beer for us! I'd invite you in," he added, motioning to the tall birch near by, "but your flesh is too coarse to pass through. Bide here in the shade a bit and we'll be back, quick as a wink. P'rhaps sooner!"

So saying, he stepped into the birch, followed by the other two. Thomas leaned gratefully against the tree, his shirt sticky with sweat, his arms and back aching with the load of that log. He was sure that he'd carried the most of it. At least his back told him it was so. He glared at the log, wondering where Haban was with his promised thorn-brew.

His hosts seemed to be taking an inordinately long time. Just when Thomas was despairing of ever seeing the three—or his refreshment—again, they popped back out of the tree.

Cory and Jold balanced large trays laden with huge mugs—at least by their standards—of the brew which was foaming over the rims with their unsteady movements. Haban waved them into place and gave a low bow to Thomas who'd sat up, one hand reaching out to steady Jold whose tray was leaning over most precariously.

"Cakes," Haban said importantly, "as well as brew. For with the labour done, it's time for merriment, hey, friend Thomas?"

A mug and a cake were thrust into the youth's hands. His three hosts waited expectantly while he tasted them. Thomas smiled broadly to show his appreciation.

"See?" Haban asked his companions. "Now where's the gob' that can eat tree-food I ask you? He's a man, sure enough. *Our* man," he added possessively.

The three settled down before Thomas and fell to. For a long while there was no sound save that of eating and drinking. Thomas wondered at Haban's last remark as he ate. In the end he put it down to their excitement at having met up with someone strange. He could see himself speaking possessively of them, were they his guests in a mortal village.

"Thomas Rymer," Haban said, breaking the flow of Thomas's thoughts. The tree-man wiped his beard clean with the back of his hand and grinned. "Strong- backed you are, aye, and kind-hearted to have aided us, but I'd ask one more thing of you. We of the woods—well, we hear much, it's true enough, but little of it in verse. So would you give us a song or a poem? With a name like your own, surely you'll be brimmed full with poetry and such."

Thomas shook his head. "Little enough I know of songs. Among men we have two names—our own, mine being Thomas, and our father's, in my case Rymer. It's just a name, see? And my father's to boot."

"No poems?" Haban hid his disappointment poorly.

"No poems." Thomas sighed. "But would a tale do?"

The three quickly nodded their heads.

"Oh, aye," Gory said, bubbling so much with excitement that he forgot his shyness. "Give us a strange one!"

"Yes and yes!" Jold agreed. "One about mortals!"

Thomas had to smile. Well, it was neither marketplace nor inn, but he had his audience now. Taking another sip of thorn-brew, he sat back and thought of a tale. Satisfied—and after another drink—he began.

"There was an innkeeper once who had three daughters…"

It was a common enough tale, but one of the very few that Thomas knew that dealt wholly with mortals. His own taste led to his collecting fey tales. But his audience of three roared with appreciation when he was done.

"What of the pig?" Cory asked through his laughter.

"Oh, the elder daughter must marry it," Thomas answered.

The tree-men roared again and rolled about in the grass, unable to contain their mirth. When they could laugh no more, mugs were filled anew and Haban turned to Thomas.

"That was a good tale, friend Thomas," he said, "and a better we've not heard in years. But now—you've helped us and amused us and, so's not to have you think we're ungrateful, is there anything that we can do for you?"

"You could give me directions," Thomas said. He'd almost forgotten the very reason he'd approached the three. "I seek the tower of the sea-lord Aylwin."

Haban paled at his words and the other two got a look about them as if they'd sooner be anywhere but where they were.

"Why?" Haban asked in a strained voice.

So Thomas explained. The tree-man shook his head, obviously dismayed. He tried to dissuade Thomas but soon found that he might as well try and make a river flow uphill. No matter what he said, Thomas would go. Haban sighed.

"There is one thing Aylwin does not have," he said at last.

"And that is?"

"A rune. The rune that will topple his tower in the sea. For the merrings built his tower and it's their way to both build and build strong, but leave one thing undone. And with the tower they spelled a rune—a rune that Aylwin his own self knows nothing of. But there's no use in your seeking it for even would he trade that for Lucan's horn, he'd never deal with a mortal anyway. So that's that and you might as well give it up now, friend Thomas."

"Where would that rune be?" Thomas asked stubbornly.

"It's in the keeping of a priest of the New Faith."

"In the south?"

Haban shook his head. "No. Northward. On Kirrimuir Shore. Kirrimuir shore that looks out on Aylwin's tower when the moon rises."

"A priest that far north?" Thomas asked in disbelief.

"Oh, aye. He seeks to spread his faith. And he's a strange one, friend Thomas, truly he is. He treats kindly with even the wee ones—speaking no doomings on them nor their holdings—and if folk will not listen to his teachings, why then, that's that. He uses no force to sway them. No. He but lives there quiet as you please and his faith spreads after all. He plants seeds, the wood-folk have heard him tell men, and by his Lord's will they grow or fail."

"How came he by this rune, then?"

Haban shrugged. "Ah, who can tell? But have it he does and it's of the old wisdom, Thomas, not his own faith. Now Aylwin's tower is mighty—did I tell you the deep merrings built it? Aye? Well, not even the priests of the New Faith could topple it down. Only the rune can—and the priest has that."

Thomas stroked his chin, thinking.

"Thomas," Haban said earnestly. "Forget this thing. No good will come from it. Perhaps you could gain this rune from the priest—being a man, he can't wither your soul like he might a fey's—but Aylwin. He will slay you out of hand before you could even speak a word."

"Is he so evil?"

"No. He lets us tree-folk alone, for we've been here as long as he and maybe longer to hear my da tell the tale. But his heart's as bitter as an adder's. Three sons of his Lucan slew, aye, and his own heart's treasure—his only daughter. Don't go, Thomas."

But Thomas only shook his head. He stood up.

"I must go," he said. "The whys and wherefors are not mine to understand, for it's on me like a geas and I can't be free until the thing's done. I began it to be a part of a tale—a great tale, I thought. Now, it's simply there for me to do and I can't say when it changed from the one to the other."

"Then this is farewell, Thomas Rymer," Haban said softly.

The three gathered up leftover cakes, the mugs and trays, and disappeared into their birch, leaving Thomas alone in the suddenly silent wood. Sighing, he began his journey once more.

— 🌿 —

TWO WEEKS fared by and a new moon was striding the sky when Finan the harper stood before that birch.

"You what?" he asked softly, but his words rang and echoed between the trees.

Haban stood fearfully before the angry elf-lord, his knees knocking together. Hiding behind him were Cory and Jold, speechless with fright.

"How could we know?" Haban asked. "We meant him no harm, lord. We *liked* him—truly we did—and begged him to stay. But he wouldn't take no and it's go he went."

"Aye," Finan murmured grimly. "But not before you pointed him the way."

He shook his head, stemming his anger. The tree-folk were not to blame. Only his late arrival was to fault.

"Too late for blames," he said and leapt to the back of his mount to look down on the trembling three. "Be at peace, friends. I promise you no harm, no matter what lies at the end of this ride."

As he gathered his reins, Haban spoke softly.

"We wished him well, lord. Truly. Moon and twilight be with you."

Finan nodded. "Aye. I'll be needing them."

He spoke a word in his mount's ear and they were gone, swift as the day's light sinking from a storm.

— 🌿 —

HABAN HAD one thing wrong, Thomas thought as he approached the priest's hut on Kirrimuir Shore. He was a man, aye, but he felt as discomforted as any fey in the presence of the New Faith's power. With each step he took, the young storyteller felt pinpricks of something he could put no name to biting into his soul. It was the witcherie in him, he realized, the twilight gift of his deepsight. It was pained at the closeness to this…other one. Every strange tale he'd ever heard told concerning the New Faith's priests rose up in his mind and he felt very vulnerable, young and alone.

The sun rose from the sea's horizon, bathing the long beach with its warm summer light. The priest's hut—a rambling throw-together of driftwood, canvas and pine boughs—was dark against the white sand, the priest a darker figure kneeling before it.

He looked up at the sound of Thomas's feet shifting on the sand and rose in a swift smooth movement. He wore a brown robe with the hood thrown back revealing a lean, lined face and a head of curly grey hair. Around his neck was the symbol of his Dead God—the crossed tree, or crucifix, as they named it. Thomas averted his eyes. Such a feeling of dread came over him when he looked at it, and yet…it drew him as well.

"Peace be with you," the priest said, raising his hand to shape a blessing in the air between them. His voice held only the slightest trace of a southern accent.

"No!" Thomas cried, feeling his throat and chest constrict. He shaped the Sign of Horns to call the Moon's consort to ward him. "Do not make your sign."

The priest nodded gravely, inspecting Thomas with a look of understanding.

"The Old Faith?" he asked in a gentle voice. When Thomas nodded, the priest smiled a little sadly. "Forgive me, then. I did not mean to discomfort you. Would you rest awhile with me?"

Thomas sat upon the sand. He kept his eyes from the crucifix that bounced on the priest's chest as the man made himself comfortable beside him.

"I am named Eustace. And you?"

"Thomas."

"Well met, Thomas. Are you hungry? Thirsty?"

Thomas shook his head and a silence fell over them. The sea murmured behind the hut, its salt tang in the air. Gulls wheeled and dipped in the sky. A kestrel floated out above Chilwich Long—the oak and pine wood that met the sea here on Kirrimuir Shore.

Thomas looked about himself, breathing slowly to steady his pounding nerves. There was a serenity about the priest that he could not fathom. He'd come expecting a wild-eyed fanatic and instead sat beside one whose spirit was as still and deep as a woodland pool, heavy with its watery secrets. There was a mystery here.

"Why are you here?" Thomas asked at last, turning to the priest.

Eustace's eyes met his solemnly. "To spread the Faith of my Lord."

"Like your brothers in the south?"

The priest showed no animosity towards the tactless remark. Instead he sighed heavily.

"There are some amongst our number who have seen the Light once, but then became blinded with their own importance. It is the Faith that is important. *It* is important. Offered, those who perceive its truth will flock to it—given time. Thrust with a sword's edge, with a burning torch…ah, what would He say of such madness?"

There was a sorrow in the priest's voice that brought sadness shining to Thomas's eyes.

"But I am not like them," Eustace continued after a moment. "I do not say that a that I am better, only that a Faith of peace should be brought in peace. So each afternoon I hold a service yonder." He pointed to where a small altar had been set up alongside the hut. "Sometimes a few come to join me in worship—fisherfolk and foresters. More often than not, there are only the sky and beach and sea. The folk in Osenthyme are kind to me. They give me somewhat to sustain me. Mostly, I am simply here. The folk know it. I can only be ready for them should they wish to come and learn. I speak with the woods and they murmur to me—it is the wind and no more, but I find it companionable. I walk the shoreline and keep a small store of the cast-offs that the tide has left for the sand. A shell, sometimes, a bit of wood…"

The priest's voice drifted off. He picked up a handful of sand and let it sift slowly through his fingers. "It may seem little, what I do, yet I do what I can. When all the thundering is done, the gentle murmuring that never ceases will be heard."

Thomas was taken aback with the priest's mild manner. And, listening, he could see the wisdom of what he'd heard. But it worried him, for the priest could well be right. He was kind-spoken enough, but what when his brothers began their northward trek? How would the land be then? Faerie driven yet further into the wilds, he realized, and fewer still would be the mortals to know the fullness of their loss.

Still the sea-lord had a tower that not even the New Faith could topple—or so it was said. If the rune was here, that would strengthen Aylwin. And if he could exchange it for the horn, perhaps Glamorgan could bring the wonder of her folk to these dales. Aye, and allying themselves with the sea-lord's people, then perhaps they would be strong enough to see that the New Faith could find no foothold here— no matter whether they thundered or were gentle.

Thomas was still young, but already his head held the tellings of many tales. He reached into their wisdoms and saw things in them that he might use to further this cause. But first there was the matter of the horn. And so the rune.

"These cast-offs," he asked idly. "Why do you collect them?"

The priest shrugged. "To busy my hands. Many and strange are the things the sea casts up from her bosom. Curious things. Some wrought by nature and the weathering of sea and land, some man-wrought... Would you like to see them?"

Containing his eagerness, Thomas nodded. "Aye. I've an interest in old things."

The priest rose and went to his hut, returning with a rough basket. He tipped it over and let its contents spill out onto the sand. Shells and bits of wood were mingled with trinkets and debris of all sort. Here and there glinted sparkles of copper and bronze, a bit of a vase—curiously carved with designs that minded Thomas of the ruined stoneworks of Those Who Had Come Before...the old folk who'd dwelled in these lands before the present races of man came to settle them.

And then he saw it.

It was no great thing—only a bit of bone with a symbol scratched roughly onto it. But Thomas sensed the power that flowed from it. His deepsight sharpened suddenly and almost he could see the scaled hand of the merring who'd shaped the rune on the bone. Such was the way of the deep sea ones, he remembered Haban telling him. To build the sea-lord his tower and then shape a rune that could destroy it—letting that rune ride the tides. For who would think to look for such a thing amidst all the debris the tide left behind each morn and eve?

And the sea-lord did not even know that the priest had this thing. There would be words of the New Faith spoken over this simple hut—words that would keep any denizen of faerie at bay. He wondered briefly how Haban had known, then realized that a gossiper such as the tree-man would gather a thousand tidbits of unrelated information. Aye, and perhaps the sea-lord knew it was in the priest's keeping as well, but could not claim it for fear of the New Faith's power.

Thomas fingered a number of the objects that lay strewn on the sand, then let his fingers linger on the bone with its terrible rune. He tossed it in his hand as he continued to pretend interest in the remaining objects, making small comments as to what might the history of this armband be? Or from what ship or mighty tree on what distant shore had this smoothed driftwood come from? Then he looked at the bone in his hand.

"Do you fancy that?" the priest asked. "I'm not sure why I picked it up, for each time I lay eyes upon it I feel a strange stirring in my heart. Not uncomfortable, but still…different somehow. Perhaps it is an amulet of your own Faith?"

Thomas shrugged. "Who can say? Perhaps you're right. But to me it has a pleasant feel and if you've no need of it…"

Thomas could scarcely contain his excitement when the priest dismissed the bone with a wave of his hand. He thrust it into his jerkin with a casualness that he didn't feel. It had been so easy. And now there was only the sea-lord left to deal with. He began to help the priest gather the objects back into the basket, but his eyes held a far-off contemplative look.

"Of what are you thinking?" Eustace asked.

Thomas regarded him seriously and felt the sudden weight of age creep across his few years.

"The moon," he said softly. "I wait for the rising of the moon."

TWILIGHT BROUGHT the sound of hooves echoing across the sand. Thomas lifted his head, startled, but the priest gave no sign that he heard anything. They were sharing a meager meal—finishing the last of Thomas's supplies. The hoof-beats were soft—for they were of a faery-steed that rode, and the footing was sand—but in that magic moment between day and night, when the whole world seems to lean into silence, they seemed loud to Thomas's ears.

He looked up to see Finan rein in sharply where the dark woods met the pale sand of the beach. The elf-lord could go no further, not with the priest there. Silently, Thomas left meal and priest behind, to meet the harper. In his jerkin, the runed-bone was a sudden prick of cold against his skin.

"You have changed," Finan said when Thomas was close. "We met—what? A fortnight or so ago? And you were but a youth, filled with all of a youth's impressionable follies. And now. The old magic pulses through your blood and age lies like a mantle over you, no matter that your body seems unchanged."

Thomas nodded. He made a motion with his hand to where the priest still sat, peering at them—or peering at Thomas, for he did not have the deepsight to see the elf-lord.

"A glamour?" Thomas asked.

"Even so."

Finan brought out his smallharp and pulled a chord from its strings. Though Thomas felt nothing, he knew that now he, too, walked the Middle Kingdom and that the priest could see neither of them.

"You have the rune," Finan continued as if there had been no interruption. "I can smell its sea-age upon you. It was well-done, this getting, but now I must beg of you, let it be. No good can come of pursuing it further."

"And how can I not?" Thomas asked. "The thing is begun. Can even I end it now?"

"You can try."

"Its doing lies over my spirit like a geas."

"You cannot hope to prevail."

"But I have a plan."

Finan shook his head in exasperation. "Thomas! This is no merchant with whom you could haggle as though you were in some marketplace. This is a lord of faerie you must deal with—bright and wild. So far the moon's own luck has been with you. Do not press it further. Those who deal with faerie reap strange rewards. And trite as it may sound, there *are* fates worse than death. Would you meet one of them this evening?"

Thomas looked away from the harper, down the strand.

"The moon rises," he said, ignoring Finan's arguments. "Will you give me a ride there,"—he pointed with his finger—"or must I run to catch the moment?"

Harper and youth eyed each other. Sighing, Finan swung his harp back and gave Thomas a hand up. The faerie steed exploded into motion and the sands of Kirrimuir Shore sped beneath them so that, just as the moon was rising, they were come to the place. Out in the sea, in the tide-land that neither sea nor earth rules, the tower of the sea-lord Aylwin formed—a dark finger of sea-deep stone that shimmered in the moonlight.

"Give me the summoning word," Thomas whispered to Finan as he slipped from their mount.

Finan was tempted to hold back this last necessary piece of knowledge that would set the whole of this final event into motion. But as a geas lay over the youth, so did he feel compelled to speak. He leaned across his mount's neck and murmured the word into Thomas's ear.

Thomas held that word inside him for a long moment, savouring its heady wonder, before he cried it aloud, out into the night, to the sea, to where the tower stood. That tower would bide where it was for just as long as it took the moon to make its first rising and slip across the world's heart. But the word Thomas spoke held the stone's shimmering disappearance at bay.

A long silence drifted over the strand. Sea's murmur and wind's whisper stilled. Finan and his mount stood as still as though the two made up a longstone, hushed and expectant as it awaited an old wonder to loose its long inheld breath. Then from the tower came the sea-folk, drawn by the summoning word.

Foremost was Aylwin the sea-lord. He was tall and grim-eyed. His mail was the scales of silver fishes. His helm was carved in one piece from a whale's rib—those creatures that were the oldest sea-masters of all. At his side was his lady Wenmabwen, she of the sea-green hair and movement like water, whose skin was all pearl-white and eyes were as deep as the ocean's own thoughts.

These two stepped from the tide-land to face Thomas. Behind came others of their kin, more and more until it seemed that the sea had taken elf-shapes and returned as an early tide.

Unlike mortals, the emotions of the Elder Folk have a power unto themselves. Gay, their joy is the wild reckless laughter of a summer's storm; angry, and the very mountains seem to tremble under their wrath. Finan astride his mount—a part of, yet not a part of this tableau—felt fear course through his veins. It was fear for Thomas as well as for himself. He could still ride—wind-swift indeed—and be away and never caught, but he was bound by his honour and his growing love for this youth who so bravely faced the sea-lord. So he remained.

Thomas knew fear, too, but he knew another thing as well. A storyteller he would be, aye, and had spent many's the long night these past few years learning tales to tell. But a story must be more than the simple retelling of events. There were lessons to be learned amidst the tale itself, wisdoms to be garnered. Inside himself, within his own poor store of tales, he had remembered a thing. Now he would learn the truth or falseness of it.

He bowed to the company gathered before him and spoke mildly.

"Greetings, lord, lady, and all wave-riders that have come here this eve."

The sea-lord fixed him with a glare. "Fair the feasting was, with no need amidst it to be reminded of the mundane world that scrabbles without our walls. We could not deny the summoning word. Aye, but though easily summoned we might be, we are not so easily bound. Prepare, mortal, to meet your pale life's ending."

Thomas's confidence washed from him to leave his knees knocking against each other, his throat thick and dry.

"I came to ask," he began haltingly, but the sea-lord cut him off.

"I do not deal with mortals."

It was then that his lady Wenmabwen touched his arm.

"Let him speak," she said softly.

The sea-lord stared at her, then inclined his head to her.

"So be it," he said. "Speak then, mortal."

Thomas drew on the ragged remnants of his courage and tried to stand straighter under the sea-lord's piercing gaze.

"I came to ask," he began once more, "if you would accept this gift from me, freely given."

From his jerkin he drew forth the bone with its dire rune and handed it to the amazed sea-lord. Aylwin looked at the thing in his hand, then back to the youth.

"Freely given?" he asked in disbelief. "I never knew this thing existed. And you…do you know what it is you have given me?"

"I know," Thomas replied, relaxing a little as the sea-lord's anger began to run from him. The anger was replaced with a strange look that Thomas could not read.

"Freely given," the sea-lord said once more, then he closed his fist about the rune. He looked at Thomas with new respect. "I had all, save this one thing. And I never knew it. I can see wisdom in you, mortal, beyond the few years that line your face. You know too, then, that you may ask of me a boon, and that I may not deny its honouring."

Thomas nodded, keeping his face free of emotion. He took a deep breath, then told of his meeting with Glamorgan and her company, how they yearned for these dales that were held by Lucan, the stag-browed one.

"Your war with Lucan is an old thing now," Thomas finished, "though the bitter memories of your losses therein you can never forget. This I understand. Yet if Lucan were freed to rejoin his kin on the Far Shores, the memories…would they not fade as well? Glamorgan and her people are gentle folk—Finan here can vouch for that. Would they not make you good neighbours? Aye, and better neighbours than you have now?"

When Aylwin nodded slowly, Thomas concluded his speech. "So I would ask you for the Horn of Plenty—Lucan's horn—that he may depart these dales and the last of the warring be a thing of the past."

Blind wrath flamed in Aylwin's eyes. Once again, before he could strike Thomas or speak a spell, Wenmabwen laid her hand on his arm and understanding dawned on the sea-lord. He was honour-bound, and to break honour would lose him the respect of both kith and kin.

Fires died to smolders in his eyes, died until they were sea-deep and quiet once more. He spoke a word to the folk gathered behind and a sea-elf stepped forward with a small pouch, placing it in the sea-lord's hand. He thrust his newly-gained rune into his belt, and opened the pouch, dropping a small curling horn into Thomas's waiting palm.

"I fulfill my bargain," Aylwin said slowly, "but there is yet one last dooming to fulfill. There is a magic laid upon that horn—I laid it in my anger in the chance that it be stolen from me. I cannot undo it. So this I tell you, mortal. Can you but hold that horn for the space of five breaths passing, then indeed may your hopes become more than mere dreams."

Thomas raised his eyebrows questioningly. He meant to ask for an explanation, when the horn burst into flame. At the first sear of pain, he opened his hand to let the horn fall. But no! cried a desperate voice inside him. Then it would all have been in vain. He steeled himself to grip the horn firmly. He held an inferno in his hands.

His mouth was open and he was on his knees, never remembering how he'd come to fall. Silent screams tore from his throat. Then the flames were gone.

An adder twisted in his hands, slippery and escaping. How could the charred ruin that was his fingers, his hands, hope to hold anything? Yet blackened bones gripped the adder. The flesh of his forearms shrank as the creature sank its fangs deep into him. He could feel the heady poison rushing through him.

Five breaths, he moaned inwardly. I will die ere....

The adder became water. It washed through the black finger-bones held impossibly together. Then Thomas knew. Pain blossomed and flared through him, his mind screamed his agonies, but through it he knew. His deepsight deepened still more. He saw more than a host of sea-elves where others would see but foam, more than a mounted harper where others would see only a strange shadow on the moonlit sand. He saw through what seemed like ruined hands and water dripping to the ground. He saw beyond the mind-numbing pain that was all he could seem to focus on. What he saw was the horn held in hands that were as hale as ever and knew the whole of his pain for yet one more fey illusion.

He looked up from his hands to lock eyes with the sea-lord. As two more breaths passed, a sudden energy that he'd not sensed before slipped away.

"Few even in the Middle Kingdom could have seen through that spelling," the sea-lord murmured. "I honour you, mortal. In my tower, in my realm, there will ever be a welcome for you."

Thomas shivered. The sweat soaking his shirt was suddenly cold and clammy in the brisk night air. He felt anger course through him, but forced it back. The sea-lord had honoured his bargain, though not quite as Thomas had expected. To let anger run its course now would be to destroy all that he'd accomplished. But the illusion of pain was burned on his mind as surely as if it had been real.

He felt hands lifting him to his feet. On one side was the lady Wenmabwen, her eyes filled with warmth for him. On the other was Finan, and his eyes held pride mingled with awe. But Thomas felt a fever upon him. His head was spinning in the aftermath of what he'd been through.

"The priest," he mumbled without reason. "He's not so bad…"

Finan nodded solemnly. "Aye. For everything there is, there can be good and bad and all the many shades between. Rest easy, friend Thomas." He looked to the sea-folk, asking, "By your leave, I would ride while there is yet the night to speed my mount."

Thomas saw the sea-lord nod, then knew no more.

SO IT came to be that Lucan the stag-lord fared for the Far Shores and the Dales of Tickhill were no longer ruled by a lord of the Elder Folk. Rather the lady Glamorgan held those lands and gentle was her rule.

She and Finan and Thomas stood on Eldale Hill one night, weeks after Thomas's ordeal on Kirrimuir Shore. There were halls in the hill below them now and fair steadings in Cragby Wood. And still a peace, for the New Faith had marched no further north as of yet.

"I've a gift for you, Thomas Rymer," Glamorgan said, looking away from the dark woods. "I saw the spark within you and longed to flame it into life. But my people already call you the Rhymer, for your tales have that wonder that only the great poets of the Middle Kingdom are said to have. Your quest widened the narrowness of your spirit, giving it the will and courage and strength to grow. What can I give you now?"

Thomas shook his head. "I want nothing. Nothing, save for new tales. I have told your folk all I know and now must road-wend awhiles, to bring those few to ears that have never heard them. Aye, and to learn—perhaps live—still more."

Glamorgan drew a golden apple from a small pouch at her side and held it up so that the glistening skin shone in the moonlight.

"And yet I would give you something, you who have given us so much. We had a tree in our homeland, and such were its fruits. It withered under the advance of the New Faith and this is the last of its harvest. Take it and it will give you a tongue that will never lie. Beauty in words is a fair thing for a storyteller, but truth is the final measure. Whether it be a tale growing from within you, or one retold, it must ring true.

"This fruit's wonder is such that it draws the truth from the hidden places within you. And the folk who hear you will *know* that what you tell is more than mere glamours to amuse them."

Wordlessly, Thomas took Glamorgan's gift. He remembered how the few tales he'd known had aided him and knew her words to be true. Such would be a fair thing, to help others to learn, through the tellings. He met Glamorgan's gaze and the lady smiled, accepting his silent thanks.

Finan coaxed a breathy chord from his harp then, and spoke softly over its ringing.

"And they will name you True Thomas," he said. "True Thomas the Rhymer."

Gipsy Davey

"It's late that night that the lord came home,
enquiring for his lady;
his servants all replied, 'She's gone,
she's away with the Gipsy Davey...'"

—from "The Gypsy Laddie";
traditional ballad (Child 200).

IN THOSE DAYS LIVED one Thomas Rymer, a wandering storyteller. He had the witch-sight of one born in the twilight, the deepsight that could pierce the borders between this world and the realm of faerie. And it was the Elder Folk themselves that gave him the gift of a tongue that could not lie.

Welcome he was wherever he traveled, be it a Lord's high-walled keep or a husbandman's rude cot. But the fairest guestings of all were in the wild places—sea-keeps, wood-halls, hollowed hills, wherever the Elder Folk were known to gather. For like calls to like, and fey was True Thomas the Rhymer.

THOMAS RYMER frowned, though his lips shaped a smile.

The easy bustle of Fairdfore's marketplace clamored about him. Smiling farmlads jostled for space with village merchants, tinkers and sharp-tongued hucksters. Goodwives chattered by the gossip stones. Young maids flirted. Smells rose and mingled—the sweat of honest toilers, their wool and leather, with spices, roasted nuts and sweetmeats. A sense of camaraderie and goodwill surrounded Thomas, but he felt only a sense of dread.

The priest repeated his question. "I asked: Will you guide us?"

Thomas regarded him. The priest's eyes were as piercing as any hawk's, deep-set in a face that was lean and thin as a weasel's. Behind his robed form stood a half-dozen men-at-arms. They were well-weaponed, with shields hanging from their shoulders and mail glinting through the folds of their mantles. Thomas felt his smile slipping. For a moment the priest's face seemed to shift into a grinning skull with maggots crawling from its empty sockets.

He hid a shudder and asked mockingly, "Cannot your god show you the way?"

He watched anger slide across the priest's face, quickly veiled with a smile as false as his own. We are two masked men, Thomas thought, but as different as night is to day. Yet where the Rhymer's heart held the grey wonders of faerie, he could not tell whether the priest's held the bright light of a noon sun, or midnight's darkest shadow.

He need not go with them. He had only to raise his voice and help would come. Tinker blades would wink in the sunlight. Burly farmlads would flex muscled shoulders and raise callused fists at his word. For he was Thomas the Rhymer who walked the old ways. True Thomas who told no lies and whose tellings let his listeners be as much *in* his tales as they were his audience. But he loved folk like these too much. To raise his voice now would only send many to their deaths. Fists and knives were poor substitutes for the long swords that hung at the belts of the priest's soldiers.

Thomas realized suddenly that the priest had been speaking and he'd not heard a word. He could tell from the hawk eyes that the words held no truth, no matter that the lips smiled reassuringly. Thomas plucked a fluff of wool from the sleeve of his jacket and watched it flutter to the ground. His gaze rose abruptly and locked onto the priest's.

"I will lead you," he said softly.

The priest's smile widened into a satisfied grin. "The Lord bless—"

"No!" Thomas said, cutting him off. "Where we walk, keep that one's name to yourself. This I swear: I will lead you. But speak his name only once and my own knife will find lodgings in your throat."

The priest paled. Thomas himself was startled at the intensity of his words. But at that naming he'd felt the coldness in his heart—a chill that was only a shadow of what the Elder Folk would feel—and knew he spoke the truth. Where they meant to go, there was no place for the holy words of the Dead God.

He could see anger brimming in the priest and could almost read his thoughts. Strike him down, the priest longed to cry out to his soldiers. But he didn't dare. The church knew the power of martyrs and would not give those who followed the old ways another. The dhruides and wise-wives were one thing. But to slay one such as Thomas Rymer would set back their gainings a good ten years.

"So be it," the priest said, regaining control of himself. "Let us be on our way."

Thomas fell into step beside him, all too aware of the six heavy-footed men-at-arms who took up the rear.

"Thomas?"

The Rhymer turned at the soft touch on his sleeve to recognize a boy from the lodging house where he guested this week. He could feel a sudden tension in the air. The priest's presence became a dark shadow across Thomas's heart. The men-at-arms touched the hilts of their swords.

"It's alright, Janny. Tell your mum that I've a road to follow and won't be back for a fortnight or so."

The boy nodded uncertainly, stepping aside as the small cavalcade moved on. A silence followed in their wake as the folk of Fairdfore became aware of Thomas walking amidst the priest and his soldiers. Thomas breathed a sigh of relief as they left the last of Fairdfore's stone-walled cots behind them. He'd averted trouble in the marketplace, but now he was alone. He had a long walk before him, in company he would never have chosen, had he been given a free choice. He wondered bleakly if he would ever see Fairdfore again.

"WHY," THOMAS asked as they camped that night, "do you seek Davey Faw? Surely your god can find a worse heretic to burn than that poor lad? I myself have done your kind more harm than ever Davey might have, priest."

"Yared," the priest said. "My name is Yared, Thomas Rymer."

Thomas nodded acknowledgment.

The priest continued. "I do not seek him for my god, but rather for Aldhelm, the Lord Huntling. Davey Faw stole his wife Jeannie in the dead of night. As she was under my care, so it becomes my burden to return her to Huntling Hall."

"Stole her?" Thomas murmured. Then he was remembering. The border minstrels had a new song and the highroads were ringing with it. *Rattle for the gipsy gipsy, rattle for the gipsy Davey.* Aye, Davey Faw *had* stolen Lord Huntling's wife, but it was willingly she'd gone with him—or so the song had it.

"Aye, stole her," Yared said. "She must be returned and Davey Faw punished as befits his crime."

Thomas shook his head. "Ill would that be done. Davey's the son of Johnnie Faw and he's the King of the Gipsies. Punish him and they'll burn Lord Huntling's keep down about his ears. You have men-at-arms, and the magic of your Dead God, but the gipsy folk are not fey, fearing iron and holy word. They have numbers and their own magics. The tale goes 'round that Huntling's wife went willingly. Take her back...punish Davey...and you will give them cause for a blood-feud that will not end until the whole of the Lowlands lie in ruin."

"Willingly?" the priest cried. "Assuredly, she'd go willingly! And with anyone. Thomas Rymer, I'll tell you this. Jeannie Huntling is a half-wit. She looks as fair as any new bride, but she hasn't even sense enough to wipe the drool from her own chin. She has the mind of a babe."

Thomas felt a chill go through him.

"Then why," he asked grimly, choosing his words with care, "why did Lord Huntling take her as wife?"

"His lands border Addleworth's dales," Yared began.

"Enough!" Thomas said, cutting him off. "I know the tale. I know it all too well. A bitter rivalry, border raids and battles...ending in a wedding. But never a care do the Lords give for anything but themselves." Sorrow twisted into futile anger. "Damn these Lords for their unthinking ways! And damn your ways, too, priest! It was a cleaner land we dwelled in before you came with your saints and holy writs…your marriages of convenience." He stabbed a finger before the priest's face, forestalling the angry retort.

"Know this, priest of a Dead God. *I* know Davey Faw, and I know him well. He is a kind soul with a gentle heart, be he gipsy or not. Better-treated this Jeannie could never be than in his company. I will not lead you to him. Slay me if you will, but I go no further."

Yared smiled. This time his eyes smiled as well and Thomas felt the chill in him deepen.

"I think you will, Thomas Rymer," he said. The soft certainty in his voice echoed like the tolling of a dooming bell. "Do you think me a fool? I know why you agreed to aid us so quickly in Fairdfore. Your own soft heart betrays you.

"You have spoken your mind. Now hear me. Lead us to Davey Faw, or all Fairdfore burns. Inhabitants, town and fields will be only so much charred ash do you not obey me. Do you think me harsh? There are reasons.

"Lord Addleworth visits Huntling Hall at the month's end. And what will he think when his daughter—no matter how feeble-minded she may be—is not there? I will tell you. He will cry treachery. He will cry for revenge and those same border raids that a wedding ended will escalate into a full war. Would you have that, Thomas Rymer?"

Thomas shook his head numbly, not sure what to think. What cared he for the petty warrings of Lords? Yet good people would die in them, just as good people would die in Fairdfore…ah, just as Davey Faw would die when this priest returned him to Huntling Hall. And then the gipsies would ride.

It seemed at that moment he could look ahead into the years to come and see only smoke and bloody ruin. But what could he do?

They fared into Glamorgan's lands, she who was a queen of faerie, and Cragby Wood about them was a fey and wild place. Priest and men numbered only seven. A small company, but large enough to hold one storyteller until…until what? What if Glamorgan's people came and met with the cold iron and holy words?

Rattle for the gipsy, gipsy, rattle for the gipsy Davey…

The words ran through Thomas's head, borne on their cheery tune, but they brought him no cheer. Ah, Davey, he thought. Did you ever think when first you did the deed? One small act, who could ever say where it would lead? Turn a corner, where normally you'd fare straight through, and your whole life could change. On such small doings rested the weight of many futures.

Thomas looked at the priest. The Rhymer's eyes were shining with unshed tears.

"The power is in your hands, priest," he said slowly, adding to himself: for now. Ah, let it be only for now.

Yared's face shifted in Thomas's gaze and again he saw a bleached skull. Shuddering, he turned away, fumbling for his blankets. He lay awake for a long while, listening to the soldiers' snores, trying to shake the vision from him. But when he did sleep, the skull-headed priest walked grinning through his dreams.

— 🕭 —

ON ELDALE Hill, overlooking Cragby Wood, a fair-haired harper bent his lean form over his harp, thin fingers drawing a sweet strange melody from the strings. A woman danced before him, long chestnut hair shimmering in the moonlight, her deep eyes seeing only him. Her beauty was the aching wonder that burned in a poet's visions.

They were of the Elder Folk, these two. A glamour was upon them, freely laid, and the whole of the world was their splendor. Suddenly, the harp rang discordantly. Slim feet faltered in their steps as the two looked at each other.

"Finan? the woman asked.

The harper looked away to stare at a broken string, curling and bloodied from where it had struck his hand when it snapped.

"It's Thomas," he replied softly. "Ah, Glamorgan, it's Thomas." He raised his eyes. "Come walking with death."

Glamorgan kneeled before him. "You are *seeing*?" she prompted gently so as not to break the spell.

"Death comes walking with iron in the one hand, runes of the Dead God mouthing from its lipless mouth. It's the gipsy they want... the gipsy and his wee wise maid..."

"We must warn them," Glamorgan said. "But Thomas...?"

Finan shook his head. "The choice was never his."

He laid aside his harp and stood, lifting the lady to her feet. A silent call summoned mounts for them both and the half-dozen riders that would accompany them. Finan took up the hunting horn from his saddles prow and lipped it. Far and wide the cry rang and mortals stirred uneasily in their sleep. And those few, those very few who *knew*, rose from sleep to stare out into the night and murmur, "The faeries ride."

— ⟨⟨ —

DAVEY FAW would never be considered a tall man, but standing at the door of his small cot he towered over his two guests. Bleary-eyed, he ran his fingers through his mop of bright red hair and smiled a welcome. The grim smiles that Finan and Glamorgan returned woke him with the suddenness of a bucket of cold water. He ushered them to seats by the hearth and shot a worried glance to where Jeannie Huntling's slim form lay curled up in his bed.

Finan and Glamorgan took their seats in silence while Davey busied himself, first setting a pot of water to boil by the fire, then pulling the blanket up about Jeannie's chin. She stirred in her sleep and Davey's brows met in a frown. Outside he could hear the faint stirrings of unshod ponies' hooves that were there one moment, the next seeming to be only a trick of the wind. He brushed a lock of pale yellow hair from Jeannie's cheek and turned to his guests.

"What's a-foot, then?"

Their uncomfortable expressions spoke volumes.

Davey sighed. "So the hunt's up again, is it?" Absently, he took the water from the fire and poured it over rose-leaves and herbs to steep. Setting the pot down he found a seat himself. His shoulders slumped and again he looked to the bed. Ah, Jeannie, he thought. And where'll we go now? The Highlands are no place for you, all lonely and wild as they are.

Finan began to speak of what he'd seen while Davey listened with half an ear. His mind was more preoccupied with the young wife of Lord Huntling, she'd stolen from the Lord's own halls.

They called her a halfwit. But different—slower—than other folk as she might be, she still had the same hopes and desires. She would live in the world, not be locked in barren rooms with her only company being a priest of the New Faith. Somewhere between her inner self and the outer world a barrier had risen—from birth—and she could no more express herself than she could fathom what went on about her. But still…in her eyes Davey could see burning a flicker of intelligence, and it was growing stronger. He never laughed at her, never made comment as he helped her through the day's smallest troublings. She trusted him. She loved him. He could tell. And in turn, he loved her.

Finan had fallen silent and Davey looked up wearily to meet the harper's eyes.

"We would aid you," Glamorgan said. "You know that. But what this one bears…"

Davey nodded. "Aye. Iron and the holy words of his faith."

"Perhaps Thomas could…"

"No, Finan. Thomas is as bound as you—else why would he be leading them to me? No. Against this priest there is little you two can do. But I…" Davey looked to the door where his cloak hung under the weight of his sword's scabbard. "Do this for me. Hide Jeannie in your hall under Eldale Hill. I will go to meet the hunters. And if…if I should fail…send Jeannie north to my kin. Tell them the full tale. Huntling will learn then what it means to arouse the wrath of the gipsy folk."

Davey pictured his father in his mind as he spoke—tall, dark-haired Johnnie Faw, with a storm's fury building in his eyes. It would be a bitter lesson that Lord Huntling would learn.

"We would do more," Glamorgan said.

Davey shook his head. "With iron and holy word before you, there is no more you can do." He stood and crossed the room. Cleaning three cups, he poured each brimful with steaming tea. "Drink with me, friends. The dawn is fast approaching when you must away. I'll wake Jeannie, now, and tell her what I can."

— ❦ —

DAVEY FAW stood outside the door of his cot. For a moment he saw the riders—the gossamer hair and billowing cloaks atop the prancing ponies, and Jeannie cradled tenderly in Finan's arms. Then there were only shadows and the hoof beats became wind. Wearily, Davey entered the cot and strapped his sword belt around his waist.

Jeannie had been dreaming when he'd gone to wake her. As it happened so often before, he was drawn into that dreaming. The outer world lost focus as his eyes glazed and the dream became reality. The hill was there, as ever, and Jeannie sat in the deep green grass at its foot. Silhouetted against the sky was the departing figure of he they named the Grey Man. He raised a hand in salute to Davey. Then he was gone and the hilltop was empty.

Davey had never learned who he was, this Grey Man. Sometimes he came to them as an old gaffer, jolly and stout; again as a middle-aged scholar, white-haired and wise; other times as a youth with a harp, playing tunes for them. But always there was the grey depth hidden in his eyes, and by that they knew him, no matter what shape he wore.

Jeannie had known him for a year. Once she'd strayed from another dream, one of the New Faith's hell that her keeper-priest never tired of describing to her. The dream had shattered and she'd found herself here—wherever here was—with the Grey Man waiting to meet her.

Here Jeannie had everything nature had denied her in the real world. Here she could speak so that her feelings passed lips that never stumbled. Her own hand could brush a lock of her yellow hair from her forehead with a grace she'd never known. She could dance and run and sing, do all the things she'd ever yearned to. Here her mind itself was free of its bindings and her thoughts were coherent—not twisted mazes wherein logic disappeared behind a veil of fumbling thoughts.

Watching the Grey Man vanish, Davey remembered why he'd come into the dream. He turned to Jeannie and told her what had befallen. She clung to his arm, her eyes rising to stare into his.

"Don't go, Davey," she whispered. "The Grey Man said we shouldn't go."

"We? Or only you?"

"Me," she replied in a voice so low he could hardly hear her.

Davey stroked her hair, understanding. She was a brave lass in this dream world—always striving not to remember how it would be again when the dream ended, when their communication was no longer so free. She knew as well as he did that she could do him no good where he went now. And it was the pain of being a burden that cut her most deeply of all.

She wanted to help him, to stand by him no matter what, yet she couldn't. For when the dream ended, she was locked inside her luckless body once more, thoughts entangled, scarcely able to care for herself, little say help him.

"He said three truths would stop him, Davey. The Grey Man did. Three truths and you must bind them in an ash wand."

Davey nodded, not really understanding.

"Glamorgan will keep you in Eldale Hill until I return," he said. "Will you go?"

"I'll go, Davey. I'll go. But you'll come back, won't you? Say you will."

"I'll come back," he promised, hiding his own fears from her. "Now wake, Jeannie. The time's at hand…"

Davey finished buckling on his sword belt and stood staring around the cot, still remembering. Again he saw Jeannie's frightened eyes, looking at him over Finan's shoulder before the shadows drew dark and the faery host was gone. He cursed under his breath and walked to the door. The first rays of dawn were glimmering pink over the eastern hills. Jeannie was safe in Eldale by now, while he…

Taking up his staff, he cursed again, louder, and set out, dark thoughts brewing in his mind.

DAVEY WALKED the morning into noon. The hills rose and fell underfoot and he paid no mind to anything about him, except for stopping once to rest under the large spreading crown of an ash tree. He remembered Jeannie's strange words…*three truths, bound in an ash wand*. Wondering still at what it meant, he looked amongst the leaves and tall grasses until he found one wind-blown twig, curved like a crescent moon.

Somehow he knew—from his grandad's tales?—that the twig must be wind-blown, not torn from the tree. Smiling, he picked it up and pocketed it.

"Thank you," he murmured to the tree.

He felt foolish but sensed that this was right as well. Did the leaves whisper acknowledgment? Davey only shrugged and walked on, lost in his thoughts again.

The Grey Man of Jeannie's dreams. He wondered about him often, remembering at times how he'd first met him. He'd been road-wending north to the Highlands and home, stopping to camp near the keep that was Huntling Hall. He was not fool enough to ask there for guesting. The folk of the Lowlands had strange ideas concerning the gipsy folk, thinking them nothing better than thieves or worse. So wrapped in his cloak, hidden under a thicket of willows with his sword at hand, he'd slept, and sleeping, dreamed an odd dream.

First he'd seen the very riverbank where he slept. It was strangely luminous—as though lit from within more than from moon and stars. The scene shifted towards the stone-walled keep in the distance until he'd found himself drifting inside like a phantom—which to his mind he was. He accepted it all as one does in a dream and felt simply curious. Then a darkness came winding about him, drawing him to the keep's main hall…in and upward…to where a priest knelt by a bed.

It was on that bed that Davey first laid eyes on Jeannie Huntling.

The priest was muttering and Jeannie writhed on the bed. Davey stood in the shadows, pinpricks of fear running up and down his spine as he listened to the voice of the cloaked, kneeling figure. The words were unintelligible to the gipsy. When he looked again at Jeannie, her writhing had quietened. He was drawn to her, his ethereal form floating across the room. As he reached the bed, he struck a barrier like an invisible wall. Searing pain exploded inside him. His mind reeled. He felt as though he were falling into a chasm that yawned underfoot, a darkness to which there was no end. Then he lay on the riverbank once more.

He remembered sitting up, thinking the dream ill-omened, then making a warding sign when he found that he sat beside his own sleeping body. But shocked though he was at that, he could only think of the lass he'd seen in Huntling Hall—she and the cloaked priest. His heart went out to her, sensing something inside her that was trapped and longed to be free.

"They call her a half-wit," a voice said from behind him.

Rising, Davey turned. That was when he first met the Grey Man.

He stood leaning on a long white staff, the folds of his grey cloak fluttering about him. There was a sad smile on his lips and a wonder in his eyes that made Davey look away, for they drew him and he was afraid of losing himself in that gaze. Neither old nor young, the Grey Man reminded Davey of the Elder Folk his mam had never tired of telling him about when he was a babe.

"Nature played her a cruel trick," the stranger continued. "Young Jeannie. She's cut off from the world. But she has an inner sight that cuts deep into the Hidden Lands and her spirit's a bright star, all on its own. There are some who'd cut her off from even that."

"The priest of the New Faith?" Davey asked, finding his voice.

In this dream—for dream it must be and no more—he felt at ease with this stranger, trusting him where, if he were awake, his gipsy instincts would never have let him.

"So he is cloaked," the stranger said. "But the White Christ is not his master. Christos is a reflection of the Gods of Light, the Tuathan—like the Norse folk's Baldur, like so many before. This priest serves a darker purpose, that of the shadowed ones, the Daketh. Harm for harm's sake…chaos. They feed on such."

Davey struggled with the concepts, only half-understanding.

"And you?" he asked. "Where do you stand?"

The Grey Man smiled. "Somewhere in between—or perhaps a step sideways. My folk are the Wild Ones, the twilight-born, children of the Moon-on-Earth and the starry piping of the Horned One."

They stared at each other then, the Grey Man holding to his thoughts, Davey trying to gather up the reins of his own scattered ones.

"You could do worse," the Grey Man said.

"What do you mean?"

"Already you are drawn to her. Pursue this thing to its end. Aid her. Steal her away from this half-life and let her truly live."

Davey nodded. The thought had been in his mind. His heart went out to her with more than pity.

"I will do it," he said.

But he spoke to the air, for he was alone again and in his own body. He stared about himself, his eyes drawn to Huntling Hall, the stone walls shining in the setting moon's pale light.

"I will do it," he had repeated, and he had.

He had crept within, stolen her from under the very nose of the sleeping priest and ridden into the woods on one of Huntling's own proud steeds, the lass wrapped in a blanket and held in his arms.

The chase had been long and hard, but all Huntling or his men caught was Davey's laughter ringing mockingly through the trees. When they gave up, he rode on to Eldale Hill and friendly guesting. Glamorgan's folk welcomed them—and surely Jeannie blossomed under their kindness towards her. In the end, rather than faring north and homeward to the Highlands, he set up their lodgings in a deserted woodsman's cot.

They set it to rights, he and Glamorgan's folk. And in the end, Jeannie and he had a cozy home of their own, safe from their foes, close to their friends. Or so it had seemed.

Davey's thoughts returned to the present again. A husbandman's holding lay before him. The noon was past and the afternoon drawing on. Perhaps the folks there would lend him a horse. Then he laughed. Aye. Lend a gipsy a horse. And apple trees grew on the ocean's floor!

Davey sighed. He'd never stolen a thing, until that night at Huntling Hall. But now he must add fuel to the old lie once again. The gipsies were thieves, it was said. So be it.

He checked first to see that his ash twig was still in his pocket. Then, taking to the thickets, he crept forward. He wondered again at Jeannie's message. Three truths, eh? And an ash wand. Then all contemplation washed away and he bent his mind to the task at hand. If his own hunting went well, he could return the horse before a week was up.

— 🔥 —

THOMAS RYMER walked under those same sunny skies, though leagues separated his party from the holding where Davey was stealing his horse. There was a bitter burden in Thomas's heart that grew heavier with each step he took. He'd let his deepsight awaken as they walked and the world came into sharper focus. First the here and now, then the deeper hidden world of the faerie. But the woods were empty of Elder Folk. He would find no help here.

Yared stalked at his side, oblivious to the Rhymer, assured of his control. When Thomas stole sidelong glances at the priest, his deepsight stripped the flesh from Yared's skull so that the bleached bone gleamed in the sunlight, white and grinning, with red fires burning in the empty sockets. Was this true-seeing? The grotesque skull a reflection of the priest's soul? Thomas could only shudder and let the deepness fall from his sight so that the skull was fleshed again, Yared's thin features shimmering into view.

When they camped that night a question hounded Thomas, keeping him from sleep. Which god did the priest serve? He delved into his store of tales—for the tales of True Thomas were histories and wisdoms cloaked as stories—and searched for meaning. In the end he could find no understanding and fell into a fitful sleep. He saw Davey's Jeannie in his dreams. It seemed she was…underground? Dead then? Surely not. And Davey he saw too. The gipsy rode his stolen horse like a wild man, his bright red hair streaming behind him, his mount's sides lathered with sweat.

You'll kill that horse, Davey, he told the gipsy in his dream.

But his only reply was a bitter laughter that rang through the woods and, beneath it, the strains of a tune and that too-familiar refrain:

Rattle for the gipsy, gipsy, rattle for the gipsy Davey…

THE THUNDER of hooves was loud in the still night air. Yared and his men heard Davey coming long before the gipsy was in view, long before he knew his danger. A soldier knelt by Thomas. Grasping the Rhymer by the throat, he held a blade so close that Thomas could feel the cold edge of it against his skin. He could scarce breathe, little say give a warning shout. The hoof beats grew louder, then Davey burst into the glade where they were camped.

Men-at-arms came at him from both sides while another dropped on him from a tree. Before Davey could get in a blow, he was tumbled to the ground, the breath knocked from him. The hard edge of a shield caught his head with a dull crack and he lay as one dead. When he woke, he was securely trussed with ropes from his stolen horse's saddlebags, lying beside Thomas.

His gaze swam and spun. He saw Thomas, but his eyes were drawn to Yared. They went hard as he recognized the priest. Yared stared down at him, his weasel-thin features twisted into a grin. The priest spent little time gloating. He merely said:

"We have the one. The second won't be nearly so difficult to acquire. And think on this, gipsy. Your death's at hand. You're to swing from Huntling's gibbets, but there's none to stop me killing you here and now if you try to escape." The grin grew wider. "So sleep while you can. We have a long march on the morrow."

Sickened, Davey looked away. His heart pounded, dulling the throb in his temples. His only hope lay now with Glamorgan and Finan. Surely they'd spirit Jeannie away? To the north and his father's halls…

"I'm sorry," Thomas said at his side, his voice low. "I wished you no harm, Davey Faw, truly I didn't. But they'd've burned the whole of Fairdfore had I not led them."

Davey turned to the Rhymer and tried to smile. "What could you have done? I don't blame you, Thomas. But surely there's an ill star hanging over me and my luck's gone."

He cocked a wary eye to where their captors were, then whispered the tale of what had befallen him since Finan had farseen the priest's coming.

Thomas listened with growing amazement. There were a thousand tales and old knowledges in Thomas the Rhymer. Young though his years still were, he had walked the Hidden Lands himself, counting faeries as friends, and with each journey his store of kennings grew. But for all his dealings with those of the Middle Kingdom, for all the mysteries of the world that he'd unraveled, there was always a deeper layer, always more to learn. And this…That two could share one dream…that Jeannie had a realm within her…and this Grey Man… As Davey spoke of him, Thomas felt a strange stirring in himself. Somewhere, somehow, he knew of this one, though he could not place the knowledge.

"What did you hope to gain, coming alone?" Thomas asked the gipsy when he was done.

Davey shrugged and the ropes bit into his wrists painfully.

"An ending," he said bitterly. "Somehow, an ending to it. And now it's come, though not what I'd wished for. I tell you that the luck's gone from me and where's the gipsy without his luck? I only hope that Glamorgan can keep Jeannie out of that foul priest's grasp."

"She'll try. But this Grey Man. He said nothing, gave no clue as to how you might have bested the priest?"

"Only riddles," Davey replied. "What I told you. The wand. Three truths bound in an ash wand." He shook his head. "There was a madness on me, Thomas. I rode as though all the fetches of the Barrow Lands were on my trail. Like a madman, aye, and never a thought did I give that your company was this close. Ah, there's a wildness afoot this eve, Thomas. The very air speaks of it."

Thomas had raised his deepsight as Davey spoke and knew the gipsy spoke the truth. The woods about them muttered and stirred, and far off in the distance he could hear Tywys the Huntress and her wolf pack, trailing a wild hunt across the distant skies. The air was charged with tension, as though a thunderstorm were imminent, ready to roar across the heavens. Wildness walks the night, Thomas agreed, and then he knew. Three truths bound in an ash wand. A wild magic. He let his mind search out the tale he only half-remembered and, finding it, he knew what they must do.

"The wand," he asked softly. "Do you still have it?"

"In my pocket."

Eyeing their guards, Thomas edged around until his own bound hands could work their way into Davey's pocket. He touched the slender ash wand—no more than a twig—and felt a tiny shock. It was like a longstone's power, touching the spirit more than the body. With the wand clasped firmly in his hand, Thomas regained his former position.

"When the moon sets," he said, speaking more to himself than to Davey. "Ah, then we'll see."

— ❧ —

THE MOON set.

Thomas was dozing and struggled with heavy eyelids to wake. The ash wand was slippery in his suddenly sweaty hands. He would have only the one chance to try this thing and if he was wrong…He looked to Davey stirring beside him and sighed, raising his deepsight. Then he spoke aloud, his voice ringing with a storyteller's resonance.

"Yared!"

The priest turned. The bleached white skull gleaming in the pale starlight.

"You do not seek young Jeannie for Lord Huntling's sake," Thomas said.

It was the first truth. He needed the half-witted maid as a focus for his dark magery. The wand moved in Thomas's hand. Yared started. Flesh swam over his skull—an indefinable expression on his features before the skin peeled back again. Thomas's deepsight cut sharply into the darkness around them. There was motion and stirring in the dark, something that longed to wake and needed only a certain key to free its bindings.

"The White Christ is not your god."

The second truth hung in the air, stark and grim. Yared rose, sensing for the first time the other forces that were stirring. The wand moved again in Thomas's hand. Yared closed the distance between them in swift strides. His hands grabbed the Rhymer's jacket and lifted him from the ground. The third truth caught in Thomas's throat as Yared shook him. Red flames blazed in the skull's eye sockets. Gipsy and soldiers were frozen where they watched, their mortal eyes glazed as they stared at priest and storyteller.

"Too late your foul spellings!" Yared cried.

He threw Thomas from him. The Rhymer struck a tree trunk and his breath whooshed from him. Yared pointed a long claw-fingered hand at him and spoke a word. Dark fires blossomed in the priest's palm. But Thomas croaked the final truth before they were loosed.

"The wild protects its own."

Something else was in the glade. The wand twisted and bucked in Thomas's grip. He opened his fingers and the wand flew from his grasp. Like an arrow it sped, plunging into the ground between Yared and the Rhymer.

Gnarled and hunch-backed was the figure that grew from the ash wand. Stag horns like branches sprouted from its brow, twisted legs ended in sharp hooves that raked the ground.

"Too dark this night for your kind," Yared said. The dark fires were an intense blackness in his palms. He raised his arm above his head, cocking it back. "What Lord of Light has power in the heart of the night?"

The stag-browed figure shrugged. "How should I know, priest?" His voice boomed hollowly. Silver sparks flowed about him, changing to gold, deepening into topaz. "What matters dark or light, when the grey wild ones wake?"

Yared's arm faltered and he stepped back.

"Whatever you are," he said, "you have still not the power to slay me." His tone belied the assurance of his words.

"Slay you?" the other mocked. "I am an ash lord, dark one. The earth embraces my roots, the moon hallows my boughs. The ash does not destroy. I heal. Your presence festers the very essence of the night. You are a canker on the earth's sweet breast. Summoned I was. I can only heal."

He reached out a gnarled arm. As Yared backed another step, the arm became a bough that twisted about the priest. Yared fought to use his own summoned power, but could not drop his arm to cast it from him. It burned down into his palm, coursing through his body like a sudden storm upon the moorlands. The priest had time for a shriek of soul-maddened pain before the darkness blackened his skull. The ash bough loosened and a heap of blackness crumbled to the ground where it lay smoking.

Thomas stared with his deepsight, shaking as he huddled against the ground. The stag-browed one turned, deep eyes upon the Rhymer, smiled sadly, and was gone. But in Thomas's mind he saw again and again the priest's death, the images swelling and burning in his head. The glade shivered. His whole body quivered with it. Then he found himself in another glade and here his body was not bound. He was alone. At first, he was alone.

Was it a raven winging through the shadows, or a wolf come padding from the dark woods? Feathered or furred, before him formed a cloaked figure that could only be the Grey Man of Jeannie's dreams.

"You?" Thomas asked foolishly.

The Grey Man nodded. "I, indeed, Thomas Rymer," he agreed. He threw back his hood to reveal strong handsome features. His grey eyes regarded Thomas warmly, his lips shaping a slow smile. From his brow curled two small horns.

"Have you a name?"

"Many," the Grey Man said. "Meanan will do as well as any."

Thomas shook his head, trying to clear it. "Why are you...we... here...wherever here is?"

"Here is the silhonell, Thomas. The spirit realm."

"Have I died then?"

"No. We are here that I may thank you for the part you played, unwittingly, these past few days."

Thomas felt an anger growing in him that he could not quite focus. But he kept a firm rein on it. He had been used, but so it was when one dealt with those of the Middle Kingdom. But surely they knew him well enough by now? They had only to ask...

"No time, Thomas," the Grey Man replied, reading his thought. "Events sped swift. It needed doing. And who better to speak the summoning truths than True Thomas the Rhymer?"

"You could not?"

"I could not. As you speak only truths—for how could *your* tongue lie?—so do I have my own geas. With time I could have spoken clearer. But a spirit was at stake and Yared could well have gleaned the plan from your mind, had I spelled them directly to you."

"Jeannie," Thomas asked. "She is so important?"

The Grey Man smiled sadly and answered as though chiding a thoughtless child. "She lives, she breathes, but of greater importance, she has a spirit that sees through to the depth of the wild heart that drums under the skin of the world. Is not every innocent soul of equal importance and deserving a champion?"

Thomas bowed his head, understanding.

"There is yet one more thing," the Grey Man said. "In Huntling Hall…"

"I know," Thomas broke in. "It will be done."

"Then I can only thank you once more. Farewell, Thomas Rymer."

As the Grey Man spoke the world swam around Thomas again. Amidst the sense of vertigo, he sensed hands upon him, felt a dull ache in the back of his head where it had struck the tree when Yared flung him. He opened his eyes to look into Davey's concerned features. The gipsy was loosening the last of Thomas's ropes.

Thomas sat up groggily. "The soldiers…?"

"Gone," Davey said. "They fled when the…the stag-man… vanished…"

The gispy's voice was filled with awe.

"Then how are you free?"

"They left my sword," he explained. "I had only to crawl across to it and saw through the ropes. How are you, Thomas?"

"Alive."

"And Jeannie. Is she…"

"She'll be well now."

Davey grinned. "Then all's well. Will you be coming to Eldale Hill with me, Thomas?"

"I can't Davey. There's a war still brewing along Huntling's borders. He deserves no help, but many others will die if that war breaks out."

"I'll come," Davey began.

"You'll do no such thing. You'll fare straight to Eldale Hill and set your Jeannie's worries to rest. Huntling won't harm me. Though he might with you at my side. Go on, Davey. Go now."

Davey stood uncertainly aside as Thomas swayed to his feet. The Rhymer forced a smile to his lips. Davey looked at him worriedly, but held back the hand that he would have used to steady the Rhymer. Thomas's face had a fierce look on it that would stand no argument.

"Go, Davey."

"So be it," the gipsy replied with a sigh. "But when you're done with Huntling…"

"I'll be coming to see you," Thomas finished. "Now go, Davey."

Davey shrugged his shoulders. He looked once about the glen. Gathering up his sword and belt, he buckled them about his waist. His stolen mount was long fled.

"Then farewell, Thomas," he said.

"Farewell, Davey."

Thomas watched the gipsy stride off into the wood. Dawn was lighting in the eastern skies and the birds were awaking in the trees about him. As he set off himself, he heard, through the birds' chorus, Davey's whistling.

— ❦ —

"…AND SO fell Yared," True Thomas the Rhymer finished, "who was neither priest of the New Faith nor holy man. Let his fall be a lesson to us all."

Thomas looked about the smoky interior of Huntling Hall's main keep, his gaze coming to rest on the Lord himself, and his guest the Lord of Addleworth. They stirred uncomfortably under the Rhymer's steady gaze.

"I will have the marriage annulled," Lord Huntling said at last. He turned to his guest. "You understand?"

Lord Addleworth dropped his eyes from Thomas's face.

"Aye," he said, turning to Huntling. A thought flickered across his features and he smiled broadly. "I have a cousin—a first cousin," he said, "whose daughter—fair and of a whole mind, I might add—will be of age before the Beltain fires are lit…"

Thomas shook his head. Already Huntling was nodding in agreement. With a heavy sigh, Thomas slipped from the dais, down the hall and out into the night. Outside, the moon gleamed high above him and his eyes went northward. Buttoning up his jacket, he began the long walk to Eldale Hill.

The Cruel Sister

IN THOSE DAYS WHEN the telling of tales was for the most part the province of the wandering storytellers, there lived one Thomas Rymer who, in time, became the most renowned storyteller of all. He was named True Thomas, for his tales touched moon-high wisdom. He was named the Rhymer, for those same tales held all the lyrical beauty of a barden lay, though instrument he played not.

Whether it was his twilight-sight that pierced the borders between this world and the realm of Faerie, or that he lived so many of his tales, such was his skill that he was welcome wherever his road-wending took him, be it a Lord's high-walled castle, or a husbandman's rude cot. And even in the wild places did he find a welcome—the sea-keeps, the wood-halls, the hollowed hills…wherever the Elder folk were known to gather. For like calls to like, and fey was True Thomas the Rhymer.

THE SEA gives, the sea takes.

Thomas Rymer was walking Kirrimuir Shore, that half-world that is neither land nor sea, but the tide's own. The sand underfoot was still wet from the receding waves and he left a long trail of footprints behind that would be gone with the morning's tide. The twilight was fast becoming night as the sun set behind the sea's horizon. Thomas quickened his steps. Soon the moon would rise and the tower appear amidst the waves. He must be at its gates within three breaths of its appearing or look forward to a gloomy night alone on the strand.

A shadow flitted through the air and a raven landed on his shoulder, feathers rustling, talons grasping the leather padding fixed to Thomas's coat for that very purpose.

Not alone, he amended, ruffling the raven's feathers. Yet still he hastened. Galthor was a dear friend, but it was not often that a sea-lord invited a mortal to a feast in his halls. And for all the smell of fish and kelp, it would be warm in there.

Thomas smiled. The winter was coming, sure enough, but still it was a fair thing to walk the twilight, the road never still under one's feet. Sometimes he felt his age with winter a-coming. He'd remember the bitter cold that pierced marrow-deep, the icy winds. Old bones could only take so much. And yet, guesting the winter in a keep or cot, he'd fret to be road-wending within a week, while faring southward, he'd hunger for the cold northlands amidst all of summer's pomp.

Galthor nuzzled his black beak against the old man's cheek and cawed as if in agreement.

"Aye, and you'd fret, too, wouldn't you?" he told the raven. "That's if you'd even come south with me."

The north was in their blood. The wild places where faerie had not yet dwindled, or been exorcised by the priests of the Dead God's faith. When there was a world merry and free about one, Thomas often wondered, why spend that wonder in the solemn worship of a dead god? Though how much of these new teachings belonged to the White Christos and how much to his priests, Thomas couldn't say. He knew only that through all the rants of hellfire and damnation, there still rang a kernel of truth, a shining wonder.

Thomas was a storyteller. He knew well enough how a tale's truth might be shifted so that the truth was still there, but interwoven with lies and half-truths. The lies served someone's purpose. The truth that remained might only be present so that the whole of the tale would still ring true in a listener's heart. Thomas told true tales, and no other, but he could recognize when a story had been tampered with.

Galthor cawed again and drew him from his musing. It was a warning cry this time and the raven lifted from his shoulders to vanish ahead into the darkness. Thomas peered ahead. Was Aylwin's Keep here so soon? In the starlight he could make out the rising cliffs of

Berwyn Head still a fair distance ahead of him. Galthor cried again. Following the sound with his gaze, Thomas looked seaward.

The tide was fully out now, the sea shining with a faint phosphorus gleam. He could see Galthor circling, dark wings blocking stars. He looked to what had drawn the raven's attention.

Thomas had the witch-sight, for he was born in that time between day and night, when the faerie hosts ride forth. So he saw the maid more clearly than might another mortal. It was as though she had her own light about her as she knelt in the sand, a slender form, head bent, long golden hair falling to her knees. There was sea-weed in her hair, green woven amongst the gold, and all of it wet. Her shift clung to her and yet—for all the chill in the air—she didn't shiver.

At his footstep, she looked up. Her eyes were the sea's own green-blue, and on her lap, half-hidden by her hair, he saw a small harp. It was carved from bone, plain and undecorated, and each of its three octave strings was wound of hair, as golden as corn, as golden as her own.

Thomas stopped a half-dozen paces from her and Galthor returned to the perch on the storyteller's shoulder. She was too fair to be mortal, this girl, but she had none of the features of the Elder Folk, and Thomas was undecided as to how to proceed. This was a mystery, but he sensed a great danger hovering nearby. He was no hero, only the teller of tales of heroes. And already the moon was rising. In moments Aylwin's tower would form amidst the waves. If he ran, he could still reach it in time. This maid…she was a sending, perhaps, or a siren, come to woo him to a watery grave. And yet…

Her sea-eyes were brimmed with sorrow. They drew on his compassion so that he had to steel himself to not rush to her side, not take her in his arms and comfort that deep sorrow as best he could. He looked away. Was that the tower taking shape? There, amongst the waves. Turning back to the maid, he shaped a ward-sign in the air between them—one that the sea-folk had shown him.

She remained unmoved, giving no sign, showing nothing but her sorrow.

"How are you named?" he asked at last.

His voice sounded harsh in the silence that was unbroken save for the soft murmur of wave on sand.

She opened her mouth as if to speak, but no sound came forth.

Thomas shook his head. She was mute. He looked away once more. The tower *was* forming now. Sighing, he knelt on the wet sand. Galthor flew from his back with a protesting squawk as the storyteller took his small pack from his back. He pulled out his only blanket and walked to the girl. She watched him approach without fear and didn't move when he laid the blanket over her shoulders. Her skin was like ice where his fingers brushed against it. He shivered as though a chill wind had blown over his soul.

Helping her to her feet, he gathered up the harp and his pack with one hand. Steering her with the other, he led her inland a ways to where the ground was drier. In a hollow between craggy stone and dune, he built up a driftwood fire and positioned the girl before it. Then he sat down opposite her and tried to think.

He had tea brewing. That would clear his thoughts and warm the maid. But what was she doing here? This strip of shore was a good three leagues from any village, for the folk hereabouts knew it as fey, knew that the tower of the sea-lord appeared in its waters on certain nights.

So where had she come from? A shipwreck? Or had his first feeling been a-right? *Was* she a siren? Her beauty was enough to give truth to that, but her features were not—he was assured of that much with the firelight bright upon her—and she appeared to have no voice.

The tea water boiled in its pot. Thomas dropped a handful of leaves and herbs into the water, setting the pot on a warm stone for the tea to steep. When it was ready, he poured hers into his one mug, meaning to drink his own from the pot, but as he stepped around the fire and offered her the cup, he saw a glisten of metal at her throat. He set the tea on the sand and moving slowly so as not to startle her, he reached out and lifted the pendant so that he could see it better.

It was circular, made of gold, and upon it was a crest that any save a stranger to Kirrimuir Shore would recognize.

"Avertorc," he said in a soft voice. "The seal of Avertorc."

The maid lifted her head at the sound of the name. With so little distance between their faces, he thought he might lose himself in the ocean depths of her eyes. He let the pendant fall back to her cold skin and moved back to his own place across the fire.

"Avertorc," he repeated a third time.

The Lord of Avertorc's keep was a good hundred leagues away, north along the coast.

"What shall I do with you?" he asked the silent girl. "Are you kin to those in Avertorc? Would you return there?"

And what else could he do? Leave her here on the shore where he'd found her? Take her to some village where folk would be as ill-prepared as he was to make the journey? No, he realized. With winter fast approaching, there was too much preparation that needed to be done for any village to spare men for the journey. But he, he was only a road-wender. So it was up to him to take her to Avertorc.

"I will do it," he said aloud, and thought he read a silent thanks in her sad gaze. "And I will give you a name until we reach your kin, for everything needs a name. From the sea you came, so a sea-name I'll give you: Moryth. Sea-freed, in the old tongue."

The maid smiled at the name. She bowed her head then, closing her eyes, and Thomas felt alone once more, except for Galthor. The raven perched on an outcrop, eyeing the maid with an unreadable look. Thomas knew the raven of old. There was a feyness a-foot in the air this eve. That look was Galthor's reprimand for his drawing them into its weaving. The sea-lord's tower—long since returned to the waves now—was one thing, this maid another entirely. Thomas had his own misgivings, but he could see no way around them.

He stared out across the sea. On his own he could make the journey in half a month's time. But the maid seemed frail—it was obvious she had been through much—so it could take a month.

He thought of being winter-bound in Avertorc and the thought was disquieting. The folk of that keep were a strange folk, not given to the merry ways of most northern folk. Still….

The sea gave, the sea took.

He could do no less for the maid than reunite her with her kin. If all went well, if the first storms held off for long enough, he could hopefully find a fairer lodging before the winter was fully set in.

Yet a foreboding had woken in him from the first moment he'd seen the maid, and he couldn't shake it from him.

The night deepened and still he stared seaward, worrying.

— 🖉 —

THEY REACHED the small fishing thorpe of Osenthyme the following afternoon. There Thomas bartered for new clothes for Moryth, outfitting her in high fur boots, woolen breeches, shirt and tunic. Last, he added a pair of cloaks—one for each of them. With winter nigh, they would need such gear, faring northward as they did.

Moryth never did speak. She followed Thomas meekly, never protesting at whatever pace he set. She walked steadily, not seeming to tire, with her harp clutched close against her breast.

By the time they were quit of Osenthyme, and Galthor came winging from the woods outside the town to perch on Thomas's shoulder, the storyteller was assured of one thing. Moryth was not mortal. Whether she was faerie, or a ghost of the dead arisen, she was not mortal. She spoke not, she tired not, she ate and drank nothing offered her. Yet strangely, Thomas had no fear of her. She meant him no harm, of that he was sure. And being with her, he felt a youthful spring enter his own steps, a lightness in his heart.

The sorrow she'd carried that first night passed away as soon as they began their journey. Always she smiled, or laughed soundlessly. She was like the sea, full of mystery, a riddle whose depth could not be guessed at, and again light as merry waves dancing in the sun.

When they camped that second night, having put many miles between themselves and Osenthyme, she drew forth her harp and played for him. The weariness that had bade Thomas to stop—for if she wearied not, he still did—washed away under the magic of her music. The harping was brisk and gay, betimes, again bittersweet, always filled with a sense of the sea, of tides and swelling waters, dolphins and seals frisking in the waves, the quiet majesty of a whale's thoughts.

Thomas could only sit quietly and marvel.

But her harping woke tales in him. When they came to Cogges-on-Sea, he must ply his storytelling trade that he, at least, find sustenance.

They entered the town's one tavern and when Thomas bespoke the innkeeper, he was given food and drink, and welcomed with favour. The word soon spread through the small burg, and by evening, the tavern was crowded with silent folk, all gathered to honour and listen to True Thomas the Rhymer.

There was a feyness on Thomas that night. He told a deep old tale—one the muryan tell each other in their hollowed hills under the moors. He stood by the hearth, his old frame straight, his eyes bright with the telling upon him. Moryth sat, silent as ever, by his feet, her harp on her lap. When Thomas came to a part in the tale where the young Harwich was set his first task, the faint sound of a harp stole up behind his words.

Never a glance to Moryth did Thomas make, but his words took on a new flavour, his voice a youthful strength, and the tale flowed as he'd never heard it before, not even when Tatter Holdhill had told it, deep in his hill, he and Thomas alone with warm rosebrews wilding their spirits.

At the tale's ending, the folk of Cogges-on-Hill were still as death. The harp's last echo faded and then the tavern erupted in a thunder of applause. Thomas stood before them, a blush creeping from under his collar. This was life…the road behind and before one, the tales to be told, the folk listening with open hearts. He bowed and pulled Moryth to her feet, applauding her as loudly as the rest.

Smiling, Thomas refused the coins that were pressed into his hands. All he asked for was a place they might sleep and some provisions to see them on their road tomorrow.

He was not denied.

Later that night, he lay abed, staring at the ceiling. Moryth sat sleepless by the window, her own gaze on the sea. Galthor had come to the unshuttered window, finding a perch on the bedpost behind Thomas's head. The Rhymer felt at peace. His misgivings were fled. Strange though Moryth might be, he counted it a fair eve the night they met. Whatever she might be, he had lost all fear of her. His only regret was that they were yet bound for Avertorc and whatever lay in store for them there.

Thinking of that grim keep, a small shadow stole across his heart, a misgiving that roused Galthor. The raven shifted uncomfortably;

Thomas forced the worry from him, calming the pounding in his own heart. By the window, Moryth sat unmoved.

Sighing, Thomas rolled over and searched for sleep.

THEIR JOURNEY slowed as they fared further north. Each step drew them closer to some dread thing that lurked perhaps only in Thomas's imagination. He could not put aside the strangeness of his companion, though it no longer troubled him as it had before. Then he had feared Moryth; now he feared for her. And whether it was selfish of him or not, he could not help but feel sorrowed with the foreknowledge that their arrival in Avertorc would sunder them.

But still they fared northward.

They stopped at each thorp, village and town that hugged the coast, some only a poor collection of fishers' cots, others prospering small burgs with more trade than those born of the sea. Sometimes they bided a few days in one or two of them. South Deeping and North Deeping. Withershap. Kinside. Corbham. Kirky-on-the-Water. Thomas plied his trade in each of them to the tune of Moryth's harping. In time he began to wonder how he'd ever fared without her. Yet stall though he might, their route took them ever closer to where the Highlands meet Shottery Head, where the Keep of Avertorc and its village stand.

THE VILLAGE of Avertorc was in the center of a crescent bay. Behind it, built into the cliffs of Shottery Head, was the Lord's Keep. Beyond the cliffs were the Highlands, league upon league of wild country, some of which Thomas and his companions had recently travelled through. Avertorc was a bustling town, for not only were its folk sailors and fishermen, but it was through Avertorc that the Highland folk brought their goods to trade with the merchants who docked their vessels in the still water of the bay. It was a prosperous town, and on that morning when the travellers looked down on it from the headlands, a town dressed out in festive finery.

"I wonder what they celebrate?" Thomas said.

He'd taken to talking to Moryth though he knew full well that she could not answer him. But he sensed that that she enjoyed listening to him.

"It's too late for a harvest festival," he continued, "and too early for the midwinter. Well, there's only one way to find out."

With that he set off, Galthor winging above his head. He took no more than a half-dozen steps when he realized that Moryth wasn't following.

"Are you coming?" he called.

She shook her head.

All of Thomas's fears arose within him once more as he returned to where she stood, but cajole as he might, she would not budge. He took her by the arm; she was immovable as Shottery Head's huge crags themselves.

Exasperated, he shook his head. "Then what would you? A month and a half we've journeyed to reach this place, and now you'll not come down into the village?"

Her face remained expressionless.

Sighing, Thomas asked, "Where shall we go, then? Point me. I've no love for yon' burg myself, truth to say. Shall we leave the coast and strike out into the Highlands? I know a place or two where we could winter comfortably…"

Moryth shook her head firmly. Stepping up to Thomas, she placed her harp in his hands and motioned him to go down to the village. A chill went through Thomas as he held the harp, and he began to tremble from head to foot. He tried to loosen his fingers to let the harp fall, but found he only gripped it the harder. Moryth touched his cheek with a cool hand, and leaning forward, kissed him with lips that were like ice. Her sea-eyes brimmed with deep sorrow and sadly she pointed again for him to go.

"Then…then this is farewell?" Thomas asked, his throat thick with emotion. "We'll not meet again?"

Moryth touched his cheek once more, then turned and walked to the sea. Unable to speak or move, Thomas watched her go.

She strode swiftly and purposeful, a gliding vision of breath-taking beauty. Tears brimmed in his eyes and trickled down his cheek when she reached that part of the shore that is the tide's own. She turned at the brink of the sea's edge, with the waves lapping at her feet. There she drew off her garments—tunic, trousers, shirt and boots—until she stood in the frosty air clad only in her white shift, her gold hair trailing with the wind's breath.

Lifting her hand in a final farewell, she walked into the sea.

Thomas watched, the tears frosting on his cheek, standing silent and sad long after the waves had swallowed her. He clutched the harp until his knuckles stood out as white as the bone that formed its supports. When Galthor gave a sharp cry, he finally turned to look at Avertorc below, all decked in its festival finery.

Sighing, he wrapped the harp in his blanket and placed it in his pack. Shouldering the pack, he followed a narrow path down the hill. He was unsure what Moryth meant for him to do with her harp. He only knew that there was a geas upon him now, and he must see it through to its end.

— ❧ —

"AYE, WELL, it's for the wedding, isn't it?" the innkeeper of the Longsway House explained to Thomas. "Though not the one we expected. But what do townsfolk know of lords' ways?"

"What do you mean?"

"See, she was to have wed young Peters—that's Jankin's son from over Dunmowe way—and the next thing anyone knows, she's betrothed to some southerner with a nigh unpronounceable name, and where does that leave Peters, I ask you?"

"She?" Thomas asked.

"You sure that bird's tame?"

"Yes, yes. But this wedding. Who was to have wed with Peters?"

"Why, Missie Gwyn—Lord Keldron's daughter? Who else would we be talking of?"

"As I said," Thomas began, "I'm a stranger and—"

The innkeeper chuckled. "And from a long ways, too, I'd say, not even knowing of the fairest flower in all the northlands. But I tell you, it's queer, her wedding this foreigner and all. Not proper, somehow.

But what's a commoner to do? March up to the keep and say, 'Yes, m'lord. I've come to protest your wedding your daughter to yon fop.' Not likely."

Thomas had trouble quelling his impatience. But he was a storyteller, and so he could listen as well as he could speak. Where else to get the tales, if one didn't listen? He took a long pull from his ale mug and feigned disinterest.

"What's so queer about her marrying a foreigner?" he asked at length.

"So queer?" The innkeeper spluttered and fixed Thomas with a fierce eye. "I'll tell you what's queer. She and Peters were betrothed, I tell you, in the old way. Under the high moon and before the sea they made their vows. And now this. Her husband-to-be's done worse as well. Brought up one of those priests from the southlands—have you heard of them? Aye, well, it's he that's to perform the wedding I've heard tell."

Thomas searched his memory.

"What of Coddon?" he asked, remembering at last the name of Avertorc's druid.

The innkeeper gave him a suspicious look.

"I thought you were a stranger," he said. "How do you come to know our druid's name?"

"I'm a storyteller," Thomas told him. "And any storyteller worth his salt knows the tale of Coddon of Avertorc and the Silkie."

Appeased, the innkeeper nodded, but his eyes went grim.

"Coddon's dead," he said.

"But how?"

"Who can say? The one evening he was as hale and sound as ever, the next morn he's stone dead. And you'd know the worst? The Lord's not sent to Harpenden for a new druid, neither. Laid to rest he was, with none of the old faith to speak over him. It was ill done."

Thomas nodded. There was something shaping inside him, a teasing riddle that he didn't fully understand as yet.

"And the wedding?" he asked.

"This eve," the innkeeper replied, his demeanor glum. "In the keep. The whole village is invited, and we'll go, though there are many who'd rather not. We've no room for this new faith here. We live by the sea—for all the merchants we have. But how to ship goods if the sea's against you? How to fish when the fish are gone? I tell you, the sea-folk will be wroth with us if we let this thing happen."

Thomas nodded again.

"But business goes well?" he asked, steering the conversation on to other grounds.

"Oh, aye," the innkeeper said. "As well as could be expected, what with every inn full, stables and all. And the hubbub…"

Thomas let him ramble on, only half-listening. His mind was fixed on solving the riddle Moryth had laid before him. The innkeeper had spoken of the sea-folk's wrath and he could see a truth in that. Yet what was there for him to do?

Suddenly he felt terribly old and alone, the harp in his pack a danger to him, but he could see no way clear of it. What he had begun, he must finish. So it went with a geas.

The sea gives, and the sea takes.

He felt an ache inside him and wished he could know what it was that Moryth expected of him.

THOMAS SENT Galthor winging into the air when he left the Longsway House. The raven cawed once, then sped away over the rooftops. Thomas watched until the bird was out of sight, then began to weave a path to the main market square, hoping to learn more of what was going on in Avertorc.

The streets were busy, and he fared slowly, ignoring the cries of vendors and beggars alike, pausing only where folk were gossiping. In such manner he made his way through the bustle of the marketplace to where the streets ran in an incline down to the sea. The keep towered above him and Thomas gazed at it thoughtfully.

He'd not learned much more on his walk. Most of the town's folk repeated what he'd already learned from the innkeeper. Yet there was an undercurrent that boded ill, and much that he'd only ventured to guess at had become more clear. Slowly, a pattern was unfolding.

The suitor's name was Valvanoris, hailing from Croalth, a kingdom that lay in the south. He and the priest—whom no one could name—had struck a bargain with Lord Keldron. They would buy all the minerals and timber that Avertorc could ship, providing transport south. The hills of the Highlands were rich in untapped wealth, they claimed, and the great oaks of Olney Wood—a forest track that bordered Avertorc's south-eastern boundaries—were much in demand and would fetch top prices on the southern market. They would also help in making both the mining and timber industries more efficient. All they asked for in return was that Avertorc deal only with them, and that the land be brought under the cross of the priest's dead god. To seal the bargain, Valvanoris and the Lord's daughter would wed—after she had been baptized.

How could the Lord pass on such a bargain? Rich—compared to the rest of the north—Avertorc might well be, but it was like a country cousin when compared against the fine kingdoms of the south. Keldron must deem it a small price to pay, giving away his daughter's hand and taking on the new faith. His only stipulation was that the marriage be held in the evening—as the northern customs would have it, for it was ill luck to do otherwise.

Small difference that would make, Thomas thought. By far the greater danger lay with the sea-folk, aye, and the Elder Folk of both moor and wood. They would not stand aside to let their lands be destroyed. And yet what could they do? It was known that the priests of the new faith wielded great powers. They could exorcise the Elder Folk with ease. Already many of their kin had fled northward as the lands here grew overcrowded with mortal folk.

Thomas shook his head. All this was politics. Disquieting though the news might be, it gave him no clue as to where he or the maid fitted in. High magics were a-foot here, but he could not pinpoint them. Perhaps he could fare himself to Harpenden and lay this all before the druids, but he felt time pressing like a cold hand and besides…only a Lord could summon a druid.

There were rumours, as well, concerning the Lord's daughter. How she had changed these past months, taken up southern ways. Her hair was dyed a dark brown, where erstwhile it had been gold.

She whitened her face, rouged her lips and cheeks, highlighted her eyes with other paints. She had become harsher in temperament as well as in looks. But even this explained nothing to Thomas. There was no maiden missing from Avertorc. And the Lord had but the one daughter.

Thomas sat by the roadside, leaning against the white daubed wall of the last house before the Keep. He stared at the aged stone walls of Keldron's holding, hoping to pierce the mystery that lay over all. He put his hand to his shoulder to stroke Galthor's feathers, but then he remembered that he'd sent the raven away so that he might pass through the market without the need for fending a dozen questions as to how he'd tamed a great raven of the Highlands. He whistled a shrill, almost soundless, note. Galthor dropped from the sky as though he'd been hovering overhead just awaiting that summons.

"What do you think?" Thomas asked the bird once it was settled on his shoulder.

The raven cocked its head and peered into the storyteller's eyes.

Thomas preened the raven's wings and nodded.

"Aye. Whether we understand or not, it's into the Keep we must fare. Moryth's harp holds the key to this riddle, and only therein can that key unlock what must next befall."

He stood abruptly. Galthor protested with a flutter of wings, then regained his perch. The day had lengthened into the dusk and a steady stream of people were passing before them, making for the gates of the Keep. Thomas fell into step with an old couple and tried to still the pounding of his heart as they passed through the wide-beamed gate. There was a look of resignation in the old storyteller's eyes when they entered the main hall.

HIGH WAS the roof of the inner keep, cut with beams of oak and hung with cloth banners dyed in every imaginable hue. Tapers blazed on the walls amid a wild splendor of tapestries. The Lord's hearth behind the dais had a roaring fire in it that dwarfed those in the smaller hearths set throughout the length of the hall. On the high table of the dais were candles and glass goblets—those priceless items surely a gift from Valvanoris' homeland.

The hall was choked with people. Near the dais were set the guest tables for the the Lords from the neighbouring holdings. The rest of the chamber was filled with long tables for the keep and townsfolk that ran the length of the hall. There was wine and mead and bitter ales flowing for the cups, and such provender upon the tables that surely they would soon buckle under the weight of it. For all the muttering and gloomy rumours Thomas had heard throughout the afternoon, the folk gathered here this eve were merry, their voices raised in laughter and wild jokes.

The couple Thomas had entered with joined a table of friends so that he stood alone by the door, surveying the whole scene. Galthor was restless on his shoulder and he stroked the raven to comfort it. The bird garnered many curious glances, but no one approached with questions.

Amid the general hub-bub, Thomas' gaze was drawn to the dais where sat Lord Keldron and his guests. The Lord was a middle-aged man with a nose like a hawk's beak and a piercing gaze that roved restlessly. There was power in the set of his shoulders, in the tilt of his head as he listened to some remark of his daughter.

Looking upon her, Thomas felt the geas laid upon him tighten across his heart. She was like a twin to Moryth the sea-maid, save her features were set into harsher lines, her hair dark. The cosmetics she wore and the strange cut of her gown set her apart from the northern ladies gathered at the guest tables. The same she was as Moryth, yet as different as night might be to day.

On her father's left sat her betrothed, clad in the robes of the southlands, his skin pale, his hair jet-black. At his side was the priest of the new faith in a humble brown habit, his hands folded piously before him on the table. In his glass goblet there was only water. Yet for all the humbleness he wore like a mask, Thomas saw through it to the greedy fervor that underlaid the priest's every small movement.

Thomas frowned. He remained standing by the door, refusing both wine and seating from the pages that ran about the hall. A strange fear was growing in him—akin to what the Elder Folk felt when confronted with those of the new faith. What was it that these priests held that they could wake such fear in breasts that feared nothing save the ending of the world's days?

The feast went on and Thomas silently observed it. His pack—with its stranger burden—was heavy upon his shoulder. He wondered if the lad Peters was here and what he thought of his betrothed's betrayal. He wondered if these folk were truly merry, or were only losing themselves in the occasion, knowing they could do nothing to stop it. When the Lord rose and called for quiet, Thomas straightened, hoping for some sign as to what he should do. There must be something, or else why did the geas lead him here?

He saw the priest rise and walk to a small table set to one side of the dais. There were white and red cloths lad over it, forming a cross, a small bowl—the holy water?—and large tome that would be The Book that spelled the laws that those of the new faith must abide. The priest lifted a crucifix from the table and Thomas shuddered. His witch-sight was upon it, and he focused on the small figure nailed to that cross—seeing it as clearly as though the whole of the hall did not lie between him and it.

A sadness came over Thomas, looking at that helpless man—for surely he must have been a man at one time—nailed to a cross, and for what? Did this Christos look down from the otherworld and shudder as well? To be reminded of that horror through all eternity...

Thomas forced his gaze away from the object.

His witch-sight pierced the walls of the keep, pierced the night without. A storm was gathering. He could see the sea lashing the rocks of Shottery Head. But the whites of the waves were not foaming water. Rather they were sea-folk, mounted on steeds of wave and wind, hundreds of them gathered, drawing near to land. Thomas looked inland and saw the moors stirring. Muryan stepped from their hidden halls, girt for war. Forest folk—green and woody—marched at their side.

The maiden Gwyn stood before the priest now. The words he intoned over her struck like blows against Thomas' soul. It was not that the new faith was evil—he knew that—only that it was somehow wrong for these northern lands. It was a religion of deserts and empty hills, man-held lands that no longer held the glamour of faerie. Here, where men lived by the sea, they must keep peace with the sea, not with this White Christ who had dwelled all his days in the sun-scorched desert, where the great inland sea bordering that same desert was tamed, not a wild thing like the waters of the north.

The priest spoke on, and then Thomas knew what he must do. He stepped from the doorway and began to walk between the tables, aiming for the dais. He cut a strange, almost piteous figure as he strode. The crowd as all dressed in their finest clothes, bright and festival merry, while he was as shabby and ragged as a tinker. But he held his head high and word went round like wildfire.

"True Thomas is here."

"Aye, it's Thomas the Rhymer."

With his feyness upon him, eyes gleaming with otherworldly lights, it was not hard to recognize Thomas Rymer for who he was. The priest looked up at the storyteller's approach and his eyes widened strangely. They studied each other, priest and storyteller, and their spirits clashed—old meeting new.

The priest finally stirred. He shook his head and looked to Lord Keldron.

"How dare you allow one such as he in here?" he cried.

But Keldron stared at the approaching storyteller and felt a doubt enter him. He knew well the tales surrounding Thomas Rymer. For all his power, for all that Avertorc was his Holding—and had been his family's for the turn of so many longyears—he knew too that there was none that might deny the Rhymer guesting. He walked with the Elder Folk. The power of the priest's faith seemed small beside the sudden remembrance of what powers those Elder Folk held. So he ignored the priest and remained silent, watching with a sense of dread hovering over him.

"Send him from here," the priest demanded.

Keldron shook his head, anger in his eyes. "Do not seek to rule in my Keep. Ill-done would it be for me to turn away Thomas the Rhymer."

"Then I will do it," the priest said.

He lifted his hands and began to intone words that sent daggers shooting through the old storyteller's heart. Thomas continued on, though each step made the pain sharper.

"Be still!" Keldron roared and the priest fell silent.

When Thomas reached the foot of the dais, he knelt down and laid his pack on before him. Galthor lifted from his shoulders and winged his way to the rafters above. Slowly Thomas undid the pack's straps and brought out the harp, wrapped in his blanket. The blanket fell aside and Thomas set the strange harp on the stone floor, then stood. He locked his gaze with those on the dais—Keldron, half fearful and puzzled; the priest, simmering with anger; Valvanoris, unsure of what was befalling. Strangest of all, though, was the Lord's daughter. She sat straight-backed and tall, her face bleached, her gaze darting left and right, yet always returning to the harp.

The bone supports shone yellow and aged in the brightly lit hall. The bronze strings gleamed, but strangest of all were the three octave strings, each woven from golden hair. Outside the winds howled and rain battered the walls of the old keep. But while the folk gathered inside heard only wind, Thomas heard the keening of the Elder Folk. He looked away from the dais, back to the harp. At the touch of his gaze, the first octave string rang out high and piercing, and words spilled into Thomas' mind.

"Lord Keldron had two daughters," he said, his voice carrying throughout the hall, though he spoke low. "Only one survived their double birthing. The one that lived knew the tale of her sister, how she'd died at their birth, and she was full-sorrowed, for merry it would have been to share the world with a twin. She eased her grief by playing beside her sister's grave, laying flowers upon it, hallowing it in the old way with gathered stones and the fruits of hedgerow and seashore."

As he spoke, each person in the hall could see the images in their own minds. The young Gwyn by the graveside on Shottery Head, the sweet seriousness of her mien, the love in her for one who never had the chance to live.

"A person dies," Thomas continued, "be they full-grown or child, and their spirit fares to the otherworld and from there...who can tell? But this love of Gwyn's held her sister's spirit earth-bound. At first the spirit loved her sister, but then she came to envy and hate her. For Gwyn had life, and the fullness therein, and what had the poor nameless maid?

"So years passed, and there came a time when Gwyn was grown to womanhood, and took to her the love of young Peters. Betrothed they were, before the sea, and the sea held witness thereto. But the nameless one, her hatred overflowed, and she meant to bring ruin to her sibling."

The Second octave string rang out through the hall, lower in pitch. Strange dread awoke in the breasts of all who heard. The storm outside the keep renewed its fury, and it seemed that the very stone walls shivered and shook under its onslaught.

"On Samhain night, when the new year begins its turns and spirits walk the land between the sun's setting and rising, young Gwyn rose from her bed to walk abroad. She was drawn by her sister's power—full-waxed on that night of all nights—and when she came to her sister's grave, her spirit was drawn out of her body and cast into the sea where it was bound with ghostly spells and hounded by the wind. And when Gwyn returned to her bedchamber, her body housed another spirit."

"Slay him!" Keldron's daughter screamed.

But none made a move. Horror was etched plainly on their faces for the truth could not be denied. It was True Thomas who spoke.

The daughter made as if to leap from the dais, but the shutters of the Keep burst open under the storm's onslaught. Winds roared in, winds that touched none save Keldron's daughter, and they pinned her to the wall beside the hearth.

"But Gwyn was under the sea-lord's protection. Always she followed the old ways, aye, and she was betrothed before the sea, therefore under its protection. She came to me upon a wave-swept shore, where I was bound to the sea-lord's feasting. No chance was there in that meeting. No chance in my invitation. She came to me and we fared north, north to Avertorc, with a sea harp of old bone and Gwyn's own hair woven into its strings.

"Now the Elder Folk demand justice."

Thomas fixed Lord Keldron with a strange look.

"You cannot *see*, Lord," he said, "but the Elder Folk are outside your keep, ready to storm it. Your greed has raised their ire, and to wed your daughter in this manner…

"Yon priest's chants will avail you naught against their numbers,"
Keldron was white as a ghost. He stared at Thomas, shaking his head.
"What…" he asked. "What do they demand?"

The maid fought the winds that bound her.

"No!" she cried. "Do not believe him. I beg you free me!"

The priest strode to stand before Thomas, his crucifix held high.
He opened his mouth to cry out, but Thomas shook his head.

"Too late, priest," he said. "The sea gives, the sea takes."

As Thomas spoke, the lowest string rang forth.

It echoed and rang through the hall like thunder. Folk cowered,
clapping their hands over their ears, but the deep sound of the harp's
ringing went on. The priest tumbled to his knees, holding his crucifix
before him, silently mouthing a litany that was lost in the tumult.

So it was that none saw, save Thomas. The spirit of a dark-haired
maid was drawn from the body of Lord Keldron's daughter. Through
the windows that faced the sea came Moryth, hand in hand with the
sea-lord Aylwin and his green-haired Lady Wenmabwen.

Gwyn's form stumbled, then righted when Moryth slipped into it.
The cosmetics flaked away to fall at her feet, the dark hair lightened into
moon-gold tresses. Wenmabwen raised her arms, and as she brought
them down, the southern-styled gown shifted in shape to become a
fair weaving of the Elder Folk.

Time within the hall seemed to stand still. Aylwin turned to Thomas
with a sad smile.

"This time we have won a victory," he said, "but the followers of
the dead god shall gain in strength until in time there will be no place
in this world for our kind. Yet more than luck was with us. There was
a rift in the balance of what is. Now Keldron's nameless child has fared
on to her peace beyond the otherworld, and his living daughter is with
him once more. She will wed Peters and the south will be held at bay
awhile longer."

"We are sorry," Wenmabwen added, "to have treated you, so,
Thomas. But the White Christ's priests are sly and if we had told you in
advance what we had planned, he might well have found a way to win
that knowledge from you. That we couldn't risk, for if he baptized that
poor dead child in Gwyn's body, then Gwyn herself would been forced

to wander the world without hope. Not truly dead, she could not fare beyond. Not truly alive, she would find no peace in this world. It was you we needed, True Thomas. Who could gainsay your words?"

Thomas nodded, mutely. It was always so with the Elder Folk, not trusting even their own friends.

He looked to where Gwyn stood and saw his road-companion Moryth. A lump filled his throat. Aylwin stooped and lifted the bone-harp. Its strings of gold hair were now plain bronze.

"Come," he said to Thomas. "We promised you guesting, and I would not have it said that sea-folk go back on their word."

"What," Thomas said. "What would you have done if the other had been baptized?"

Aylwin fixed him with the deep, impenetrable look of the Elder Folk.

"We would have tumbled this keep into the sea," he said. "But that is behind us. The muryan return to their moors, the forest-folk to their woods. Come now, Thomas. Let us return to the sea."

Thomas nodded once more. He called to Galthor and the raven winged down from the rafters to his shoulder. He looked to Gwyn and the maid stepped forward. They stood in arm's reach of each other, then the maid threw her arms around the old storyteller's neck.

"Fair it was to travel with you, Thomas Rymer," she whispered. "I thank you and will remember you in all the days to come. Visit us, Peters and I, when next your road brings you this way. Aye, and perhaps you can meet with our child then. If it's boy, we'll name him Thomas."

She kissed him lightly on the brow and ruffled Galthor's feathers, then stepped back. Her lips on his brow, her hand when it was in his, were both warm. Mortal hands.

"Aye," Thomas said. "Perhaps I'll take you up on that."

He joined hands with Aylwin and Wenmabwen and then the sea-folk took him away to that tower that can be seen on certain nights, just when the moon rises.

—❦—

SPRING FOUND Thomas Rymer walking along Kirrimuir Shore. Galthor winged high overhead as the old storyteller scuffled the sand at his feet, his gaze on the sea. Always when he told his tale now, he heard a faint harping. Within him. A part of him. And he never did stray long from the sea, no matter where his road-wending took him.

A Miscellany

The Fane of the Grey Rose

The fateful slumber floats and flows
About the tangle of the rose;
But lo! the fated hand and heart
To rend the slumberous curse apart!

—William Morris

I REMEMBER WELL THE day I first set eyes on her, the maid I named the Grey Rose for the blossom she wore in her rust-brown hair. Fresh-plucked it seemed, and this a wonder, with traces of morning dew yet clinging to its fragile petals. Aye, a wonder, for it was at even-tide that she first came to Wran Cheaping, during the mid-summer of my twentieth year, as the sun slipped steadily westward to settle at last in the bosom of the low hills that girded the town. She was clad in a mantle the hue of twilight, with stars glistening in her dusky eyes and the breath of autumn wrapped about her, filling the air with a sweet and heady scent.

I had taken myself from Farmer Here's fields earlier than was my wont, and was standing bemusedly amidst the bustle of the closing market. The chapmen were busily securing their shops against the approaching night and the husbandmen were loading their wagons with unsold wares when she swept by me, her mantle rustling like wind-blown leaves. She was not tall, though something about her lent her the appearance of height, and she walked with a loose easy stride, here buying a sack of grains, there a handful of fresh vegetables, all carried in a wicker basket upon her arm.

Spellbound, I watched her go about her business. I longed to speak with her, but I was shamed at my appearance, aye, suddenly very aware of my rough woolens and shabby cloak and the dirt of the fields that yet clung to my skin. As she reached the far side of the market, I turned as if to go, but not before she stole a glance my way, her eyes catching mine in such a way that we seemed to share a secret that only we two might partake of. She smiled and I cast my eyes to the ground, feeling a flush 'neath my collar. When I lifted them once more, she was gone.

Slowly I wandered homeward, my mind a-whirl with visions of this strange maid. Home! I laughed mirthlessly at the thought of the stable corner I called my home. Even Farmer Here's dog had a kennel that was more luxurious. I shook the bitterness from me and returned my thoughts to the maid of the Grey Rose until I reached the door of the stable. I busied myself with sweeping the floor, and when at last the chore was done, I crept to my corner at the rear of the stable. Sitting in the straw, I drew forth a rudely-carved harp. It was no work of a proud craftsman, for I had labouriously fashioned it myself. The supports and sound-box were cut from weather-worn barnwood, and it was strung with cow-gut that I had pilfered from the back of Ralen's meat-mart. Still, I could coax a tune from it, and it filled the long hours that I spent on my own.

As I tuned it, I thought again of the parents that I had scarcely known, for I was but four when the sickness took them and I was orphaned here. My mother Eithne had been a Harper of the old school, revered and respected until she was cast from the Halls of Wistlore for wedding an outlaw from the Grassfields of Kohr. It was not often that a woman was taken into the Harper's Guild, but so skilled had she been that not only was she of the Guild, but she bore a high rank therein as well. Then she met Windlane, outlawed from his tribe and as wild as the Grassfields themselves, and he captured her heart.

The Guild would not allow her wedding him, and when she set herself against them, she was banished from the hallowed Halls of Wistlore, where the Harpers have e'er held sovereign with the Loremasters, Wyslings and other wizard-folk. Whither they were bound when the sickness took them here in Wran Cheaping, I fear I'll never know, but when they died, I was taken in by Farmer Here and his goodwife, and as soon as I turned eight, I was set to work in the fields. Ah! but my mother's blood runs strong through my veins and e'er have I longed to learn the minstrel craft, aye, and my father's blood has sowed a seed of wander-lust within me, and one day I will reap its harvest.

When I reached my fifteenth year I left the farm and moved to this stable in town. Poor it might be, but I may call it my own home. At morn and eve I would clean it to pay for my lodgings, and for my toil in his fields, Farmer Here paid me three good coppers a week so that I might feed myself. Hidden in the straw, in a small leather pouch, I had thirty coppers saved, and now with that, and my heart set a-longing for new lands and faces from the brief glimpse of the fair maid in the market place, I resolved to make my own way out into the world at summer's end.

All the days of my short life I have dwelt in Wran Cheaping, yet ne'er have the folk of this burg made me o'er welcome, and so I, in turn, have spurned them. I had but one friend, Old Tess the witch-wife, and I was first drawn to her more as a result of our both being outcasts than through friendship. Ah! but she was a kindly soul, and as the years fled by, I came to love her as I might have loved my mother, had she but lived.

Still I was determined to go, though I was loath to leave Old Tess behind. But perhaps I would make a name for myself and then return to show the folk of Wran Cheaping what sort of a man I had become. Aye, and if that maid dwelt here yet, perchance I'd go a-courting her with a fine harp strapped to my shoulder and tales worth the telling to delight her ears.

I laughed softly to myself at my fancies, and so bemused, with my fingers trailing quiet melodies on my harp, I felt a weariness come over me. I played one last tune, then rose and stored my harp safely in the straw before I gathered together a bed, and so slept.

IT WAS another week ere I had a day free from the fields. I arose early on that morn, and with my harp in a burlap bag, I made for the Golden Wood that lies just north of Wran Cheaping on the edge of the downs.

There was a loaf of fresh bread and a slab of cheese in my wallet, and the sun was bright and fair o'erhead, when at last I reached its trembling shade. Soft-footed, I wandered 'neath the summer-rich boughs of the beech and elms, pushing my way through stands of thin maple and silver birch, till I came to the banks of a brook filled with clear bubbling water. I cast my clothes on the cat's-tail and watercress that ridged the stream and plunged in, the cool waters washing the dirt of my week's toil from me and refreshing my limbs.

When I tired of the sport, I clambered up the bank and caught fast of my clothes to give them a good scrubbing. Soon I was sitting in the sun, my clothes drying where they hung on a blackthorn bush nigh by, and I dreamt lazily of the world outside the West Downs. 'Twas said that the Aelfin folk dwelt in those hills, aye, and made their homes in the dark glades deep within the Golden Wood as well. I thought of Aelves, and the tales that Old Tess told me of the folk of the elder days who once held this land, ere man made it his own, and I longed to see an Aelf, or any sort of magical being.

With a sigh, I rose and clad myself, and fared deeper into the wood. I walked for perhaps two hours, full of dreams and dreamy thoughts, until I came to a dell as sweet as ever there was, with orchids and red campions, light blue columbines and other wild flowers shimmering in the grass underfoot. A hawfinch rose chittering before me and swept into the canopy of tall oaks and elms that encompassed the dell, and there were mushrooms growing in their shade, of which I picked a few to eat later with my bread and cheese. Then I sat myself down, and taking my harp from its rude sack, I tuned it. Soon, I was deep into a new tune and I lost myself to the wealth of harmonies I could imagine within its measures; aye, here the tumbling breathy timbre of a flute might add a trill, and there the lift and lilt of a fiddle's tone could strengthen the flow. This was for the maid of the Grey Rose, I decided, as the tune took firm hold of me. I began to hum to myself until words came spilling from my tongue, ill-shaped perhaps by a Harper's standard, but fair sounding to me.

Imagine my surprise when I heard another voice, low and sweet, joining mine. I stopped in mid-tune and glanced about only to see the self-same maid of my new song standing by my side. She was clad in a short white kirtle that briefly outlined the sweet shape of her form and contrasted sharply against the sun-brown of her slender limbs. I scrambled to my feet, hot with embarrassment, my harp falling to the grass with a discordant ring.

"Wh-what do you here?" I asked, and then wished I hadn't spoken as I stumbled over the words.

A low chuckle escaped her throat and she favoured me with a smile.

"Why, I'm picking mushrooms for my supper, Harper," she said. She brushed a willful lock of her rusty hair from her brow and added: "That was a brave tune you were playing. How is it named?"

For a moment I thought she was mocking me and my only thought was to flee the glen, but her smiling face seemed without guile and her words so generous, that I gathered my courage and said:

"M'Lady, 'tis but a new tune that I've begun to shape today. When 'tis done, I thought to name it for you...for the Grey Rose."

I could feel my cheeks redden as I spoke, but the maid smiled again and gracefully settled herself on the sward, slim legs tucked underneath her kirtle. Looking up, she said:

"You honour me, Harper. Will you play it again?"

Numbly I nodded in agreement and sat down beside her. I picked up my harp, and nervously, plucked the opening chords until, haltingly and with many false starts, I began the tune again. I dared not sing the half-formed words that I had sung before she had come, but I strove to play the air as best I might. When I came to a complex sequence, I suddenly forgot my shyness for the tune took hold of me once again, and then I played with an assurance and confidence unknown to me, save when alone in my corner of the stable or in some secluded wood or field.

Once more she began to hum the air with me and my fingers fairly flew o'er the strings as her voice set my spirit all a-tremble. All too soon, the moment passed, and the last strains of our music faded into the quickening day. She sighed and asked:

"How are you named, Harper?"

"Cerin," I replied, but I dared not ask her the same.

"I've barley-bowl and mushrooms a-waiting us upon my supper table. Will you come then, and share my meager meal with me?"

Right gladly I agreed, my heart thumping in my breast, and I quickly gathered up my harp and its sack to follow her through the woods to her home. Her slight form slipped through the trees with an Aelfin grace and, though she was not tall as I have already told, for the top of her head reached but to my shoulder, still when she stood by me, it seemed as if I must look up to see her.

We came at last to another glade, bounded by gnarled ash trees and thickets of birch and young oaks. In its midst there was a tiny cottage, vine-draped and wrought of stone, with a garden of wildflowers before and a well to one side. As she went within to fetch us some tea, I stood in the sun and gazed about myself, marveling, for I had been to this glade aforetime, aye, perhaps three months past when the spring was in the air, and though this cottage had been here, true enough, it had been all a ruin and the glade itself overgrown with weeds and brush. I puzzled at the mystery of this, yet when she came without, balancing a tray laden with two mugs of steaming tea and a platter of fresh-baked bannocks, I soon forgot the riddle, forsaking it for the victuals and her company.

That afternoon, and the even that followed, will ever be among my fondest memories. We dined on simple fare, 'tis true, but we spoke and talked long into the night, and that conversation was better to me than all the meat and drink of a noble's table.

When first I had seen her in the market, this maid of the Grey Rose, I yearned for her as any man might yearn for a maid that warmed his heart, but as the evening slipped away, I realized that we could never be lovers. Yet the thought did not sadden me, for here in the Golden Wood, I had met one with whom I could share my innermost thoughts without fear of ridicule, and if I lost a lover, I gained a speech-friend that was thrice as dear.

It was much later, after I laid my harp aside, for we sang many a song that eve: ones that I knew from Old Tess, and strange wistful tales and airs that the maid taught to me, that I asked her how long she had dwelt here and from what land she was come. She was quiet and a long silence wrapped itself about us. She glanced at the shadows playing on the walls of the cottage, born from the dim glow of the hearth fire, and said at last:

"There is a geas upon me that drives me like a wind throughout many lands, aye, and there is a shade of the dark that follows me and strives to undo all my deeds and make me its own. Long roads have I wended until, at the waxing of the Dyad Moon, I came to this wood, weary from wandering and yearning to rest for a spell . But not for long, no, not for long…"

Her voice trailed away as she lapsed into a thoughtful silence. I, for my part, felt a tremor of fear stir my heart at her words. I wondered again at who she might be and how she had raised this cottage from a ruin, aye, and her dark talk of a geas and the threatening shade made me anxious for her sake. I worried at these riddles, but she smiled suddenly, and our conversation and my thoughts turned away from the puzzle and fared on to gentler things.

When it was well past moonrise, I rose reluctantly to begin my journey homeward. The maid accompanied me to her threshold, and there she bade me a good eve.

"Will you come again, Cerin?" she asked, and I said I would, readily enough.

I was very thoughtful on my return to Wran Cheaping through the darkened Golden Wood. There was a mournful wind upon the West Downs with a chill in its breath, but I bore yet the afterglow of the maid's company warm in my breast, and my thoughts were on her and when next I might have a free day to see her, so the wind I minded not.

— —

SO THEN, passed the summer. I worked in Farmer Here's fields by day, dreaming of the Grey Rose, and at night I sat writing tunes for her, or adding airs to the tales she told me and setting them to rhyme. Aye, and oft I would fare to that glade in the Golden Wood to spend an eve or a day with her. At summer's end, I had thirty-nine coppers saved, but now there was no wish in me to leave Wran Cheaping. With her coming, the Grey Rose made my life fuller than I had deemed it possible, and I would not have this joy come to an end.

But there came a day, upon the edge of autumn, when the countryside was filled with the glory of the leaf-fall, that my idyll came to an end. I walked from Wran Cheaping that day with a new tune at my fingers and basked in the wonder of the season. The harvests were all gathered, aye, and we worked hard in that gathering, and all the world seemed a-bloom with the autumn. Seas of rusts and golds, browns and singing reds swept across the West Downs, and the Golden Wood was so bright that I must needs almost turn my eyes from it.

Underfoot, bright melyonen bloomed violet amidst the fallen leaves and nuts, and the bushes hung heavy with berries, thick splashes of colour against the growing somber attire of the wild. My heart was light and I hummed to myself as I strode along. A quickening confidence had blossomed within me, along with the growth of the barley and corn fields, and I harvested it more eagerly than the farmers might their crops. This was my gift from the Grey Rose, for she sowed this sureness of spirit within me, aye, and had she not been my speech-friend, yet would I have thrice-blessed her for this.

I came at last to the sweet glen wherein her cottage stood, and paused in mid-step. Although I could not define it, some subtle change was wrought therein that went beyond the simple turning of the seasons. It was as though a malevolent shadow overhung the glade; a brooding darkness wrought in some nether region beyond mortal kenning. Hurriedly, I crossed the glade. When I came to the door, it stood ajar, and I peered through to see the Grey Rose sitting disconsolately at her kitchen table, a half-packed journeysack set upon it before her. I stepped within.

"What betides?" I asked, and my heart fell as I spoke, for I knew well-enough by the look of things that she was making ready her departure. She had spoken of it oft enough, but I took no heed of it, deeming that the day would never truly come. She looked up at my words and tried a brave smile.

"Ah, Cerin," she said, "I must away. Too long have I tarried here, for though time seems to pass but slowly in this wood, it speeds by in the world without, and I have a geas that is overdue in its fulfilling, aye, and a bane that will soon come a-knocking on my door."

"What do you mean?" I asked. "What befalls? Can I aid you?" The words spilled from me in a jumble, and I tried to still the thudding of my heart.

"I fear not, kind friend," she said. She sighed and took my hand. "Sit you down, Cerin, and I will tell you the tale of my life, aye, and the sorry end that it comes to."

Her words filled me with foreboding. What did she speak of? It seemed that the time for answers to the many riddles surrounding her had come, and now, curious as I once was, I wished this time had never come.

"Have you e'er heard tell of the Cradle of the Kings?" she asked.

"Aye," said I. "It was a great city in the elder days, though it lies in ruins now. Twas Old Tess told me of it, of the bright lords that ruled there and sought the wisdoms of the world. More revered than Wistlore was it, but now naught remains but fallen towers and the shades of the dead. She said that it lay just above the western entrance of Holme's Way, on the edge of the Perilous Mountains, and fell in some great war. Twas another name she had for it as well, but it escapes me…"

"Banlore," said the maid.

"Aye, that was it. But what has that haunt of daemons to do with you?"

"I am hand-fasted to one therein that you might well name a daemon. Yarac Stone-slayer he is named. Aye, a Waster, a child of the Dakath, the Dark Gods, is what I am to wed."

I was stricken with horror at her words. I opened my mouth to speak, but she raised her hand and went on.

"No, list first to my tale, Cerin, ere you voice your protests. Long ago it was that I pledged my hand to him, and in return for that pledge, I gained the promise that no harm would come to the Hill Lords, those who reigned in the Trembling Lands at the end of the Elder Days. It was a cruel war that raged for longer than long is, and this was its only ending, for the Hill Lords were pitiful in number by then, though their hearts were brave and true, and they would have soon fallen, had we not this offer to make to the Waster. I am of their kin, you see, though distant are the ties 'tween my folk and the Hill Lords, and it was my will that this be, hateful as it might prove to me.

"But then, on the eve of our wedding, Yarac sent a plague of were-riders and yargs into the Trembling Lands and slew nigh all of the Hill Lords, never deeming that I would learn of it until it was too late. But word came nevertheless, and I flew from Banlore, for so was it named when Yarac wrought its ruin, and he pursued me. Yarac met with the remnants of the Hill Lords on the hills nigh the city, and they were slain, but I escaped, aye, and I flee yet. Three year-turnings past, he stole from me my spirit's shadow and so gained a control over me. I cannot live longer without it and tonight, I know, he will come for me."

I shook my head in bewilderment. I knew the tales of the Wasters, aye, and shuddered at their tellings, and I knew as well of wars in the Trembling Lands that had even touched the West Downs and the Golden Wood...but the time of their waging was ages past. There had been no strife in these lands within living memory. That she might speak of these things as though they were but yesterday...for that she must needs be ten score ten years herself, and this could not be. The undying dwelt but in tales...

My scalp prickled, and I felt the cold sweat of fear upon me.

"Who are you?" I asked her, almost loath to hear her answer.

"To you," she said with a sad smile, "I would e'er be the Grey Rose."

It was no answer, and I was about to say as much, but she continued to speak.

"They are all gone now: the Hill Lords and their people, aye, and the were-beasts and their riders, the yargs and goblins...all gone, save for Yarac. He and I, we are the last to remain from those years of struggle."

She shook her head slowly and fell into a brooding silence.

"I like it not..." I began, and she glared at me.

"And do you think I do?" she said bitterly. "Do you think I welcome the honouring of a broken pledge and to have that creature foul my flesh as he beds me?" Her eyes flashed fire from their dusky depths and I drew back from her. Then she sighed and said in a gentler tone: "But no, Cerin, I wrong you. You should not feel the brunt of my anger. That I will save for when the Stone-slayer comes for me this eve, little good that it might do."

"I will aid you," I said. "I know not how, but I will stop him."

"'Twas bravely spoken, Cerin, but better it were if you were not here when he came. To face him is death, perhaps worse."

"I will not leave," I said.

I marveled at my courage. Had this been the early summer, I would never have dreamed that such things might betide, aye, or that I would be facing them. Fearful I was, indeed, but not so fearful that I would not try.

We sat at the table and slowly the day wore by. As the long shadows of dusk darkened the room, the maid I named the Grey Rose, stood from the table and lit a candle. Wearily, she finished packing her journeysack, by its light and the wan light that yet caught the glade without in its grasp. When she was done, she sat again, gazing out of the still open door. Quietly I arose and closed it, dropping an oak bar the width of my thigh in its place. Returning to the table, I saw tears glistening in her eyes.

"Cerin, Cerin," she said, "I would not have you die. Flee now, I beg you, for you cannot know what you will be facing. This is no tale to be told before a roaring fire, with hot mugs of tea in hand and a harp plucked softly behind the telling. There is more to the world than the ways of mankind. North of the Perilous Mountains there are wide rolling lands, hills and downs, aye, and long tracks of unbroken wood and dark moors where the old ways are not forgotten, and there legends live and breathe the same air as might you or I. There are Aelves in those woods, Wessener in the moors, aye, and Dwarves in the mountains. And where there are beings of Light, there are the minions of the Dark as well

"Yarac Stone-slayer is real, and if you bide here with me, he will slay you as easily as he may crush stone!"

"That may be," I said, "but still will I stay. I am not as the folk are here. My mother was a Harper, aye, and my father was a warrior from the great Grasslands of Kohr. My kin are from those northern lands, and though I may not have the knowledge of magical power, I have yet the strength of my limbs. There may not be much meat to my frame, but the long hours I have toiled in the fields have not left me a weakling. I will face this Stone-slayer, aye, and perhaps I will fall, but I will not flee."

The darkness had grown as we spoke and a look of despair came into the maid's eyes when she realized that my resolve was hardened and I could not be swayed to leave. Without the cottage, I could hear a wind rising, rattling a loose shutter and tearing at the autumn-dried vines. For all my brave words, I felt the cold hand of terror upon me, and I prayed that my courage would not forsake me.

It was almost fully dark now, and the wind became like a thing alive, howling about the cottage. Naught but an autumn storm, I thought, a common enough thing, but my thoughts dwelled more on the Waster of which the maid had spoken than on the naturalness of this growing storm. Soon it would be moonrise, the rise of the Blood Moon. As the wind still howled, I wondered at the ill-omen of this moon's naming, for my thoughts were now filled with the maid's tale.

Suddenly, she rose, so swiftly that her chair fell with a clatter to the floor behind her.

"He calls," she said in a strained voice. "Oh, Cerin, he calls, and I am afraid."

I stood, striving to hear that of which she spoke, but all that came to my ears was the raging of the wind. She groaned and took a step toward the door. I put out a hand to stop her. No sooner had I touched the sleeve of her gown than the door burst asunder and shards of wood whipped about us. And something was there. The candle blew out as the wind tore into the small cottage, but I had no need of light to see the maid moving toward the threshold where the intruder awaited her.

"No!" I cried, and pushing her aside, I leapt at the thing. All my strength I put into that assault, yet I fell from him to the floor, the wind screaming in my ears. Then a flash of lightning ripped across the heavens and I saw the shape of the Waster clearly silhouetted against the sudden light. Nigh eight feet in height, he towered like a monolith wrought of living iron, with coals of red fire smoldering where his eyes should be. He picked me up from the floor with one huge hand, and as I pummeled his chest, he threw me across the room where I landed with a jarring crash, the breath struck from me and a pain running through me as though each and every one of my bones was shattered from the impact.

I sought to rise, but found that I could not. Helplessly, I watched him take up the maid of the Grey Rose and turn from the threshold. Raging and gnashing my teeth, I managed to crawl across the litter-strewn floor, my body shrieking in agony at each movement I made. Ages seemed to pass before I reached the threshold and glared out into the ensorcelled night. The wind whipped the trees into a frenzy, and as I watched, a sheet of rain erupted from above and I could see no further than my hand. But it fell not so soon that I could not see that the glen was empty. Both the maid and her abductor were gone. Bitter tears laced my cheek as I realized my failure. Then I fell forward, a darkness washing o'er my consciousness, and I knew no more.

WHEN I regained my senses, it was just before moonset. The glen, and the wood beyond, were as silent as a held breath. My clothing was soaked from the rain that fell upon me while I was unconscious and I ached from a thousand bruises, though I could feel no broken bones. Cautiously, I stood and made my way from the threshold. In a corner I found the candle where it had blown from the table, and I lit it with unsteady hands. Dragging a chair to the table, I slumped in it and sat dejectedly there, trying to gather my thoughts.

I awoke with a start, and realized that I had slept through the night. In the bright morning light, the stump of the candle seemed to stare at me and mock my failure. Brave words they were that I spoke last eve, aye, but only words. What had I done to aid her, and she my friend, this maid of the Grey Rose?

I must follow them. She had spoken of the Cradle of the Kings, the ruined city that was now named Banlore. There I must go. But first I needed knowledge. To defeat the Waster I must know his weaknesses, be there any; I must learn how to destroy him. And there was only one I knew of that might have that knowledge stored away within her: Old Tess. To Wran Cheaping I would return then, for though the townsfolk named her mad and shunned her company, yet was she my friend. All my tales of old I had from her, for the old wisdoms were hers, aye, and learnings and knowledge that even the Wyslings of Wistlore might yearn for were locked away in her mind.

With my course resolved I drew myself up from the table and hobbled to the door. I leaned against the twisted remains of its frame for a moment, drawing deeply into my lungs the crisp autumn air, then I made for the woodpile on the far side of the cottage. There I searched through the yet unchopped wood and kindling for a length of wood that might serve me for a cane. After much prying and scrabbling, I came upon a thick staff cut from a rowan tree, and this I strove to break into a suitable length for my cane. Either my strength was more depleted from my encounter with the Waster than I thought, or the wood was especially resilient, but I could not break it. I glared at it, as though my gaze might serve where my limbs could not, then I realized that it would serve me admirably as a staff, just as it was. So leaning heavily on the length of its white wood, I made my way back to Wran Cheaping and a meeting with Old Tess.

— 🖋 —

THOUGH I fretted for each moment of the time, it was still a week ere my strength returned sufficiently for me to hazard the journey. Always my thoughts were on the Grey Rose, and it grieved my heart sore that she should be in the clutches of that fiend, Yarac Stone-slayer. Yet the week served me well, for my limbs soon felt as hardy as ever. Still, I turned more in my sleep at night than was my wont: partly from stiffness, aye, but partly from unfamiliar and dark dreams that took hold of my sleep-bemused spirit and filled it with shadowed omens.

On another clear day, with the autumn well at hand, I left Wran Cheaping once more, and this time for good. Whether my quest go well or ill, I would not be returning. As I walked the way across the downs to the maid's cottage in the Golden Wood, my purse with its thirty-nine coppers jingled at my belt, and I thought on what Old Tess had told me.

"Oh, aye," she had said, her brow wrinkled in thought, "there's ways to lay low the Wasters or any that are kin to the Dark Old Ones, but it takes a brave heart and a sturdy one to see it through. Do ye have the strength, Cerin? Eh, do ye now? No matter. I can see that ye mean to give it a try, and I'm too old to stop ye, or go with ye, aye, but not too old to give ye a word or two of counsel, m'lad. It's Heart's-sure ye be carrying in yer belt, and when ye face him, it's a deft thrust with a dead king's sword, a sword of shadows. Ah! And how would I be knowing where ye might get yerself a sword such as that? Search a barrow, m'lad, search a barrow. And mind ye be sure that ye've the dead one's blessing, or it's more sorrow ye'll be reaping than sowing. Aye, so say the old tales…Heart's-sure and a dead king's sword…aye, and was there one more thing? Ah! I can't recall it now…"

I shook my head as I strode along. Riddles, always riddles. First there was the maid herself: that riddle I had forsaken, for sweet was her company and I had been loath to spoil it with prying questions. Aye, I knew not even her true name. Then there was the Waster, the city of ruins, those tales of old wars…and now yet more riddles, these from Old Tess. Heart's-sure I knew of; it grew along the mountain slopes and I would be passing that way. But a dead king's sword…I knew of no barrows in these lands, though the downs were said to be hollowed in places, and there were hills that might harbour a barrow nigh the Cradle of the Kings itself. Mayhap, if luck favoured me, I would find one along my way. But what else had Old Tess said? I sent my thoughts questing back and remembered. I was just leaving when she called me back, saying:

"And, Cerin, look for aid along yer way, and in strange guises. Mark this rede of mine, for the lands beyond the Perilous Mountains, aye, and those Mountains themselves, are filled with queer folk, unlike us, and there's one or two might treat ye kindly."

Her words had filled me with foreboding, as though she were far-seeing the future. Now as I fared along, the rowan staff in my hand, I tried to puzzle it all out until I gave it up at last, my mind too bemused and weary to think clearly any longer.

I was soon come to the cottage then, planning to stop only long enough to gather my harp. But I went through the maid's journeysack, and setting aside the food that was spoilt, I added the fresh produce and breads that were in my wallet. I looked around then for something of the maid's that I might bring with me as a token, and saw fallen by the door the Grey Rose that she e'er wore in her hair, still flourishing as though it were but newly plucked. It was sorcery, surely, that kept it so, but I knew that I must familiarize myself with magics, aye, and as this was the maid's, I had no fear of it. Still, I felt a strange tingle run up my spine when I took it in my hand and placed it inside my tunic where it lay cool against my skin.

I took up her journeysack and shouldered it with my harp. So burdened, and with my staff in hand, I set my steps westward for the Perilous Mountains and the days that were to come.

— 🌿 —

THAT NIGHT I camped in the midst of the West Downs and watched the twilight settle o'er the gaunt hills. Silence hung heavily in the air, broken only by a whispering lean wind that was as subtle as a moth's flight, aye, and as gentle in its touch. The dusk was poised upon the land for but another moment, then the deep night swept o'er all. I watched the stars begin to twinkle in the sky, first one, then the other, as though some chambermaid was among them lighting them as an earthly maid might light candles. Before moonrise, I fell into a dreamless sleep that lasted till the dawn.

I lay awake for a few instants, savouring my new freedom. No more toil in Farmer Here's fields, aye, no more of any of Wran Cheaping was there for me now. Then a thought of the Grey Rose intruded into my musing and I scrambled to my feet and set out, munching a small loaf of corn bread that I bought the day before in the market of my old hometown.

To my right, the side hills of the mountains began their clambering rise, to end at last in their final heights, towering and glistening in the morning sun. Along their base, my path led through the foothills until I came to Holme's Way, and I resolved to make that pass ere the nooning was upon me.

The sky became overcast by the time I came to the cleft that marked Holme's Way, and I took shelter 'neath a ledge to break my fast ere I essayed the pass. As the morning went by, the gorse and heather-topped hills had given way to a rough and wild land, strewn with granite outcrops and patches of shale o'er which I slid at times, breaking sure falls with my staff. Finally, even that was left behind, and the land was now like one solid root of the mountains, with only the hardiest weed and brush growing here in the patches of soil that were clumped in rills and folds of the rock.

Rising from my meal, I took the left-hand side of the pass and stepped briskly, trying to outdistance the growing storm that I could see gathering itself o'er the downs. I fared for no longer than an hour when I heard a rumbling that I took to be thunder from the storm behind me. I paused to listen more closely, and then I realized that the sound came from before me, not my rear. Aye, and it took on a clearer meaning as well. It was the sound of horses' hooves.

Now, no matter what Old Tess said, I looked to meet none in these lands that I might call friend, and I cast my eyes hurriedly about in search of refuge. The sheer walls of the canyon met my frantic gaze, too high and steep to scale, and I felt trapped until I saw an opening in the walls some three hundred paces ahead, on the right side of the pass. Taking a firm hold of staff, harp and journeysack, I sped for it, heedless of the rubble strewn in my path. I just reached the mouth of the opening, when I slipped on the loose rocks and fell in a tangle of limbs.

The breath was knocked from me, but still I had sense enough to gather my belongings and scramble the last few yards. Once within the opening, I turned and peered cautiously without, hoping for a view of the oncoming riders so that I might know what manner of men they might be. No sooner did I cast my gaze in the direction of the hooves' rumbling, than five riders came thundering from around a turn in the pass, and I saw them clear enough then.

Bright mail glittered, even in the dull light of the approaching storm, and I could see that they were well-weaponed, what with swords and spears, and two bearing great axes. It might be wrong to judge a man by first sight—aye, it's not as if I, myself, didn't look a ruffian in my travel-stained clothes and rude equipment—yet I felt that I would not be far off my judgment in deeming these men to be outlaws, or brigands of some sort. So I was congratulating myself on my good sense, when disaster struck.

You did well to hide yourself from the likes of them, manling.

To this day I can still recall my shock as that gruff voice resounded within my mind. Sick with dread, I twisted about and my eyes went wide with shock as I beheld the dim outline of the huge bear-like form that had so addressed me. I backed away from it, only to stumble once more, and this time I fell without the opening and in plain view of the approaching riders.

I cursed myself for a blunderer, but it was too late. Already they saw me. Aye, and from the opening shuffled the figure that I had seen within, the thing that mind-spoke to me. Disbelief ran through me, for by the gods, it was a bear. Nigh ten feet high it stood upon its hind legs, all grizzled brown fur, topped with a shock of steel-grey hair above its dark eyes. Its two immense forepaws cut the air before it as it neared me, and I felt that my doom was upon me.

By my hand lay my staff, and I reached for it ere I stood. Slowly I backed away from the bear, but behind me, I could hear the riders pulling up, and I knew not which was the worst I must face. Mayhap the riders would aid me against this beast, I thought. Aye, but what then? One of the riders spoke as I was puzzling this out, and my decision was made for me.

"Ho! Here's sport, indeed. A man and a beast to feed our blades, comrades. What say you to that?"

As he spoke, and his companions joined him in laughter, I turned to them, my staff raised chest high and held loosely in my shaking hands, much as I had seen the lads of Wran Cheaping prepare their quarter-staves for mock combat. Yet this was no play-fight, and with my death sure upon me, my thoughts turned to the maid of the Grey Rose, and I grieved that she should have no champion now. Poor enough of one I made, it's true, yet I was all she had.

Behind me, manling.

Again the voice spoke in my mind, and I glanced o'er my shoulder to see the bear almost upon me. But his blazing eyes were for the riders only. They shifted in their saddles, till at last one broke from the rest and charged us. The bear swept by me on all fours and then rose to his full height just as the rider was nigh him. One sweep of those terrible paws and the man was thrown from his frenzied steed, a great gash across his chest. A wail of despair was throated by another of the riders, and as one, they all bore down upon us.

I can remember little of that short battle, it all passed so swiftly. One moment there were four riders sweeping toward us, and in the next there were two more men hurt to their deaths at our feet and the others fleeing, following the lead of the three empty-saddled horses. I had wielded my staff and struck at least one of them, but the bear was a whirlwind of motion and our attackers soon lost their lust for killing. As I watched their figures rapidly dwindling in the distance, I wondered what they had hoped to gain from a poor traveler such as myself and a beast. They spoke of sport ere they struck at us, and if that was their reason, I felt no guilt at having a hand in their slaying.

I was still breathless in the afterglow of the skirmish, when the bear turned to me with his head cocked, peering thoughtfully at me. The silence grew uncomfortably between us, until at last I drew upon my courage and said:

"My thanks for your aid, Master…ah…bear…"

My voice trailed off and I felt foolish 'neath his penetrating gaze. A beast that might speak, this was something that could only be in a tale. Still, in these last few days, I had come to appreciate that the old tales held more truth than ever I thought they might.

Your thanks is accepted, marling, came his voice within my mind again. *I am named Hickathrift by the Wessener of Weir, although I was hight Trummel as a cub when first I dwelt in the Woods of Auldwen. I am lately come from Wistlore, and it's there I was given the mantle of a Loremaster by William Marrow, himself. And yourself? You are a Harper, by the looks of that sack, though mayhap not a rich one. Still, when has there been a rich Harper, save in the days of Minstrel Raven-dear, and those days are long past now, I fear.*

I was amazed at how swiftly I accepted this mind-speech, aye, and from a bear at that, and my heart leapt when he spoke of Wistlore, and that with such familiarity. Though my mother had been cast from those Halls, yet I held a longing to look upon them myself.

"I am named Cerin," I said to him.

He shook his head thoughtfully and answered: *The name is not familiar to me. Is it listed in the record scrolls?*

"I'd think not," I said, "for never have I looked on any of the northlands, though my mother, aye, and my father, too, were from that land. My mother was a Harper, in times past. Eithne was her name, and my father's was Windlane. Have you heard tell of them?"

Aye, the bear replied with a nod. *Their tale is written out in the lore books, though what became of them has not been recorded. Nor is it mentioned that they had a child.* He shot me a piercing look. *They were not well-loved at their leave-taking, it seems. Did you know of that?*

"I knew," I said, and there must have come a look to my face that showed my displeasure with those who would send from them one of their own, solely because she found a love that they frowned upon. Aye, and had that not occurred, I might have been raised in other lands, far from Wran Cheaping, and might have been a Harper in truth. I was bitter, though not toward my parents. Should I ever reach the Halls of Wistlore, that was one matter that I longed to confront those elders with. But still, had I not dwelt in the West Downs, would I then have met with the maid of the Grey Rose?

But what of yourself? asked Hickathrift, breaking into my thoughts with his gruff voice. *Are you bound for Wistlore, then?*

"In time," I answered, and I told him a little of what had befallen, dwelling longer upon the fate of the Grey Rose and the words of Old Tess, than on the rest of my tale. Hickathrift was quiet while I spoke, stopping me only once or twice when my words ran ahead of themselves, and then I must backtrack to explain some matter. At last, when the telling was done, he shook his head gravely and spoke.

I would like to meet this Old Tess of whom you speak, aye, and the maid you name the Grey Rose, for the lore books are largely silent as to that war between the Stone-slayer and the Hill Lords of the Trembling Lands. To all accounts it was a dread time, and northward, there was none who knew its ending, aye, or the brave sacrifice of this maid. I think that I would accompany you upon this quest, if you will have my aid.

This I had not imagined. If I would have his aid…ah! With his aid I might have an actual chance of success. I said as much to him and he laughed, deep and throaty.

Do not think too highly of me, Cerin, for I have not the power to stand up against a Waster. Yet I will try, and there are other matters that I can assist you with. You know of Heart's-sure, but as to a dead king's sword…there is a barrow not far from the very outskirts of the Cradle of the Kings, hidden in the side hills. I was within it and explored it thoroughly, but there was no sword within. Still, mayhap you will find something where I saw naught, for I was not searching for aught in particular when I was there. I wonder what that other thing was that Old Tess could not recall. Aye, and how are these to be used against the Stone-slayer?

I shrugged my shoulders for I knew not myself and worried about it oft.

No matter, he replied. *When the time for their use is nigh, let us hope that the knowledge will become apparent. For now, we have a need to gather these things first.* He lifted his muzzle and sniffed the air. O'erhead dark clouds were gathering, roiling and scudding in a turmoil. *We have yet an hour or so, ere the storm strikes. What say you that we leave this place of death and fare onward for that hour? I can recall other caves, further on up the pass, and within one of them we will spend the night and take further rede as to this coming struggle.*

We left the dead brigands where they lay, though I took a sword from one. I knew naught of the art of sword-play, yet I felt a little more confidence with such a weapon tucked into my belt. We fared on down the pass and came, in time, to the caves of which Hickathrift had spoken. Soon I was sharing my victuals with him by a fire set just far enough back from the opening of the cave that its glow and reflection might not be seen from without. Therein, while the storm howled the night through, we slept deeply and unheeding of it.

THE NEXT morn, we arose with the sun and fared the remaining length of Holmes Way without further mishap. We stood in the jumble of strewn rock and boulders that marked the western gate of the pass while Hickathrift cast his gaze about, searching for a landmark. Once found, he led a winding way through the rough foothills and brought us at last, with much scrambling upon my part, to the barrow where it lay half-hidden in a small gully choked with brush and thick-bladed grasses.

The dusk grows, he said as we stood before the dark opening, flanked by two weathered stones. Strange runes ran up and down their length, but I could not read them, my knowledge being limited to what Old Tess taught me, and she stored most of her learning in her mind, scorning books and writing.

I asked Hickathrift as to their meaning, but he shook his head.

Though the runes are familiar enough, they spell words in a tongue of which I have no knowledge. I was bound for the Trembling Lands, and meant to make copies of them upon my return so that the Wyslings in Wistlore might puzzle over them. But now, and he pointed to a narrow cleft at the far side of the gully with his paw as he spoke, *let us take our rest and essay this barrow on the morrow. There are spirits that dwell in barrows that come awake when the sun sets, and they do not care to be disturbed.*

I shook my head at his counsel, for I tallied the days since the Grey Rose was stolen, and that tally was too high.

"No," I said, and I fell to searching for a length of wood to serve me as a torch. There was nothing nigh, so I gathered an armful of the tall grass and sat down to twist their tough fibers into a serviceable taper.

"Time runs out," I said to Hickathrift as I worked on it, "and I feel that even now it might be too late. There is only a need for haste now.'

So be it, replied Hickathrift, *on your head be it, for that haste may well lead you into ruin. The counsels of the wise are specific in their warnings, and if you will not heed them, let the dooming fall upon you. I will await without and guard you from mortal foes, but I will not chance a curse of the dead.*

I shrugged, for though I was not feeling overly brave myself, a desperation of sorts set itself upon my spirit, swamping my own feelings of fear, aye, and the counsels of the wise as well. My torch was soon ready and I lit its end with flint and steel. Then I turned again to the mouth of the barrow's entrance and entered, with a dead outlaw's blade bared in my hand, in search of a dead king's sword.

Luck go with you, came Hickathrift's thoughts, then there was silence, save for the scuffle of my boots upon the stone floor and my own laboured breathing. Within, the passage was narrow and I soon felt cloistered, and the walls seem to press in upon me. It was an unpleasant feeling, treading this dark confined space with but the light of a taper of twisted grass. I glanced at my torch and saw that it was burning swiftly, perhaps too swiftly, and I felt that its illumination might not last me for as long as I hoped. It flickered and burnt unevenly, sending strange shadows scurrying ahead of me down that narrow passageway. I thought of returning for a few tapers, but instead I pressed on, for ahead I could see that the passage was opening up into a large space of some sort.

When I stepped within, my torch was half-burnt and lit an empty chamber. To the left, I saw the threshold of another passage, and on the floor, I could make out the prints of Hickathrift's heavy paws etched in the dust. To that opening I went then, hurriedly crossing the chamber, and soon I was in another corridor, though this one was a little wider. Still, my heart was thumping in my breast as I walked on, for the weight of the rock about me seemed to bear down, aye, and an oppression crept in upon me so that I glanced nervously about, with many a look o'er my shoulder.

This passageway, too, came to an end, and then I stood within the heart of the barrow. All about there was a litter of broken rock and shards of what once must have been weapons and other finery, and the stone slab, where the remains of the barrow's inhabitant should have lain, was chipped and empty. Peering closer, I could see a snarl of bones by its side, and the remnants of age-rotted cloth and rusted armour. My torch spluttered, and I looked around myself, searching for something with which I might replenish my dwindling light. In one wall there was set a torch, blackened with tar, and to this I touched my poor grass taper. The tarred wood took fire readily and soon the whole chamber was lit with a brighter illumination.

The minutes slipped by as I took stock of the barrow's holdings. Weapons there were, or at least the heads of axes and spears, their shafts broken and lying in a tangle. Of riches there were none, but there were plenty of clay-shaped bowls and dishes wrought of stone and rough metal, some of which were painted with now fading colours, though once they must have been fair.

I shook my head despairingly, for nowhere saw I a blade or sword, or even a dagger. The silence hung leadenly in the stuffy air. And then a sound. At first I thought it was Hickathrift, come to aid me after all, but I soon realized that it came from the wall that faced the passageway. All my fears rose within me in an overwhelming wave, and I turned to run back to the outside and safety, but a keening wail resounded throughout the chamber and my limbs froze.

As suddenly as the keening rose, it fell, and silence once more encompassed the barrow. Then a voice broke that silence, so loud that the stones of the burial chamber shook as it spoke, and I covered my ears to lessen the din.

"WHAT DO YE IN MY BARROW, MORTAL?"

With shaking knees, I turned to face the owner of that voice.

"ARE YE SO WEARY OF LIFE THAT YE HAVE COME TO JOIN WITH ME IN THESE HALLS OF THE DEAD?"

No matter that the torch cast its light about the chamber, for I could see naught before me save a darkness etched against the already black shadows that shrouded that end of the barrow.

"N-no…" I managed at last, my throat tight with fear. I struggled to overcome my terror and added, as I backed away from the darkness toward the threshold of the corridor behind me: "I sought but a sword, for there is a geas of sorts laid upon me, and the sword of a dead king I must have to fulfill it."

"A SWORD?" said that bodiless voice, and I caught a hideous chuckle behind its words. "AND WHAT WOULD YE GIVE ME IN EXCHANGE FOR A SWORD? WHAT DO YE HOLD MOST PRECIOUS IN ALL THE WORLD OUTSIDE THESE COLD WALLS?"

I was dumbfounded and stopped my backward movement to peer closer into that darkness. Would this spirit but bargain with me, and mayhap, allow me to flee its barrow with that which I sought? What did I hold most precious? I racked my mind, seeking for something that I possessed that might please this shade of the dead. There was little I had, save my harp, the brigand's sword and the clothes on my back…and then I thought of the rose that was yet cool against my skin, hidden within my tunic. Loath was I to give it up, but to save the maid…Slowly I pulled it forth and laid it upon the burial slab.

"I have this," I said. The torchlight caught its petals, still damp with glistening dew, and I marveled again at its flourishing.

"WHERE GAT YE THIS?" the voice boomed with anger and I saw the darkness move away from the wall toward me.

The force of its anger tore into my mind and I staggered back 'neath its brutal attack. Through the twisting horrors that lapped on the boundaries of my consciousness, I tried to form words with which to explain how the blossom came into my possession.

"WHERE GAT YE THIS?" the voice boomed again. "THIS WAS MY DAUGHTER'S OF OLD, ERE THE COMING OF YARAC THE WASTER, AYE, ERE THE WARRING FELL UPON US. LAST WAS I TO FALL, HERE SO CLOSE TO HIS CURSED HOLD, LAST AND TO NO AVAIL. HOW DARE YE STEAL THE GREY ROSE FROM HER

AND OFFER IT TO ME, HERE IN MY TOMB THAT THE DWARVES WROUGHT FOR ME, ERE THEY FLED NORTH. I WILL SLAY YE! I WILL REND YE! SPEAK, MORTAL! WHERE GAT YE HER POWER FROM HER?"

The darkness was nigh upon me, and babbling, I told of what had befallen the maid of the Grey Rose, and what I meant to do to aid her. Rapidly I spoke, my heart thumping in my breast, aye, and I was on my knees, for there was no strength in me to stand, with the dead bandit's blade held uselessly before me, as though I might fend off his wrath with it.

Then the darkness lashed me and swept o'er me, and I felt an unfamiliar mind probing my own, weighing my words for their truth. Not gentle was that unspoken questioning. The shade of the dead Hill Lord tore my memories from me, and I writhed in my terror, striving to tear away from him, to retain my sanity. Then, as suddenly as the horror fell upon me, it was gone, and the voice of the shade resounded throughout the chamber.

"YE SPEAK THE TRUTH, AND I THANK YE FOR WHAT YE WOULD DO FOR THE CHILD OF MY FLESH, OF MY BLOOD. TAKE YE THE ROSE THAT YE MAY RETURN IT TO HER, AND I WILL GIVE YE A SWORD, AYE, A SWORD AS NE'ER THE WORLD HAS KNOWN SINCE THE FALL OF THE LAST OF THE HILL LORDS. BATHE IT IN SMOKE, MORTAL, THE SMOKE OF HEART'S-SURE BURNING IN A FIRE OF ROWAN WOOD. BLOOD RED FLOWER AND WHITE WOOD…THAT IS HIS BANE, AND HAD I BUT KNOWN IT IN MY TIME, IT IS HE WOULD BE LYING IN THIS FOUL TOMB, AND I THAT WOULD BE FREE.

"GO, MORTAL, AND LAY HIM LOW. WITH HIS DEATH, MAYHAP, I WILL KEN PEACE AT LAST. TAKE THE SWORD, AND GO!"

My ears were pounding with the volume of his voice and I lay prostrate upon the floor, not quite realizing that he was gone. Slowly I rose to my feet, shaking my head numbly. I looked about and saw the rose yet lying on the slab. I picked it up and thrust it into my tunic, then searched for the sword that the Hill Lord's shade said he had left for me. But there was none to be found. Unbelieving, I looked again and again, tearing at the rubble strewn o'er the floor in vain. Then, when at last I had given up, I saw it. Reflected on a wall was the shadow of a sword. With a cry of triumph, I spun about, albeit wobblely, to where the blade that cast that shadow must be. Yet there was nothing there.

I shook my head in bewilderment. Riddles, always riddles! Then I recalled my talk with Old Tess again. What had she said? Slowly the words returned to me. "...a dead king's sword, a sword of shadows..." Uncertainly, I approached the wall and put out my hand to the hilt of the shadow-blade...and felt a solid hilt beneath my fingers. Filled with wonder, I grasped it and drew my hand back from the wall, aye, and the sword came with it. Here was magic, I thought, as strong as any that the Stone-slayer might wield.

Slowly, I retraced my steps to where Hickathrift awaited me without the barrow. I bore no torch, only the shadow-blade in my hand, yet I stumbled not, and made my way without the fears that plagued me earlier, when first I strode down this passageway. When I stepped from the entrance, Hickathrift stared at me, and the dim outline of the sword that I held in my hands, with disbelief.

You have it! he said, *by my ancestors, you have it! I thought you were slain when I heard those muffled sounds, and then a cry as though a spirit were being rent from its body.*

I could not recall that scream, but it must have been torn from my throat when the shade of the Hill Lord entered my mind. I told Hickathrift of what befell me within, and he nodded his heavy head calmly as I spoke, though I could see excitement gleaming in his eyes.

A Hill Lord's barrow! he said when I was done. *I should have guessed it by the unfamiliar runes. Now I will do my part and search out a stand of Heart's-sure while you take some rest. But the rowan wood...I cannot recall any rowans in these parts. Where we will find the wood...your guess is as good as mine.*

The thought struck us both at the same time. Rowan wood...why my staff was cut from the wood of a rowan! We shared a smile then, the bear and I.

"So now I have a chance, indeed," I said to myself as Hickathrift padded off in search of the Heart's-sure. "I only pray that it's not already too late." The words were scarcely spoken, ere sleep washed o'er me and I fell eagerly into her welcoming arms, the shadow-sword clasped firmly in one hand.

ON A rounded hillock that o'erlooked the ruined city of Banlore, once the Cradle of the Kings, we laid a fire with the broken shards of my staff of rowan. Where my strength had failed earlier, Hickathrift soon broke that resilient wood, and with flint and steel, I set a flame to it. One by one, I dropped the Heart's-sure that he gathered while I slept into the heart of the fire.

It was the mid-afternoon of the day following my experience in the barrow, and we had hurried throughout the morning till at last we came to this spot.

Do you see that spire, or at least what remains of it? Hickathrift had said, pointing with his paw toward the northernmost part of the city. *That is where he will be…that is where we must go.*

So here on the hillock we built our fire and began our preparations.

The flames lapped around the Heart's-sure as I dropped them in, and smoke bellowed from those flames. I drew the shadow-sword from my belt and held its blade in the smoke. In awe, we watched grey runes forming upon the dark blade.

"What do they say?" I asked, but Hickathrift knew little more than I.

They are writ' in the tongue of the Hill Lords, was his answer, *and they alone know the kenning.*

I held the blade in the smoke till the last of the rowan wood and Heart's-sure were but coals, then I withdrew it and held it aloft. We gazed at it for a long while, but at last I slipped it back into my belt and we made ready to essay the ruins below.

A long howl broke the still afternoon air, and I looked about in surprise.

"What…?" I began, but an answering cry filled the air, followed by another.

Wolves! came Hickathrift's thoughts to me. *The Stone-slayer must have set them as guards and they have caught our scent. Swift! Make for the city!*

I gathered up my harp and journeysack, and bolted for the city with Hickathrift loping at my side. Howls rent the air again; many of them, and they came from all sides. Glancing o'er my shoulder, I saw their dark forms on the hilltop. They stood silhouetted against the sky with their muzzles lifted in the air. Their new cries were still echoing when they quit the hill and came speeding toward us.

From the right and left, more dark forms were now ringing us about, and my heart sank. There were at least a score of the beasts in this pack and I saw no hope for us to outrun them, aye, or mayhap, even out-fight them. I stopped my mad flight, and stood panting. Hickathrift brought himself up short by me.

What do you? We must make for the ruins!

"We'll not reach them in time," I replied. "We must stand them off here, rather than have them pull us down from behind as we flee."

Then if they must be faced here, let it be me who faces them, and you go on with our quest.

"No! We succeed or fall together," I said.

Fool! came his gruff voice roared into my mind. *Think of the maid, your Grey Rose!*

Aye, I thought, think of the Grey Rose, but already the wolves were closing in, and I could hear their snarls and growls as they prepared to charge. The hackles were risen along Hickathrift's back and a low warning rumble issued from his throat as the wolves came nearer, almost ringing us.

I held the shadow-sword in my fist, and with a cry, I leapt forward and swung it at the nearest beast. It dodged my blow with a deft movement to the side and its head darted for me as I stumbled off-balance, its teeth snapping. A blow from Hickathrift's claws sent the creature reeling backward, dead ere it fell. Then they were all upon us, and we were kept busy against their insane bloodlust.

My harp and journeysack I dropped at the beginning of this onslaught, and as the wolves struck, I was backing from one when I put my foot through the soundbox of my harp. It splintered 'neath my weight and I cried out at the sound. Rude and poorly-crafted it might have been, but it was all I had. I returned to the fray with renewed fury, but the sheer number of them was overwhelming us.

Already Hickathrift's magnificent coat was torn from dozens of cuts and my sword arm was weary, so weary. The blade seemed to fight on its own, true enough, for I had no skill in its use, but still it was my arm that bore it, and I soon felt as though I could scarce lift it any longer.

There came a lull in the struggle, and we stood breathing heavily as the wolves regrouped for another attack. Hickathrift turned to me and mind-spoke, the force of his words stinging like a blow.

Go now, and I will hold them off!

I began to shake my head and say that I would not leave him, but he bared his teeth.

Go! he roared.

I backed away, my heart filled with worry for him. But overriding that was the thought of the Grey Rose in the clutches of Yarac Stone-slayer. Cursing, I spun and ran for the city. The wolves sent up a howl and made for me, but Hickathrift threw himself upon them. When I was at the edge of the city, I glanced back and saw him born down beneath their numbers, then I ran on, in among the ruined buildings, with tears stinging my eyes. I would have vengeance, I vowed, aye, I would revenge the death of proud Hickathrift, who in the short while we were together, had become very dear to me, but first, so that his sacrifice might not be in vain, I would deal with the one that was the cause behind all my grief. Aye, Yarac would pay.

On I sped, my thoughts filled with anger and sorrow, and I made for the crumbling tower we had spied from the hillock without the city. The day was beginning to fail now, and a wan light pervaded these deserted streets. The buildings, all ruined as they were, cast strange shadows across my way, their darkly weathered stones brooding and filled with dim secrets. Through the growing dusk, I made my way, my footsteps slowing as I neared the tower.

Curiously, though time sped by as I fared onward, the twilight yet wrapped these still streets, as though the night were to be held at bay by its half-lit greyness. In my tunic, the maid's rose grew even colder against my skin, and in my hand, the grey runes that ran along the shadow-sword's blade began to glow with a golden hue. Soon they were too bright to look upon with comfort, and the sword itself tugged me in the direction of the tower. Aye, and still, though the night should be well upon me by now, the twilight yet held sway.

Now a sluggishness entered my limbs, so that it seemed as though I was forcing myself through water, and I felt tendrils of thought touching the boundaries of my mind, much as in the Hill Lord's barrow, but these touches were tainted with a foulness that made me bolster all of my inner strength to draw back from their questing. Ever onward I fared, yet at a slower and slower pace, so that it seemed I scarce moved. The foul mind-touches grew stronger and washed into my mind, and needs must I concentrate with all my might to force them from me. As those moments passed, I would find that I had not moved, and then I would set one foot ahead of the other again, and so go on.

How long that hellish journey continued, I have no way of telling, for throughout it all, the unnatural twilight soaked the avenues of the ruined city. Though mostly it was fallen down, in places walls still reared, and in others I must clamber over the heaps of rubble that blocked my path, aye, and always the mind-touches battering away at my consciousness. After one, I found myself lying prostrate upon the ground, when at last I forced it from me. All that kept me going was the sacrifice that Hickathrift made for me and the thought of the maid of the Grey Rose trapped in the clutches of the Waster, for my courage was spent and nigh fled from me.

At last I was come to the base of the tumbled structure that was all that remained of a once proud tower in the elder days, when this had been the Cradle of the Kings. I stepped though the portal and a blast of power struck me upon the threshold so that I staggered back and fell to my knees, a scream of pain wresting itself from my throat. Tears blinded my eyes as I struggled to my feet and fought the evil from me. At a snail's pace, I lurched through the doorway and a foul stench hit my nostrils so that I near gagged.

Within, all was dark, and I crept across the debris-strewn floor, fighting that dark mind-power each step of the way. Then it struck. One moment I was forcing my way through utter shadow, and in the next an over-bright glare lit the inside of the tower. Sickly-ochre it was, as foul to my eyes as the stench was to my nose. I lifted my gaze to where a ravaged dais yet stood at the far end of the room. There they stood: the Grey Rose and her tormentor, Yarac the Stone-slayer.

I moved forward, the shadow-sword gripped firmly in a sweating palm. The power that had pounded my mind was gone and nothing hindered my approach so that elation began to grow within me. Was he defeated already? Ah! My heart leapt at the thought, only to be dashed in the next moment.

From beside the still form of the Waster, the Grey Rose spoke, and as I turned my gaze to her, I stepped back at the hate reflected in her eyes.

"Scum!" she cried, her voice laced with venom. "Do you think that if I wanted your presence, I would not have bided with you? How dare you follow me here? How dare you profane this place with your farmer's body? Harper!" She laughed at the word and the sound of that laughter sent a chill of horror down my spine. "You would be a Harper, would you? Why not try your tunes on the wolves without the city? They have a need for dinner music I should think!"

A rage burned in my heart that she should speak thus of Hickathrift. Against my breast, the rose was like ice, and I lifted the sword as I stepped nearer. Standing before her, I shivered 'neath her withering gaze, for hell-fires burned in those once dusky eyes, eyes that had looked upon me with friendship. I ignored the Waster then, for I saw that all I had strove for was of no avail. There was no need of rescues, for she was his willing bride.

"I loved you," I said, the words spilling from my heart. "Not as a man loves a maid, but as a companion loves his speech-friend. There was a fane in my heart where you once dwelled, but now its foundation crumbles, and all that was holy, is now like a dead thing. I had thought—"

"Go!" she cried out, breaking into my words and pointing toward the door. "Go, or my mate will break his patience and slay you at my command. You live now only for what was between us once, but that is no more, and soon, it too will mean nothing. Go!"

I looked at her with pity, and glancing at her companion, I turned to go, the shadow-sword trembling in my hands. Then suddenly, I whirled about and plunged it into her breast. A scream tore that chamber, a scream so fearful and filled with pain that the walls themselves began to crumble and fall in upon us. The ochre light flared to a blinding brilliancy, and stark against it was the darkness of the shadow-sword, buried to its hilt in the chest of Yarac Stone-slayer.

"No!" he howled. His fingers plucked at the hilt of the sword. "How could you have known…"

There was another flare of light and the room plunged into darkness. Swiftly I sped to where the form of Yarac had first appeared to stand when I entered the chamber, and 'neath my questing hands, I found the still form of the maid I knew as the Grey Rose. I lifted her in my arms and bore her from the tower as it fell to pieces about us. Once without, I saw that the night had finally come, and in a star-flecked sky o'erhead, the proud vessel of the moon rode the heavens. Gently I laid the maid down upon the stones, and with shaking hands, I reached into my tunic and drew forth her rose. She was like one that is dead, but the shade of the Hill Lord had spoken of the rose as though it held some power, and I only prayed that it held what was needed to revive her.

I placed the blossom upon her breast, and then took up her body again and bore her without the walls of the city. From behind, there came a deafening roar as the Waster's tower fell in upon itself, burying the monster in his death, aye, and so becoming the tomb he did not e'en deserve.

THE MORNING was rising o'er the hills, and I was standing nigh the ruined walls of that city once named the Cradle of the Kings, lost in thought as I had been for most of the night, when a low voice broke into my musing.

"Cerin?"

I turned to see the Grey Rose attempting to sit up, and I hastened to her side. She pushed aside my protesting hand and stood, albeit shakily, and took a deep breath.

"Ah! Sweet life!" she said, and she smiled at me. "How did you free me, Cerin? How did you best Yarac the Waster?"

I sat down and she lowered herself by my side, then I told her of all that had befallen since the night she was taken. There was a deep silence when my telling was done.

"Who are you, in truth?" I asked at last.

She took my hands and said:

"Look into my eyes, Cerin, if you would know me for what I am."

Hesitantly, I lifted my eyes to hers and was lost to the swirling depths locked within the dusky lights that were therein. There were all the shades of grey there, gold and dark mingled in perfect harmony, and tales that would take years for the telling. At last I dropped my eyes from hers, and she whispered:

"Aye, my father was the Hill Lord whose shade you met, but my mother was of the eldest race, for I am the Spirit of Twilight, aye, the Dark that is Light. The Aelves name me *Mar wel na frey Meana,* and long have I been trapped in this form I wear, trapped by a broken promise and the might of a Waster."

She rose with a graceful motion and lifted me to her side.

"I have another journey to make, one that has no ending that I can see now, for I must search out my kin and take up once more the mantle of my naming. You have proved a true friend, Cerin, and you will always wear my thanks for what you have done. This now I will foretell: your life will be long, longer than any of your kind has ever known, and in those days to come, you will be the most renowned of all the Harpers. Today I name you Song-weaver, but for now I must bid you farewell. We will meet again one day, I pray..."

As she spoke, her form began to shimmer and fade from my sight. Sadness welled up in my heart at her parting and I longed for something I might say, something I might do at this moment, but my mind was numbed and empty.

"Cerin?" came her voice from her fading form.

I looked up expectantly.

"How knew you that the form you slew was not mine?"

"Because," I said with a laugh, "when Yarac was berating me, I glanced at the form I thought was his, and saw that it had your eyes."

She laughed then as well.

"So much for his trickery," she said. Her form was almost gone, when she added: "There is one awaiting you on the hillside, Cerin, aye, and a parting token from me as well. Ne'er let the fane within you die, my friend, for it would grieve me sore. Fare ever well."

"Farewell," I said, and she was gone.

Slowly I walked up the hillside to where she pointed and then I saw him.

"Hickathrift!" I cried, and ran the remaining distance between us.

He was battered, aye, and so cut with wounds that I feared for his life, but he smiled and said: *Gaze around you, manling. There are others who fared not half as well as I.*

And he spoke the truth, for the hillside was littered with the corpses of the wolves that had attacked us. And then I saw something else. By Hickathrift's side was a leather bag. Eagerly I made for it and loosened the bindings. As the leather fell away, I saw the Grey Rose's parting gift: a harp carved from the wood of a rowan, with figures and mythical beasts carved all along its sides that appeared to live and breathe, so skilled and true was its craftsmanship. Its strings were of a glistening metal that I could not name, and at its top, where the curving wood met the sound box, was set a Grey Rose. And though it was set into the wood, it had the appearance of being fresh-plucked, with dew yet damp upon its petals.

With a smile, I replaced it within the leather bag and turned to help Hickathrift with his wounds. North to Wistlore I would fare with him, once his hurts were healed, aye, but first, after I had seen to them, I must finish that song that once I began, so long ago in the Golden Wood. I had a name for it as well, now. I would call it "The Fane of the Grey Rose".

A Kingly Thing

i.

IT WAS THE TIME of the haysel, but there was an expectancy in the air that belied the approach of year's end and, with it, the winter. Over the Greylands a pall of autumn cloud hung heavy in the distance, lending a sullen appearance to its already grim heaths. Still, the thin scrub and laden meadows that edged that drab land held the bright festive colourings of the season so that the overall impression was one of warmth, though it be summer's end.

Emrys returned to his work. He was seventeen summers this year and longed to be away from his father's holding. The world was wide, yet he was trapped in a narrow scope of endless toil. The sameness of his life bore on him with an unrelenting weight.

Southward, the great tracks of the Lodowick Forest spread. On its southmost edge the market-town of Tinsmere lay and beyond it sprawled the Southern Kingdoms. Yet for all their wonder, they held no longing for him. His heart was drawn to the north; to the Greylands that stretched endlessly, shrouded in mystery.

Emrys recalled tales of a monstrous mountain range that lay beyond its reaches where age-old treasures awaited he who was either brave or foolish enough to cross the moors. Someday he…

With a start, Emrys realized that he'd been daydreaming again. Guiltily, he glanced over to where his father laboured and half-expected a tongue-lashing. But his father was preoccupied and hadn't noticed.

The yellow corn was high and they had yet half a field to reap before dusk. With a sigh, Emrys put his thoughts from him and swung his sickle with a sure well-practiced motion.

— 🌿 —

THAT NIGHT when the household was asleep, Emrys forced his weary body from a warm bed and crept downstairs. From its place above the mantle, he took down his grandfather's sword. It was a plain blade in a worn scabbard, the peace-strings of which had not been unbound for a score of years—which was longer than Emrys could remember.

The kitchen yielded bread and cheese, which he stuffed in his journey-sack, and he filled his water-bag at the well in the yard. Then he was ready.

High in the night sky, the Barley Moon hung and cast a pale glow upon his preparations. Northward, he could see the Greylands, a strange glow pervading its hollows and rises. His heart leapt at the sight and he started forward. On its border, where sprightly bushes became gnarled mockeries of themselves, he paused and looked back. Just the one glance he allowed himself, then he stepped resolutely forward and entered that eerie land of glowing mists and hidden wonders…

ii.

IT WAS a strange dream that came to Emrys on his third night in the Greylands. He had marched steadily through that first night—his grey eyes shining with the excitement of his new-found freedom—and on until the evening of the second day. He soon discovered that the glowing he had seen was merely the moonlight on moor-mists, but each waking moment was filled with other sights to entrance him. The land itself seemed intent on refuting its grim name.

Gnarled copses of thin stunted trees wove spider-like webs with their branches and held him so bemused that he often stumbled in some hidden hollow that rilled the ground. Sweeps of rich purple heather were interspersed with gorse and strange heart-shaped golden flowers for which Emrys had no name. Brackish dark-watered pools caught the sun by day, the moon by night, and reflected a dazzling sheen, while mica glinted in granite boulders with a hint of further riches if one would but take the time to examine them more closely. But Emrys pressed on.

On his third day, he came across huge standing stones that towered high above him or lay in long broken lines along his way; menhir and dolmen that seemed to watch him as he passed them by. They stood or squatted along faint tracks that began and led to nowhere. In his mind, they appeared to be not so much the remnants of some elder race, but rather sentient beings in their own right—somehow frozen and doomed to remain silent and watchful until the end of days.

By sun's light they were impressive enough—those grey monoliths with their age-old secrets—but in the night, as the waning Barley Moon cast her witch-light upon the haunted moor, they seemed to take on life, indeed. At times, Emrys swore he could see them tremble in their eagerness to rise and accompany him. Then he would shudder and hurry on.

The evening of his third day found him on a long barren stretch of the heaths and he felt a sudden weariness take hold of his senses. He cast himself down upon a waiting bed of heather and fell into a deep and troubled sleep. And then he dreamt.

At first, he was home again—the holding stood out in sharp relief in his mind's eye—and then he seemed to almost fly across the moors. Onward he sped until he came to a great range of mountains that brooded under a storm-heavy sky and clawed at the clouds with a singular intensity.

Then he was come to the gaping maw of a cavern and he stumbled within. Eerie runes glowed from the walls and lit the dark with a pulsating sickly-green light. Far within, the runes' shine seemed to take on a further depth and beckoned to Emrys with an almost sultry appeal. With half-focused eyes, he stepped forward.

When he reached the point where the light was strongest, he perceived a door in the stone wall of the cavern. He pushed at it— shrinking inwardly at its clammy touch—and found himself inside a small chamber. There was a throne in its centre, carved from the living rock of the mountains, and in that throne sat a decaying corpse. Upon its skull was an iron crown.

Emrys stared at the thing with a growing wonder. Suddenly, heedless of all care or caution, he grasped the crown and set it on his own brow. A shudder of ecstasy ran through his body and each fibre of his being seemed to be delightfully on fire with a passion too strong for words. He took hold of the mouldering corpse and cast it from the throne. Then he sat upon it.

In that instant, a stately music filled the chamber. With it came a diffused golden light. The corpse faded away and young maidens bearing purple flowers appeared and laid their blossom-gifts at his feet. Courtiers came as well, wishing him a long reign and…

Emrys awoke with the sunlight overly bright in his sleepy eyes. He looked about himself with a sudden panic, then slowly re-oriented his befuddled senses to his surroundings. He was yet in the Greylands and it had all been…a dream…

He shook his head and ran a stocky hand through his dark hair. It had been so real, that dream. Perhaps it was a premonition of things to come? A far-seeing of his own future? He shrugged and pulled a crust of bread from his journey-sack to munch thoughtfully in the morning light.

It was the last of his food, but he gave no thought to that. There was more for him in the remembrances of his dream than in any immediate worry for sustenance. When his meager meal was done, he was on his feet and eagerly upon his way.

iii.

WITH DUSK, on his fifth day, Emrys saw a fire on a small rise in the distance. The sharp tightness in his belly persuaded him to investigate on the off-chance that a fire meant a fellow traveller and, therefore, food.

There was indeed a figure hunched over the fire. The thin wind of evening blew him the savoury smell of a stew. He stepped closer and was about to call out when the figure arose and turned to him, saying:

"Greetings."

It was a young girl and the suddenness of her movement startled Emrys so that he backed up a pace. In the dim glow of her fire, it was hard to make out her features, but he saw that she had hair that was darker than his—blue-black and almost waist-length—and her skin was the same colour as the rich earth of the moors themselves. Her eyes seemed to shine golden in the uncertain light and she was clothed in a shift of the purest white. Overtop, she wore a dark cloak.

She returned his gaze steadily and then, with her hands on her hips, she asked: "Do I frighten you?"

Emrys approached the fire cautiously and said: "Why no, it's just that...well...I hadn't expected to meet anyone and..."

The girl laughed at his halting speech.

"Well, I'm no troll, if that's what you fear," she said. "My name's Megan. Are you hungry?"

"No. I mean yes," he mumbled.

What was the matter with him? Why was he so nervous?

He sat down by the fire and added: "I'm called Emrys. What are you doing here?"

"I might ask you the same thing," she said, "but your business is your own, as mine is mine. Briefly, I'm traveling across the moors and I'm about to have my supper. Will you eat with me?"

Emrys agreed readily enough and they soon fell to spooning up the thick stew. Megan offered him bread and wine as well. To Emrys' empty stomach, the simple fare seemed like a feast.

As they ate, he continued to stare at her, trying to fathom what she was doing in the Greylands. She appeared so frail and her clothing unsuitable for this grim land. Young breasts peeked through her thin shift and a long expanse of thigh was bared and golden in the glow of the fire. Emrys felt an unfamiliar stirring in his loins and turned from her with sudden embarrassment.

When he glanced at her again, there was a broad smile on her lips. She stretched sensuously—savouring his discomfort as her breasts pressed against the flimsy material of her shift.

Then she said: "My journey's wearing on me, I'm afraid. I will see you in the morning."

It was a half-statement, half-question. Emrys nodded but the gesture was wasted on her. As she spoke, she turned from him and, rolling herself up in her cloak, seemed asleep already.

"Sleep well," murmured Emrys.

"Mmm," was her only reply.

Emrys stared at her sleeping form for a long moment. Then with a sigh, he unrolled his own cloak. He lay wide-awake with the stars in his eyes for so long that he thought he would never sleep. But as the moon rose—thin and waning—those strange unbidden desires that the girl had awoken in him faded and sleep came.

IT WAS Emrys' sixth day in the Greylands. In the morning, he looked to his companion where she lounged by their fire sipping tea. He hadn't been mistaken last night: her eyes were golden in colour—sultry eyes with large black pupils even in the broad daylight—and her skin was, indeed, a deep brown. She looked, if anything, still more alluring this morning.

Long midnight hair brushed against the pure white of her shift and with the sun upon the flimsy fabric, more was revealed than hidden. She had high cheek-bones and her lips—wet with tea—seemed eminently suitable for the awakening of desires. And awaken them, they did. Emrys tried to concentrate on his breakfast.

"Which way are you faring this morn?" Megan's voice broke into his thoughts.

He glanced up and said: "Northward."

"Well," said she, "if you'll have my company, I think I'll journey a ways with you."

"I'd like that," said Emrys, wondering at the same time if he should remain in her company. Somehow, his desire for her seemed a threat to his dream-throne. That the throne was real, he had no doubts. That he craved the delights that Megan was obviously offering, he could also not deny. But he felt, instinctively, that the two did not blend.

And so they set out: Megan walking with a sensuous flowing motion, while Emrys trailed along, heavy with thoughts and yearnings.

—〰—

IN SUCH manner, they fared ever northward across the Greylands. The days passed them by and soon, high in the night sky, the Blood Moon replaced her sister and waxed ever fuller. With each night, Emrys' desires for Megan grew stronger.

One evening, he told her of his dream. His eyes glowed in the half-light of the dusk as he spoke to her and there was a tremor of unsuppressed excitement in his voice. When he was done with his telling, Megan laughed.

"Ah! Emrys," she said, "you're a fool, I fear. And do you really expect to find a kingdom in the wastes to the north?"

She loosened the fastenings of her shift and it fell from her, revealing her proud young body—his if he would but take it.

Opening her arms to him, she said with a smile: "Here is a kingdom for your taking!"

But this was not the way to entice Emrys. With her mocking laughter, all desire for her had fled him and, as she stood before him, he closed himself to her and turned away. A strange look of pain passed fleetingly over Megan's face and then she redid the fastenings of her shift. They slept and when Emrys awoke in the morning, she was gone.

He felt a sense of loss at her leaving, yet at the same time, an increased commitment to his quest. With a sigh, he gathered his cloak and Megan's journey-sack, which she had left with him, and walked on.

iv.

NOW THE days passed with a singular regularity. Emrys missed Megan and her easy company and longed, at times, for her return. But, yearn as he might, he pressed ever northward, stopping for rest less often and, when he did, for shorter periods of time.

The rich heather and flowers gradually faded, and in their place, grey-brown vegetation covered the rolling land. The sky was almost always overcast during the day and in the night, the red glow of the Blood Moon hung oppressively in the star-laden dark above him.

It was on the last day of his third week in the Greylands that Emrys came across more standing stones. They stretched north for as far as the eye could see. Walking amongst them, all of his old fears returned to him. Surely, the stones were alive. Towering menhir reached for him. Dolmen shivered and appeared prepared to loose their highmost stones at him—huge stones that could crush him to the earth with little or no effort.

Emrys shuddered and fingered the hilt of his grandfather's blade that rested in its sheath at his side. The hilt comforted him with a faint warmth and he continued along his way.

— 🌿 —

LATER THAT day, he was yet faring through the reaches of the standing stones. The dusk was fast approaching as thin mists spread over the low hills, rising from the hollows between them. Then before him, in the shadow of a tall menhir, Emrys saw a cloaked figure resting against its base.

Megan! he thought.

He missed her more than he had thought. Not enough to forsake his quest, but enough to be eager for the comfort of her company. He ran toward her, calling her name, when the figure suddenly turned to him, revealing a weathered face framed by long white hair and a scraggly beard. It was an old man.

"Who are you?" Emrys almost shouted as he skidded to a stop before the stranger. "And where's Megan?"

The old man peered at him from underneath shaggy eyebrows and muttered: "Ah! Megan. And am I to succeed where she has failed?"

Emrys glared at him and said: "What do you mean by that? Succeed at what?"

The old man shook his head slowly and said: "I am Taragon, of course. And you, you're Emrys?"

Emrys was taken aback at the sudden turn in the conversation.

"I am he," he answered finally. "But how do you know my name? And what do you know of Megan?"

"What do I not know?" said Taragon. He scratched his beard and added: "She didn't succeed, you see, so I've been sent to dissuade you from your foolish quest."

"Sent? Sent? Sent by who?"

"By whom, you should say."

"By whom, then?"

"Ah! But that would be telling, wouldn't it?" replied Taragon with a cryptic smile.

"By the Gods! Will you answer my question?" cried Emrys.

"It's by the Gods," said Taragon, "that I answer it not. Now come, lad, be not so hasty. All questions are answered in time, you see. Now, I'm here to tempt you, so would you be kind enough to at least listen to me without shouting and interrupting?"

As the old man spoke, Emrys clutched at his throbbing temples, for his thoughts were spinning and confused.

"Now, where was I?" continued Taragon. "Ah! Yes…temptations! And what have we? Bodily lusts? No, I think Megan covered that as well as she could and I'm rather ill-equipped for that sort of thing. So what's left, then? Death? No, that's a bit too final and it's Wystan's field really. So that leaves wealth and power, and perhaps, rather doubtfully, wisdom." He looked up at Emrys and asked: "Well, what's it to be then, lad? Wealth, power, or wisdom?"

Emrys shook his head. The man was mad, that at least was all too obvious. There was only one thing he really wanted and that was the throne of his dream. It beckoned to him; it called him every waking moment and filled his dreams. This doddering madman was of no concern to him. He took a last look at him. Taragon's fierce eyes met his and Emrys staggered back with the shock of their intensity. Then he turned from the cloaked figure and strode away.

"Your answer, lad?" Taragon's voice followed him and a sudden rage welled up in Emrys' mind.

"I want nothing from you or anyone, old man!" he shouted. He wheeled about to see only the grey menhir standing before him. Taragon was gone as if he had never been. A gust of wind shook the furze at the stone's base. Emrys rubbed his eyes, and, unbidden thought, *Am I the madman?* He cast that thought from him as best as he was able and, facing northward once more, fared on.

v.

WHEN HE was a month's journeying into the Greylands, Emrys beheld a sight that made him reel. It was the eve before the full waxing of the Blood Moon and northward, in the distance, the great mountains of his dreams could be seen through a haze of mist and brooding dusk. He stood and gazed at them and could go no further that even.

In his mind's eye, his promised throne stood stark and waiting. He cast himself upon the brown coarse grass of a small hillock and let his spirit fill with the wonder of their closeness and the expectation of what he hoped to find within their darkened caverns. And then, at last, he slept and dreamt his dreams again.

HE AROSE with the sun's first light, though it was hidden with an overhanging of grey cloud. By mid-afternoon, he was come to yet another stretch of standing stones. In his eagerness to reach the mountains, he was not so intimidated by them. As he passed through them he recalled an old rhyme he had heard sung by a minstrel in Tinsmere one market day…

> come, hoary rootman, tell the tale
> of hollow hill and lore-deep dale
> where sullen Old Ones brood and weep
> and curse the stone that binds their sleep
>
> should all the moors be rent asunder
> hill-backs broken, storm and thunder
> would they be freed? would they be fallen?
> or lost in darkness, beyond calling?

The words held little meaning for him, but they seemed to verify his own feeling toward these old stones. In fact, it was more than likely that the subconscious memory of that rhyme had caused his fears in the first place. And yet…they seemed alive and waiting. Still, he felt they posed no threat to him and it was with a lighter step that he continued on his way.

When the twilight came slipping over the heaths, the Blood Moon rose full and swollen in the darkening air. He was in the foothills of those distant mountains now and pressed ever forward—not even the night could stay him, for he was too close to his goal.

He walked until his legs could no longer bear him and then he collapsed where he stood. At dawn, he rose and pressed on again.

AT LAST there came a time when he judged that he was no more than one day's journey from his goal. Scarcely suppressing his excitement, he had still enough wisdom to realize that he mustn't push himself beyond his own capabilities. He bided where he was then and broke out the last of his food from the journey-sack that Megan had left with him. As he ate, he felt a small sadness that she wasn't with him to share in this, his glory moment.

For the first time since her hasty departure, he attempted to solve the riddle of her presence on these moors. Could she be some essence of the Greylands, itself, some spirit of this grim land come to life? And the old man—Taragon he had named himself—he had known her as well. He had spoken of temptations…Silently, he pushed the thoughts from him. And it was then that he became aware that he was no longer alone.

He turned and faced the strangest sight he had yet beheld in this fell land. A warrior stood before him, a warrior of gigantic stature, for his height was eight feet, if not more. He was clad in furs and leathers with a breast-plate of burnished metal. In one hand he bore an immense sword that Emrys would have had trouble lifting, little say wielding.

Long yellow hair fell to his breast in two braids; his eyes were the blue that shimmers on the ocean at sunset and there was a grim set to his square jaw. For long moments they confronted each other in silence. Then the giant spoke.

"I had hoped not to meet you, Emrys."

Emrys stared at him, slowly comprehending the threat. With fumbling fingers, he undid the peace-strings on his grandfather's sword.

Then he asked: "Why threaten me? I have done you no wrong, stranger."

"No wrong to me," agreed the giant. "I am called Wystan and I guard the last frontier. There is that which you seek—hidden in a cavern in the Mountains of Melaren—and you must not have it. Strive and you will be slain. Depart and you may leave in peace."

"I cannot," said Emrys. "I must go onward."

He had half-drawn his blade, but then with a curse, he thrust it back into its sheath. Slowly he redid the knots of its peace-strings. He had realized, even as he drew the sword, that he would not win to that throne with his hands soiled with another's blood. There was a wrongness therein.

He said to Wystan: "I won't fight you. Let me pass by in peace or slay me where I stand. I have no quarrel with you and should you cut me down, it is you who will be cursed in the eyes of the Gods."

As Emrys spoke, a sad smile crossed the giant's face.

"Well-spoken, Emrys," he said. He sheathed his great sword and then spoke further, saying: "There is a curse that lies within the Mountains of Melaren, though dwarven-home it was of old. Our weird—for aye, my companions are indeed Megan and Taragon—was to dissuade any who approached."

"Do you mean the *temptations* they offered?" asked Emrys, accenting the word with distaste.

"Aye," said Wystan, "that was their way. I have nothing to tempt you with and now I see that I cannot bar your way with violence. I had hoped that the mere threat of my presence would sway you from your quest, even as Megan and Taragon offered you what was in their power. When you have gained your throne, I ask you to remember one thing: that we tried to turn you from it. More I cannot say."

With that, Wystan turned from Emrys and stalked off into the growing night.

— ❦ —

At first, Emrys felt a great relief that he had been spared the ordeal of combat with the giant—for surely he would have fallen 'neath that huge blade. But then he thought upon Wystan's speech. The giant seemed honest, though obscure. What curse? And what of the throne… if Wystan knew of it, why had he not claimed it already? Was it for one man only, and that man was himself?

It was with a much troubled heart that Emrys prepared himself for sleep. And his dreams were many and strange…

vi.

HE WAS come to the threshold of the Mountains of Melaren. His feet had led him swiftly this past day and now, at last, he was here. The mountains towered above him, not so much grim and brooding as grave and stately. Monuments of living stone, they were, the greatest works of Avenal, Mother of the World. Upon them the sky could rest its burden and those mountains would never weary of it. Like a unicorn's horn, they were the beauty of the world, and like bone, its very foundations come to taste the air and lands above the depths of the earth.

Emrys stood awed and speechless as the night fell upon him. The waning Blood Moon rose into the dark sky, and yet he stood. The stars faded and grey streaks of light cut the sky to herald the coming morning, and yet he stood.

Then the sun rose, unfettered by clouds, and Emrys stirred and walked along the base of the mountains. He scrambled over heaps of fallen stone, leapt over small crevices, and was come at last to the yawning entrance of the cavern in his dreams.

Reverently, he stepped within. The weight of the mountains bore down upon his soul and he had to stand still for a moment to catch his breath. The runes were there, green and brightly glowing and more sharply delineated than he recalled, but his dream had moved swiftly and there was much that was hazy in his memory of it.

The runes beckoned him inward and gained in their intensity until their seductive call was more than he could bear. He ran and then came to the small door set in the granite walls. There he hesitated.

What was the curse?

He felt he should bide until it was revealed, but the throne drew him. Slowly, he pushed the door open—its surface was dry to his touch, not clammy as in his dream—and stepped within the small chamber. There it was! The throne that had drawn him—at first unknowingly from his father's holding and then across the Greylands in his dreams.

He held his breath as he stared at the thing that sat in it. Once, it had been a man, but now…Its flesh hung from its bones and upon that naked skull sat the crown of iron that he coveted. He walked closer until he stood no more than an arm's reach away. Waveringly, he reached for the crown, and then it was in his hands.

Cold…it was so cold to his touch. But now he moved swiftly. Suppressing his repulsion, he dragged the corpse from the throne and sat himself down upon it. His trembling hands held the crown above his head. With one last sharply indrawn breath, he set it on his brow and…screamed…

Pain tore through his mind; pain ripped his soul into shreds; pain ravaged his heart until a darkness came welling up from somewhere deep within his spirit and he knew no more…

— 🕯 —

WHEN HE regained his senses, there was a numbness in his soul as if some part of his spirit had died, to be no more. Fearfully, he tried to rise from the throne, but could not. He was snared as surely as if he were chained to that granite throne.

He cast desperate eyes about the dimly lit chamber. The runes on the walls were feeble, their unearthly green light slowly but surely fading. Then his eyes fell upon the corpse. It lay where he had dragged it—but there was a difference in its position. Then he stifled another scream for…the thing was stirring…

With stiff unnatural movements, it rose to its feet. Rotted strips of skin held its bones together and the impossibility of its living burnt into Emrys' mind and brought him to the brink of madness. It seemed not to notice him where he sat on its throne.

Facing the door through which Emrys had entered, it spoke and said: "I am free! After millennia, I am free!"

Slowly it turned and faced him and Emrys shrank back against the stone of the throne. There was a malice in the features of that skull that defied description.

Then the thing spoke again, saying: "My thanks, Emrys, though it's an ill deed you have done upon yourself, this day. Aye, an ill deed for you, but freedom for me! I have a vengeance to wreak against three who have seen to it that none would come to free me. Three who guard the Greylands... ah! the Greylands... I can recall a time when those grim heaths bore another name and fair then was the land... By the Gods! How long has it been?"

The creature lapsed into silence. For long moments all Emrys could hear was the wild pounding of his own heart.

"I went mad at first," the thing continued, "and perhaps I'm yet mad... but no matter... for I am free now! Free!"

Its voice rose until the echoes resounded in that small chamber like thunder. Then the half-fleshed skeleton bent to Emrys until its skull was an inch from his face. Empty sockets bore into Emrys' eyes as it spoke on: "But there is hope, Emrys, there is hope of a sort. Perhaps in time—" the thing chuckled at the word "—aye, perhaps in time, you'll gain the strength to lure some unsuspecting fool to take your place so that he may be damned for all time. As was I... as was I... but now I'm free!"

As it spoke, Emrys discovered that although he could not rise from the throne, he could move about within it. He squirmed under the creature's awful sightless gaze.

"Ah! I weep for you, Emrys," it was saying, "but my sorrow is not so overpowering to let me set you free. Here you must bide, even if it be for ever and for always."

Emrys' throat was swollen with terror. Labourously, he said: "What... what are you... doing to... me?"

There was a blind horror in his eyes and he shook with his fear. His thoughts ran wildly through his mind...

O Gods, aid me!

But there came no answer. Then his mind filled with images of those ancient standing stones that were strewn over the Greylands and he recalled that rhyme...

Where sullen Old Ones brood and weep…

"Have you not guessed the answer?" asked the thing, unaware of the fact that Emrys was only half-heeding what it said. "If not, I will make it clearer: you wear the Iron Crown of the Ages and your throne, your throne is the Throne of Time!"

As it spoke, Emrys sent out a pleading cry…aid me, Old Ones, aid me…and there came a trembling in the ether…O aid me, aid me…

"You are a king now, in truth: the ruler of the Kingdom of Time…"

I beseech thee, Folk of Stone, aid me…

"And here you must bide for all the days that are to come—"

"No!" cried Emrys, and his cry rang against the barren walls.

NO! cried a thousand voices of stone, and their power crackled in the air of that small chamber.

Emrys grasped the skeleton creature that bent over him, and his strength was the might of the moors. It was born of hollow hills and standing stones; of tall menhir and brooding dolmen; of the Old Ones and all things trapped in time…

For the briefest of seconds, time stood still, and Emrys grasped that moment with a fury beyond his ken. In that moment, the throne and its crown held no power over him. He ripped the iron obscenity from his brow and, twisting about, forced the thing that had used him back into its own throne. Savagely, he pounded the crown against its white skull and then the moment was past…

His strength ebbed from him, but he was free. He knelt upon the cold stone of the cavern and gave thanks to those of the wild that had come to his aid. And on its throne, the thing gnashed its teeth in anguish…and screamed…and screamed…

THERE WERE three who greeted Emrys outside that cavern and there were four that fared southward across the grim Greylands. Behind him, Emrys left his youth and gained new dreams. Behind him, Emrys left the Throne of Time for he had found that it was not such a kingly, a kingly thing…

Woods and Waters Wild

Where the wave of moonlight glosses
The dim grey sands with light,
Far off by farthest Rosses
We foot it all the night,
Weaving olden dances,
Mingling hands, and mingling glances,
Till the moon has taken flight…"

—W.B. Yeats

IT'S KILTY LARKIN WAS a young man, that night the sidhe took him for their own. On Beltane Eve, from the midst of their revels, they bore him to their halls hid deep in the hollow hills and kept him for a year and a day, till his own foolish tongue cast him forth.

In Ennis, County Clare, he was born—the how and why of his faring north being a tale in itself. He crossed the River Shannon into Galway, strode long-legged through the flat pastures of Roscommon, to come at last to the gentle hill-lands of County Down. Perhaps he sought work, or a fortune, for he was the youngest of four brothers and had no hope of receiving aught when his father passed on, or perhaps some fey fancy caught hold of him and drew him northward—who can say?—but Down was not a rich land, there being little work for her own sons, and no fortune awaited him there.

He was walking along the hedgerows one eve, his thoughts filled with this and that. The twilight hung heavy in the air, when through the hawthorns and brambles that bordered the roadway he saw a young maid gathering flowers in the field. A pretty lass she was, in a blue dress, with her brown hair hanging down as she stooped to pluck here a bright blue harebell, there a scarlet-tipped pimpernel. What he hoped for he couldn't have said at that moment, yet still he stood there, bemused and staring, until he caught her eye and a warm smile welcomed him on her sweet lips. A sudden sure longing took hold of him so that he pushed through the hedge to have words with her.

Thorns tugged at his coat, nettles stung him through his thin socks. To his eyes, her form seemed to shimmer in the growing dusk as though she were some sending of the Hidden Folk, caught stationary for the briefest of moments in an unexpected lapsing of the ever-present breeze. Aye, and when he stood in the field with her, the glamour appeared more fey than ever, her form so gossamer that he swore he could almost see clean through her.

"Cross o' Christ about us," he murmured, stepping forward.

No sooner did the words escape his lips, than the maid disappeared as though the very earth had swallowed her up. Crossing the short cropped grass to where she'd stood, Kilty looked about himself in bewilderment. Never a trace of her was there, save for the broken stems from where she'd plucked a flower, aye, and a sweet heady scent of apple blossoms, though there wasn't an apple tree in sight.

"She was of the sidhe, right enough," he said to himself, "and it's my speaking of the one they can't abide did send her from me."

It's in Newry he was staying, above Brendan O'Grady's bar, and he took to wandering the hills in the evening, searching for this maid. In tiny glens he stood for hours, or strode through the long boreens, down the hedgerows, even climbing among the rills and rises of the Mourne Mountains. Not a whisper of her did he find. The dust of the roads clung to his coat, his hair hung unkempt to his shoulders, while the stubble on cheek and chin grew into a beard. A haunted look crept into his eyes so that when a man or woman passed him on the road, they would cross themselves and look away, muttering that he was like one fey. And so he was.

Brendan O'Grady took him aside one night, speaking soft in his ear:

"There'll be a ruin on you, me boyo, and you keeping this up— forsaking all honest folk, mooning through the hills after a sending of the sidhe…"

"Bethershin!" Kilty replied, "and it might be true. But there's not a mortal girl would please me now, aye, or at least not till I've tasted the one kiss from that maid's lips."

"And that may be," O'Grady said, "and it's all your life you'll be wasting."

"Aye, that may be," Kilty said.

Brendan O'Grady left him to himself and went to pull a draught for a customer, shaking his head all the while. As for Kilty, he stepped from out the close warmth of the bar to stand gazing at the moon until the long night passed.

It went like that till the evening he found himself by the laneway of a rambling house just outside of Rathfriland. He'd walked a long way, with the thirst growing in him and a lonely feeling worrying away at his very marrow. The music slipped down the lane, the sound of laughter and dancing feet seemed so gay, that he turned from the road, stepping toward the house. Past somber yews he walked, straight to its door. Within, he stood by the threshold. The music flowed over him, the flushed faces of the dancers glistened in the light, ah, and the longing in him grew till it felt like a hound straining at its fetters.

There came a pause, as the fiddler stopped for a drink, and from without the house, an echo of the music lingered on. Sweeter still it was, with a wild quality that bespoke the land itself—dark woods, lonely moors, high windswept mountains, peat bogs and memories when an older race held sway over its acres. Kilty turned to step back into the night.

"And where are you going, Kilty Larkin?" cried out a young man who recognized him. "The night's young upon us and, sure, the faeries are abroad. You'd best watch they don't steal you away."

A chorus of laughter joined his words and even Kilty smiled.

"Aye," he said, "it is their night...but theirs is the fairer music, and it's their company I've been longing for."

"Ah, and has someone put pishrogues on you, Kilty Larkin?" asked one named Sheamus, with the fiddle yet in his hand. "Have the faeries called you for their own?"

"Sure it is," Kilty replied, "that if it's so, I welcome it all the more."

He passed through the threshold, while the crowd within laughed again. They returned to their revels, thinking no more of him till the next day was upon them, and they heard he was gone.

When Kilty stepped out of the door, the sweet scent of apple-blossoms was in the air, and his heart skipped a beat for the joy of it. He hastened down the lane to where it met the roadway. By the fairy thorn, where lane and road joined, stood the maid of the sidhe that he'd seen before. She laughed as he came nigh, calling out in a lilting voice:

"Ah, it's thrice welcome you be, Kilty Larkin. Come, for the moon's on the rise, and if we don't shake the dust from our feet, the dance will begin without us!"

She took his hand and led him along the road; to him it was as if they flew, so swift was their faring. Oft and again, he'd steal a sidelong glance at the pretty maid who led him. His heart thumped in his breast, aye, and there was a gleam of happiness in his eyes so that they shone like they were whiskey-warmed, though he'd not a drop the whole of the eve.

They came to a small glade, girded with blackthorns and rowan, with a stream bubbling nearby. The whole of the dell was filled with little folk, capering and scrambling about. A piper blew up his pipes, when he saw them coming, the fiddlers put bows to their fiddles. As the music was struck up, they all shouted: "Welcome, welcome!"

The dance was begun.

Kilty Larkin looked about himself with wonder, a grin upon his face. Tossing his cap into the air, he threw himself into the dance. In honour of him, they played a set of old tunes: *The Lark in the Morning, The Lark's March, An Fuiseog ar an Trá*, ending with a reel the piper named *Kilty Larkin's*, newly composed. All the little folk lilted that tune with him, their voices like so many linnets and thrushes.

The moon was still high when Kilty flung himself by the stream to take a drink of water, the thirst being on him from his dancing. He stooped over the water, when who should be by his side but the young maid with a cup in her hand. He took the offered drink and lifted it to his lips. A long swallow sent the sweet liquor slipping down his parched throat and set all his nerve-ends a-tingle.

"And how're you named?" he asked the maid.

"Mim," she said with a smile.

She drew him to his feet and they joined the dance once more. Round and round they spun, limbs flashing in the silver light of the moon. Ah, and Kilty Larkin…as the liquor coursed through his veins, he forgot his mortal ways. He danced more wildly than the sidhe, he raised his voice higher and sweeter than theirs. A strangeness swept over him in the midst of the dancing so that he began to recite a tale in verse, as did the bards of old. The words spilled from his mouth in measured cadences. The dancers fell from their capering, the music was stilled, and all the little folk gathered round him to listen to the tale.

On he spoke, wrapping his words with such finery that the sidhe sat hugging their knees with delight. Ever and again, he would pause to sip from Mim's cup. The liquor shook his very soul and the words would flow even more freely.

His tale came to an end just as the moon took to its setting. The little folk toasted him, repeated parts of his tale to themselves, and asked where he'd got such a way with words. Kilty only shook his head.

"Musha," said he. "Surely it was not me speaking so?"

But yes, they all said. Now nothing else would suffice save that he must come with them to their Hidden Land and be their *file*, their poet. Kilty Larkin, with his hand clasped in Mim's, said:

"Sure it is, I'll come."

They all arose in a flurry and bustle. The piper and fiddlers put their instruments into little cloth sacks. Still lilting tunes, they made a ring, hand in hand, arm in arm, and dancing to the sound of their own voices, they sped off in a chain over the woods and hills and hedgerows.

The liquor yet warming him, and he dizzy from the dancing and talking, Kilty Larkin was swept along with them, for when the sidhe choose one to be their own, he was taken to their hallowed halls within the very earth, there to be welcomed and live in all comfort.

How long he dwelt with them, Kilty never knew. There was always mirth and music, the finest of ales and whiskey, and for company, sweet Mim stood him in good stead. If it was not for a hundred years, sure it seemed so at times, though at others, it was like the passing of but the one evening.

Still, there came a day when a stranger entered the rath of the sidhe where Kilty Larkin was staying, and all the little folk drew as far away from him as they might. Though his limbs and hair were like those of a young man, there was an age about him that bespoke of times when even the land was young. Black and curly the hair, white the limbs, and his face was as pale as that of a corpse. His eyes were sewn into that face like two black beads, and there was an evil of the godless in him, not the merry cheer of the sidhe.

"Tis a shade of the dead," said Mim to Kilty, "and pay you him no mind. It's our merriment called him from his grave, and he'll return soon enough. But first he seeks to spoil our fun..."

For all her words, she still drew back as she spoke. Kilty looked with horror upon the thing.

"The good Lord save us from all hurt and harm," he muttered.

All the little folk gave a shriek and a wail, and the ghost turned to Kilty with a mocking smile.

"There's one now," said the dead thing, "that'll have no more joy. For that I'll rest content a little while."

Kilty stared at it, uncomprehendingly.

"Och, musha, and it's bad luck to you, Kilty Larkin, for calling on Him in our halls!" cried one of the sidhe.

There was a great roaring and rushing of air that whipped about Kilty, spinning him till he was dizzy and knew not up from down. Just as the darkness swept over him, he knew what harm he'd caused.

"I meant no ill!" he cried over the howling wind and encroaching dark.

There was no reply.

Kilty Larkin awoke to find himself alone on the brow of a low hill overlooking Milltown. The sky was blue above him, the grass green, and nowhere the sound or smell or touch of the sidhe. He hammered on the hill, crying:

"Let me in! Let me in!"

When there came no answer, Kilty bowed down his head and wept. He was forsaken now, for calling upon the name that the sidhe may not hear. Aye, it's a broken man was Kilty Larkin. Having tasted the pleasures of the Hidden Folk, he'd never find joy or comfort in mortal ways again.

Slowly, he stumbled along the hedgerows till he came to Newry and Brendan O'Grady's bar. He walked in, and it's a long face he wore.

"Och, and what's the matter with you, old timer?" asked O'Grady as he brought Kilty an ale.

Kilty looked up astonished and said:

"Do you not know me, Brendan O'Grady?"

O'Grady peered closer and shook his head.

"You've the familiar look about you," he said at last, "like a lad that hung about these parts a year or so back. Ah, but you'd have to be his grandfather, for he'd no more than twenty years on him. Na, I can't say's as I know you."

"It's Kilty Larkin I am," said Kilty, standing up. As he spoke he looked in the mirror that overhung the bar. He saw his reflection therein, and it's an old man, weighed down in years, he looked in truth.

"Mille, murdher!" cried he, "they've cast me out and stole' my youth!"

He fled the bar, leaving Brendan O'Grady behind staring at his fleeing figure.

"It can't be..." O'Grady said to himself.

The thought that was born in his mind he stilled swiftly. Scratching his head, he sighed, and took to wiping the bar, striving to keep the picture of a young man named Kilty Larkin far from his mind.

It's Kilty Larkin walks the wild woods and hills. Searching and searching, though he never finds what he seeks. He has the touch of the poet about him now, and is always welcome at parties and such. Folk think him fey, though, and keep their young from talking too long with him, for he is a man that's forsaken the good Lord, aye, and the tale of his forsaking breaks the heart to hear—sometimes putting wild fancies into an impressionable child's head so that he would go to seek the sidhe as well.

Kilty Larkin minds them not. Ever he waits to hear the wild strains of music that the Hidden Folk alone may draw from an instrument. Along lonely roads and boreens, over hills and dales, the length and breadth of Ireland he walks in his seeking. His sadness is not such a visible thing now, save in the spring, when the sweet scent of apple-blossoms fills the air...

The White Road

THE EARLY WINTER SKY was a dirty grey the day Nordendale's men returned from the war. They had marched and ridden out, banners unfurled, helms gleaming in the sun, but returned as stragglers, grimy with the dirt of the road and battle, their uneven column stretched out for a quarter of a mile. They returned victorious, having helped drive the Hounds of Alizon from High Hallack, but their haunted eyes, the wounds they bore, the very stoop of their shoulders, bore witness that even in victory, they had lost.

Their Lord and his heir were dead. The Dales they returned to had felt the sting of the invaders' attack; the harvest was poor and more fields lay untilled than had been seeded. And not one family had emerged unscathed from the final battle at Ruther's Pass.

Saren had left her work in the inn when the call went up. She joined the others to watch the men return, her hair tied back in a long braid and wearing men's clothing that hung a size too big on her bony figure. Having turned sixteen this past autumn, Saren had known nothing but times of trouble in the Dales. The war with the invaders had dragged on for a score of years, coming to a head this past year when Were Riders from the Waste and the men of High Hallack, combined with the fleets of the Sulcar, had finally put an end to the Alizon menace.

She watched the men pass, here Gully with his arm in a sling, avoiding her gaze, there the haywright Capper carried on a stretcher for he'd lost both legs. Big Ran Jenner went by, reduced to a frame as skinny as her own. Theodric's son Nichol, walking alone and carrying his father's axe.

There were no cheers raised to greet them. Only gazes as haunted as those of the returning men; gazes that searched the ragged ranks and turned quickly away when a loved one's features were not to be found.

Saren watched, then turned away herself. A sick feeling rose in her, but it was revulsion at herself. The face she missed was that of her betrothed, Erard, and her first thought at that discovery had been, by the Hunter's Cup, I'm free! But the gladness quickly soured into guilt. It didn't matter that the marriage had been arranged to serve the needs of their fathers, nor that—the Moon knew why—Erard himself seemed pleased with the bargain. A man had died in defense of his land and that was no cause for joy. Was she so small-minded that she set another's life above her own happiness?

"Your pardon...?"

Saren started at the touch on her elbow to find a stranger regarding her with an apologetic look on his face. He appeared to be a few years older than her, worn and thin, his clothes threadbare. He leaned on a crutch. Saren looked down and saw that one leg was shorter and thinner than the other. Another victim of the war.

The stranger pointed to the battered sign that hung above the door. "Is this still an inn?"

"The Herdsman's Halt," Saren replied. "Finest in the Dale. The only one in the Dale, actually."

A brief smile touched the stranger's lips. "Can I get a meal—and a room for the night?"

Saren nodded. "You've picked a poor time of year for traveling," she said as she stepped aside to let him enter.

Inside, the smell of food mingled with that of sour ale and old body odour. The room was dark with a broad hearth at one end. A trestle table with benches, an ale barrel by a smaller table stacked with plates and tankards, and a pair of wooden settles near the hearth were the only furnishings.

"I thought it a good time," the stranger said. Awkwardly, he shook out his cloak and laid it across the back of one of the settles, then sat heavily down. "What with the invader finally defeated."

"I meant the weather."

The stranger shrugged. "I had nothing before I marched to war and less now. Winter, summer—it makes no difference the season when you have no home."

"But you can at least camp out-of-doors in the summer."

"One can camp out-of-doors in the winter as well—it's just harder." He stretched out his crippled leg, moving it with his hands until it was in a comfortable position. Looking up, he caught her glancing away from it. "I got this three years ago," he said. "There's not much work for a soldier who can no longer march."

"You were a Sword Brother?"

"No. But I sold my sword all the same. I was a guardsman in Jorby for awhile. Later I rode with Elsdon. Then I got this." He touched his leg. "A wise woman took me in and let me stay on while I healed—fetching and carrying and the like. The work, little though it was, kept my leg from healing worse than it did. It was she that told me..." He paused and that half-smile touched his lips again. "Your pardon. I talk too much sometimes. But it's been a lonely road. I came in with your men, and they weren't much for talking."

What did the wise woman tell you? Saren wondered, intrigued. But aloud she only said: "We never had much either—and have less now as well."

The stranger held a coin out in the palm of his hand. "I can pay."

"I didn't doubt that."

She regarded him contemplatively, wondering at the things he'd seen and done. If she'd been born a man, instead of being locked into a Dalesgirl's narrow life, if she'd been free to wander and see the world...

The stranger mistook her look for sorrow. "Did you lose someone?"

"My betrothed."

"I'm sorry."

And she was not, she thought again. Erard's father had a farm and liked his drink. Her own father had seen the profit to be gained in an alliance with a family that could provide cheap provisions for the inn and had a gawky daughter underfoot. A simple bargain had been struck, with her as the coin.

But that was over now. Her father had died last year, defending the Lord's cattle against a far-ranging band of the invaders. Her betrothed had died at Ruther's Pass. All bargains were finished with and there was no one but her mother left to make new ones. But Saren didn't intend to be coin anymore. If a crippled man could travel the Dales in winter, then so could she. She could…She blinked, realizing that the stranger was still regarding her.

"We've fresh stew," she said brightly, "and home-brewed ale. Will that do?"

The stranger nodded. "I'll take them here by the hearth if I may. My bones need warming."

Saren brought him a plate of the stew and drew an ale from the barrel for him, then left him to his meal while she returned to her chores.

THE NEXT morning she watched him go, trudging off under another dirty grey sky. He went up the Dale, towards the mountains where only herdsmen tended their sheep, instead of south towards the sea where life was somewhat easier. Where had his wise woman bid him to go? she wondered, fingering her braid.

Perhaps he meant to turn off to Grimmerdale. There was a place of mystery there—one of the Old Ones' ruins, standing stones called the Circle of the Toads. But he hadn't seemed the kind to trust such a chancy site and it was not a place that a wise woman would bid a Dalesman to seek out. Then where? If he went far enough he'd come to the Waste and there was nothing there for anyone but a Were Rider.

After awhile, Saren put his destination out of her mind and concentrated on her own troubles. She could go—there was nothing stopping her. Only go where? Be what? If she was a man…She touched her braid again and thought, who was to say she couldn't look like one? She didn't have a woman's shape and with her hair cut short…A pleased cat's smile touched her lips. Oh, she liked it.

She went around to the back of the inn and set about her morning chores, humming a tune under her breath that made her mother give her a frown. Saren paid her no mind. To her mother, she was only free labour. This last day Saren meant to go about her chores, but come tomorrow, her mother could look for new help and would find that it didn't come so cheaply.

IT WAS snowing when Saren slipped out of the inn that night. She closed the door softly behind her and turned her face to the sky, letting the snowflakes melt on her skin. She couldn't have asked for a better night to go. Even if there was pursuit—though it was unlikely that anyone would search for a runaway inn-brat—this snowfall would soon cover up all trace of her passage.

Shouldering her wallet, she set off, taking the same path that the crippled stranger had followed earlier in the day. The wallet was stuffed with provisions and a change of clothes, with a blanket tied on top and a water sack hung below. It made for a heavy load, but she was a strong girl, used to long hours of hard work.

Her journey up the Dale that night passed in the utter silence of a snowfall. The snow tapered off towards the earlier part of the morning, but it looked as though it would stay, for the temperature had dropped. The wind was busy sweeping drifts into hollows and up against the sides of outcrops and trees. Saren's calves had begun to ache. She hadn't thought she'd get footsore so soon—after all she was used to being on her feet all day—but she'd been up early and worked hard all day and evening, then left without getting any sleep.

She marched on until the trail dipped into a small valley thick with pines. Slipping and sliding down the incline, she was soon padding noiselessly under their snowhung boughs, across a carpet of pine needles that still was dry. When she reached the far side of the little forest, where the trees thinned out as they began their march up the slopes once more, she let her wallet fall with a thump and leaned against a tree.

She wolfed down two dried apples before she remembered that what she carried would have to suffice until who knew when. She had a few coins in the purse at her belt—taken from a pot in her mother's room and fair payment for the years of work, she had decided—but in the wilderness, places to buy provisions would be far and few between.

She would have to set snares and live by her wits, see how much she remembered from all the tales of travellers and trappers and the like that she'd listened to in the Herdsman's Halt over the years.

But she wasn't worried. With her head filled with her newfound freedom, her guilt forgotten, she had no room for worry. Everything was too new. She was warmly dressed against the weather—from the fat herdsman's hat on her head, complete with ear flaps that tied down to her chin, to her thick cloak and the boots of sheepskin with the wooly side turned in to her feet. She had provisions and a few coins. And, by the Hunter's Cup, she had her freedom! Only one thing remained to completely sever her past from the days to come.

She drew the sharp knife sheathed at her belt and, removing her cap, began to cut away the long locks of her hair. Sharp though the blade was, it still hurt at times, but eventually her hair lay in a tangled pile on her lap and what remained on her head was barely an inch or two at its longest. She shivered as the cold touched her scalp and quickly replaced her hat. Digging a hole in the frozen dirt with her knife, she buried her hair and covered it over with pine needles. Now her freedom was complete. Unrolling her blanket and, well-bundled against the cold, she fell into a deep, well-earned sleep.

SHE PASSED the road that led to Grimmerdale around mid-morning and paused there to munch a stick of dried meat. Had yesterday's stranger taken that route? Considering his crippled leg, she didn't think he could make very good time and had half-expected to come upon him today. But she had the hills to herself. Well, if he'd gone to Grimmerdale, he was welcome to it. Saren meant to see something of the world beyond Nordendale's closest neighbours. Eyes gleaming, she passed the road by and continued north.

Just before night came to the snowy mountains, she found a herdsman's croft set snugly into the side of a hill. The stone walls and turf roof almost appeared to be a part of the land itself and if it hadn't been for the tell-tale smoke from its chimney and the two men chopping wood outside, she might well have passed it by. She called out to the men in a friendly fashion, taking care to keep her voice somewhat gruff, and was cheered at their welcome.

They were father and son, she decided. Wiry, dark-haired men, bearded like goats in big sheepskin coats. The older man introduced himself as Forwood, his son as Abear.

"My name's Sardul," Saren told them. "I'm from Jorby, originally, but what with the war…" She gave a weary shrug.

"That's two of you then," Forwood said, "and in as many days! Is the whole coast moving to the mountains?"

"Two of us?"

Forwood nodded. "There was another lad here yesterday—older than you, with a crooked leg. His name was Carnen—do you know him?"

"Yes…yes, I met him—in Ulmsdale, I think it was. I didn't know he'd come this way."

"Looking for a white road," Forwood said.

His son laughed. "And a good time he picked for it! All roads are white, this part of the year."

Saren laughed with them, but she had to wonder. How had the stranger—Carnen, she corrected herself—managed to come so far, so fast?

"You'll be wanting to stay for the night?" Forwood asked.

Saren shook off her thoughts and nodded. "I've coin," she began, but the herdsman shook his head.

"Give us a hand with this wood," he said. "That'll be payment enough."

Saren set her wallet down by the croft's door and accepted an axe from the son. The herdsmen returned to their work and Saren bent to the task with them, though her mind was more on what Forwood had told her about the crippled stranger than on the work at hand.

Looking for a white road.

Carnen himself had begun to tell her something about what a wise woman had told him to look for. This white road? It didn't make any sense.

— ❦ —

SHE MET Forwood's wife Signe and their toddling daughter Torrie later, both as dark and slender as their menfolk. After a meal of mutton stew, they all sat around the croft's fat hearth, drinking mulled home-brewed honey ale and talking. Saren passed on what news she could, gleaned from customers of the inn, but found that Carnen had already told most of it before her. When Forwood began to tell stories, she settled down, pleased to have someone else do the talking, and listened with delight and some small amount of dread as he told of That Which Runs the Ridges, and then a tale of snow faeries that made them all laugh.

"Are you looking for a white road, too?" Signe asked her as they went to their beds later.

Saren looked up from where she was unrolling her blankets by the fire and shook her head. "I don't even know what it is."

"Some remnant of the Old Ones, I think," Abear said. "That's what I got from Carnen. They used a pale stone for their roadworks—did you never see them down by the coast?"

"Not that I remember. We were told to avoid such places."

Forwood nodded. "It's well you did. They're chancy at the best of times." He scratched at his beard and gave Saren a considering look. "Are you looking for a place to winter, Sardul?"

"Well…"

"We don't have room here, but Bindon has a bigger place—about three days' march north. He might take you on. Tell him I sent you, lad. Maybe it will help."

"I…thank you."

The herdsman said a gruff goodnight and then the family went to their beds, leaving Saren to the hearth. She stretched out on her blankets, but found sleep hard to come. She kept wondering about Carnen's swift traveling and this white road he was looking for. When she finally slept it was to dream fitfully of wise women and ancient ruins, of a crippled man and something that called out to her from a circle of stones to which a white road led.

— ❦ —

IT HAD snowed again overnight and the day dawned cold with threatening grey skies. Saren said her goodbyes and took a north trail through the white slopes, blinking at the brightness of the snow. The winter had come to stay.

She passed a number of herdsfolk's crofts during the morning. A word or two with the friendly folk told her that she was on the right trail. Carnen had passed ahead of her, still traveling quickly for all that he had a crippled leg. What Saren tried to decide now, as she continued to tramp northward, was why she was following him.

Looking for a white road.

Some remnant of the Old Ones...

What promise had Carnen's wise woman given him? What did he look to find at the end of his white road? She thought of the dreams that had troubled her sleep last night. Something had called to her from a stone henge. It had promised her. . .what? A whisper of summer air in the middle of winter. A hint of wonder. Some marvel stood between the stones, if she could only find the road that would lead her to them.

Working in the Herdsman's Halt, Saren had heard all the old tales. Danger lay in wait for those who meddled with the Old Ones' places of mystery, more so than any gain. Bargains were kept in those sites, but not always in a manner that the seeker had expected. I'm not a seeker, Saren thought. I'm just...curious.

At the end of a white road, the memory of last night's dreams whispered to her. *In a circle of stones...*

She began to feel as though she'd been enchanted. By Carnen, perhaps, or by whatever it was that lay at the end of the white road. What she *should* do was turn around and make for the coast. Instead she kept trudging on through the snow, traveling until the night fell, and she couldn't have said why she was continuing. She only knew that it was something she had to do.

She slept in a hollow that night, curled in her cloak and blanket, face hidden from the cold. It snowed lightly around midnight, but she was caught fast in her dreams and never noticed.

She dreamed of the road and her footsteps ringing on it. The pale white ribbon of stone sounded hollow underfoot as it led her on and on through a shifting dreamscape. She moved along it like a ghost, or one of the great silver cats that haunted the mountains, quick as a thought, until suddenly the henge was looming over her. The sense of a green promise, summer scents and birdsong, came to her from between the stones, but all she could see inside the henge was a thick grey mist.

A wooden crutch lay on the pale stone at her feet. She thought of Forwood and his tales. That Which Runs the Ridges. Monsters. All the unknown. Underneath the promise of warmth, she sensed something menacing, but there couldn't be any horror in there, she realized. A wise woman had told Carnen to seek it out. A wise woman would not knowingly send someone into danger.

Yes, the voice of her fear whispered inside her. *But that wise woman sent him, not you.*

It was cold where she stood. Her teeth chattered against each other. And there was a promise of warmth beyond the swirl of mist. She took one step, then another. The mist clung to her face like cobwebs. A third step in and it began to clear. The cold disappeared. She saw a woodland glade, held fast in summer. Her mouth formed a delighted "O," but then rising from the fresh green sward underfoot, pushing aside the sod with skeletal fingers that were curled like claws, were dead men.

Fear held her motionless until the first fleshless hand rasped across her boots. She took a quick step back, her skin crawling with revulsion. Something snapped under foot. A sharp crack of shattered bone. The clawing hands of the dead swarmed up her legs and she flailed at them only to—

—wake up screaming.

The echo of her scream rang in the still mountain air as she sat up, hugging herself. The cold had settled deep in her bones and she shivered as much from it as from the terror she'd woken from.

"Dream," she muttered through chattering teeth. "J-j-just a dream."

She built a fire and huddled over it, waiting for snow to melt in her pot so that she could make tea. Not until the scalding liquid was spreading its warmth through her was she able to relax. Sweet Gunnora, the dream had been vivid. She was not usually given to having nightmares. It had most likely grown from the indecision inside her and the cold, but it had seemed more a warning. She knew as well, without knowing how she knew, that the place she had dreamed was real and that she would go on until she found it. What she didn't understand was why.

It was close to dawn now so, rather that trying so sleep another few hours, she packed up her blanket, doused the fire with handfuls of snow and was on her way by the time the sun came creeping up above the eastern horizon. She learned that Carnen was still ahead of her from a family of herdsfolk she met later in the morning, but Carnen himself and his white road continued to elude her until she stopped at yet another croft late in the day.

"Bindon's holding is a day and a half's journey from here," the father of the household told her. "But there's nothing in between. Just..." He hesitated.

"Just what?" Saren asked.

The herdsman looked uncomfortable. "A road," he said. "Left over from the time of the Old Ones."

That decided Saren. "Where does it lead?" she asked.

The man shook his head. "No one knows. No one's been fool enough to follow it."

"All the same," Saren said. "I have to go on."

"There's a storm brewing," the herdsman warned, looking skyward with a frown.

"I'll be careful."

"It's not care that's needed to survive a storm in these mountains," he told her. "It's shelter and warmth. Blind luck won't get you through."

Saren thought of Carnen who was still ahead of her and of her dreams that held both threat and promise in their strange turns.

"I'll have to trust to luck," she said. "It's all I've got." The herdsman shrugged. "Well, luck go with you then—with the both of you. I warned your friend as well, but he wouldn't listen either. With a crippled leg, he won't make Bindon's keep by nightfall—that's for sure."

"Thank you for the tea," Saren said. Then before the herdsman could continue with his warnings, she set off, leaving him standing by the door of his croft and shaking his head as he watched her go.

— 🦋 —

SHE FOUND the road of the Old Ones before midnight. The storm still gathered in the night skies above her, clouding the stars. Wind dusted sharp pellets of snow against her skin so that she wore a strip of cloth torn from her blanket as a scarf to protect her against their sting. Drifts filled hollows, making for deceptive footing. But she found the road. Weary, she sighted down its length, scuffing the toe of one boot against the snow until she'd cleared a slab of the flat rock that formed the road's length.

Easy to find, she thought.

If it was so easy to find, what made it special? Anyone could seek it out, even a crippled man in the first storms of winter. But that didn't gainsay the promise that might lie at its end, for how many *would* follow it? Only the brave or fools sought out the places of the Old Ones. Or those with hidden knowledge. Carnen might have such, gleaned from his wise woman. What did she have? A dream—half promise, half warning. Sighing, Saren set off along its length.

The road was easy to follow, even when the storm finally came blustering down about her. Thick flakes were driven in swirling gusts all around her, but something about the road kept her from straying. The cold wasn't as easy to deal with. Her limbs went numb, as much from the bitter chill as her weariness. She shuffled forward in a state somewhere between somnolence and sleep. When the snow let up, the cold came creeping through the layers of her clothes in earnest. She unwrapped her blanket with stiff fingers and wore it around herself, over her cloak. It helped only a little.

It was hard to see with the cloud cover hiding the stars and the wind-driven snow. When the wind finally died down, she stopped in her tracks to look around. The mountains were gone. Instead, she was on a vast plain, an empty white expanse that stretched out from where she stood for as far as the eye could see. She scuffed at the snow, clearing a spot. The road was still underfoot. The sky had cleared. Stars speckled the night sky, but the constellations they formed didn't seem familiar.

Carnen's white road. It had taken her…elsewhere.

She shivered with the cold and the strangeness, then sighed and began her forward shuffling motion again. The past was gone. Nordendale, her mother, the inn. The crofts of the herdsfolk and the mountains. What lay ahead, she didn't know, but it had to be something. Perhaps better, perhaps worse that she'd known, but with the past gone, she felt she had no choice but to go on.

Her mind drifted to the memory of the men of Nordendale returning home from the war and she felt a kinship with what they had experienced. Soldiers were coin, spent on a battlefield. Her own life had been a kind of dying as well; a coin, its value lying in what it could be bartered for, not for what it was itself. This kind of thinking made her head ache. And Carnen, she wondered. Was he his wise woman's coin?

She paused again, slowly lifting her head. The wind dusted her face with a sharp sting of snow and her headache made it hard to concentrate. She blinked, eyelids moving so slowly she was sure they were almost frozen, rimmed with frost. The henge stood in front of her, tall and brooding.

The stones were darker than she'd pictured them to be, more foreboding. A summery scent came to her from between the stones where a mist moved slowly to the breath of a different wind than the one that tugged at her clothes. She looked down at her feet and saw Carnen's crutch lying there.

She bent down and picked it up, feeling the hard wood through her mittens. Was he inside now, his wise woman's coin spent? Another whiff of summer escaped the space between the stones. Apple blossoms, a faint smell of roses, the scent of grass and wildflowers and green growing things. Strawberries and lilacs.

She stepped forward, determined to see it through. The mists clung to her as she stepped between the stones. She shivered, anticipating the touch of skeletal fingers.

Once inside she had a momentary glimpse of the summer glade shown to her in her dream. She saw apple trees in blossom, yet bearing fruit at the same time. Rose bushes with both bud and flower on their thorny branches. She heard a birdsong, sweet and clear. At her feet, yellow and red and pale blue flowers grew in a circular scatter amongst the grass.

She took another step forward, then everything flickered. A rushing sound filled her head. Scent and sight vanished. She made a small noise in the back of her throat, then her weariness came over her in a rush. She tried to use Carnen's crutch to keep to her feet, but it slipped from under her when she put her weight on it and she pitched forward into the darkness.

— 🕯 —

WHEN SAREN woke it was to find herself in a long dark hall, a gloomy light coming through windows set high in its walls. A hearth stood at its far end, cold ash inside. Two carved chairs stood on the dais, both empty. Three trestle tables ran the length of the room with rough benches along their either side. Mouldering tapestries hung from the walls, too much in disrepair for whatever they had depicted to still be visible.

Saren pushed herself up from the stone floor and sat on her haunches. A winter chill still lay in her bones and she trembled despite herself. Where was she now? In some ruined keep of the Old Ones? Dreaming? Dead?

The hall's one door began to creak open and Saren scrambled to her feet, backing away. She tripped against the dais and fell backwards, quickly pulling her legs up over the lip of the dais. Crouching there, biting at her lower lip, her gaze centered on the slowly opening door.

It hadn't been foolishness that brought her here, she thought, watching that door. It had been utter madness. True, Carnen had preceded her, but she didn't doubt that his wise woman had let him know what to expect. There would be formalities to observe, certain approaches that the seeker after the Old Ones must take, secret knowledge—none of which she had. Where Carnen must have had some idea as to what he faced—by the Hunter's Cup, he'd know *why* he was on the road in the first place and what he sought at its end—she was only muddling along. Toying with disaster. And now—

Her worst fears were realized as the door opened wide enough for the hall's inhabitants to enter. Raw fear clawed through her. She knew now where she was. In a hall of the dead.

Corpses, like those from her dream, shuffled in to take seats at the various tables. Some were newly dead, their wounds still inflamed. Others were white-fleshed and swollen—corpses that had lain a week or so in their graves. The worst were those whose flesh was so mouldered that the white bone showed through its tattered remnants. Skeletal figures with skull faces.

Sweet Gunnora, she moaned. I never meant...

"Meant what?" one of the dead demanded. It stepped close to the dais and bent down until its ravaged features were only inches from her own. A maggot hung from the corner of its mouth, wriggling into the flesh. "Never meant to wish me dead?"

"I..."

Bile rose in Saren's throat as she recognized the creature for her betrothed Erard. Behind it another figure approached and this one she recognized not so much from its features—for there was little recognizable in that skull-face with the tatters of flesh and scalp still hanging from it—as from the clothing she'd last seen it wear when it was alive. Her father.

"Is this how you repay the years of love I gave you?" the dead thing demanded. "To come here in your flesh and mock me?"

"You...you never loved me..."

"Small wonder. What father was ever cursed with such a poor excuse of a daughter? One that would steal coins from her own mother."

Fear and sickness warred inside Saren, but she shook her head slowly. "*I* was the coin," she said.

"Hard times," Erard said. "War makes for hard times. We all had our part to play, our coin to spend and be spent in turn."

"No!" Saren cried. "It wasn't for love of Nordendale that I was to be spent, but for my father's greed and whatever use you meant to make of me."

"Witch blood," Erard said. "A wise woman told me you had witch blood and that if our lines joined, I would prosper. Yet you denied me, Saren. You let the war take me and spend my life in battle with your ill-wishing."

"I never ill-wished you! I never loved you, but I never wished you harm."

"You never sprang from my loins," her father said. "A bard spilled his seed in your mother, but I wed her all the same. I raised you as though you were my own, but what return did you give me?"

"Lives are not to be bartered and sold."

"No?" Erard asked. "Then what are they for?"

More of the creatures were pressing forward now to hear her answer. Saren stared at their ruined visages, fear thrumming in her. Her head spun with what she'd just heard.

Witch blood.

A bard spilled his seed in your mother.

A bard's witch blood. Was that what the road had snagged from inside her and used to draw her into this trap?

"Tell us," one of the dead demanded. A half-fleshed face pushed forward, ravaged fingers held out to her. Fat white grubs fell to the floor as it moved its arm.

"What are lives for?" another asked.

"Coins to spend—what else!" a third cried.

The voices came hard and fast, a jeering, demanding cacophony that made her press her hands against her ears. She wept and her tears froze on her cheeks. The stink of rotting flesh and the proximity of the dead made her empty stomach lurch and boil with acid. Skeletal fingers plucked at her clothing.

She screamed when the dead flesh and bone touched her face. The corpses began to pull her into their midst and she huddled into herself more. Dead hands grabbed at her arms, pulling them from her ears. She flailed at the creatures. Where she struck them, bones shattered, arms were tugged from shoulder sockets to fall to the floor.

"What is life?" her father demanded.

"We had life," another of the dead told her, "but our coin was spent and we have nothing now."

"If not coin, what is it?" Erard shouted at her.

"A gift!" Saren wailed. "A gift—do you understand? Not coin to be spent. Not something to be bartered for profit. But a gift, freely given!"

The grip of the creatures loosened and she was able to pull free and stumble to her feet. She staggered back a pace or two and stared at them. Mist roiled about their feet. The rot smell of opened graves was thick in the air.

"Nothing is freely given," one of the corpses said. "There is always a payment that needs paying, or else why are we here? Why do we die? What sent us here?"

Saren shook her head, trying to clear it. How could she be here, discussing philosophical concerns with the dead? By the Hunter's Cup, she *had* gone mad. But she thought on what the corpse had asked her and an answer slowly formed inside her all the same. Right or wrong, she didn't know, but it was all she had.

"Did you never give a bouquet of flowers to a loved one?" she asked.

Here and there, gruesome heads nodded.

"And when the flowers withered—did that make less the moment of giving? A life is like that gift of flowers. While we bloom, we make the best of the promise in it. When we die, it's not a gift taken back, but a natural progression."

"Words!" her father spat. "In this place—"

"You're in this place because you can't see the gift!" Saren broke in. "Because life is just coin for you and nothing more. That is what you made of the gift's promise, so you must abide by it."

The creatures began to advance on her again, muttering and waving their stick-thin arms at her. She backed away until the wall was there and she could go no further. She heard the rushing sound again, as though a great wind blew by her ears. Dizziness swept over her, corpses and hall spinning in her sight. She lowered herself down until she was sitting on her ankles, back against the wall. She tried to stay erect, but she couldn't.

The dead creatures came boiling up over the lip of the dais, but Saren fell over on her side, great clouds of darkness swimming in her sight and taking her away once more. But just before she was gone, before the dark took her or the dead touched her, she saw a woman's face in her mind's eye. It was a broad, good-natured face, blue-eyed and framed by a spill of corn-yellow hair. There was a hint of a green dress on a rounded shoulder, a breath of summer fields that cut across the grave stench in the hall.

"Oh, well-spoken, daughter," the woman said.

Then the darkness swam up and took Saren away.

WHEN SAREN'S eyes fluttered open, she found herself warming by a friendly fire that blazed merrily away in front of her. The hall was gone and she was inside the henge, stone under her blankets. The tall pillars didn't seem so foreboding in the flickering light. Sitting beside her was the crippled stranger that she'd followed from the Herdsman's Halt, always a day or so out of step with him.

Seeing him, she felt a sudden calm. She sat up, held out her hands to the fire, and studied her companion. He was sitting in a way that made her think that perhaps the crutch she'd found hadn't been dropped so much as thrown away because it wasn't needed any longer.

"Hello, Carnen," she said.

"And you're the girl from the inn," he replied. "I didn't recognize you when I first found you here. What brought you?"

"Your white road."

"But I said nothing of it to you."

Saren shrugged. "You told the herdsfolk and they told me." She pointed at his leg. "You seem to be in better shape than when I first met you."

"It was a charm of Andnor's," he explained. "The wise woman I told you of. Each step I took on my search helped to ease it—the charm being completed if I reached the end."

"So that's why you made such good time—your leg kept getting better."

He nodded. "And you—was it your witch blood that brought you?"

Saren lifted a hand to touch her cheek, then let it drop to her lap. She told him of her experience, following the road. "But I don't feel as though I have witch blood."

"I saw it in you when I first met you—a small trace, but there nevertheless. Without it, you wouldn't have survived the white road."

The henge they were in, Saren realized, was not the one the road had led her to. This one stood in the mountains, high on a ridge. The night skies were clear above them, dotted with familiar stars. The slopes were white with snow, but the henge itself was clear.

"Was it all a dream?" she asked. "The plain, the other henge, the…" She shivered. "The hall of the dead?"

Carnen shook his head. "The stoneworks of the Old Ones are connected. It is possible to step from one to the other in the blink of an eye. The road tests us, you see. That's what Andnor told me. I…I went to my own hall of the dead, though it was different from yours."

"And the woman in green—the one that called me daughter?"

"I never saw her," Carnen said. "I saw a man—a man with stag antlers springing from his brow. He never spoke at all." He poured tea from a pot by the fire and handed it to her. "What will you do now, Saren?"

"If life's a gift," she said, "then I want to use its promise wisely. I want to…" She looked at him across the top of her mug. "To follow a green road, I think. One into summer. I want to give of myself to others, freely, with no bartering and no coin. I'd like to tell stories, maybe, or learn to play an instrument. Become a healer. I don't know. I just want to do something useful."

Carnen lifted his mug. "I think I'd like to travel that green road with you—if you wouldn't mind the company."

"Together, instead of me trailing a day or so behind you?"

Carnen smiled.

"To the green road, then," Saren said, clinking her mug against his. "Good fortune to us both!"

"Good fortune," Carnen repeated and they drank to the toast.

IN A green wood, in a place Saren might have called "elsewhere", a corn-haired woman sat back from a pool that held an image on its surface, an image of a henge and two well-worn travellers toasting each other. She looked at her companion, a tall, broad-shouldered man with stag's antlers sprouting from his brow.

"There's one for each of us now," she said.

The antlered man nodded. "And there will be more. The Dark has had its time, holding the land in the thrall of war. I think its coin is spent."

"For awhile at least."

"And our coin?"

The woman in green put a finger against his mouth and shook her head. "We have no coin—only gifts," she said. "And a gift can only prosper."

"Is that a promise?" the antlered man asked.

"A hope," she replied. "Nothing more."

Looking at the two figures still reflected in the pool, the longstones rearing above them, the light of their fire flickering against the grey stone, she sighed.

"I pray it will be enough," she added.

The Graceless Child

I am not a little girl anymore.
And I am grateful and lighter
for my lessened load.
I have shouldered it.

—Ally Sheedy,
from "A Man's World"

TETCHIE MET THE TATTOOED man the night the wild dogs came down from the hills. She was waiting in among the roots of a tall old gnarlwood tree, waiting and watching as she did for an hour or two every night, nested down on the mossy ground with her pack under her head and her mottled cloak wrapped around her for warmth. The leaves of the gnarlwood had yet to turn, but winter seemed to be in the air that night.

She could see the tattooed man's breath cloud about him, white as pipe smoke in the moonlight. He stood just beyond the spread of the gnarlwood's twisted boughs, in the shadow of the lone standing stone that shared the hilltop with Tetchie's tree. He had a forbidding presence, tall and pale, with long fine hair the colour of bone tied back from his high brow. Above his leather trousers he was bare-chested, the swirl of his tattoos crawling across his blanched skin like pictographic insects. Tetchie couldn't read, but she knew enough to recognize that the dark blue markings were runes.

She wondered if he'd come here to talk to her father.

Tetchie burrowed a little deeper into her moss and cloak nest at the base of the gnarlwood. She knew better than to call attention to herself.

When people saw her it was always the same. At best she was mocked, at worst beaten. So she'd learned to hide. She became part of the night, turned to the darkness, away from the sun. The sun made her skin itch and her eyes tear. It seemed to steal the strength from her body until she could only move at a tortoise crawl.

The night was kinder and protected her as once her mother had. Between the teachings of the two, she'd long since learned a mastery over how to remain unseen, but her skills failed her tonight.

The tattooed man turned slowly until his gaze was fixed on her hiding place.

"I know you're there," he said. His voice was deep and resonant; it sounded to Tetchie like stones grinding against each other, deep underhill, the way she imagined her father's voice would sound when he finally spoke to her. "Come out where I can see you, trow."

Shivering, Tetchie obeyed. She pushed aside the thin protection of her cloak and shuffled out into the moonlight on stubby legs. The tattooed man towered over her, but then so did most folk. She stood three and a half feet high, her feet bare, the soles callused to a rocky hardness. Her skin had a greyish hue, her features were broad and square, as though chiseled from rough stone. The crudely-fashioned tunic she wore as a dress hung like a sack from her stocky body.

"I'm not a trow," she said, trying to sound brave.

Trows were tall, trollish creatures, not like her at all. She didn't have the height.

The tattooed man regarded her for so long that she began to fidget under his scrutiny. In the distance, from two hills over and beyond the town, she heard a plaintive howl that was soon answered by more of the same.

"You're just a child," the tattooed man finally said.

Tetchie shook her head. "I'm almost sixteen winters."

Most girls her age already had a babe or two hanging onto their legs as they went about their work.

"I meant in trow terms," the tattooed man replied.

"But I'm not—"

"A trow. I know. I heard you. But you've trow blood all the same. Who was your dame, your sire?"

What business is it of yours? Tetchie wanted to say, but something in the tattooed man's manner froze the words in her throat. Instead she pointed to the longstone that reared out of the dark earth of the hilltop behind him.

"The sun snared him," she said.

"And your mother?"

"Dead."

"At childbirth?"

Tetchie shook her head. "No, she…she lived long enough…"

To spare Tetchie from the worst when she was still a child.

Hanna Lief protected her daughter from the townsfolk and lived long enough to tell her, one winter's night when the ice winds stormed through the town and rattled the loose plank walls of the shed behind The Cotts Inn where they lived, "Whatever they tell you, Tetchie, whatever lies you hear, remember this: I went to him willingly."

Tetchie rubbed at her eye with the thick knuckles of her hand.

"I was twelve when she died," she said.

"And you've lived—" The tattooed man waved a hand lazily to encompass the tree, the stone, the hills. "—here ever since?"

Tetchie nodded slowly, wondering where the tattooed man intended their conversation to lead.

"What do you eat?"

What she could gather in the hills and the woods below, what she could steal from the farms surrounding the town, what she could plunder from the midden behind the market square those rare nights that she dared to creep into the town.

But she said none of this, merely shrugged.

"I see," the tattooed man said.

She could still hear the wild dogs howl. They were closer now.

EARLIER THAT evening, a sour expression rode the face of the man who called himself Gaedrian as he watched three men approach his table in The Cotts Inn. By the time they had completed their passage through the inn's common room and reached him, he had schooled his features into a bland mask. They were merchants, he decided, and was half right. They were also, he learned when they introduced themselves, citizens of very high standing in the town of Burndale.

He studied them carelessly from under hooded eyes as they eased their respective bulks into seats at his table. Each was more overweight than the next. The largest was Burndale's mayor; not quite so corpulent was the elected head of the town guilds; the smallest was the town's sheriff and he carried Gaedrian's weight and half again on a much shorter frame. Silk vests, stretched taut over obesity, were perfectly matched to flounced shirts and pleated trousers. Their boots were leather, tooled with intricate designs and buffed to a high polish. Jowls hung over stiff collars; a diamond stud gleamed in the sheriff's left earlobe.

"Something lives in the hills," the mayor said.

Gaedrian had forgotten the mayor's name as soon as it was spoken. He was fascinated by the smallness of the man's eyes and how closely set they were to each other. Pigs had eyes that were much the same, though the comparison, he chided himself, was insulting to the latter.

"Something dangerous," the mayor added.

The other two nodded, the sheriff adding, "A monster."

Gaedrian sighed. There was always something living in the hills; there were always monsters. Gaedrian knew better than most how to recognize them, but he rarely found them in the hills.

"And you want me to get rid of it?" he asked.

The town council looked hopeful. Gaedrian regarded them steadily for a long time without speaking.

He knew their kind too well. They liked to pretend that the world followed their rules, that the wilderness beyond the confines of their villages and towns could be tamed, laid out in as tidy an order as the shelves of goods in their shops, of the books in their libraries. But they also knew that under the facade of their order, the wilderness came stealing on paws that echoed with the click of claw on cobblestone. It crept into their streets and their dreams and would take up lodging in their souls if they didn't eradicate it in time.

So they came to men such as himself, men who walked the border that lay between the world they knew and so desperately needed to maintain, and the world as it truly was beyond the cluster of their stone buildings, a world that cast long shadows of fear across their streets whenever the moon went behind a bank of clouds and their streetlamps momentarily faltered.

They always recognized him, no matter how he appeared among them. These three surreptitiously studied the backs of his hands and what they could see of the skin at the hollow of his throat where the collar of his shirt lay open. They were looking for confirmation of what their need had already told them he was.

"You have gold, of course?" he asked.

The pouch appeared as if from magic from the inside pocket of the mayor's vest. It made a satisfying clink against the wooden tabletop. Gaedrian lifted a hand to the table, but it was only to grip the handle of his ale flagon and lift it to his lips. He took a long swallow, then set the empty flagon down beside the pouch.

"I will consider your kind offer," he said.

He rose from his seat and left them at the table, the pouch still untouched. When the landlord met him at the door, he jerked a thumb back to where the three men sat, turned in their seats to watch him leave.

"I believe our good lord mayor was buying this round," he told the landlord, then stepped out into the night.

He paused when he stood outside on the street, head cocked, listening. From far off, eastward, over more than one hill, he heard the baying of wild dogs, a distant, feral sound.

He nodded to himself and his lips shaped what might pass for a smile, though there was no humour in the expression. The townsfolk he passed gave him uneasy glances as he walked out of the town, into the hills that rose and fell like the tidal swells of a heathered ocean, stretching as far to the west as a man could ride in three days.

"WHAT...WHAT ARE you going to do to me?" Tetchie finally asked when the tattooed man's silence grew too long for her.

His pale gaze seemed to mock her, but he spoke very respectfully, "I'm going to save your wretched soul."

Tetchie blinked in confusion. "But I...I don't—"

"Want it saved?"

"Understand," Tetchie said.

"Can you hear them?" the tattooed man asked, only confusing her more. "The hounds," he added.

She nodded uncertainly.

"You've but to say the word and I'll give them the strength to tear down the doors and shutters in the town below. Their teeth and claws will wreak the vengeance you crave."

Tetchie took a nervous step away from him.

"But I don't want anybody to be hurt," she said.

"After all they've done to you?"

"Mama said they don't know any better."

The tattooed man's eyes grew grim. "And so you should just... forgive them?"

Too much thinking made Tetchie's head hurt.

"I don't know," she said, panic edging into her voice.

The tattooed man's anger vanished as though it had never lain there, burning in his eyes.

"Then what *do* you want?" he asked.

Tetchie regarded him nervously. There was something in how he asked that told her he already knew, that this was what he'd been wanting from her all along.

Her hesitation grew into a long silence. She could hear the dogs, closer than ever now, feral voices raised high and keening, almost like children, crying in pain. The tattooed man's gaze bore down on her, forcing her to reply. Her hand shook as she lifted her arm to point at the longstone.

"Ah," the tattooed man said.

He smiled, but Tetchie drew no comfort from that.

"That will cost," he said.

"I...I have no money."

"Have I asked for money? Did I say one word about money?"

"You...you said it would cost..."

The tattooed man nodded. "Cost, yes, but the coin is a dearer mint than gold or silver."

What could be dearer? Tetchie wondered.

"I speak of blood," the tattooed man said before she could ask. "Your blood."

His hand shot out and grasped her before she could flee.

Blood, Tetchie thought. She cursed the blood that made her move so slow.

"Don't be frightened," the tattooed man said. "I mean you no harm. It needs but a pinprick—one drop, perhaps three, and not for me. For the stone. To call him back."

His fingers loosened on her arm and she quickly moved away from him. Her gaze shifted from the stone to him, back and forth, until she felt dizzy.

"Mortal blood is the most precious blood of all," the tattooed man told her.

Tetchie nodded. Didn't she know? Without her trow blood, she'd be just like anyone else. No one would want to hurt her just because of who she was, of how she looked, of what she represented. They saw only midnight fears; all she wanted was to be liked.

"I can teach you tricks," the tattooed man went on. "I can show you how to be anything you want."

As he spoke, his features shifted until it seemed that there was a feral dog's head set upon that tattooed torso. Its fur was the same pale hue as the man's hair had been, and it still had his eyes, but it was undeniably a beast. The man was gone, leaving this strange hybrid creature in his place.

Tetchie's eyes went wide in awe. Her short, fat legs trembled until she didn't think they could hold her upright anymore.

"Anything at all," the tattooed man said, as the dog's head was replaced by his own features once more.

For a long moment, Tetchie could only stare at him. Her blood seemed to sing as it ran through her veins. To be anything at all. To be normal…But then the exhilaration that filled her trickled away. It was too good to be true, so it couldn't be true.

"Why?" she asked. "Why do you want to help me?"

"I take pleasure in helping others," he replied.

He smiled. His eyes smiled. There was such a kindly air about him that Tetchie almost forgot what he'd said about the wild dogs, about sending them down into Burndale to hunt down her tormentors. But she did remember and the memory made her uneasy.

The tattooed man seemed too much the chameleon for her to trust. He could teach her how to be anything she wanted to be. Was that why he could appear to be anything she wanted *him* to be?

"You hesitate," he said. "Why?"

Tetchie could only shrug.

"It's your chance to right the wrong played on you at your birth."

Tetchie's attention focused on the howling of the wild dogs as he spoke. To right the wrong...

Their teeth and claws will wreak the vengeance you crave.

But it didn't have to be that way. She meant no one ill. She just wanted to fit in, not hurt anyone. So, if the choice was hers, she could simply choose not to hurt people, couldn't she? The tattooed man couldn't *make* her hurt people.

"What...what do I have to do?" she asked.

The tattooed man pulled a long silver needle from where it had been stuck in the front of his trousers.

"Give me your thumb," he said.

GAEDRIAN SCENTED trow as soon as he left Burndale behind him. It wasn't a strong scent, more a promise than an actuality at first, but the further he got from the town, the more pronounced it grew. He stopped and tested the wind, but it kept shifting, making it difficult for him to pinpoint its source. Finally he stripped his shirt, letting it fall to the ground.

He touched one of the tattoos on his chest and a pale blue light glimmered in his palm when he took his hand away. He freed the glow into the air where it turned slowly, end on shimmering end. When it had given him the source of the scent, he snapped his fingers and the light winked out.

More assured now, he set off again, destination firmly in mind. The townsfolk, he realized, had been accurate for a change. A monster did walk the hills outside Burndale tonight.

— ❧ —

NERVOUSLY, TETCHIE stepped forward. As she got closer to him, the blue markings on his chest seemed to shift and move, rearranging themselves into a new pattern that was as indecipherable to her as the old one had been. Tetchie swallowed thickly and lifted her hand, hoping it wouldn't hurt. She closed her eyes as he brought the tip of the needle to her thumb.

"There," the tattooed man said a moment later. "It's all done."

Tetchie blinked in surprise. She hadn't felt a thing. But now that the tattooed man had let go of her hand, her thumb started to ache. She looked at the three drops of blood that lay in the tattooed man's palm like tiny crimson jewels. Her knees went weak again and this time she did fall to the ground. She felt hot and flushed, as though she were up and abroad at high noon, the sun broiling down on her, stealing her ability to move.

Slowly, slowly, she lifted her head. She wanted to see what happened when the tattooed man put her blood on the stone, but all he did was smile down at her and lick three drops with a tongue that seemed as long as a snake's, with the same kind of a twin fork at its tip.

"Yuh…nuh…"

Tetchie tried to speak—what have you done to me? she wanted to say—but the words turned into a muddle before they left her mouth. It was getting harder to think.

"When your mother was so kindly passing along all her advice to you," he said, "she should have warned you about not trusting strangers. Most folk have little use for your kind, it's true."

Tetchie thought her eyes were playing tricks on her, then realized that the tattooed man must be shifting his shape once more. His hair grew darker as she watched, his complexion deepened. No longer pale and wan, he seemed to bristle with sorcerous energy now.

"But then," the tattooed man went on, "they don't have the knowledge I do. I thank you for your vitality, halfling. There's nothing so potent as mortal blood stirred in a stew of faerie. A pity you won't live long enough to put the knowledge to use."

He gave her a mocking salute, fingers tipped against his brow, then away, before turning his back on her. The night swallowed him.

Tetchie fought to get to her own feet, but she just wore herself out until she could no longer even lift her head from the ground. Tears of frustration welled in her eyes. What had he done to her? She'd seen it for herself, he'd taken no more than three drops of her blood. But then why did she feel as though he'd taken it all?

She stared up at the night sky, the stars blurring in her gaze, spinning, spinning, until finally she just let them take her away.

SHE WASN'T sure what had brought her back, but when she opened her eyes, it was to find that the tattooed man had returned. He crouched over her, concern for her swimming in his dark eyes. His skin had regained its almost colourless complexion, his hair was bone white once more. She mustered what little strength she had to work up a gob of saliva and spat in his face.

The tattooed man didn't move. She watched the saliva dribble down his cheek until it fell from the tip of his chin to the ground beside her.

"Poor child," he said. "What has he done to you?"

The voice was wrong, Tetchie realized. He'd changed his voice now. The low grumble of stones grinding against each other deep underhill had been replaced by a soft melodious tonality that was comforting on the ear.

He touched the fingers of one hand to a tattoo high on his shoulder, waking a blue glow that flickered on his fingertips. She flinched when he touched her brow with the hand, but the contact of blue fingers against her skin brought an immediate easing to the weight of her pain. When he sat back on his haunches, she found she had the strength to lift herself up from the ground. Her gaze spun for a moment, then settled down. The new perspective helped stem the helplessness she'd been feeling.

"I wish I could do more for you," the tattooed man said.

Tetchie merely glared at him, thinking, haven't you done enough?

The tattooed man gave her a mild look, head cocked slightly as though listening to her thoughts.

"He calls himself Nallorn on this side of the Gates," he said finally, "but you would call him Nightmare, did you meet him in the land of his origin, beyond the Gates of Sleep. He thrives on pain and torment. We have been enemies for a very long time."

Tetchie blinked in confusion. "But…you.…"

The tattooed man nodded. "I know. We look the same. We are brothers, child. I am the elder. My name is Dream; on this side of the Gates I answer to the name Gaedrian."

"He…your brother…he took something from me."

"He stole your mortal ability to dream," Gaedrian told her. "Tricked you into giving it freely so that it would retain its potency."

Tetchie shook her head. "I don't understand. Why would he come to me? I'm no one. I don't have any powers or magics that anyone could want."

"Not that you can use yourself, perhaps, but the mix of trow and mortal blood creates a potent brew. Each drop of such blood is a talisman in the hands of one who understands its properties."

"Is he stronger than you?" Tetchie asked.

"Not in the land beyond the Gates of Sleep. There I am the elder. The Realms of Dream are mine and all who sleep are under my rule when they come through the Gates." He paused, dark eyes thoughtful, before adding, "In this world, we are more evenly matched."

"Nightmares come from him?" Tetchie asked.

Gaedrian nodded. "It isn't possible for a ruler to see all the parts of his kingdom at once. Nallorn is the father of lies. He creeps into sleeping minds when my attention is distracted elsewhere and makes a horror of healing dreams."

He stood up then, towering over her.

"I must go," he said. "I must stop him before he grows too strong."

Tetchie could see the doubt in his eyes and understood then that though he knew his brother to be stronger than him, he would not admit to it, would not turn from what he saw as his duty. She tried to stand, but her strength still hadn't returned.

"Take me with you," she said. "Let me help you."

"You don't know what you ask."

"But I want to help."

Gaedrian smiled. "Bravely spoken, but this is war and no place for a child."

Tetchie searched for the perfect argument to convince him, but couldn't find it. He said nothing, but she knew as surely as if he'd spoken why he didn't want her to come. She would merely slow him down. She had no skills, only her night sight and the slowness of her limbs. Neither would be of help.

During the lull in their conversation when that understanding came to her, she heard the howling once more.

"The dogs," she said.

"There are no wild dogs," Gaedrian told her. "That is only the sound of the wind as it crosses the empty reaches of his soul." He laid a hand on her heal, tousled her hair. "I'm sorry for the hurt that's come to you with this night's work. If the fates are kind to me, I will try to make amends."

Before Tetchie could respond, he strode off, westward. She tried to follow, but could barely crawl after him. By the time she reached the crest of the hill, the longstone rearing above her, she saw Gaedrian's long legs carrying him up the side of the next hill. In the distance, blue lightning played, close to the ground.

Nallorn, she thought.

He was waiting for Gaedrian. Nallorn meant to kill the dreamlord and then he would rule the land beyond the Gates of Sleep. There would be no more dreams, only nightmares. People would fear sleep, for it would no longer be a haven. Nallorn would twist its healing peace into pain and despair.

And it was all her fault. She'd been thinking only of herself. She'd wanted to talk to her father, to be normal. She hadn't known who Nallorn was at the time, but ignorance was no excuse.

"It doesn't matter what others think of you," her mother had told her once, "but what you think of yourself. Be a good person and no matter how other people will talk of you, what they say can only be a lie."

They called her a monster and feared her. She saw now that it wasn't a lie.

She turned to the longstone that had been her father before the sun had snared him and turned him to stone. Why couldn't that have happened to her before all of this began, why couldn't she have been turned to stone the first time the sun touched her? Then Nallorn could never have played on her vanity and her need, would never have tricked her. If she'd been stone…

Her gaze narrowed. She ran a hand along the rough surface of the standing stone and Nallorn's voice spoke in her memory.

I speak of blood.

It needs but a pinprick—one drop, perhaps three, and not for me. For the stone. To call him back.

To call him back.

Nallorn had proved there was magic in her blood. If he hadn't lied, if…

Could she call her father back? And if he did return, would he listen to her? It was night, the time when a trow was strongest. Surely when she explained, her father would use that strength to help Gaedrian?

A babble of townsfolk's voices clamored up through her memory.

A trow'll drink your blood as sure as look at you.

Saw one I did, sitting up by the boneyard, and wasn't he chewing on a thighbone he'd dug up?

The creatures have no heart.

No soul.

They'll feed on their own, if there's not other meat to be found.

No, Tetchie told herself. Those were the lies her mother had warned her against. If her mother had loved the trow, then he couldn't have been evil.

Her thumb still ached where Nallorn had pierced it with his long silver pin, but the tiny wound had closed. Tetchie bit at it until the salty taste of blood touched her tongue. Then she squeezed her thumb, smearing the few drops of blood that welled up against the rough surface of the stone.

She had no expectations, only hope. She felt immediately weak, just as she had when Nallorn had taken the three small drops of blood from her. The world began to spin for the second time that night, and she started to fall once more, only this time she fell into the stone. The hard surface seemed to have turned to the consistency of mud and it swallowed her whole.

WHEN CONSCIOUSNESS finally returned, Tetchie found herself lying with her face pressed against hard packed dirt. She lifted her head, squinting in the poor light. The longstone was gone, along with the world she knew. For as far as she could see, there was only a desolate wasteland, illuminated by a sickly twilight for which she could discover no source. It was still the landscape she knew, the hills and valleys had the same contours as those that lay west of Burndale, but it was all changed. Nothing seemed to grow here anymore; nothing lived at all in this place, except for her, and she had her doubts about that as well.

If this was a dead land, a lifeless reflection of the world she knew, then might she not have died to reach it?

Oddly enough, the idea didn't upset her. It was as though, having seen so much that was strange already tonight, nothing more could surprise her.

When she turned to where the old gnarlwood had been in her world, a dead tree stump stood. It was no more than three times her height, the area about it littered with dead branches. The main body of the tree had fallen away from where Tetchie knelt, lying down the slope.

She rose carefully to her feet, but the dizziness and weakness she'd felt earlier had both fled. In the dirt at her feet, where the longstone would have stood in her world, there was a black pictograph etched deeply into the soil. It reminded her of the tattoos that she'd seen on the chests of the dreamlord and his brother, as though it had been plucked from the skin of one of them, enlarged and cast down on the ground. Goosebumps traveled up her arms.

She remembered what Gaedrian had told her about the land he ruled, how the men and women of her world could enter it only after passing through the Gates of Sleep. She'd been so weak when she offered her blood to the longstone, her eyelids growing so heavy...

Was this all just a dream, then? And if so, what was its source? Did it come from Gaedrian, or from his brother Nallorn at whose bidding nightmares were born?

She went down on one knee to look more closely at the pictograph. It looked a bit like a man with a tangle of rope around his feet and lines standing out from his head as though his hair stood on end. She reached out with one cautious finger arid touched the tangle of lines at the foot of the rough figure. The dirt was damp there. She rubbed her finger against her thumb. The dampness was oily to the touch.

Scarcely aware of what she was doing, she reached down again and traced the symbol, the slick oiliness letting her finger slide easily along the edged grooves in the dirt. When she came to the end, the pictograph began to glow. She stood quickly, backing away.

What had she *done*?

The blue glow rose into the air, holding to the shape that lay in the dirt. A faint rhythmic thrumming rose from all around her, as though the ground was shifting, but she felt no vibration underfoot. There was just the sound, low and ominous.

A branch cracked behind her and she turned to the ruin of the gnarlwood. A tall shape stood outlined against the sky. She started to call out to it, but her throat closed up on her. And then she was aware of the circle of eyes that watched her from all sides of the hilltop, pale eyes that flickered with the reflection of the glowing pictograph that hung in the air where the longstone stood in her world. They were set low to the ground; feral eyes.

She remembered the howling of the wild dogs in her own world.

There are no wild dogs, Gaedrian had told her. *That is only the sound of the wind as it crosses the empty reaches of his soul.*

As the eyes began to draw closer, she could make out the triangular-shaped heads of the creatures they belonged to, the high-backed bodies with which they slunk forward.

Oh, why had she believed Gaedrian? She knew him no better than Nallorn. Who was to say that *either* of them was to be trusted?

One of the dogs rose up to its full height and stalked forward on stiff legs. The low growl that arose in his chest echoed the rumble of sound that her foolishness with the glowing pictograph had called up. She started to back away from the dog, but now another, and a third stepped forward and there was no place to which she could retreat. She turned her gaze to the silent figure that stood in among the fallen branches of the gnarlwood.

"Puh—please," she managed. "I...I meant no harm."

The figure made no response, but the dogs growled at the sound of her voice. The nearest pulled its lips back in a snarl.

This was it, Tetchie thought. If she wasn't dead already in this land of the dead, then she soon would be.

But then the figure by the tree moved forward. It had a slow shuffling step. Branches broke underfoot as it closed the distance between them.

The dogs backed away from Tetchie and began to whine uneasily.

"Be gone," the figure said.

Its voice was low and craggy, stone against stone, like that of the first tattooed man. Nallorn, the dreamlord's brother who turned dreams into nightmares. It was a counterpoint to the deep thrumming that seemed to come from the hill under Tetchie's feet.

The dogs fled at the sound of the man's voice. Tetchie's knees knocked against each other as he moved closer still. She could see the rough chiseled shape of his features now, the shock of tangled hair, stiff as dried gorse, the wide bulk of his shoulders and torso, the corded muscle upon muscle that made up arms and legs. His eyes were sunk deep under protruding brows. He was like the first rough shaping that a sculptor might create when beginning a new work, face and musculature merely outlined rather than clearly defined as it would be when the sculpture was complete.

Except this sculpture wasn't stone, nor clay, nor marble. It was flesh and blood. And though he was no taller than a normal man, he seemed like a giant to Tetchie, towering over her as though the side of a mountain had pulled loose to walk the hills.

"Why did you call me?" he asked.

"C—call?" Tetchie replied. "But I...I didn't..."

Her voice trailed off. She gazed on him with sudden hope and understanding.

"Father?" she asked in a small voice.

The giant regarded her in a long silence. Then slowly he bent down to one knee so that his head was on level with hers.

"You," he said in a voice grown with wonder. "You are Henna's daughter?"

Tetchie nodded, nervously.

"*My* daughter?"

Tetchie's nervousness fled. She no longer saw a fearsome trow out of legend, but her mother's lover. The gentleness and warmth that had called her mother from Burndale to where he waited for her on the moors, washed over her. He opened his arms and she went to him, sighing as he embraced her.

"My name's Tetchie," she said into his shoulder.

"Tetchie," he repeated, making a low rumbling song of her name. "I never knew I had a daughter."

"I came every night to your stone," she said, "hoping you'd return."

Her father pulled back a little and gave her a serious look.

"I can't ever go back," he said.

"But—"

He shook his head. "Dead is dead, Tetchie. I can't return."

"But this is a horrible place to have to live."

He smiled, craggy features shifting like a mountainside suddenly rearranging its terrain.

"I don't live here," he said. "I live…I can't explain how it is. There are no words to describe the difference."

"Is mama there?"

"Hanna…died?"

Tetchie nodded. "Years ago, but I still miss her."

"I will…look for her," the trow said. "I will give her your love." He rose then, looming over her again. "But I must go now, Tetchie. This is unhallowed land, the perilous border that lies between life and death. Bide here too long——living or dead—and you remain here forever."

Tetchie had wanted to ask him to take her with him to look for her mother, to tell him that living meant only pain and sorrow for her, but then she realized she was only thinking of herself again. She still wasn't sure that she trusted Gaedrian, but if he had been telling her the truth, then she had to try to help him. Her own life was a nightmare; she wouldn't wish for all people to share such a life.

"I need your help," she said and told him then of Gaedrian and Nallorn, the war that was being fought between Dream and Nightmare that Nallorn could not be allowed to win.

Her father shook his head sadly. "I can't help you, Tetchie. It's not physically possible for me to return."

"But if Gaedrian loses…"

"That would be an evil thing," her father agreed.

"There must be something we can do."

He was silent for long moments then.

"What is it?" Tetchie asked. "What don't you want to tell me?"

"I can do nothing," her father said, "but you.…"

Again he hesitated.

"What?" Tetchie asked. "What is it that I can do?"

"I can give you of my strength," her father said. "You'll be able to help your dreamlord then. But it will cost you. You will be more trow than ever, and remain so."

More trow? Tetchie thought. She looked at her father, felt the calm that seemed to wash in peaceful waves from his very presence. The townsfolk might think that a curse, but she no longer did.

"I'd be proud to be more like you," she said.

"You will have to give up all pretense of humanity," her father warned her. "When the sun rises, you must be barrowed underhill or she'll make you stone."

"I already only come out at night," she said.

Her father's gaze searched hers and then he sighed.

"Yours has not been an easy life," he said.

Tetchie didn't want to talk about herself anymore.

"Tell me what to do," she said.

"You must take some of my blood," her father told her.

Blood again. Tetchie had seen and heard enough about it to last her a lifetime tonight.

"But how can you do that?" she asked. "You're just a spirit.…"

Her father touched her arm. "Given flesh in this half-world by your call. Have you a knife?"

When Tetchie shook her head, he lifted his thumb to his mouth and bit down on it. Dark liquid welled up at the cut as he held his hand out to her.

"It will burn," he said.

Tetchie nodded nervously. Closing her eyes, she opened her mouth. Her father brought his thumb down across her tongue. His blood tasted like fire, burning its way down her throat. She shuddered with the searing pain of it, eyes tearing so that even when she opened them, she was still blind.

She felt her father's hand on her head. He smoothed the tangle of her hair and then kissed her.

"Be well, my child," he said. "We will look for you, your mother and I, when your time to join us has come and you finally cross over."

There were a hundred things Tetchie realized that she wanted to say, but vertigo overtook her and she knew that not only was he gone, but the empty world as well. She could feel grass under her, a soft breeze on her cheek. When she opened her eyes, the longstone reared up on one side of her, the gnarlwood on the other. She turned to look where she'd last seen the blue lightning flare before she'd gone into the stone.

There was no light there now.

She got to her feet, feeling invigorated rather than weak. Her night sight seemed to have sharpened, every sense was more alert. She could almost read the night simply through the pores of her skin.

The townsfolk were blind, she realized. *She* had been blind. They had all missed so much of what the world had to offer. But the townsfolk craved a narrower world, rather than a wider one, and she…she had a task yet to perform.

She set off to where the lightning had been flickering.

THE GRASS was all burned away, the ground itself scorched on the hilltop that was her destination. She saw a figure lying in the dirt and hesitated, unsure as to who it was. Gaedrian or his brother? She moved cautiously forward until finally she knelt by the still figure. His eyes opened and looked upon her with a weak gaze.

"I was not strong enough," Gaedrian said, his voice still sweet and ringing, but much subdued.

"Where did he go?" Tetchie asked.

"To claim his own: the land of Dream."

Tetchie regarded him for a long moment, then lifted her thumb to her mouth. It was time for blood again—but this would be the last time. Gaedrian tried to protest, but she pushed aside his hands and let the drops fall into his mouth: one, two, three. Gaedrian swallowed. His eyes went wide with an almost comical astonishment.

"Where...how...?"

"I found my father," Tetchie said. "This is the heritage he left me."

Senses all more finally attuned, to be sure, but when she lifted an arm to show Gaedrian, the skin was darker, greyer than before and tough as bark. And she would never see the day again.

"You should not have—" Gaedrian began, but Tetchie cut him off.

"Is it enough?" she asked. "Can you stop him now?"

Gaedrian sat up. He rolled his shoulders, flexed his hand and arms, his legs.

"More than enough," he said. "I feel a hundred years younger."

Knowing him for what he was, Tetchie didn't think he was exaggerating. Who knew how old the dreamlord was? He would have been born with the first dream.

He cupped her face with his hands and kissed her on the brow.

"I will try to make amends for what my brother has done to you this night," he said. "The whole world owes you for the rescue of its dreams."

"I don't want any reward," Tetchie said.

"We'll talk of that when I return for you," Gaedrian said.

If you can find me, Tetchie thought, but she merely nodded in reply.

Gaedrian stood. One hand plucked at a tattoo just to one side of his breastbone and tossed the ensuing blue light into the air. It grew into a shimmering portal. Giving her one more grateful look, he stepped through. The portal closed behind him, winking out in a flare of blue sparks, like those cast by a fire when a log's tossed on.

Tetchie looked about the scorched hilltop, then set off back to Burndale. She walked its cobblestoned streets, one lone figure, dwarfed by the buildings, more kin to their walls and foundations than to those sleeping within. She thought of her mother when she reached The Cotts Inn and stood looking at the shed around back by the stables where they had lived for all of those years.

Finally, just as the dawn was pinking the horizon, she made her way back to the hill where she'd first met the tattooed men. She ran her fingers along the bark of the gnarlwood, then stepped closer to the longstone, standing on the east side of it.

It wasn't entirely true that she could never see the day again. She *could* see it, if only once.

Tetchie was still standing there when the sun rose and snared her and then there were two standing stones on the hilltop keeping company to the old gnarlwood tree, one tall and one much smaller. But Tetchie herself was gone to follow her parents, a lithe spirit of a child finally, her gracelessness left behind in stone.